ROAD

OF

CLOUDS

Written by
Eric Loren

Book 4
Ways of Camelot

Reader Hill
Yucaipa, California

Published by
Reader Hill
PO Box 490
Yucaipa, CA 92399
readerhill.com

Dedication

To my beloved wife. You are such a blessing in my life, enriching my days and filling them with laughter. Thank you so much. I will love you always.

ONE

Avoiding the Guild

"Journeyman Thomas, I have need of you."

Thom looked up from spreading an ointment on his injured side to find Brother Colwyn beckoning him. The monastery's librarian was acting as the leader of the monastery in the abbot's absence.

He carefully wiped off his fingers on a rag and then lowered his shirt. "How can I help?"

"You are the best magician we have left at the monastery and the only one who is guild trained. We have some visitors from your guild demanding to see the Father Abbot and I would like you near when I meet with them. You will be out of sight but close enough to know if they are using any magic. I do not want them to know you are sheltering with us but we also cannot allow them to do any of their tricks to find out more about the Father Abbot or the league."

Thom nodded agreement, getting to his feet and following the monk out of the makeshift barracks in Mousehome. Because it was less than an hour after dawn, the shadows were long and the air still cool. He wondered how early these visitors had set out to reach this distant end of the city so early. It was peaceful as Thom followed Colwyn across the compound, but he was very aware of the dangers not far away. The city around the monastery was still in turmoil, with herds of marauding centaurs in the streets and vicious griffins in the sky overhead. The sorcerers had all fled, taken with them most of their human army, but some squads had been left behind and they were looting what they could as they tried to find a way out of the magically-encased Camelot. King Arthur's men were still concentrated at the castle, leaving the rest of the city to fend for itself. Merlin and his fellow magicians had reclaimed Clas Myrddin, but they too were hunkered down after all the fighting, ignoring the needs of greater Camelot. The turmoil beyond the monastery's walls was very real and not something he wanted to deal with while injured. Thom wanted to linger here while healing. That a group had come through all that chaos just to find Abbot Justin was worrisome. The sorcerers had imprisoned the leader of Saint Barnabas and now the magicians' guild was looking for the abbot.

As he followed the monastery's temporary leader, his mind raced over the possibilities for himself. He ought to be going back to the guild house and returning to his constrainment to the servants' quarters, but he had no desire to do so. He doubted the guild council would believe that the sorcerers seized his magician's box and imprisoned him for a time. He would simply be accused of losing it. He worried about returning but he also worried about staying away too long. Almost everyone at the guild house had been scattered by the invasion of sorcerers, but the wizards would be expecting the students and servants to return soon.

Brother Colwyn led him to the chapel, which was empty of petitioners this early in the morning. "Step into the confessional," he whispered to Thomas. "You will be able to hear us without being seen. They will not be able to sense you otherwise, will they?"

Thom shook his head. "The cream I was lathering on was the one from Mercenary Marcus, not the magical bone healer balm from Wizardess Bronwen that is for my ankle. Nothing about me will alert them."

"Good! Now get in here," ordered Colwyn, holding the door open to the screened booth.

Thom stepped in, sitting down and latching the door. It felt wrong that he was in the seat used by the ordained to take confessions, but the monk had ordered it. Through the lattice work he could vaguely see around him and he watched as another monk ushered in a handful of visitors that included one in black robes and another in a hauberk and bright blue cape with a long sword hanging at his side. Thom recognized the wizard as one of those on the guild council.

"Thank you for seeing us, brother," said Wizard Varus. "The king has sent us to retrieve Abbot Justin. Where is he?

"He is not here. The Father Abbot was forced to flee the invaders, taking the Road of Waters days ago," replied Colwyn. "In his absence, I am in charge of the monastery. How can I be of service?"

The knight stepped forward, towering over the librarian, his hand on the hilt of his sword. "Are you certain about his absence? My liege desires to converse with him."

"He is not here and we are uncertain of where he has found refuge. Please understand, sir knight, that Abbott Justin suffered imprisonment by the sorcerers and vile threats from them. He was able to escape before the king restored order to fair Camelot, so he fled as far away as he could to avoid recapture. I should think that as soon as he hears Camelot is safe, he will return to this enchanted city."

"Are there any sorcerers at the monastery?" questioned the wizard.

"No."

"Any from the guild?"

"Wizard Osiris was here for a time and stayed with the nobles who sought refuge in our guest house, but they all left when there was a break in the fighting. Last I heard, he was on one of the galleys that escaped King's Harbor before the sorcerers attacked there and destroyed numerous ships. I heard many of the nobles were on one of the vessels that sank."

Thom was impressed how the librarian told the truth yet guided the conversation carefully to keep from revealing anything about the league and its other magicians.

"I saw the hulks pulled out of the water," replied the knight. "Do you know how many boats escaped?"

"I do not, sir knight. You may want to question the harbor master for your answer. That happened near the start of the invasion and it was then that our Father Abbot was captured. As you can imagine, we were rather distraught about that. When he was later freed, we were glad to escort him to King's Harbor and find him a berth on a departing galley. Some of our brethren went with the Father Abbot to see him to safety."

"We do not care about shipwrecks or who travels with the abbot. You need to make certain that he learns that King Arthur and Wizard Merlin expect his presence before them as soon as possible."

"I will have a message sent after him this very night," assured Colwyn, "but realize it could take weeks to catch up with the abbot and for him to travel back to the city."

Thom could not see any of their faces clearly through the screening but he sensed that the wizard and the knight were upset. The wizard fidgeted with a pouch at his side. It was a lead-lined material of some kind because as soon as he opened the pouch Thom heard magic. Its contents were already crafted and stored, which was usually a dangerous thing to do. Varus pulled out a handful of powder and then blew it into the face of Colwyn, who pulled back and coughed, but the wizard grabbed his arm to keep him near.

"Once again, monk. We have a few more questions that you will answer honestly. Are there any sorcerers or sorcerer students at the monastery?"

Colwyn replied angrily. "No."

Before the wizard could ask anything else, the knight stepped forward and blurted his own questions. "Do you shelter any of Mordred's men? Do you have any magical beings hiding here like those awful centaurs?"

"No and no," snapped Colwyn, then he coughed again.

"Impetuous of you," growled Varus at the knight. "The enchantment only allows three questions."

"Then douse him again and get another three," replied the knight in a miffed tone.

"It does not work like that. Done a second time it will bring nightmares and other imaginings on him. Done a third time in repetition and he will go raving mad for a day or longer."

The knight grabbed Colwyn and spun him around so that warrior was directly behind him and then drew his sword and set it to his throat. "I do not need foolish magic to get answers. What else do you want to ask him?"

The wizard sighed. "No more questions. Rather, I will give some warnings and I expect you to share them with all your brethren. First, this monastery must not offer succor or refuge to any of the king's foes, be it sorcerer or soldier. Is that understood?"

Thom saw the monk nod slightly, the blade at his throat drawing a drop of blood.

"Second, we remind the church that they are called to heavenly service. Neither the king nor the guild will tolerate the church interfering with the rule of the land or with the practice of magic. Spar in our arena and you will get speared."

Thomas wondered what brought on that warning.

"Third, we are searching for a runaway student named Thomas of York. He may or may not be dressed as a journeyman. You are to consider him dangerous. If you encounter him, send word to the guild house immediately so that we can bring him to justice. Is that understood?"

Thomas froze on that hard wooden bench. Was he now a fugitive from the guild? What kind of justice were they planning to do to him? Wizard Varus called him dangerous!

"Understood," gasped Colwyn. "This student is a threat to the guild and its mighty wizards. Should he appear here, we are to bar the gates and send a messenger to the guild house so that your men can overwhelm and capture him."

The knight chuckled, pulling his sword away from the librarian's throat but still holding him close. "The monk has you there. You have mentioned this Thomas at every establishment we have visited yesterday and now you are at it again. How frightening is this aspirant that even wizards cower at the mention of his name?"

"We do not fear him," spat Varus, "but he is rogue without a master to control him. He is a danger to others and it is our responsibility to see that he is no longer a threat."

Thom wondered how they planned to do that. He feared this might be more than just banishment from the guild. He wanted to protest. He had done so much to help the realm, even rescuing the king and queen, and now they want him removed just because they thought his master was dead. He felt anger toward the guild and toward Levitanus for putting him in this situation.

TWO

Leaving Camelot

The wizard and the knight left soon after issuing their warnings, but Thomas was slower in leaving the relative safety of the confessional. He waited until Brother Colwyn returned and called for him.

"Thank you for not telling them about me. I assure you that I have done nothing wrong."

"I am well aware of your actions, Thomas. The king even rewarded you for your deeds. I do not understand why no other wizard came forward to take you as his new student nor do I understand why the guild leaders despise you. From what I have heard, you have crafted enchantments far beyond your known skill level, so maybe they fear you like a woodworker or smith fears an overly talented apprentice who might steal their reputation and customers. Whatever the cause of their envy or consternation, we will not be handing you over to the guild."

Colwyn motioned for Thomas to follow him, for the brethren had reopened the chapel for the community and some were already coming in to pray. Once they were outside, Colwyn continued. "You may remain at the monastery as long as you want, but I would suggest joining those who are going down the Road of Waters tonight."

Thom nodded. "I think that would be best too. Can I travel with those of the league even though I am not a member?"

"You are practically one of us already. You need only swear to the league's code on conduct to join. Talk to the next league master you meet."

"I think I will."

"Good," replied the librarian. "Now we have to speed up the packing. Everyone who is to leave the monastery needs to be out tonight. Will you work with Brother Michael today?"

"I will do all that I can," said Thomas, determined to help despite his many ongoing pains.

* * *

Thomas grimaced as a jolt of agony went through his left ankle, proof that he wasn't completely healed from the abuse he'd suffered, in spite of three days of using the magical bone-knitting balm he'd received from Wizardess Bronwen, the Keeper of Camelot. He stopped walking and set his boot on the ground at an angle and stepped down, forcing his ankle to snap back into place. It briefly hurt more, then it became just a dull ache that he could ignore. He had no time to be resting his injuries, especially when it was still so early in the day. There was just too much to get done evacuating those who belonged to the League of

Barnabas.

"Are you in distress?" asked Brother Michael, who was carrying the other end of the large crate. He was one of the monks who Vivien had been training as a magician's apprentice.

"I'm fine. I apologize for stopping," replied Thom, shifting his grip and continuing on.

They were carrying masonry tools to the monastery's stable.

As he and Michael carried the crate past unworked gardens and unpicked vines, he realized the emptiness of the monastery. As had been explained to the visitors, Abbot Justin was already gone, having taken a galley down the Road of Waters the very night that he was rescued. With him went Marcus the Mercenary and six of his warriors for protection, along with four monks including Brother Canon, one of Vivien's apprentices. Another ten brothers left the next night, taking along supplies and the manuscripts that had been salvaged from the previous week's wreckage. Thom had no idea where they were going, only that once they exited the Road of Waters on the upper Thames, they would get further instruction on how to reach the retreat house that the League of Barnabas was establishing somewhere in the backwoods of the realm.

Those Benedictine monks still here in Camelot were either helping to gather the final load to be sent south or were providing aid to the distressed citizens of the city. It left the monastery gardens neglected for now, but that would be short-lived. Thom expected it would go back to being a normal monastic compound within a few days, once all the league members left.

Thom no longer wore his battered journeyman's robe, for it wasn't safe to do so. As for the magician's staff he had inherited from his torturer, he had left it next to his sleeping mat in a small room at the Mousehome compound because he saw no reason to carry around something he didn't even know how to use. Besides, he no longer had a magician's box. He was a journeyman magician without any way to craft magic.

Thom and the monk carried their crate full of masonry tools around the back of the chapel and into the yard of the stable. As they approached the open doors, they ran into Thom's beloved Adele and the two nuns who were also magicians in training.

Thom smiled at her, since his hands were too full to offer a hug. Besides, the nuns would probably start beating on him if her tried to touch the fair lady, no matter how much Adele welcomed it. "What are you hauling to the wagon?"

She smiled back. "We brought blankets from the convent and now we have boxes of dried fruit to retrieve."

"You still intend to be on tonight's galley?"

She nodded. "The castle is no place for me, even if I wasn't a magician in training. I doubt the other queen's ladies will return any time soon; they have returned to their fathers' estates to await calmer times. I have sent word to the king that I am well and that I intend to travel down the Road of Waters to join the queen at her refuge. The sisters will come with me as escorts as well two of

Marcus' men. Once they deposit me into the queen's hands, they will go on to league's new keep. What of you?"

Thom understood why the league's leaders wanted Adele to stay with the queen's court, but that meant he would see little of her. It was a depressing thought. "Me? I just found out that I cannot return to the guild, for they have declared me a dangerous runaway. I will help here at the monastery as I can, for I have nowhere else to go. I've lost my teacher and my craft, so I am thankful that the monastery is providing me with food and a place to sleep. I will work here as long as they need me then I will go down the Road of Waters myself. From there, I don't know where I will go or be welcomed."

"Please do not linger in Camelot too long," she implored. "All is still in shambles in the city, so the guild hasn't had a chance to start hunting for you, but they will soon. Leave as soon as you can and please join the league. The league will give you a new place to call home and will continue your training in the craft you love. Promise me."

Thom nodded agreement because he knew that she was right, even though it meant he would likely never see her again. He wanted to tell her to come with him, to leave off being a queen's lady. He wanted to be with her for the rest of his life, but he knew he had nothing to offer her. He had no work prospects and the land the king had granted him would likely be rescinded. Still he longed to be with Adele and he whispered, "I will always love you."

Adele didn't hear him because at that moment Sister Harmony came up behind her and touched her shoulder so that Adele craned her neck to look back.

"Come along," said the nun loudly, unaware that she was interrupting Thom's confession of love. "We still have much work to do; there is no time to dally here."

Adele turned more fully toward her. "Of course. If we are to sail tonight, we need to get everything done quickly."

She began walking off with the nuns, but looked back toward Thom once more, still unaware of what he had just tried to confess to her. "Please leave here soon, Thomas. I worked too hard rescuing you from imprisonment to have you get yourself captured again."

She smiled and he couldn't help but smile in return even though his heart felt heavy.

"Pick up the pace," ordered Harmony. "God frowns on slothfulness."

Adele looked skyward in frustration at the nun's nagging and then gave Thom a wink. She did start walking again though and said, "Indeed, Sister Harmony, you are always so diligent. Let us get on to our next task."

Thomas stared after her for a time, until Brother Michael cleared his throat. "Shall we get these tools loaded into the wagon?"

"Once again, I've broken your work pace. My apologies," said Thom, indicating with his chin that the monk should lead on.

They entered the stable, heading over to the two wagons parked in the middle of the large stable. As the two came into the dusty place, another monk leaned over the side wall of one of the wagons and motioned them over. It was Brother Francis.

"Over here with the tools. I have a spot in this wagon."

They did as asked, setting the heavy crate into an open space against the side wall.

"What do we retrieve next?" asked Thom. They would be doing this all day, as were another five pairs of helpers.

Another voice spoke up. "Nothing at the moment."

They all turned to find Brother Colwyn entering the stable with Adele. "Climb down from there, Francis. You and Thomas and Adele have been summoned. Brother Michael, can you take over the packing of the wagons?"

Thom's partner of the day agreed, quickly consulting Francis about what was still needed and who was retrieving what.

Soon, Colwyn was leading the three of them outside. "Apparently, today is the day for visitors. There is a pixie waiting at the chapel to escort all of you to the City Keeper's House. Wizardess Bronwen sent nothing written and gave the messenger no details; I only know that it is urgent."

Thom's eyes looked up to where the city's dome of magic still showed damage. It was not as easy to see during the bright day, but with his inner ear he could easily pick up the discordant sounds in the enchantment that protected Camelot. The Keeper was responsible for maintaining the magic and she had been working hard for days now trying to repair the damage caused by an explosion that happened too close. All of the magic had almost unraveled, which would have destroyed the whole city, killing everyone in it. It had been so dire that Wizard Merlin and Sorcerer Dalrake had stopped their fighting to temporarily unite and prevent the catastrophe. The two Founders had done what was necessary to stop it and then had gone back to their fight over the city, leaving it to Wizardess Bronwen to complete the re-crafting of the city's enchantment.

"I hope she will not ask for help with that," said Francis, gesturing to where Thom was looking. "Neither you nor Adele should be doing any magic according the guild and they would notice if new magicians joined Bronwen in her crafting. The City Keeper's House is the last place we should be when trying to hide from Merlin and his guild."

"Brother, I already told you that she provided no details, but it says much that she risked one of the few pixies left in the city to come here and fetch you. The three of you should at least hear what she has to say."

"We will go," said Adele firmly, "but we will go with much caution. I will not have either Thomas or Brother Francis recaptured, for they have already been through enough. Besides, all three of us are supposed to be on a river galley tonight."

Colwyn smiled at her and then said with sincerity, "You are a fierce one, Lady Adele. I trust you will make sure they reach the Keeper without harm and get back in time to join those taking the Road of Waters tonight."

THREE

City Keeper's House

The pixie messenger waiting at the chapel's door was a woman with gray-touched hair and fine wrinkles that added to her facial tattoos. She sized up the taller humans in a way that made Thom feel like he had come up wanting. "How am I to travel back to the City Keeper's House unnoticed with three disparate humans?" She looked at Brother Colwyn with a raised eyebrow of accusation. "Are they truly monk, warrior, and noble woman?"

Thom never would have thought of himself as looking like a warrior, but he did have a sword hanging at his side and his face and arms showed obvious bruising and scabs from recent wounds.

"These are the three that the Keeper requested," replied the librarian. "They are who they are."

"Well then, let us get moving. The Keeper is not known for her patience and we have a chaotic city to cross to reach her."

The pixie turned and trotted across the courtyard, toward the monastery's main gate. Thom and the others had to stride quickly after her. There were still many people sheltering in the area and some noticed the pixie and the trio of humans pass by, but most paid them no attention.

Thom realized he hadn't even learned the pixie's name, but she didn't seem the type of person who wanted polite conversation.

* * *

A few hours later they were in the heart of the city. They would have traveled faster, but Thom still needed the occasional stop for his painful ankle. He almost wished he had taken the time to retrieve his journeyman's staff as a walking aid, but the staff would have drawn too much attention even with its jewel head unlit. So he endured the walk without it, leaning at times on Francis or Adele when the cobblestones became too uneven or their route caused them to hurry to avoid a patrol.

They made it to the heart of the city without being challenged. On the edge of the large central market square sat Camelot's imposing town hall with marble pillars on either side of its overlarge doors. It was a three-story building with a copper dome whose green patina set it apart from the typical slate roof tiles of most larger buildings in the rich city. Behind the town hall stood another three-story building that seemed like a wing of the complex but was actually separate from it. Instead of a copper dome it had a square tower, but otherwise it seemed like just an extension of the town hall. That was the City Keeper's House. There was no obvious entry to the place, for the magicians wanted to discourage casual visitors.

The pixie led them through a wrought iron gate into a narrow garden behind the town hall. As they entered the garden, Thom looked up at the section of sky that could be seen between the tall buildings. He saw blue sky and a sliver of the clouds that were the Road of Clouds, but not any of the damaged areas of the city's encircling enchantment. His inner ear still heard that damaged area though, still distinct over the usual rhythms of Camelot's dome of magic. Were they being called here to somehow help with that repair work?

The path meandered around the plants and up to an imposing oak door with iron hinges. The pixie reached for to the heavy door knocker that was set high for her grasp, raising and dropping it precisely three times. Then she waited, saying nothing to the three who were with her.

Finally, the door opened and a girl in apprentice gray let them in.

"Is she in the tower?" asked the pixie.

The apprentice nodded.

Without another word, the pixie led them across the spacious foyer and up the sweeping stairway. She gave them no time to observe the artwork or furnishings and she certainly didn't allow them time to see what rooms were beyond the entry hall.

Thom swallowed hard as he looked up the stairwell.

"Lean on me as we climb," suggested Adele. "Francis is still sore from your imprisonment, so it would be better for me to help."

"Thank you," he sighed, hating that he was still so weak.

Thom and Adele went up together. His right hand held the railing and his left arm was draped over his shoulders. Francis followed them. They passed each landing without pausing as they tried to catch up with the pixie, until they came out at the top of the tower. The pixie asked them to wait there as she approached Keeper Bronwen alone.

Thomas let go of Adele, though he would rather have shifted his arm from her shoulder to her waist. He took the moment to catch his breath and to look around. The top floor was one large room, with views in every direction. The wizardess was standing with her arms crossed, looking out the open northern windows toward the area where the city's enchantment had been damaged. From this high up, Thom could now tell that the damage had occurred very near to the gate fortress where the Short Roads connected to the city.

The room was sparsely furnished with a scattering of tables and chairs, with the tile floors bare and the roof beams exposed overhead. A half-dozen unlit lanterns hung from those rafters.

Adele touched Thom's arm and drew his attention to another pixie in the room, this one laying on a cot beyond one of the tables. At first Thom thought him dead, but then realized his eyes were open and he was watching the woman who had led them here, though he did so without lifting his head. Thom wondered if the man was ill or injured.

"It was a bloodletting," whispered Francis. "There is great power in pixie blood, which they probably need in helping to rebuild the damaged enchantment. Can you hear the elemental pulse of his blood from that stoppered container?"

"They drained his blood?" asked Adele, sounding appalled.

"Not too much to hurt him," replied the monk. "I would guess he supplies it voluntarily, for his people usually support Merlin's magic."

Bronwen had nodded to the pixie woman and now turned to look at them. Thom quickly noticed that she looked older and more weary since he last saw her at the monastery. "Thank you for coming. I have grim news to share with you."

She motioned them closer and then turned to the pixie woman. "Salai, can you help Aram to a more comfortable bed? It gets rather breezy up here as the day wanes and I would not want him to get chilled."

"I will do so," the pixie replied. "Has he eaten anything since he gave of his power?"

Bronwen shook her head. "I think he worried too much about your safe return. There is a covered bowl of soup that you might be able to get into him now that you are back. I will have Letitia take it down to your room."

"That would be good." The pixie woman walked over to her prone mate and stroked his face, bringing a tired smile to the man's face.

"Can we help move him?" asked Thomas as they all came closer.

"No need," replied the pixie woman as she helped the man to sit up.

"We can at least carry the soup down for you," said Adele.

"I will take care of that, my lady," replied the apprentice who had come up the stairs behind them, unnoticed until now.

Aram seemed to regain more of his strength from the touch of his beloved, for he was soon able to stand and then walked down the stairs while leaning on Salai. The apprentice girl followed the two pixies, carrying a tray that held a covered bowl and a mug.

"What dire news do you have?" asked Francis. "Has something happened to the Father Abbot on the Road of Waters?"

"God forbid anything more afflicts the abbot or that Road," replied the wizardess. "As far as I know, Waters remains clear to travel. No, this is something that has happened on the Road of Clouds."

"Levitanus?" asked Thomas, speaking the name of his former master.

"As far as I know, he is still in the hands of Dalrake but alive. No, this news is about the two who set out to rescue him. Kane and Vivien are trapped on the Road of Clouds and need someone to free them."

"And you call us?" Francis' tone revealed his disbelief. "None of us are master magicians that can walk the wizards' road."

Bronwen sighed. "Nonetheless, you are my best hope for them. I cannot go without sacrificing all of Camelot, and I am not about to do so. Weakening the Roads as Levitanus did is one thing, but if I were to stop the repairing of the city's enchantment it could kill everyone inside the city. I cannot allow that."

"Merlin is back. Tell him to send another to relieve you," suggested Francis.

"Even if I could craft a story that would fool him, he has no masters available. Wizard Gilead, who was my helper here, has been tasked with trying to restore the Short Roads after the sorcerers yanked it to Mordred's bidding. Others still work on restoring the Road of Leaves and the Road of Waters. I hear the guild council are now at Castle Camelot to provide the king with what protection they can. Only Merlin is uncommitted and he is not about to take over my duties. I am fortunate that he spares me what time he can, maybe a few hours every other day to help rebuild the city's shield."

"Only a master can walk that Road," reiterated Francis.

"Yet you have walked it before, Brother Francis."

"I renounced magic long ago."

For a moment, the two stared at each other, both defiant in their stance.

"Could you ask Merlin to free them?" asked Adele.

Bronwen shook her head at Adele's question. "You are not thinking clearly, Apprentice Adele. What do you believe will happen when Merlin realizes that the two are a sorcerer and a renegade journeywoman? Would they not go from one confinement to another? This rescue must be done by the league itself, or friends of the league."

"Where is Osiris?" asked Thom, mentioning another wizard of the league. Osiris was on one of the few river galleys that escaped Camelot when the sorcerers attacked King's Harbor.

"He is too far away to be of any help. He works to set up the protections around the league's new refuge. It would take weeks just to get him a message and I know that we do not have that long. You are the ones who need to rescue Vivien and Kane. Will you not help them?"

Francis raised his hand to forestall her. "Please tell us what has happened to them. Maybe we can think of another solution to this."

"Someone else should tell that story," said Bronwen, who then whistled a collection of notes like a songbird.

After a moment there came a response from outside the open windows and then Thom saw three small birds fly toward them in the morning sunlight. They soared into the tower and that it when he realized it was two birds flanking a small winged person. All three were whistling back to Bronwen, circling the wizardess a half-dozen times before the two birds flew up to perch on one of the exposed roof beams, while the fairy settled on the edge of the nearest wooden table.

FOUR

Fairy Message

The two birds seated above were Azure Nightingales, similar to their mundane cousins whose songs filled the fields and forests of the land. But unlike their normal tawny-colored, yellow-beaked relative, the Azure Nightingales' feathers were a dusky blue and these were more petite. There was magic in their encouraging song and in their feathers that allowed the birds to stay airborne for hours on end. The pair chose to perch but they were not relaxed. He realized that they were focused on protecting their fairy companion. They were tiny yet fierce.

Thom's focus went to the tiny fairy that was shorter than the length of his forearm. She had butterfly-like wings that were twice her body length, a purplish-blue with white spots. The fairy's face and body were human-like and with flowing hair on her head in a color to match her wings. She wore a short dress in a muted gray that was cut low in the back to not interfere with the motion of her wings. Her hands and feet were bare and human-like too. She studied them as much as they studied her, her wings slowly folding and unfolding in apparent agitation that for some reason reminded Thom of a twitching cat's tail.

She spoke and it was trilling voice. "Only one black robe and that is such a rough garment. Are these truly master magicians?"

"I wear the robe of one dedicated to the service of God, not wizard's black," corrected Francis. "I am Brother Francis, a monk of the Benedictine Order."

Her wings fluttered faster, definitely more aggravated, and she shifted her gaze to Bronwen. "What is this? I cannot guide humans who will slip off the ice and fall through the mists."

"All three know how to do enchantments and one of them has already walked the Road of Clouds numerous times," assured the wizardess. "Now please tell them the tale you told me, Rainflower. They need to know what has happened."

She raised an eyebrow, looking at the three of them with doubt on her face, but she still obeyed. "There are two humans trapped in Dripping Branch Wayrest, kept in by harpies." She looked back at Bronwen, crossing her arms in defiance. "There, they have the gist of it."

Bronwen sighed. "I have no time for silly offenses. Do not act like you have just broken free from your chrysalis and your wings are still wet. You are not

15

fragile, Rainflower. You have flown through storms and withstood gales; you can endure not having your questions answered for a short time..."

"Why my queen sent me to you rather than the Keeper of the Clouds, I cannot fathom."

"You question your queen now?"

Rainflower didn't respond but her wings stopped moving.

"Please explain fully to these three what has happened, then they will explain to you who they are and how they can help. You can start with the sorcerers and their captive."

The fairy gave the slightest of nods, her wings once again fluttering slowly. "It is a lengthy story best told over dandelion tea or an acorn cup of lavender nectar, but I will try to condense it for you hasty humans.

"Three days ago, I was on my way to harvest hail crystals when I saw Founder Dalrake walking the Road, which he does often with his fellow magicians, but this time his large entourage included Founder Levitanus, who I had not seen in many years. Rudely, none of them responded to my welcoming trills. Why are you humans so impolite?"

She paused, crossing her arms and staring at them for an answer.

Thom was at a loss on how to respond, but thankfully the wizardess intervened. "Rainflower, we apologize for the rudeness of our race, now continue your tale."

The fairy raised a dainty, blue eyebrow at the Keeper but uncrossed her arms. "You must admit that it was improper behavior. After they insultingly ignored me, I returned the favor so I do not have anything else to say about the Founders or the other magicians accompanying them. They went their way and I went mine. However, a half-day later two more magicians came through, a lovely couple. Though her accent was stilted, I appreciated her effort to trill as a fairy." Rainflower sighed. "If only the harpies had gone after the Founders instead of them."

"Harpies attacked Kane and Vivien?" asked Adele. "Are they in trouble? Where are they now?"

"Can you not find some patience, young lady? I am not yet to that part of the story," replied the fairy.

"Humans are impatient," agreed Bronwen, "but do not let that pause your tale. Please continue, Rainflower."

The fairy did continue, telling a long-winded story about the challenges of hail harvesting, the degradation of the Road's stepping clouds which she has to use even though fairies fly, because *no one can fly forever*, the gossip mongering of fairies from the village of Mistkiss, because she traveled through the village on that day, and on and on.

Thomas wondered how long she would meander, but finally the fairy got to the part of her tale where Kane and Vivien came to Cloudholder Mountain and through Rainflower's village as they followed the trail of Dalrake. Rainflower shared how the two couldn't determine which direction the sorcerers had taken from the mountain, so they bargained with the village elders for a guide. She had been chosen for that duty because she was the village's best cloudfinder. She took the time to decipher the Road's path from the day before and then helped them redirect it to again take that same path. The weather was not very helpful and it ended up becoming a climber's path. (Thom had no idea what that meant, but he wasn't about to interrupt the fairy to ask.) After a long hard day, they spent the night at Dripping Branch Wayrest. When they sought to continue their journey in the morning, they found a pair of harpies blocking their path. Rainflower was able to skirt past them and escape, but the two humans are still trapped in the wayrest.

"There you have it. That is the hurried version of the tale." The fairy looked at the Keeper of the City. "But I do not understand why you have me explain all this to them, because they do not look like master magicians to me."

Bronwen nodded. "That is because they are other than wizards or sorcerers. You should know Francis from when he was a journeyman magician, or do you not recognize the Fair Defender of Laddenfree?"

"Truly?" The fairy sprang into the air and flew closer, hovering only two feet away from Francis' face. The pace of the wing strokes sped up so that she could float like a bee over a flower. Her tongue flicked in and out as if she were tasting the air around him. "I do remember you, for I was there when our queen presented you to the gathering of the Fair. I would be honored to guide you to our queen on Cloudholder."

"I no longer craft magic," replied Francis, "so I cannot walk the clouds."

Rainflower pulled back and gave a puzzled look at him and then at Bronwen.

The Keeper quickly explained, "He has taken vows to God, but these other two are both magicians."

"But they aren't masters," protested Francis. "Adele is barely an apprentice."

"I have no one else to send, at least not in time to free Kane and Vivien in time for them to hope to succeed at their mission. You have the knowledge and Thomas the skill. Together you can successfully walk the clouds."

"But of what use am I?" asked Adele. "Francis is right; I am barely an apprentice who knows only a handful of enchantments."

"You are needed for the harpies," answered Rainflower before Bronwen could say anything. The fairy fluttered over to hover over Adele's head, looking down at her. "The Keeper's intent is obvious, for those vicious things can only be approached by other females. Women they will hurt; men they kill."

Thom resisted the urge to bat the hovering lady away, for she was close to his face too and the rapid beating of her wings blew a flowery scent that tickled his nose. Instead, he stepped back one pace to get a bit of distance. "I wouldn't be fair to pull Adele into this. Is there no way Francis and I can drive away the harpies on our own?"

Rainflower moved closer to Thom and he once again got a face-full of her scented breeze. "Harpies, besides being vicious and stubborn, have long memories. They will not easily let up on a perceived enemy and something has convinced them that your friends are a danger to them. When they are so inflamed, they will not hear reasonable arguments or heartfelt pleas. They want blood." A tiny index finger pointed at Thom's nose for emphasis. "Preferably male human blood."

"All three of you will be needed," stated Bronwen. "These are not griffins or other beasts; they are beings just like us, even if they are temperamental. I would expect the three of you to do your best to drive them away rather than murder them. It will take all three of you for that to happen."

Bronwen looked specifically at Thomas and Francis. "I cannot order the two of you, for you are not league members. I can only ask. Will you take on the task of saving Kane and Vivien?"

Thom frowned in dislike of what she was asking. He looked to his companions and was surprised to see both Adele and Francis nodding. He suppressed a sigh and also gave the slightest of assents. Well, at least this time he was entering one of the Roads by his own choice, well aware that it would be a hostile path.

FIVE

Travel Plans

The fairy and her bird escorts flew out the window once Thom and the others agreed to rescue Kane and Vivien. Rainflower had promised to wait for them at the entrance to the Road of Clouds, but warned them to hurry.

As soon the fairy left, Bronwen looked at the three humans still in front of her. Thom found it a hard stare that seemed to look all the way inside of him. The silence lengthened until she finally broke it in a calm voice. "I am asking much of the three of you and for that I am sorry, but I know you can accomplish this and anything else that might be needed."

"Thomas and Adele both lack elements," stated Francis.

Francis was right. Thom's magician's cache had been taken from him during his imprisonment and then the second cache he had claimed had been taken by fire. He had nothing to craft with and not even a pestle and bowl for crushing and mixing. Adele, as a new apprentice, hadn't been issued a full supply yet.

Bronwen nodded. "I can spare some, but we have gone through large quantities trying to mend the city's enchantment."

"You know better than I that the Road of Clouds requires some very specific elements," continued Francis. "Without them we will not make it as far as Cloudholder, let alone back. We will also need whatever is required to drive off the harpies."

"You will be provided with the necessary elements, but will have to share a magician's box. Would you want a magician's staff and travel robes?"

Francis shook his head. "Thomas is the only one of us who has been awarded one and he should be the only one carrying one on the Road. As for robes, is there a way you can get us travel robes that are not black? None of us are entitled to wear the black of mastery and that would be obvious to any magicians we may encounter."

Bronwen actually smiled a bit as she shrugged. "Unfortunately, travel robes come only in black and I insist that all three of you wear one. It would be too cold without them."

Thom had never heard of "travel robes" but it sounded like they would be dressing like master magicians. The idea made him feel uncomfortable and he was sure Francis would strongly object.

Francis surprised him by simply nodded at what she had said. "What about water and food supplies?"

"That I can provide more easily than elements."

Thomas interrupted them, "How will we even get to the Road of Clouds? Isn't Clas Myrddin back in Merlin's hands? The guild guards will never let us near Sky Tower."

"I understand when you escaped you posed a guild guard," replied Bronwen. "You should do that again."

"I discarded the guard cape and staff bunting when we made it safely to the monastery."

"You will be provided with a new uniform as well as a staff, since there is no time for retrieving the one back at Saint Barnabas. Is that acceptable?"

Thom nodded, although he didn't like the idea. "If they catch me, they will do far worse than expel me from the guild."

"You were already practically exiled to the servants' quarters with rather strict restrictions, and you have already violated all of those conditions. Now the council has put a price on your head." Bronwen held up a finger to stop his protest. "I know all of it was done for the sake of others and the realm, but still it was done. You have met most of those on the guild council. How do you think they will react upon hearing that you were one of those who destroyed the classrooms at Clas Myrddin? How will they react when they learn that your master is still alive? Even if they wanted to show you any compassion, Merlin would never allow it. Thomas of York your life as a guild magician is over and the sooner you embrace that truth, the better. Your master faked his own death and will certainly be expelled by the guild, just like they did to Founder Dalrake so many years ago. As his student, the same will happen to you. It is only a matter of time. You will never get a new master assigned to you. You will never be able to earn your way to becoming a wizard of the magicians' guild. Leave off all those dreams, for they are dead to you."

The words hit him with the force of a blow. His training was truly over.

"You are being rather harsh," said Adele.

"I only state the truth," replied Bronwen. "I have no time to be gentle in this; he needs to face the truth of where he stands. He can join the sorcerers, join the league, or flee the realm. That decision can be delayed for a bit longer, just like he can deceive the guild for a few more days until someone remembers the master-less journeyman that's supposed to be in the lower levels of the keep. I doubt his pretending to be a magician-guard puts him at much more risk."

Thom grimaced but nodded. "Then I will need a journeyman's robe to wear under the magician-guard cape."

"You will have it."

"Are we really going to be doing this?" asked Adele. "What do we know about driving off harpies?"

Francis turned to her. "It is more of a convincing and intimidating them, and that is why the Keeper wants you with us. They are cruel beings, but they grudgingly respect powerful women."

"But Vivien is far more powerful than I am and they have her cornered in a Wayrest. If they don't respect her, why would they feel that towards me?"

Francis smiled, but it was a sad one. "Because you will have magic on your side. Vivien and Kane can use magic inside the Wayrest or they can craft it once they are back on the Road, but they cannot create an enchantment in the Wayrest and try to take it through the gateway to the Road. That would cause a terrible clash of magic. The harpies have trapped them by holding the gateway that connects the two, is that not correct, Keeper Bronwen?"

She nodded. "I do not have much more time for the three of you. Brother Francis, there are three enchantments that I believe are within Thomas' abilities that might work against the harpies: Fireballs, Hands of Lightning, and Twist of Air, although I would encourage negotiating if at all possible. The appropriate elements have already been set aside. I trust that you remember how they are crafted. Now, I must return to my work in restoring Camelot." She walked over to a pull rope and yanked, ringing a bell. The Keeper's apprentice came up the stairs in response.

"Letitia, take them to the supplies that were set aside for them, including the Cream of Caladrius for Thomas' ankle. If they have any other needs for their trip, do your best to fulfill those too. I need to return to my duties."

The girl gave her teacher a respectful nod and motioned for them to follow her. Bronwen turned away from everyone and walked over to look out the windows of the tower, gazing toward where the enchantment covering Camelot still pulsed and sputtered from damage done to it.

As Thom followed the young apprentice downstairs, he wondered what he had gotten himself into this time. He had no idea how to stand on a cloud, let alone how to hike among them halfway across the realm. How was that even possible?

Letitia brought them to a study that contained a wall of bookshelves, a half-dozen chairs, and a large reading table. At one end of the table lay an open knapsack and a closed magician's box. At the other end of the table lay an assortment of black robes and a dark blue one. Against one of the chairs leaned three magician staffs.

"I am to let you sort through this and then bring you to the kitchen pantry for foodstuffs," stated the apprentice girl, stepping to the side to await them.

"We are going to dress like wizards?" asked Adele in a harsh whisper.

Francis frowned but nodded. "Those robes are specifically for traveling on the Road of Clouds. Find one that fits you comfortably over your clothes but not too loose. You want it snug enough to keep in your body warmth. We will want to pack them until we get to the Road because they are too hot to wear in the city. Go ahead and find one that fits."

"You are going to wear a master's robe?" asked Thom of his friend.

"Travel robes come only in black, but that doesn't mean I will do any crafting. No one anticipated a monk walking the clouds." Francis then turned to the table to find a robe for himself.

Thom joined him, finding the garments very thick and well made. He tried on two before finding one that fit decently, which he then draped on a chair. He noticed that Adele and Francis had also found robes for themselves.

All three of them moved to the magician's box. Thom pulled it close and lifted the lid. The discordant magical sounds filled his inner ear as he started looking through the powdered elements. He pulled out one vial and found it only a thumb's width full. He tried another and also found it mostly empty. He frowned and looked up at Francis who was watching him.

"Start at the top left and examine each one," suggested the monk. "You need to see how much there is of each element in this cache. The Keeper did say that she was short on supplies."

In the end, they found only four vials that were full and those were necessary for the Cloud Walker enchantment needed to travel the Road of Clouds. All the rest of the vials were less than half full, some much less than half.

"She hasn't left any room for error," observed Francis. "You will have to be very careful in your crafting, which I know you are capable of doing."

Thom nodded but he didn't feel that confident. Instead of saying anything, he closed the box and then slid it into the knapsack. As he did, he realized the pack wasn't completely empty; it already held a bowl and pestle, as well as a jar of the bone-healing cream. Thankful as he was to have at least some supplies, he wished he had more and that Adele had a magician's cache as well. If only he had the large cache hidden in his master's suite at the guild house.

"Be sure to take a journeyman's robe, a guard cape, and a magician's staff," said Francis. "The uniform could prove helpful in getting us inside Clas Myrddin because we cannot fly directly to the top landing of Sky Tower like the fairy did."

Thom held up the three blue robes and chose the one that looked the best fit and put it on. Next, he slipped a guard cape over his shoulders and tied a guard pennon onto one of the magician staffs. "Do you really think they will let me in just because of the uniform?"

"Most likely," stated Francis. "I doubt that they have had the time to organize things at the keep. You are not the only guild magician who fled Clas Myrddin; they all did. Many went to the king's keep, but not everyone. Do you think you were the only one who hid in the city? It has only been a few days since they recaptured the city and the guild house, so others will still be returning."

"But they are searching for me. Surely the guild guards have a description of me."

"They will be looking for a scared journeyman who was living among the servants. They will not expect a confident mage-guard striding boldly through the front gate."

Thom had his doubts about that, but chose not to pursue it further. "Do you think they will have Sky Tower guarded?"

Francis frowned. "I pray not. We will have to face any such obstacles as they appear, and try to do so without wasting any of those scarce elements. There is a hidden way we might need to use to get around the tower guards."

Thom considered and then stepped close to Francis, motioning Adele over. Once they were pressed shoulder-to-shoulder he whispered so that the nearby apprentice wouldn't here. "I have another cache of elements in my master's hidden room. We would have enough to supply both Adele and I with full boxes."

"Where is this? We have no time to travel to Levitanus' cottage."

"It's in the guild house, a hidden room in his personal suite."

"Do you think it's still there?" asked Adele.

"Clas Myrddin was overthrown soon after his death, I don't think Merlin or the council ever had the time to reassign his rooms. It is likely still unknown to the guild. I think we should go to the suite before going up the tower."

"That would be worth the risk," agreed Francis. "Now let's get these bulky robes stuffed into knapsacks and then gather the rest of our supplies. We have two friends to rescue."

SIX

Return to Clas Myrddin

Clas Myrddin's main gate was still a shambles but four guild guards stood watch in the fallen wall's gap, their red capes snapping in the stiff afternoon wind. Thom, Adele, and Francis watched them from an alley farther up the road. Thom shifted the over-stuffed knapsack on his back. All three of them wore one, carrying their travel robes, water, and foodstuff. Only Thom's had a magician's cache and that one wasn't very full.

"Why is it so windy?" asked Adele, noticing something that was nagging at Thom's thoughts too.

"I can only guess that it is due to the damage above us," replied Francis, looking up at the city's invisible dome of enchantment. "Judging from the bank of clouds to the west, I would say that a storm is coming in."

"Will that storm affect the Road of Clouds as well?" asked Thomas, his eyes going to the line of clouds that led off to the southeast today.

Francis nodded. "That Road isn't as sheltered as the other Ways of Camelot. Up there, the weather always encroaches into the enchantment."

Thom swallowed. He couldn't image walking through the midst of a cloudburst or windstorm. What was he getting himself into this time?

"How will we endure it?" asked Adele, pointing at the dark clouds. "It is hard enough to walk down a street under the outpouring of a fierce storm, but how do you walk directly into the face of that?"

"I pray that we make it to the first Wayrest before it overtakes the Road. The Wayrest will shelter us until the worst of the storm has passed." Francis motioned to Thom. "We need to get moving. Take the lead because you are the one escorting us into the guild house to see one of the masters."

'To see one of the masters' was their agreed-upon story. It wasn't really a lie, since they would be seeing Kane if they succeeded and he was a master magician. Nonetheless, Thom felt nervous about the rest of the deception. He had to pretend to be one of the journeymen assigned to guild guard duty although he knew nothing about being a part of the guard. Was there an expected way to greet the men? What if there was another magician guard on duty? They would surely know he was a fraud.

"Go on, Thomas," urged Adele with a squeeze of his arm. "We need to do this because the league has no one else to send."

"No need to rush because I know you are still in pain," added Francis. "Just walk slowly but confidently and pretend you have all the authority of the

Founders behind your words. No explanations. No apologies. Just short statements and show no doubt or hesitancy."

Thom nodded, stepping out of the alley and walking purposely toward the guild house. He wanted to look back to make sure the other two were following, but he didn't. Instead, he looked directly ahead and considered how he would get inside a place where he no longer wanted to return.

The streets of Camelot were still nearly empty after all the days of fighting, so there was no sneaking up on the guild guards. The four watched them cross the cobblestoned pavement and then weave through the scattered rubble of what remained of the high wall.

"What do you have here?" asked one of them of Thomas.

Thom kept walking at them, tightening his grip on the magician's staff. "I am bringing them to see one of the masters. He wishes to talk with them. Do you have a problem with that?"

"Which wizard has summoned a monk and a lady?"

Thom gave the guard a hard stare, choosing not to answer or to stop.

"Go ahead, sir," one of the other guards said. He then turned to other. "What are you doing, Leo?"

Thom walked past them without a glance, keeping a cool expression even though his heart was pounding. He just concentrated on keep a steady pace in spite of his side starting to hurt again.

Behind him, he heard the guild guards still talking. "Don't question the mage guards. They have to do whatever the wizards order."

"I was just curious about who wanted to see those two," argued the guard named Leo.

"That will get you thrown out or worse," hissed one of the other guards. "Those two are the responsibility of the mage guard and it will fall on his head if he's brought in the wrong folk. We don't need to know what is being delivered to which master, be it a person or a package. The wizards cherish their secrecy, so never pry."

That was all said loud enough for Thom to hear, but then they lowered their voices and continued to talk even as he moved away from them. It wasn't his concern anyway. He was just thankful he had been able to get the three of them inside.

The entrance courtyard was much as he had last seen it, with scorch marks where he was almost burned during the initial invasion by the sorcerers and tumbled rock where he had sheltered when they had tried to escape from their imprisonment. It was not a place with warm memories for him.

"Keep going," whispered Francis from behind him, noticing a faltering in his step. "Take the reception doors on the right. That is the way most visitors would enter."

Thom did exactly that, for Francis was right. There were no servants monitoring the doors, but then there probably weren't that many servants left in Clas Myrddin, so he let himself in and then closed the door behind Adele and the monk.

"I would suggest removing the cape and pennon," suggested Francis, "because we are more likely to encounter other magicians now that we are inside. You should still play the role of escort, but now as a simple journeyman. I would tell you to raise your hood, but none do that indoors."

Thom nodded, swiftly taking off the red garments and handing them to Adele to stuff into his knapsack.

"Isn't it far more likely that Thomas will be recognized by someone now that we are inside?" asked Adele.

"Very likely, but I think the guild house is nearly empty. Nonetheless, we should use the servants' corridors to get as far as we can."

Thom had to agree with that. He had explored most of those routes during the first weeks of his constrainment to the keep's servants' section, so he quickly considered what would be their best route. "Follow me."

He led them to the nearest entrance to the hidden corridors and soon they were passing through the back ways of the guild house. The corridors were empty and dimly lit, until they took the back stairs up to the second floor. It was better lit as they entered the area where the master magicians had their rooms, but they still saw no one. Adele noted that fact in a whisper.

"Likely because of the time of day," replied Thomas, since it was now late morning. "In the mornings they will be bringing breakfast to the various masters, hauling fresh water, removing chamber pots, and cleaning rooms. Not as many eat in their rooms for lunch or dinner, so it is not as busy at those times. Now that it's past midday there isn't much call for servants up here. In addition, from what Bronwen had said, I doubt that there are many masters in residence."

"How close are we to your old master's suite?" asked Francis.

"I'm not certain," admitted Thom. "I explored the servants' areas after my banishment from these areas, so I didn't delve far into these routes. I risked looking down some passages, but there were servants who would have gladly reported on me so I never dared to go this far."

"Do you have any idea where we are going?" asked Adele.

A bit embarrassed, Thom tried to explain himself better. "I didn't get up to this floor, but the servants' passages have a set pattern in the other sections of the guild house. They are designed so that workers can get around the keep quickly, while keeping the worst of the bustle out of sight. We won't be able to get into Levitanus' old suite directly but there will be a door that comes out in the main hallway close to the entrance to his rooms."

Francis smiled encouragement. "Lead the way, Thomas. You still know more about these passages than either of us."

Thomas did just that, and eventually they made it inside the suite that had belonged to Levitanus. The door wasn't locked, so they slipped inside without being noticed.

"These were your master's quarters?" asked Adele. "They are well appointed."

Thom smiled at a memory, but also felt a twinge of sadness. "He rarely stayed here. He preferred a rustic cottage on the edge of the woods. Levitanus liked a simpler life than all of this, which is why he never took him here during the first decade of my apprenticeship. When I finally did stay here, I was assigned a small room behind that door over there. The master's bedroom is beyond that door."

"If he kept supplies in the magician's cabinet, then we are too late," said Francis, gesturing toward pried-open doors on the wooden furniture.

Thom frowned. He remembered that the journeyman named Sarlic had wanted to gain access to the cabinet, but there was no way to know if he had been the one to break the lock. It could have been anyone from among the guild or even one of the sorcerers when they took over the guild house. "No, I don't think he kept anything in there. Levitanus had a separate room for his supplies."

"A lead-lined room?" asked the monk, surprised.

"No, it is hidden but not shielded. The elements are kept in shielded boxes and chests. Come along and I'll show you."

He led them to the far end of the sitting room, to a richly paneled wall on which hung a series of large paintings that depicted various magical beings. He walked up to the painting of a centaur and lifted it outward, reaching behind it to trigger the hidden latch. There was a click and suddenly part of the wall opened up to reveal the room his master had secretly built so many years ago.

Seeing the darkness in the narrow room, he grabbed one of the room's unlit candelabras.

"Here, let me light that," volunteered Francis. He already had his flint and stone out.

As soon as they had a light, Thom ushered them into the secret room and shut the door behind them. He went to the far end, where there were large lead-lined chests full of elements. He pulled one out and then looked at Francis. "How can we do this quickly? As soon as I open this, it will be rather loud."

"You want two full caches," stated the monk as he looked over many shelves. A stack of four wooden boxes caught his eye. "Are these magician boxes full or empty?"

Thom had assumed they were empty, but maybe his master stored them full. "I've never glanced inside."

"Let us take a look. We will need to listen for particular elements that you will likely need, especially air elements."

"Aren't all caches the same?" asked Adele. "I know that apprentices and journeywomen have less slots filled, but I thought there was the same assigned place for each item in every box."

Francis shook his head. "No, because there are more elements than slots in even the largest cache, so a master will be selective on what to include. I have heard of wizards that have separate caches, for air or land, fire or water. Maybe these four are such."

Thom knew that there were more magical elements than any cache had room to store, but he hadn't heard of caches customized to particular types of enchantments. It made sense though. "What do you suggest?"

"You open them quickly; you will want either a typical mix or an air enchantment mix. Open. Listen. Close."

Thom nodded understanding, taking the first of the four and setting it on the chest he had already pulled out. He opened the case to a swirl of elemental sound, reminding him of merfolk and fish and rushes.

"Close it quickly," ordered Francis, which Thom did. "What did you hear?"

"That was a water cache," stated Thom, to which Adele nodded agreement.

Francis took the wooden box from Thomas and exchanged it for the next one on the shelf.

On opening the second one, Thom found the cache of air elements, filled with sounds that reminded him of pegasi and pollen, rocs and rainstorms. There were also many other magical rhythms in that box that were unfamiliar to him. He was a bit slower closing it because he was curious of the new sounds, but he still shut it quickly so that the lead-lined lid would muffle the distinct noise of raw magic.

Francis pulled down a knapsack from one of the top shelves and handed it to Thom. "Put that cache in here. Adele, can you please get a mixing bowl and pestle from over in that corner?" He indicated a neat stack of the items, probably a half-dozen of each. "Levitanus certainly kept a large supply here, considering that he rarely came to the guild house. You should open the last two caches because I think you should add the land cache to what you'll be carrying. You will recognize most of those earthly elements and know ways to craft magic from them."

Thom saw the wisdom in that, so he quickly peeked inside the other two boxes, quickly closing the one with all the exotic fire elements, even though he was curious, and taking the one that had the sounded more like a typical mixture.

"We have what we needed, now we can climb up to the Road of Clouds," said Francis.

Suddenly all of Thom's uncertainties came out. "What are we doing? I know Vivien and Kane need to be rescued, but how are we going to be able to do this? I don't even know how we are going to get onto the stairs in Sky Tower, let alone how to walk on mists."

Adele froze, staring at him. He could see her own fear in her eyes.

But Francis chuckled. "We will succeed just like we did on the other roads. As for bypassing the guards at the foot of the tower, leave that to me. You aren't the only one who knows secrets of the guild house. The masters have a second entrance onto the stairs and I know where they hid it."

His friend's smile was contagious and soon Thom was smiling too.

Adele nodded as she recovered her confidence and then she moved to the door. Before Thom could caution her, she was already opening it just enough to peek into the room beyond.

The suite remained empty, so they all stepped out into the suite, taking the now-extinguished candelabra with them.

As Thomas secured the hidden door he asked Francis, "Which way do you want to go from here?"

"Get us back into the servants' passages. If we can get to the grand hall, I can lead the rest of the way."

So the three of them slipped out of Levitanus' suite and tried to make it to the nearest entrance to a servants' passage, but just as they were about to turn the corner of the hallway, they heard others approaching.

SEVEN

Dark Places

"We shouldn't be here Sarlic. If a master finds us…"

"There are no masters at the guild house today, and I heard magical elements on this floor. Someone is where they shouldn't be."

"That's us!"

"Then leave, Patrick. We aren't the person stealing; we are here to stop whoever it is."

Thom stiffened as he realized they were about to be discovered. He turned to Francis and Adele. Adele pointed back toward the suite they had just left, but Francis shook his head. Instead, he pointed to a plain door across the hallway: the privy. Thom nodded and led the way, rushing into the small room and climbing up on the stone bench to make room for the others, trying his best to ignore the aroma coming up from the hole in the middle. He had to bend over to keep from banging his head on the ceiling above the toilet bench, but if he hadn't climbed onto it there wouldn't have been enough room for the other two to squeeze inside the small room. Francis closed the door soundlessly just before the two journeymen rounded the corner. Thom wished Francis could have left the door partially open because it was crowded in here and the smell coming up from the cesspool wafted directly up at him. Just outside the door, the two journeymen stopped to talk.

"You think it was in one of the suites?" asked Patrick. "Who would dare?"

"Someone broke into the cabinet in the old Founder's room, but I don't think they found his cache. That thief might be back."

"I thought you said that his old student did that, and he was banished from here."

"He was sent to the lower levels but no one has seen him since the sorcerers invaded. Maybe he is still slinking around and came back to steal his old master's supplies."

Thom realized who was out there: the journeyman who had escorted him away from the guild council when he was banished to the servants' section of the keep. Sarlic had been so interested in finding Levitanus' elemental cache. He was probably the one who broke into the cabinet, though there would be no way to prove it.

"Sarlic, entering a master's quarters is beyond what I will do, even a dead master's. I will keep watch out here while you check. Make it quick though. Whoever brought out those elements has concealed them again and I do not hear any active magic, so maybe they have already fled."

"I will still look." A door opened and then there was silence for a while. Finally, they heard the door closing again.

"Did you find anything amiss?"

"Nothing new," grumped Sarlic, "but it must have been that weasel Thomas. Maybe he went into one of the other suites."

"I am leaving," stated Patrick. "I do not want to be here if you're snooping elsewhere. It doesn't matter who your sire is, if they catch you in their rooms, they will throw you out of the guild if not have you executed."

"Go on, then. I'm not afraid of any black robe because they will understand that I do this for the good of the guild."

"Sarlic, you are obsessed about the dead Founder's hidden cache and his abandoned student, but the truth is that such a supply either does not exist or is still so well hidden that we will never find it. Leave that mystery for the masters to solve. Besides, anything unprotected on this floor was likely looted by the sorcerers when they came through." There was a pause, then Patrick continued. "We heard elements, so that likely means one of the masters has returned, probably to replenish elements for the repair work on the Roads. It isn't our place to question what any master is doing. We need to leave."

"You two! Why are you here?"

The newcomer sounded familiar but Thom couldn't quite place the voice, especially through the heavy door to the privy.

"We were just leaving, sir," replied Patrick.

"We heard numerous elements up here and feared there might be a thief," said Sarlic.

"What specifically did you hear?"

There was silence and then Sarlic spoke, "It was a large mixture... no three separate caches."

"One sounded very watery," added Patrick.

"Yes, and another sounded... fiery."

"Where did you hear these caches?"

"I... I am not certain," replied Sarlic. "We were passing the stairway when he heard the first one. We asked the guard if any master was in residence and he said none were, then we heard the second cache. It took some convincing to be permitted up here. He probably would not have believed us but he is one of those who can faintly hear magic. When we all heard the fiery cache, he finally relented and let us pass, with strict instructions to report back to him about whatever we found. We realized that the sound was coming from this area, but by the time we raced up the stairs and down this hallway it had all stopped. Has anyone been in your rooms, Founder Merlin?"

The leader of the guild ignored the question, but instead asked, "Did you hear any crafting or only the sound of raw elements?"

"Elements only," stated Sarlic, "but many were rare ones. Thinking back now, I would say the caches sounded like something a master would own."

At that moment, Adele almost sneezed, barely stopping it. Since the conversation continued, no one in the hallway seemed to have noticed the faint, muffled noise, but it was still distracting enough that Thomas missed the first part of Merlin's reply.

"...but I thank you for your diligence, journeymen. Most likely what you heard was one of the other wizards having returned from the Road of Leaves to replenish his supplies. You may go now, and be sure to tell the guard that you met me and have told me everything."

"Yes, sir," they both replied.

Thom shifted his stance in the alcove, pressing closer to the arrow-slit opening that was the only window to the outside and let in just a hint of fresh air and light into the murky privy. He was getting a crick in his neck from the awkward perch, but he wasn't ready to ask Francis to let them out because he worried that Merlin might still be close.

After waiting some time in silence, Francis finally whispered to the other two. "I will go out alone, with my hood up, pretending to be a confessor asked here by one of the magicians." He didn't wait for any discussion but slipped off his knapsack and then raised the hood of his robe. Silently but quickly, he opened the door and slipped out, closing it behind him.

Thomas and Adele shared a look of concern. He stepped down from his awkward perch, but that resulted in the two of them being pressed close together. As much as Thom wanted to be near her, there was no way he was going to try to kiss her in this setting. Instead, he whispered. "I pray that he finds no one. Merlin doesn't despise Francis like Dalrake does, but he certainly has no love for him."

"We should be ready for anything," suggested Adele in a soft voice, drawing her dagger.

Thom nodded, carefully pulling out his sword even while wondering what he could do with such a large blade in such a confined place. He realized that he would have to jump out of the privy to gain room to use his weapon. Even though Mercenary Marcus had told him to avoid tensing up before a fight, he still found that his muscles were tightening in anticipation.

In the end, his tension was for nothing. Francis returned and whispered through the door before opening it. "I am back and I saw no one."

Thomas and Adele stepped out and found the monk with two black robes in his arms. "I found the launderer's basket and borrowed a pair of robes, one for Adele and one for myself."

"I thought we decided not to pretend to be wizards until we had to put on those heavy travel robes," replied Adele.

"We will use these to get up the tower and then we can shed them before stepping on the first cloud. Realizing that Merlin is here has made me more cautious. He is not about to mistake my monastic garb for a master's robe, no matter the color similarity."

Thomas nodded agreement, surprised that his friend was willing to wear such garments for even a short time. He watched as the monk slipped it over his Benedictine vestments, for it was bulky enough to do so, and then re-shouldered his knapsack. When Adele put on the other one, he thought the black complemented her blue eyes and dark hair, but that raised another issue. "Put your hood up, my beloved, for no wizardess would have such rich-colored hair, unless you think we should dye your hair gray."

She raised an eyebrow at his suggestion but still pulled the cowl free from under her knapsack and covered her head. Francis raised his hood as well. Being hooded was suspicious indoors, but that was better than being recognized.

"I don't know where Merlin went, so we need to be quick yet careful in getting away from here." Francis motioned for Thomas to lead. "Get us back to the servant passages and then to the great hall and I will get us through the hidden entrance to the Sky Tower stairs."

The great hall was the largest room inside the keep. Thom had never attended any function in the grand space but he had heard it was used for balls, banquets, and important guild meetings. The huge room sat at the edge of the area he had been forbidden to enter during the time he was ostracized from the other students, so he had only looked in from the servants' doorways near the fireplace. Nonetheless, Thom was able to guide them through the back passageways to a door that came out on the great hall's mezzanine level. The three of them quietly approached the railing and looked down.

Thom saw the long wooden tables, empty of any tableware or decoration but polished to a sheen, benches pushed in neatly. The candelabras were empty as were the wall sconces, so the only light came from the twin banks of high windows above the mezzanine. On the walls hung tapestries depicting nature scenes. Either the hall had never been disturbed during the recent fighting or the keep's staff had already worked hard to restore the room, for nothing seemed out of place. At one end of the long room was a huge fireplace that lay clean and cold. At the other end was a wall of wood paneling that reminded him of the panel wall in Levitanus' suite. Above the paneled wall was a minstrel's gallery that held no musicians today. There were no people anywhere besides the three of them.

"Are we really going there?" asked Adele.

Thom gave her a questioning look, then realized she was staring out the bank of windows that was above their floor. High above the great hall was a glimpse of the Road of Clouds.

"Soon," replied Francis in a low voice, "but first we have a few steps to climb. You can barely see where the clouds end at the tower from here, but you can see how high it is. It will be a strenuous hike for certain." He motioned that they would follow the mezzanine around to the far side. "The masters' lounge is across from us, between the tower and the great hall."

So they walked around that floor, trying to move quietly. They passed through sunlight from the windows and shadows cast by the mezzanine's columns, their footsteps on the tiled floor still echoing even though they tried to be cautious, but they heard nothing else and saw no one.

Just as they completed the circuit and reached the double doors to the lounge, Thomas looked back and thought he saw a black robed, white-haired man across the hall from them. He caught his breath and touched Francis on the shoulder to warn him, but when he looked back the person was gone.

"What disturbs you?" asked Francis.

"I thought I saw a wizard on the mezzanine across from us, but I cannot see anyone now and didn't hear any magic that could have hidden him."

"We need to move faster," replied Francis, his words urgent even if barely above a whisper.

They enter the plush lounge but took no time to appreciate its furnishings or decor. Instead, Francis hurried to a wood paneled wall behind a pair of armchairs. He pushed an unlit sconce to the left and there was an audible click as part of the wall opened inward.

"No time to light a candle. We will just have to climb the stairs in the dark," said the monk.

"All the way to the top of the tower?" asked Adele, sounding doubtful.

Francis smiled in spite of the tension. "No, just to the third-floor landing, then we will open another hidden doorway and reach the tower's stairwell. Go on, Lady Adele, lead the way."

As he climbed in the dark behind Francis, Thom wondered how many hidden ways there were inside the guild house and why they were needed. "Why would the wizards need a hidden entrance?"

"My old master claimed it was for convenience, but I think many used it to avoid the guards that are always posted at the foot of the stairs."

"Are there no guards at the top?"

"Why should there be?" asked Francis. "Only master magicians and magical beings can travel the Road of Clouds and a mere guard cannot do much to stop either."

"But when the sorcerers invaded, I saw some kind of magical warfare occurring up there."

"Maybe the invaders surprised some wizard getting ready to take the Road," mused Francis, though he didn't sound fully convinced by his own words.

"Or maybe after all the antics on the Roads, the guild posted additional guards on the route we are heading toward," suggested Adele.

"Enough talking," said Francis. "Pay attention to where you're stepping. Adele, when you get to the top of the stairs, move to the right so that I can get past you and trigger the other door."

"Is it hidden from this side as well?" she asked.

"No, but it will be hard for you to find it in the dark, while I remember where to find that latch."

"You remember it that well after so many years?" asked Thomas.

"I remember everything about that journey; it was my last as a magician."

EIGHT

Climbing Stairs

They came out of the hidden stairs to a well-lit landing inside Sky Tower. As Francis shut the door behind them, Thom thought he saw some light at the bottom of the hidden stairway, as if someone had opened the lower door, but he heard no one. It was just a brief moment viewed over the monk's shoulder, so he couldn't be certain, but he whispered a warning to the others.

"We need to climb quickly then," said Francis, "for there's no way to bar the door from here."

"Should we grab one of the torches?" asked Adele as they started moving up the tower. "It looks rather dark farther up."

"No need. There will be at least one lit torch on each half-rotation and once we are beyond the next landing, there will be arrow-slit windows that let in light."

So they climbed, going as fast as they could on the steep stairs that kept circling to the right. The way darkened between torches but they could still see the steps clearly. When they came out on the next landing they paused to listen for any pursuit, but heard nothing. Thom noticed another doorway and pointed to it without saying anything.

"The door leads out onto the keep's rooftop walk," explained Francis in a whisper. "It is concealed on the other side to look like a store room for the guild guards. We will not have another exit until we reach the tower walk just below the enchantment that covers the city. Let's keep climbing."

Sky Tower was the highest spire in the realm. It would have been impossible to build without the aid of magic because no scaffolding could have reach so high, but there was no active magic involved in keeping it standing. As Thom climbed, he heard no elemental sounds from its stones, though with each rotation up the stairwell he could hear that they were drawing closer to the dome of the city's enchantment. They had to pause regularly so that Thomas could catch his breath and take the weight off his left ankle. It was throbbing constantly now but surprisingly held out and wasn't excruciating. Using the journeyman's staff to help support his weight helped.

When they finally reached the last landing within the enchantment, the sound of the magic was very loud in his ears. The landing was large but there was no furniture or window ledge to sit on. Rather than just standing there, Thom turned to the doors that led outside to the tower walk and stepped out, hoping to rest by leaning against the parapet wall. Adele and Francis followed.

Below them was all of Camelot, shining in the afternoon sun. Near to where

Thom was resting, he saw a chunk of the parapet gone from where the roc had tried to perch a few days ago. Looking out, he saw the tower where he had inadvertently seen the sorcerers releasing griffins on the city from this very walk. Looking beyond that, he could see the stout walls and towers of Camelot Castle to the northwest. Looking the other direction, he saw the glisten of the clear waters of King's Harbor to the east.

"Why can't I hear the Road of Clouds?" asked Adele, looking up at the very near puffs of white and gray.

"It is like in Mousehome," replied Francis. "We are on the wrong side of an enchantment. Once we pass through, we will hear it."

Thom nodded in agreement for he remembered the tunnel under the city and how the magic sounds seem to cease as soon as he stepped out from under the enchantment. "Francis, correct me if I am mistaken, but isn't there a level of Sky Tower that is inside neither enchantment, when both will be muffled to us."

"That is correct, but we will not pause on that floor. Maybe we can do so on our return trip, but we need to catch up with our fairy guide."

"Will we be coming back this way?" asked Adele, "or will we go on with Kane and Vivien to rescue Wizard Levitanus?"

"I would think that it would be easier for them to go on without us once we have them freed," replied Francis. "It will be hard enough for us to travel as far we must to rescue them, but the second half of the Road is far harder than the section we plan to traverse." He looked over at Thomas, who was leaning on the walk's wall. "Are you ready to go on? I know this pace is hard on you, but we need to reach Rainflower soon if we want to make it as far as the first Wayrest before sunset. That storm is still coming toward us and I would rather not be stranded on the Road when it overtakes us."

Thom nodded as he realized that it was almost midday. He pushed off the wall and hobbled back toward the door, leaning heavily on his staff.

"Does the Road of Clouds go wild after dark like the Road of Leaves?" asked Adele as she followed the two men.

"This Road is always wild," replied Francis as he held the door open for Thom to pass through, "so there is no difference between night and day, but it is harder to see where to step in the dark and missing a step will kill you."

The monk walked over to a row of wall pegs that held a few travel robes like the ones they were carrying. "It is time for us to shed these borrowed robes and put on the travel robes."

"Should I get rid of the guard trappings too?"

"I think so, but hang them behind the robes."

All three of them changed robes and soon were sweltering in the thicker ones. Thom didn't look forward to climbing another flight of stairs in such hot clothing, but it was necessary.

"We've delayed here long enough," said Francis. "Lead us again, Thomas."

But as they turned to the stairs upward, all three of them heard an enchantment below them, a sound that was steadily drawing closer.

"What is that?" asked Thomas in alarm.

Francis pushed them to keep moving. "Some masters use magic to ascend rather than climbing the stairs. Whoever is behind us is being rather extravagant with their cache."

"Do you think it's Merlin?" asked Adele.

"That is likely," replied Francis, "and he will try to ensnare us or kill us if he cannot capture us."

"You really think he's that cruel?"

"Founder Merlin does whatever he thinks is necessary and does it without any hesitation."

"Do you agree with Francis?" asked Adele of Thom.

Thom was ahead of them on the stairs and had just passed through Camelot's enchantment. Suddenly he couldn't hear anything beneath him, not Merlin's progress, not even the city-covering enchantment. The sudden change was jarring.

"Thomas? Did you hear me?"

"Sorry. I was distracted. Wizard Merlin is convinced that whatever is best for him is what is best for the king and the realm. If he sees us as a threat to himself or the realm, he will attack with as much magic as necessary to stop us, even if that causes our death."

"So you do think that... oh, that's what distracted you." She had just climbed through the top of Camelot's enchantment. She stopped as the sudden change became apparent and looked up, as if she could see something through the stone ceiling. "I still cannot hear the Road of Clouds."

"Keep moving," urged Francis from behind them. "You will hear the Road when we climb up to the top of the tower and reach the gateway. And when we get up there, remember that the fairies know nothing about the league. To them, we are either from the guild or from the sorcerers. Do not let Rainflower find out about any of this, for she seems prone to indiscriminate chatter."

"Does the Fairy Queen know about the league?" asked Thomas, wondering why Rainflower had been sent to Bronwen instead of the Keeper of the Road.

"Yes, I'm fairly certain of that, but I have never been privy to dealings of the league's inner circle. We can talk more of that some other time. I only wanted to warn about sharing too much in front of Rainflower. Now pay attention to what is above us. If there are any guards on the Road's entrance, they will be at the top. Also be careful because the stones are wet."

Although he was doubtful that he had the strength for any sword fight, Thom pulled free his blade and went first up the stairs, staff in his left hand and sword in his right. He wasn't about to try any enchantments this close to a gateway. Slowly and without much sound, he stalked up the curving stairs to the top of Sky Tower.

NINE

Into the Fog

Thom tried to rush up the last steps, but his body betrayed him. It was more of stagger. Desperately, he pointed the sword in all directions, but he found the room empty. And wet.

He kept moving to give Adele and Francis room to get up too. He spun around a few times but still saw no one. The floor flagstones were dark with moisture, much of it also green with moss as well, making it a slick surface. He slowed down when he felt one foot slip but still kept turning as he looked for any guards.

"No one is here besides us," stated Francis.

"It seems like we are in a different place altogether," remarked Adele. "Everything is so wet and it's clammy."

"That's what happens when you are inside a cloud every day," said Francis, walking past Thomas and toward an open doorway in the tower room. He slipped his cudgel back into its loop on his rope belt and seemed to relax some.

"Where's the fairy?" asked Thom.

"I expect that she's waiting on the other side of the gateway. I neither see or hear anyone up here, so go ahead and sheath your sword. You'll need at least one hand free as we approach the gate."

Thom put away his sword although he didn't understand what Francis was implying about needing a hand free.

"Is there anything we can do to block the way of the wizard following us?" asked Adele, looking back down the stairs they had just ascended.

"Not unless we collapsed the stairwell and I rather not destroy the tower with us at its pinnacle. We should hurry and get through the gateway."

"Where is it?" asked Thom, once again spinning around. The tower room had open windows all around but there was nothing to see outside. Gateways usually had a glow about them, but he couldn't see even a hint of its light. "I only see clouds beyond the doorway and the windows."

"We need to step outside and follow the wall to the right for three openings and then step straight out into the clouds. We will only see the gateway once we are right upon it. Oh, and please stay directly behind me because there is no parapet wall up here. Step too far in the wrong direction and you will plunge off Sky Tower."

"Who builds a tower walk without an outer wall?" asked Adele.

"Arrogant magicians who see everything as a test and an opportunity to show their skills," replied Francis, "at least that was what I thought when I was a journeyman."

Francis waited until the two were pressed up behind him to explain what they would do next. "Thomas, keep your staff ready to use as a weapon, if nothing else. Soon, you will have to learn how to make its jewel glow because that light will help keep the fog at bay, but for now the staff will make a decent club should we encounter any danger lurking on the other side of the gateway. Until we get there, we'll almost be walking blind, so I want Adele to hold onto the hem of my robe and Thomas to hold her other hand. As I said, keep directly behind me in a line because the tower walk is rather narrow. Now, let's go."

Last in line, Thomas did his best to stay as close as he could to the others. Adele held onto Francis' robe with her left hand, while reaching back with her right to hold Thom's hand. He had shifted the staff to his left hand and used it to stabilize his gait and to probe for the edge of the walkway. When he looked over Adele's shoulder, Francis was nothing more than a shadow and soon the clouds thickened so much that he lost sight of the monk and Adele became shadowy too. It was an unnerving experience, especially since it was so silent up here. They were outside both enchantments, so he heard nothing of Camelot or the Road of Clouds. All that he heard was their shuffling along the wet stones and his own breathing.

"I am at the third window," announced Francis. His voice seemed to boom in the silence but he hadn't spoken loudly. "I will now walk outward straight from the window. Do not try to angle behind me. Instead, make sure you are squarely between and that opening. I will move slower so that no one loses their grip as we shift direction."

They made the transition and started walking away from the tower. To Thom it felt like they were shuffling toward their death plunge. Step by step they slowly moved outward and it seemed to take forever. He looked back once but Sky Tower was nowhere to be seen. All around him was swirling dark clouds, too thick for any sunlight to penetrate. The only thing solid was the wet stones under his boots and Adele's now-chilled hand.

"I see it," came Francis' voice from somewhere ahead him.

Thom saw nothing except the uncertain form of Adele but he kept walking, trusting that Francis wouldn't lead them to a deadly fall.

"I see it too," said Adele as she slowed down.

Thom slowed too, rather than run into her. He couldn't make out the gateway, but the fog in front of Adele did seem a bit lighter.

"Let go of my robe and follow right after me," said Francis.

There was a slight pause, then Adele said, "He's gone. Can you see it yet, Thomas?"

"Not clearly, but keep moving toward it and I'm sure I will."

She took another two steps and suddenly it came into view. The gateway looked much like the ones on the other Roads, but smaller. This route didn't see ships passing through or even wagon trains. There was no need for a large entrance. It was narrow enough that Thom could probably embrace the side columns and just stick his head through, though he wasn't about to try that.

Thom let go of Adele's hand. "Go ahead of me; it's not wide enough for us to walk side-by-side. I will be right behind you."

Just as she disappeared through the portal, Thom heard a scream behind him. With wide eyes he whirled, looking disparately into the fog. He heard it again, like an overloud eagle's cry but he knew it was the voice of something far worse and it was coming towards him very fast.

Turning back toward the portal, he ran the last steps and then threw himself into it, hoping no one was standing in the way on the other side.

TEN

Icy Entrance

Thom leaped through the gate, hitting the ground hard and skidding across an icy surface. In a panic, he tried hard to stop his sliding but there was nothing to grasp.

"Grab him, Adele," yelled Francis.

Even as he kept sliding in spite of Adele grabbing his good leg, he yelled, "Everyone out of the way! There's a griffin behind me!"

A shocked Francis threw himself to the ground, just as the griffin broke through, screaming as it did.

Thom finally slammed into something… an ice-coated stone bench. He let go of the magician staff he was clutching as he tried to embrace a bench leg with both arms. Just as he got a grip on it, Adele slammed into him, for she had been sliding after him, and then Francis bumped against both of them.

The griffin screamed again and looked directly at them. It probably would have snatched one of them as a meal, but Rainflower had flown in front of it as she tried to escape the beast. The griffin switched its attention and launched into the air after her, but the fairy and her bird companions were too nimble, easily dodging the large brute. The eagle-lion screamed in frustration but did not try to turn back, quickly vanishing from sight in the lighter fog that seemed to prevail on this side of the portal.

Thom pulled himself up onto the cold bench and gave a hand to Adele to sit next to him. They both reached out to Francis and he stood in front of them, being cautious on the slippery ice. Surprisingly, the monk had somehow rescued Thom's errant staff and handed it back to him.

"Did a wizard send that after us?" asked Thomas as he leaned the staff next to him on the frigid bench.

Francis was staring at the portal as if he expected another monster to burst through. Not taking his eyes off of it, he answered, "It might have come through on its own, having tired of hunting in Camelot, but more likely the magician we heard behind us sent it through. I don't know whether that person was a wizard or a sorcerer who lingered after the failed invasion."

Suddenly Rainflower popped up behind the bench. "It was driven through by magic. It was more angry than hungry."

Thom looked over his shoulder at the fairy and realized that the bench sat on the edge of the platform. It dropped off into nothing but clouds. Rainflower flew over them and daintily landed in front of the portal. Her bird companions flew up after her and settled on the edge of a bench on the other side of the platform.

"Why is everything icy?" asked Adele, giving a slight shiver.

"The Road of Clouds is made of ice," stated Francis, "but when we reach the Wayrest it will be warm. Now, Thomas needs to craft the first two enchantments we need to walk on the clouds. We need to be quick about it to avoid the magician behind us and the storm brewing ahead of us, so get your supplies out, Thomas. Adele, you can help by holding the mixing bowl so that it doesn't skitter away from him."

Thomas swung his knapsack off and set it between his feet. He took out the cache of air elements and opened it on his lap then looked up at Francis for instruction.

"You will be doing two enchantments, one to grab the icy steps and another to help us leap and almost float across cloud gaps. They are known as Sole Grip and Sole Flight. The For the first, you will want powdered Cheviot Regal Goat hoof, Rowan root, Blue Lichen, and crushed Stickleback burs. Give those four to Adele until you are ready to craft. For the second enchantment, you will need powdered Phoenix feather, Pegasi mane, Copper Dandelion seed, and Gray Gannet feather. Give those vials to me."

Thom found all the correct vials with some direction by Francis and then started crafting the first enchantment. He worked as quickly as he could, very much aware that at any moment guild guards could swarm through the gateway and capture them. He added water from one of their waterskins and then as the last step, spat in the bowl to attune the magic to himself.

"Good. Now you need to slather this on our boot heels. Do so liberally for all three of us, because it will keep us from sliding on the ice, but do not touch any of it to the toe section of our boots. The second enchantment coats that area. Each boot's instep should remain clear of any magical pastes so that there is separation. Also, put a dab on the butt of the magician's staff, but only on the iron cap. Keep the wood clean because you will be kindling the gem at the top, and I want clear separation there as well."

Thom did as told, putting the goop on their heels and then on the butt of the staff. In the cold, the goop quickly started to harden and by the time he was done the leftovers were already hardening in the bowl.

"We can all stand on it already, but you need to get your bowl cleaned quickly or else you'll be chipping at it for hours. Wipe your hands clean too."

He did so and then looked around, wondering where to dispose of the now dirty rag.

"Fold the cloth and save it for next time. Now, get on with your next enchantment. Adele, hold onto the bowl for him because this crafting has a tendency to make the bowl and pestle float away."

As Thom started mixing the next enchantment, Francis gave an additional warning, "Keep the first enchantment active, Thomas. You will need to maintain both enchantments until we reach the first Wayrest."

He nodded understanding, for this wasn't the first time he had to keep two enchantments going at the same time, but it wouldn't be an easy task.

Thom, with Adele's help, completed the second crafting and then applied it to the toe area of everyone's soles, making sure that the two enchantments were separated by a clear insole so that there was no danger of the magics touching. When done, he once again wiped out his bowl and cleaned his hands.

"Now we should practice standing and walking," suggested Francis. "It will be awkward at first. If you go up on your toes, there will be a bounce in your steps that could send you flying off this platform. If dig in your heels, you'll barely be able to move. To simply walk you need to do a rolling motion from heel to toe with each step."

Rainflower settled on one of the icy benches to watch as they cautiously tried walking around the small area in front of the gateway. "You use older enchantments? Why is that?"

"He conserves power for what lies ahead," replied Francis, "and this way we will be quieter as we travel along the Road."

"There is some wisdom in that," conceded the fairy in a flat tone.

Thom thought she didn't sound fully convinced with Francis' choice of enchantments but he had no way of comparing the various magical ways of traversing the Road. If one of the other methods was the enchantment the other magician was using to ascend Sky Tower, then this one was definitely quieter.

"Can we go now?" asked Rainflower. "As you have already noted, there is a storm approaching and I would rather be in the Wayrest when the weather changes. I dislike getting my wings, hair, or clothes wet."

Thom wondered if the cold bothered her as well, for her tiny feet were bare and she was standing on one of the ice-covered benches.

"To the Road," said Francis, stepping between the benches to the edge of the ice. Through the mist, Thom saw two sets of whitish stepping stones laid out on the clouds themselves. "You will notice that there are two ways before us, one coming and one going. If you listen carefully, you will know which one we are going to follow."

He paused, expected Thom and Adele to follow his suggestion. Thom did so, listening to the magic until he noticed a pulsing in the two paths. One seemed to pulse toward them and one away. Thom nodded his understanding and looked to Adele, who was pointing at the path on the left, the one pulsing away from them.

"The magic helps to carry us across the heavens, much like a current would carry us across the seas. You will likely not notice the added speed to our steps, but it is what enables us to traverse distances in only days that would take weeks if we were walking on the ground far below us. Now, enough with my lecturing; we need to get going."

Francis motioned them to wait while he stepped to the very edge in front of the path Adele rightly pointed out. "Let me go first because there is a certain skill of pushing off with the front of your boots and landing on your heels. I don't want either of you to skip like a flat rock skimmed on a lake. Just watch how I launch myself and how I land. The first stepping stone is not far off and isn't at a different height, so this will be a simpler jump. Come here to edge and watch carefully."

Thom and Adele crept to the edge of the platform, neither of them feeling as confident in their walking as the monk. Thom could see the next stepping stone floating across a misty gap that he could have easily jumped if it were on the ground. He wasn't so sure how well he would manage it with the weird enchantments slathered on this footwear.

They watched as Francis walked confidently toward the edge and then rose up on his toes and jumped, flying through the air, and easily spanning the gap to the next stepping stone of ice. In mid-flight he shifted so that his heels would land first and when he hit it was hard landing that he had to absorb by bending his knees and squatting deeply. Once stable, he turned and called out to them. "I exaggerated my movements so that you'll understand what to do. Adele, you should jump next."

She nodded and tried to emulate what Francis did but she kicked off too hard and sored rather high. Awkwardly, she shifted her heels downward for her landing but was heading close to the far edge of the stepping stone. Francis helped her by grabbing her arm and pulling her downward while digging in his own heels. She landed solidly but took a moment to regain her balance, whirling her arms outward until she felt in control again.

Once she was stable, Francis motioned for Thom to follow, so he swallowed to wet a suddenly dry throat and then stepped back from the edge. He knew better than to run or even walk too fast. That would not be good with his still-sore ankle. He decided on a steady pace using his staff in his left hand to offer a bit of extra support. Backed up almost to the gateway, he walked forward as quickly as he felt his battered body could handle and then tried to push off with the same force with both legs, but his weakened ankle betrayed him at the last and he launched crookedly.

Francis quickly shifted, scooting over further so that he would be on Thom's weak side when he landed.

"Keep the enchantments going," reminded the monk. "Now, shift your heels forward."

It all happened so fast, but he made it, although his landing was uneven.

"He jumps like a one-legged frog," remarked Rainflower, who had been hovering to one side.

Thom chose to ignore her. He was just glad he made it and his ankle seemed no worse for the leap.

"Only a few hundred stepping stones still ahead," continued the fairy. "I hope your jumps improve or you will likely end up splatting on some farmer's field far below us."

ELEVEN

Walking on Clouds

Thom wanted to continue on to prove that he could jump well, but Francis put a restraining hand on his chest. "Stop for a moment. Both of you. We need to listen to the magic around us. How does the Road of Clouds sound? Does its magic beat steady? You should always remind yourself that being inside of an enchantment is almost as dangerous as being hit by one. Listen carefully but quickly. I want us to be at least five stepping stones away before whoever follows comes through that portal. At that distance they will not be able to see us though they will still hear your magic."

"Why haven't they already come through?" asked Thom.

"They fear a magical trap, so they hesitate. I expected them to charge through behind the griffin, but when they didn't, I realized we would have some time before we were followed. Whoever it was we heard ascending the tower, he's waiting to send someone else ahead of him. Maybe it will be a student or guild guard or even a servant of the keep, but it will be someone who can step back through and tell him what is waiting in here."

"Should we then go back and set a trap for anyone following?" asked Adele.

"Do you think its Merlin out there?" asked Thom at the same time.

Francis lowered his voice. "Careful in what you say. Rainflower is a guide, not a companion. We don't have the time to set and maintain a trap. As to who is out there, it could be Merlin but I've never heard that he had an affinity for griffins. In the past, only strong sorcerers developed the skill to order those monsters to do their bidding." He paused a moment and looked around them. "We need to stop all this speculation. As I asked, take a moment to listen with your inner ear. Get a feel for the enchantment's size. How does the Road's magic sound?"

Thom did so. He found it to be a steady rhythm that was also somehow wispy, as if the magic floated with the clouds all around them. That made sense, since it was said that this Road was far more capricious than any of the others. He could no longer see the route that went in the other direction but he could hear that it was close, its pulsing moving back toward the tower. He strained his inner ear even more, trying to discern if there was any other active magic, but heard nothing except his own enchantments on their boots. As for the Road, the enchantment seemed to be shaped like a "U" cupping both paths in its side walls connecting that went skyward to a height of about three-story building. There was some kind of ethereal floor below the pair of paths, but it was certainly not solid. The *roof* above it all was more subtle, like a flimsy curtain drawn taunt across the top. As for the magic itself, Thom heard nothing jarring or weakened. "I haven't listened to this Road before, but the enchantment seems strong."

"It is," agreed Francis, "so remember how it sounds."

"You expect us to encounter damaged areas?" asked Adele.

"Likely, since we've seen such on both of the other Roads we've traveled and also at Camelot. Learn how it should sound and then you will be more aware when something goes awry." Suddenly, he strode to the edge of the step and jumped to the next one, his feet brushing through drifting wisps. "Come along. We have a long journey ahead of us."

The second floating chunk of ice was longer and abutted the third one with barely a hand's width of a gap, so they were able to walk for a ways, then came another leap, another walk, another leap. And so it went for the next hour. It was almost like crossing an ice-choked river and jumping over breaks, but instead of being on top of a racing water flow they were bobbing among the ephemeral clouds. Thom tried not to dwell on the ice pavers too much, but he still wondered how thick they were and how long they lasted before the Road shifted and the clouds dissipated. Did they plunge to earth whole or would they suddenly melt? He stopped pondering when he felt his enchantments wavering slightly. "Keep focused," he muttered to himself as they got ready to leap to the next floating ice paver.

As he landed on the next sky island, Thom heard a distinctive cracking sound. He looked over at Adele, who was already standing on the ice. "What was that?"

Francis landed nearby and there was another cracking sound. "The Road is shifting. Hurry, we need to move to the next cloud."

Thom strode over to the far edge but he saw only scattered wisps and a long drop to the next layer of darkening clouds. He saw no ice islands anywhere. "Where do we go next?"

"This way," said Rainflower, hovering to the right. "The Road of Clouds shifts away from the coming storm. The new island is still hardening, so be careful in your landing."

When Thom made the leap over, he found it to be slushy. He looked questioningly at Francis.

"It will harden soon, but it is still safe to walk on. Your enchantment pastes have had enough time to set, so the slush shouldn't affect your magic. Look around for our next cloud because the Road is shifting quickly."

"I think I see it," said Thomas, having walked straight across the island, "but the route is obscured in more clouds."

"There is something over here," said Adele, indicating a cloud again to the right, "but this is different. It is more like narrow stairs."

"That's it," declared Rainflower, flying over to Adele. "The Road now wants to move higher up to avoid the worst of the storm."

"Follow the women," said Francis to Thom as he sloshed in their direction.

The jump over to the stairs was not a long one but the landing area was much smaller so they had to aim carefully. Once over, they started climbing a steep flight of ice steps as the cloud folded around them like a gray blanket. Soon they were all wet from the ambient moisture. They had to learn an awkward rolling gait letting their heels hit the ice first so that the Sole Grip would give them a firm hold, and then roll forward as they stepped up, letting the Sole Flight enchantment give them a little boost to the next step. It was an odd way to walk, but it made the steep ascent easier.

Thom climbed first, using his staff to help find each step in the growing fog. "It's getting hard to see."

"You should light your staff," suggested Rainflower from somewhere over to the side.

Thom didn't reply, not wanting to admit to her that he didn't know how.

"It is best that he doesn't," said Francis from behind him, for he was climbing last in line. "The less magic the better, to avoid easy detection."

"You fear the harpies already? They have your friends trapped at the first Wayrest beyond Cloudholder, so they will not be able to hear any magic happening this far away."

"We are more concerned about any who are coming behind us," replied the monk. Thom could tell he was being careful in answering the fairy. "I believe you know about the recent disputes between the magicians' guild and the sorcerers. That griffin bursting through may not have been a coincidence."

Rainflower flew closer and Thom could now see her blue-purple wings through the fog. "I understand, though I do not know why you humans need to quarrel so much. You are such hasty and temperamental people."

"God certainly made humans different from other beings such as merfolk and pixies, but all humans are not identical, Rainflower. Just like one fairy is different from another in appearance, affinities, and abilities, so humans are different from each other."

The fairy didn't respond but instead flew ahead, disappearing into the fog again.

They kept climbing for another fifty steps but it wasn't a straight climb, so they had to be careful where they stepped as each riser seemed to turn in another direction. It was an ice stairway that seemed to snake upward through the cloud, twisting and turning for some reason unknown to them. When Thomas finally reached the top of the stairway, he came out on top of the cloud to blue skies overhead. The view awed him and it took a poke in his back by Adele to get him moving again. He stepped forward so that the others could ascend out of the mists into the sunshine. A steady breeze seemed to push him on forward too.

"It's beautiful," whispered Adele, gazing at the expanse of blue in front of them.

"Be careful of the walkway," warned Francis. "In the sunshine the Road can get rather slick from a bit of melt, so keep your heels down. We also need to keep moving because it isn't all sunny skies up here. Look behind us."

Both Thom and Adele turned and realized there was a wall of dark clouds looming on the horizon. The storm was still there but their sense of direction had been lost in all the twisting of the Road.

"How soon will it be on us?" asked Adele.

"By sunset," replied Rainflower. They turned to see her standing on the icy walkway ahead of them. "We will feel more of its wind within the hour."

Thom kept looking around and realized something. "I can feel the Road's enchantment around us, but it seems far more ephemeral than the other Roads. Is this magic not as strong?"

"I would say it is more porous," replied Francis. "On the other Roads, if you get too close to the walls of the enchantment, you bounce back. Here, if you fall off the path you keep falling. The sides and floor of the Road give a painful jolt to any who pass through it. They say the jolt is strong enough that many lose consciousness, which might be welcome if you are plunging toward the ground. As for the ceiling above us, anyone passing through it will feel discomfort but not much more. The Road of Clouds lets in the weather and allows birds to pass through. It doesn't block the rain from reaching whatever fields might be below it today. If you misstep up here you will plunge to your death, unless you have wings like our guide."

Adele noticed the path for the other direction below them and asked if it would be possible to leap from one to the other.

"It has been done," admitted Francis, "but remember that the magic is like a flow in either direction. It might seem like we are standing still at the moment, but we are really just moving in the same direction as the windblown clouds, making it all seem to be standing still. If we were on that path over there it would seem like the clouds were roaring past us. It is all rather deceiving, but trust me that both paths are moving in opposite directions. If you were to leap from one to the other, it would be much like jumping off a careening wagon. Expect to get bruised and battered, at the least. I would suggest that we not attempt any such jump unless it is a rather dire situation."

Thom nodded agreement and was about to reply that he wanted no more wounds, when he heard something new. Someone was using magic, somewhere behind them.

"Hoods up," ordered Francis as he raised his own. "Someone sends an Eagle's Spying to see who we are. Let us keep going because it looks like the Road digs back into the next cloud and it will be harder to recognize us hidden in the mists."

Thom remembered watching the Wizard Cath craft an Eagle's Spying while they were on the Road of Waters. The tiny, purple-glowing sphere would shoot out from the magician and spy out the land for as long as the wizard or sorcerer controlled the enchantment. He pulled up his hood and started walking again, using his staff to keep a fast pace and doing his best to ignore his now-throbbing ankle and side.

In his eagerness to get away from the prying eyes of whatever magician was following them, Thom leaped hard to cross the gap to the next cloud. His toe-push sent him flying far and he plunged into the next cloud and lost sight of the path.

TWELVE

Pursued

For a brief moment Thomas thought he had overshot in his jump and was going to die, but then he hit the ice with his toes, causing another jolt up and out. Panicked, he whirled his arms and almost dropped the staff as he tried to get his heels down to catch the next landing. The second time, he hit the ice and stuck, the shock of the hard landing going up his legs and back.

"Thomas! Where are you?" yelled out Francis as the monk sprang after him.

Something blue fluttered nearby. "He is over here," reported Rainflower. "He is fortunate that the Road is straight and wide on this cloud or he would have definitely missed his landing."

The others quickly caught up with him as Rainflower settled daintily on the ice just ahead.

"Are you alright?" asked Adele, hugging him.

He hugged her back tightly, resting his head on her shoulder. A shiver ran through him as he realized how close he had come to dying.

"The Eagle's Spying nears," said Francis. "Separate and look down. That will make it hard for the spy to see under our hoods. Rainflower, please guide us across the ice, for I think Thomas was a bit shaken by that last leap. Please move slowly, for I would rather be seen in this fog than under clear skies."

The fairy gave him a little bow of agreement and then flittered ahead of them, a bit of blue in a world of gray. The three humans kept walking, following the fairy. They heard the approaching enchantment as it followed the twists and turns of the Road of Clouds.

Thom caught his breath when he realized that there was a purple glow behind him. He wasn't aware if the enchantment made any actual sound, but it certainly had a distinct rhythm to his inner ear. The purple sphere hovered nearby as its sender took his time to look at them. Once it even passed close enough for Thom to touch it, but instead he reached up and pulled his hood lower.

The purple sphere swept around Rainflower and then twice more around the three humans dressed in black robes and then it suddenly vanished, the enchantment ended. But just as they sighed in relief and dropped their hoods, they heard another enchantment being crafted. Thom recognized it from when he and Vivien helped his old master craft the same enchantment on the Road of Waters. The magician was crafting a Tarn's Call to amplify his voice.

"Hide in shame, sorcerers," boomed Merlin, for it was him who had followed them onto the Road. "Now flee after Dalrake and never again come to Camelot or I will have you imprisoned."

With that, the enchantment ended and the only magic they heard was the Road around them and the enchantments that Thom was maintaining on their boots.

"Why does Founder Merlin name you sorcerers?" asked Rainflower.

"He is mistaken," replied Adele.

"Then why dress in black robes and hide your faces from him?"

Adele looked to Francis for an answer. Thom was also at a loss for words because they were supposed to keep the league a secret.

"We are not sorcerers," replied the monk, "but we also do not have Merlin's permission to be on this Road. Keeper Bronwen sent us because our friends need rescuing, but she did so without the guild's knowledge."

"Because you are the Fair Defender, I will accept that you are not sorcerers. I will also accept that you hid your faces from the magical spying because you did not know who sent it. However, once you heard Founder Merlin's voice, why did you not call him here to help? Certainly, he of all humans would be able to easily chase away troublesome harpies. You should be sending a magical message back to him to bring him here. Why is the one you call Thomas not doing so?"

"Our friends are on an urgent task and need to be freed to pursue their duties. If Merlin encounters them, he would likely chase off the harpies but then detain our friends. They deserve the chance to finish their mission."

"What does Merlin have against them?"

"That is their tale to share, not mine," replied Francis. "We can only say that it would be best for them not to be discovered by Merlin or Dalrake or anyone else. As for us, we only want to free our friends and then return to Camelot. Nothing else."

"You are leaving much unsaid." She hovered at eye level close to the monk and her face was stern. "I will share with my queen all of my concerns when next I see her, but for now I will guide you as she bade."

"Understood," replied Francis, signaling for the other two to start walking again.

The fairy flew near them for a moment, then raced ahead, disappearing into the fog.

"We might not see her again until we reach Crooked Bough Wayrest. Fairies do not fly in bad weather and it will soon turn into quite a storm," noted the monk. "Pick up the pace, Thomas. We started our travels later than most who enter the Road, so we need to go faster than most. I want to reach it before the rain becomes overpowering and darkness descends on us. Can your injured ankle endure such a pace?"

"So far it seems to be holding me weight well and the pain isn't overwhelming. Do you want to set the pace?"

"No, you keep the lead. Just try to go as fast as you can, because I would rather not walk this Road in either storm or night, and especially not in a nighttime storm."

For the rest of that day they hiked across the skies, following the icy Road of Clouds. At one point they came to a gap that was clear all the way to the ground. Far below, they saw trees and a meadow but couldn't tell what part of the realm they were looking down upon. The jump across was no greater than any others, but Thomas certainly felt his heart race more during that leap.

About two hours before sunset the storm caught up with them, bringing gusts and sleet and they had still not arrived at the first Wayrest.

"Thomas! Stop for a moment," yelled Francis against the wind. "We need you to kindle your magician's staff or else we'll never find our way in this darkening day."

Thom stopped and the three of them huddled close in a wider spot on the Road. "I don't know how to light the gem."

"There are many ways to cause a staff to glow. I will teach you the simplest way, since you need to maintain the other enchantments as well."

"Three at once?" Suddenly he worried about fumbling all of them, which could cause them to lose their footing and plummet to their deaths.

"You are skilled enough to control that many, unless you want to hand the staff over to Adele."

"But he needs it to help him walk," protested Adele.

"Unfortunately, for this enchantment the magician must keep touching the staff."

"I will do it," said Thom, trying to sound more certain than he felt. He removed his knapsack and set it on the ice between them, pulling out main cache of elements.

"Take out the elements for crafting a Wizard Light."

Thom gave him a puzzled look. "I thought you were going to show me how to kindle the gem on the top of the staff."

"Exactly that," replied Francis. "It takes the same elements, but you will add Spotted Pine oil to make it more watery, then you will use your fingers to rub it all over the jewel until all facets are coated. They call this enchantment Wizard Bright. It is a messier way but it is easier to maintain and strong enough to help set the Road to glowing."

"The Road can glow?" asked Adele.

Francis nodded. "You will see. Watch carefully, Lady Adele, because you may need to craft the next kindling of the staff."

"Where do I craft?" asked Thom wondering how he was going to keep this magic away from their boots and from the Road's enchantment.

"You will kneel and mix in your bowl right here on the ice, just be sure not to spill any because we don't want to accidentally step in any of it while the magic is active on the soles of our shoes. The top of the ice is inert, which is why your other two enchantments haven't caused any magical clashing. The Road's enchantment is on the underside of the ice and farther out around us, as you can hear. Now get to it."

So Thom knelt in the dubious wind break of his friends as the storm grew around them. He followed Francis' directions and mixed the elements correctly, using only one hand while the other stayed clean and with a firm grip on the staff. When it began glowing in the mixing bowl, he carefully dipped his fingers into the thick liquid and began rubbing it on the greenish gem that was embedded at the top of the magician's staff. As he did all of this, he also had to keep the other two enchantments on their boots going too.

When he finished, the bowl was still half full. Francis ordered him to smear it on the ice behind them. "It cannot be dumped or it might run off the ice and splatter on the Road's magic. Smear it and we'll leave a glowing ice path that anyone following will have to avoid."

Thom did so, slathering it on the frozen path until it was empty and his hand was numb from the cold. Francis stepped forward with a rag and helped Thom to clean his hand and tools while Adele helped him pack everything back into his knapsack.

"What now?" he asked, looking at the now-glowing staff.

"You light our path," stated Francis.

Thom gave him a hard stare. He didn't appreciate the flippant tone, for this couldn't be as simple as lighting a candle, especially since he was now trying to control three enchantments at once.

THIRTEEN

Crooked Bough Wayrest

"Try again," ordered Francis as they slowly kept going.

Frustrated, Thom stopped and concentrated on the staff's glowing gem and then on the ice they were walking on. Francis said this wasn't so much crafting another enchantment but reaching out with the one already active and touching the ice with it. However, he had already tried this six times and failed.

"Do not fear the Road's enchantment. It is meant to interact with a staff's light. That is how the Founders planned it."

"Is there something he should be saying or focusing on?" asked Adele.

"He can do whatever he wants, but neither has anything to do with the magic."

Thom concentrated but couldn't seem to make the connection.

"The storm is getting worse," said Adele. "Should we just hurry on without the light?"

"Hurry into this darkness and you will soon be rushing toward the earth," warned the monk. He looked heavenward, ignoring the heavy raindrops falling on his face. "Lord, please help Thomas find a way to light our path."

He tried to ignore their talking and praying, to focus just on the enchantment that lit the jewel and on getting that magic to translate down the staff and into the ice they were standing on. He needed more light, an excess to go through the staff and light their icy path, and suddenly the jewel blazed bright and then his whole staff lit and the light kept going, seeming to ignite the ice at their feet and travel in both directions.

"Too much, Thomas!" yelled Francis. "You'll melt the ice with that much power. Try to lessen it without extinguishing everything."

Thom tried to do that even as his companions urged him to keep walking. At least it was easier to see where to step because the path now glowed a bluish-green, like his staff and the blazing gem on its tip. The light sputtered then he was able to get it to a steady glow, not too bright or too dull.

"Is that what you were looking for?" asked Adele of Francis.

"More extravagant than any wizard, but it works. He may have to renew the enchantment before we reach the Wayrest because he is burning through it rather fast, but we will address that when needed. Come on. You go first, Lady Adele, and guide Thomas. I think he needs to concentrate on his trio of enchantments to keep them steady, so please take the lead."

Thom agreed with Francis' assessment but was too busy with his enchantment to say anything.

* * *

They reached the Wayrest portal two hours later, to find Rainflower patiently waiting for them. Her two bird companions gone.

"Rainflower, why aren't you waiting for us inside?" asked Adele after she and Francis guided Thomas over the final gap and onto the ice platform in front of the gateway. All three of them were dripping from the storm that was now blowing around them in earnest.

The equally wet fairy put her hands on her hips but kept her wings furled. "I am your guide; it would not be right for me to take leisure while you still struggle through the storm. I cannot fly in this kind of weather, but I can still be vigilant."

Thom sat down on one of the icy benches nearby and then looked up at Francis. "Is there a particular order to releasing the enchantments?"

"Let go of the light first, then Sole Flight and last Sole Grip. Warn us before you release that last one because the ice will suddenly become slippery again."

Thom nodded tiredly and let the light fade from the gem, darkness dropping on them like the incessant rain. He sighed and then concentrated on letting go of what Francis had just named Sole Flight and lost that lightness in his steps. "I'm ready to let go of the last one."

Francis nodded. "We should all move closer to the gateway, just don't step through until the Sole Grip has gone silent."

He helped Thom to his feet and then all of them crowded near the shimmering gateway. Rainflower waited patiently to one side, looking out into the storm.

Thom stopped his final enchantment and it faded away, the crusted gunk on the bottom of their boots going inert. It felt like he was going to slide away as that extra gripping ended, but he was able to keep in one spot.

"Before we go in, take a final listen for any other magic on the Road," said Francis. "If there is no one near, then we'll likely have no interruptions tonight. Not even Merlin would want to travel through a night storm."

They heard nothing beyond the Road of Clouds itself, so all of them stepped through to the Crooked Bough Wayrest.

The first thing Thom saw when he passed through the shimmering archway was a gnarled tree with a wide trunk. It dominated the place. Overhead, its dense branches and leaves wove a ceiling of green and brown. At his feet, intertwined roots formed a rugged floor. How could a tree grow up here in the clouds?

He looked to Francis in astonishment and then realized there were two more trees, one on each side of the gateway. "I don't understand how trees can find anchor in clouds, but I'm grateful they're here."

Francis smiled. "Cloud Rowans are hard to cultivate. Imagine the challenge they had roping their first one and bringing it within reach."

"Roping it?" Thom imagined a group of gray-haired wizards trying to throw lines into the sky. "Who can toss a rope that far?"

Francis lost his smile. "It was a young Dalrake and he did it from Cloudholder Mountain, using trained falcons to carrying the ropes around the tree's bough."

Thom lost his grin too. "Sometimes I forget that Dalrake was so involved in creating the Roads."

"Is that a horse up here?" asked Adele, interrupting them as she pointed beyond the center tree to where a white rump barely showed.

Francis' smile returned as he stepped further into the refuge and made a clicking sound. "Wayrests shelter more than just passing magicians and fairies. The pegasi like to pasture here. They keep the grass beds trimmed and in return provide... fertilizer to the roots."

The pegasus stepped forward and looked around the tree in curiosity.

Francis moved no closer. "They are wild so they will bite or kick if you get too close, but otherwise they will share a Wayrest without any trouble." Then he motioned toward the tree to their right. "But before we do anything, we need to clean our boots. Everyone visiting is expected to scrap them off on the ledge."

Adele went first, scrapping her boots on the wooden edge and letting the debris add to the leftover gunk from others that had traveled before them. As Thom watched and then took his turn, he wondered about his old master. Just a few days ago, Levitanus would have been here, doing the same thing. That was assuming that the sorcerers were allowing him to travel on foot with them and weren't trying to carry him somehow.

"Are Dalrake and Levitanus still on the Road?" asked Thomas, wondering if it wasn't too late by now.

"The Road of Clouds takes two days to travel to Mount Cloudholder," replied Francis as he stepped up to take his turn, "and then another two to ten days more, depending on the destination Dalrake has chosen. It has only been three days since they started on the Road, so they are likely somewhere ahead of us."

"What are you saying about the Founders?" asked Rainflower, having just stepped through the archway.

"Thomas was wondering if they were still on the Road," stated the monk, standing straight now that he had finished scrapping.

"They are still on the Road," replied the fairy, adding quickly, "not that I am interested in their travels after such rude behavior."

Rainflower then stepped farther into the Wayrest, careful to avoid the puddle-filled dips in the root floor, and then she unfurled her wet wings and started fanning them to dry. Her two escort birds flew out of the lower branches and started circling her, tweeting excited greeting.

"It is much warmer in here," sighed Adele with a smile, dropping the hood of her cloak.

"The trees generate heat, helping to melt any snow or ice that might have fallen on their upper branches," replied Francis, stepping out onto the tangle of roots. "Watch your step, Thomas, and please use your staff to help. We should head toward the beds on the right side of the archway, for I think the pegasus has already chomped them to a comfortable length."

Thom had no idea what Francis was talking about. Flying horses eating beds? But he was too tired to ask for clarity. Instead, he carefully followed the monk around the trunk to their right. A more sure-footed Adele went ahead of him. Even in his tiredness, he appreciated her lithe moves as weaved her steps across the gnarled roots.

He loved her. It was a sweet thought to keep his thoughts off his aches and pains.

As they came around the bole they saw a group of five raise root beds, about thigh high. In each of those elevated basins grew grass. Thom suddenly realized what Francis meant: each grass bed was a verdant green and neatly trimmed, apparently by the grazing pegasus.

When Adele tentatively sat on one of them, Francis smiled. "You'll find it much softer than sleeping on the ground. The root bundle holding the soil bank has the slightest give to it, not enough to dislodge the earth but enough to make it feel like a firm mattress." He slung off his knapsack and placed at one end of the grass bed he had chosen and then sat down as well.

A more cautious Thomas finally reached one of the beds too, and sat down with a weary sigh. He was exhausted.

FOURTEEN

Sharing the Burden

The new day came with new aches and twinges. A frustrated Thomas swung off the grass bed and tried to stretch out some of the tender muscles. It didn't help much.

Adele, who had been looking out into the surrounding clouds, turned and smiled. "Good morning."

He smiled back because he loved seeing her, trying his best to mask his pain. "Good morning."

"Francis is getting our breakfast ready, while our guide and her bird friends are feasting on some small fruits from the tree on the left. The pegasus is already gone."

"Food would be good. I was so exhausted last night that I ate nothing before I fell asleep."

She nodded, walking over to him. "I'm well aware of that. How do you feel today?"

He almost lied, trying to conceal his suffering, but realized that would be wrong. "I hurt. The injuries from my imprisonment aren't healing as fast as I would like and all this traveling isn't helping."

She took his hand and gave it a careful but comforting squeeze. "I will help you any way that I can. Maybe we can set a slower pace today."

"We have to go even faster," corrected Francis, looking around the corner of the central tree trunk, "but I think we can lighten his burden nonetheless. I'm almost done with preparing our meal, so let's discuss it over food."

He soon came over with a plate of cheese wedges and strips of jerky, a bowl of freshly picked Cloud Rowan berries, and a basket holding a sliced and buttered half-loaf of rye bread. "We cannot have any fires inside a Wayrest, so it's a cold breakfast, but you'll find the berries sweet and the rest hearty."

As they ate, Francis shared his plan. He wanted to get to Cloudholder by late afternoon, so that they could hike across the mountain and be ready to reenter the next section of the Road at dawn. He shared his concern about getting to Vivien and Kane before some other magician did. That was why he wanted to hurry them today and also why he wanted Adele to craft the Sole Flight enchantment. That way Thom would only have two enchantments to maintain. They readily agreed.

"Now let's see those wounds." He signaled for Thomas to take off his robe and shirt.

Thom hesitated, with an embarrassed glance toward Adele, but then stripped off clothing to reveal his cut and bruised torso. At least none of his wounds were seeping any longer.

Francis looked him over carefully and gently touched some areas, but Thom was able to endure it all with little more than a wince.

"Sit down and show me your ankle."

He complied, pulling off his left boot to show his still-swollen ankle. At least the bruising had faded.

Francis grabbed his foot and moved it about to check the flexibility and strength, as Adele watched intently. Again, he bore the probing with only a few grimaces. The monk frowned but nodded. "Both ointments seem to be working, but the ankle is definitely tender from a day of walking and jumping."

When Thom moved to redress, Francis shook his head. "Let's apply some ointment now."

"Should we apply it in here?" asked Thom, concerned about how the active magic might react when he walked through the archway.

"Just Marcus' Miracle Mud, for it is medicinal but not magical. The balm from Keeper Bronwen can wait until we step back onto the Road. Her ointment wouldn't cause anything terrible, but the reaction of the two enchantments might cause skin blisters and you don't need that."

"Are the three of you ready to continue?" asked Rainflower from her perch on the central tree, raising her voice enough to be heard clearly. "This heat grows oppressive."

"We are almost ready," replied Francis. "You can wait for us on the landing if you want."

"That is exactly what I will do." The fairy and her escorts flittered through the air, all over the Wayrest, and then finally headed through the archway.

"Does she really think it is hot in here?" asked Adele.

"Fairies like colder climes," replied Francis as he helped Thomas slather on the Miracle Mud on his various injuries. "That is why so many live on Cloudholder Mountain. It is said that lowland fairies hide in cool borrows during the heat of summer days."

As Thom pulled on his shirt, he asked about Francis' injuries, because both of them had been tortured by the sorcerers.

"Mine are well on the path to healing," replied the monk. "I wasn't tortured as long nor as harshly as you. I did use a bit of your Miracle Mud last night after you fell asleep, but none of my cuts or bruises impede travel. It is you who was sorely abused."

"I am so sorry for both of you," said Adele, offering Thom help in getting his thick robe over his head. "I wish we could have rescued everyone much sooner."

"You came," replied Thom, "and that was brave of you. The others had magical training and sword skills, but you were the boldest of them all. Kane might have left us behind if you hadn't insisted on getting the two of us too."

The trio cleaned up after themselves and then shouldered their packs and stepped through the grayish shimmer of the archway to appear on the icy landing. Rainflower stood there waiting for them, the two birds perched on her shoulders and nestling into her hair for warmth. She gave them a short glance, but then returned to staring off the platform at the clouds below.

The sudden change in temperature caused Thom to shiver, but he still sat on one of the icy benches and invited Adele to sit next to him. He pulled out the balm from the Keeper and then took off his boot and applied it liberally to his ankle. He then wiped his hands clean and gently slid into the boot.

"Now we should get to the magic. Francis will watch us to check our work, but it's up to us to get these enchantments crafted."

Thom pulled out his mixing bowl, pestle, and cache of elements. She carefully watched as he chose the proper ingredients and then crafted the Sole Grip enchantment. When done applying the magic to the heel section of each boot, he helped her gather the correct elements to craft the magic assigned to her. She did well and applied the Sole Flight to each of their boots too.

All three of them then walked about the landing to test their footing. Confident that they had crafted their magic well, Thom focused on his last assignment. He kindled his staff and sent the light to illuminate the ice they were standing on, and this time he did so without it being so glaring.

"Lead the way, Rainflower," said Francis as the three of them stepped onto the first stepping stone of ice. "Please let us know how the route looks ahead of us."

"It should be fair travel today," replied the fairy as she took flight. "The storm has passed, leaving behind a sky full of clouds. I expect our route to be fairly straight today."

"That is good, for we want to reach Cloudholder by shortly after midday and to reach the far side of the mountain by nightfall."

"With those enchantments? Most magicians usually craft different magic for such a pace, but who am I to advise wizards?"

"Each craftsman has their specialty, which is also true with magicians. They craft the enchantments that fit best to their skills and temperament."

The fairy raised an eyebrow in doubt then turned away. She sped up her fluttering to fly ahead of them.

* * *

They had been traveling the Road of Clouds for hours when Francis motioned for Rainflower to come back. The fairy returned to hover directly over them, a ray of sunshine making her wings glitter while fluttering up and down. "We will stop for a rest now. It is close enough to midday."

"As long as it is not too long," she replied. "Unless you have changed your intention of reaching the other side of Cloudholder by sunset."

"That is still our goal."

"Then rest for no more than half an hour."

Thomas flopped to the ice, glad to get off his feet. He kept his two enchantments going, but it was hard to concentrate on their rhythms when his ankle was creating its own throbbing beat.

Adele sat down with more dignity, after first taking off her knapsack and digging out some food to share. She was doing a great job at keeping her enchantment strong; Thom doubted he could have done the same with as little training as she had.

As they ate, Thom noticed that Rainflower had settled on the next ice step along with her bird escorts and was sharing nourishment with them. It looked like drops of honey or nectar squeezed from a soaked cloth. He realized that he knew hardly anything about these tiny flying beings, including how they related to birds, but he was too tired to ask. Instead, he just ate and carefully stretched sore muscles.

When it was time to go on, Francis paused and lifted his hand for silence. Thom realized the monk was probably listening for magic use near them but he was too tired to try listening himself.

"I faintly hear some magic behind us. Someone has entered the Road by way of Sky Tower, and that person is using an inordinate amount of magic to hurry their journey."

"Is it Merlin or someone else?" asked Thom. He didn't know who he feared encountering more, the head of the guild or one of the sorcerers escaping from their failed attempt to take Camelot.

"I have no way of knowing, but they will catch up to us this day."

Adele settled the pack over her shoulders. "Then we need to get moving, because there's no place to hide out here unless we can fly off into the clouds."

"We should be on Cloudholder Mountain before they overtake us," stated Francis. "I just hope we can find a place to hide there."

FIFTEEN

Mists of Cloudholder

The gateway out of the Road of Clouds was just suddenly there. Thom was in the midst of carefully jumping from one ice stepping stone to another in the midst of a fog when he almost crashed one of the ice-covered benches. Startled, he looked up and barely saw the gray shimmer of the archway and the fairy that was hovering in front of it. "Is this another Wayrest or have we made it?"

"Cloudholder awaits beyond the gateway."

Thom sighed with relief, for the one coming behind them had still not caught up. He looked back for the others and gave warning. "Ware the benches; we've reached the gateway to Cloudholder Mountain."

"Finally," replied Francis as he followed Adele onto the landing. "No time to rest. Adele, please let go of your enchantment now." All of them heard the sudden ceasing of that particular rhythm as she let it fade away. "Thom, your turn."

With the enchantments gone, the ice suddenly felt slippery and their footing uncertain. Taking short steps, they passed through the gateway's shimmer and into more fog. But at least they now stood on stones instead of ice.

"Watch your step," stated Rainflower, who could barely be seen through the mist as she hovered before them. "You are on a narrow promontory. There are cliffs to either side of you. Please walk straight toward me until we are on the actual slope of the mountain."

"Once again, the guild saw no need for railings or walls," stated Francis as he scraped the residue off of his boots. "Clean off your soles quickly, because we need to get into the covering of the forests. We still need to reach the far side of the mountain before nightfall and light will fade quickly if the fog doesn't dissipate."

"What about whoever is coming behind us?" asked Thom. "Is there only one road across the mountain, or can we take a different path to avoid him?"

"There are no roads or paths on Cloudholder," replied Francis. "Fairies fly more than they walk. Also, there are no wagons or carts here, nor much in the way of beasts of burden. You will find no hedgerows or boundary walls. You will understand it better when we pass through one of the fairy villages. Some have said they look more like a collection of birdhouses or beehives."

"Birdhouses? Beehives? Who would say such a foolish thing?" asked Rainflower.

Francis smiled at her. "I know that Fairy settlements looks nothing like either, but they are hard to explain to someone who has never seen one."

"What is so hard? It is a fairy village, like every fairy village that has ever existed."

"Your people are good at hiding their settlements, so not many humans have seen them. That is just a way to help others get an idea of what to expect. How would you describe a merfolk cavern or the great nestings of harpies that they call the Harp?"

"Harpy homes are foul places that no fairy would ever approach and how would I know what merfolk do under the water? I am no fish. We are not birds, fish, or bees. Nor are we harpies or sea beings. Why would you try comparing us to any of them?" She shook her head at his apparent ignorance and flew off ahead.

Thom was growing a bit tired of her attitude. She hadn't been much of a help in the last two days. "Why do we need the fairy?"

"You will understand better once we reenter the Road of Clouds," replied Francis. "From here on, the path is more like a spiderweb, with many possible routes but few ways that won't snare us in death."

"That doesn't sound encouraging," remarked Adele as she started walking in the direction the fairy took. "But we still need to keep going. Let's get away from this cliff and start crossing the mountain. I want to get to Vivien and Kane as soon as we can."

Thom said nothing; he just started following her. Francis was soon at his heels.

* * *

Once off the promontory, they found themselves walking into a forest where the fog thinned to a mere mist that left everything a bit damp. Rainflower didn't say anything, but whenever they caught up with her, she would fly a bit farther and settle on another tree branch or boulder to watch as they followed on foot.

They talked in hush tones, the mist dampening their words even as it did the forest around them.

"How are you feeling?" asked Adele of Thom.

Rather than complain, he simply said, "I'm still able to keep up. The ointment has really helped my ankle to endure all of this."

"But it still hurts," she stated. "I wish you were lounging on a river galley going down the Road of Waters rather than suffering here."

"I'm here with you, though, and that makes it worth enduring. Once we travel down the Road of Waters, we'll be separated and I don't know when I would see you again. You're going to join the queen while I'm going to this new, hidden place for the League of Barnabas."

Adele reached out and took hold of his free hand as they kept walking. "I'm glad you're joining the league. It fits you better than the guild ever did."

Thom nodded but said nothing. For some reason, his thoughts went to that wilderness cottage where he spent so many years as Levitanus' student. Those had been simpler days, just the two of them and the wonder of magic. Now it was so much more complicated and dark.

Francis suddenly spoke up from behind them, since the fairy was too far ahead to hear. "I agree with Lady Adele. You are a better suited to the league."

Thom looked over his shoulder and gave his friend a smile of thanks, but as he was about to respond he heard magic. They all did. It came from behind them.

"What is it?" asked Adele.

Thom wasn't certain. The sound happened and then stopped, like some short-lived enchantment or minor explosion. Now he heard nothing.

"Hide!" ordered Francis, motioning frantically at Rainflower. "Get under the thickest trees before the beast flies over us."

"What comes?" asked Thom as he and Adele scrambled between two close-grown trees.

Francis was focused on the fairy. "Ware the skies, Rainflower! Something large has flown out of the Road, far larger than the griffins."

She must have heard, because she fluttered off into the woods and was soon out of sight.

Francis ran over to Thom and Adele and hunkered down with them.

"What comes?" repeated Thom, this time in a whisper.

"Something large has burst out of the Road. As I told you earlier, the Road of Clouds is unlike the others; it is permeable, but every time something breaks through it will make a noise. Even rain makes a sound, though so faint that hardly anyone hears it. What we heard was something flying through the enchantment, something much larger than a griffin or a pegasi."

"Is it the roc we saw in the skies over Camelot?" asked Adele.

"Possibly. Whatever it is, I fear that it's large enough for a magician to ride, and certainly big enough to easily kill us. No more questions, for it will be on us very soon."

Francis went still, looking up through the leaves at what little of the drizzly sky peeked through. Thom and Adele followed his lead as they waited.

Suddenly, they heard a deep roar and then the sound of massive wings laboring in the clouds overhead.

"Do you see it at all?" whispered Francis sharply.

Thom shifted to see better in the direction of the sounds, but it didn't help. "Nothing."

"The clouds are too low," replied Adele.

"That was no roc screech," he muttered as he rose from where he hunkered and stepped out to a clearer area. "The wings sound huge, almost ponderous, but it moves quickly."

Rainflower flew close. "That was a dragon."

Francis shook his head in doubt. "Are you certain?"

"You doubt a fairy's eyesight?"

"No, but it is hard to imagine a dragon on the Road. I would think the way would be too restrictive for such a large beast."

"It was likely summoned. We did not hear it break into the enchantment because we are outside of it now, so we only heard when it flew back out."

"Who can call a dragon?" asked Thom.

"Whoever was riding on its back," replied the fairy.

"Did you recognize who it was?" asked Francis.

Rainflower frowned. "I recognized a human shape. Beyond that, I cannot say. Everything seems a blurry shadow when the clouds are this thick. It is already raining in earnest at that altitude and will soon be falling around us."

"You saw much more than we could," stated the monk. "Whoever it was, the dragon has carried them far past us." He took a moment to shift the knapsack that lay over his back. "We should continue our journey."

In less than a minute the rain reached them, a strong soaking that had hidden the dragon's passenger from recognition, but likely kept that person from looking too closely at the land being flown over. Thom thought the rain protected them from being noticed but also protected whoever that was from being recognized. Was that passenger a wizard or a sorcerer?

* * *

The rain stopped less than an hour later but the skies remained brooding. They had been trudging across the damp slopes of the mountain for hours when they noticed a settlement in a clearing below them.

"That is no fairy village," stated Thom, looking down at the muddy encampment. Rather than just stopping to look, he instead sat down on a wet boulder to ease his aching ankle. "I had no idea that pixies lived up here too."

"They are refugees from the Road of Leaves," replied Rainflower. "Our queen has granted the pixies and dryads permission to settle there after all that happened."

"I hadn't heard that it was so bad," remarked Thomas.

"They say no one travels that Road anymore, even after so many wizards have worked at restoring the great enchantment. It is said that hundreds of pixies have already died and it still is not enough."

"Why have the pixies died?" asked Adele as she sat down next to Thomas.

"They are an essential part of the enchantment," replied Francis sadly, "and not all want to give that ultimate sacrifice, which is probably why they have fled here."

Thom watched as Adele's countenance fell, for she realized what the monk was implying.

She turned to Thom and asked in a ragged whisper, "The wizards kill them for their magical essence?"

He nodded. "Apparently, there's great power in them that master magicians can't resist."

Adele cursed, surprising Thomas with her vehemence.

"How can they be so evil? Does all magic lead to this?"

Before Thom could answer, Rainflower did. "No, it does not. All fairies have innate magical abilities of flight and farsight. Do you think I am evil because of that?"

"No, of course not. I'm talking about human magicians who use elements to make their enchantments."

"The power is a great temptation," replied the fairy, as she settled to the ground next to them, "but even humans can resist temptations."

"There are still good magicians," added Francis, who just leaned against the wet stone. "Thomas is one of them, and I think he will remain so even when they finally recognize him as a master."

Thom appreciated his friend's confidence in him, but he wondered if he would ever attain the rank of master. "I am not that skilled..."

"Lying does not become you, Thomas of York," interrupted the fairy, lifting off the ground to hover in front of him. "You are very skilled. They all name you journeyman, but I have seen the enchantments you craft even while suffering from obvious injuries. I have guided wizards and sorcerers along the Road who have had less skill than you."

Thom met her stare but didn't know what to say. He was no wizard. Of that, he had no pretensions. So, for a time, he and the tiny fairy held each other's eyes. It was not in defiance or affection; it was a measuring of each other. Thom found the diminutive woman fierce and wondered what she saw as she seemed to look inside of him.

"We should keep moving," stated Francis softly, pushing off the boulder. "The day grows older and we still have half a mountain to cross."

Thom looked over and nodded, struggling back to his feet with the help of his staff. He had only taken four steps before he heard a griffin's scream further up the mountainside.

SIXTEEN

Fairy Ring

Rainflower flew higher and then hovered there as she stared northward for a time. When she dropped back down to the humans, she reported, "The griffin is still far away, but the echo off the slopes makes it sound much closer; I cannot even see it. At such a distance, the monster will not have our scent."

Another griffin called out, from somewhere behind them.

"Do you think they are looking for us?" asked Adele.

"Maybe, but griffins are not hounds," replied Francis. "They hunt by sight not by the scent of our trail, so as long as we stay well ahead of them, they will never find us."

"I will do my best to keep up," said Thom. "Lead the way, Fairy Rainflower. We have a mountain to cross and the day grows old."

* * *

An hour later they came upon the dead pegasus. Some wild beast had eaten from it, leaving a bloody mess in a clearing. Francis insisted that they detour to look at the carcass.

"So sad," mumbled Adele through a cloth-covered mouth as she tried to hold off the stench. "They are such majestic animals. What do you think caught it?"

"A magician," said Francis in a calm voice that belied his frown. "That's no animal kill. The pegasus was rendered, leaving the rest to whatever beast found it later."

Thom looked more closely and saw that most of the wing feathers had been plucked and the long mane sheared. Maybe some of the blood was drained, leaving the rest to run freely on the grasses. "Who would do this?"

"Many magicians. Pegasi are rare and not easily caught, so elements made from them are precious to those who craft air magic."

"They are magical *beasts* and not *beings*, yet this is a waste," stated Rainflower, keeping her distance. "Most of what was taken from this animal could have been attained without killing it or ruining its ability to fly."

"We should keep going," stated Francis through lips tightening with anger. Thom understood his fury; magic was too often abused.

"That would be best," agreed Rainflower, rising in the air and heading off. Her bird companions appeared from the nearest trees and joined her.

* * *

The sun broke through the clouds for the last two hours of the day, adding

73

a bit more light and long shadows to their path. The group had stopped for a brief rest. The humans sat on a fallen tree, while Rainflower lazed on a limb above their heads. "Where did you want to overnight, Brother Francis? Fair Oakwood is within walking distance."

"No fairy villages."

"Then we will have a cold camp, for the queen forbids open fires in our woods."

"Is there any nearby gathering circles?"

Rainflower just stared at him for a moment, surprised by his suggestion. "We do not camp at gathering circles."

"It is not forbidden and we can have fire there."

"We do not do such things." She crossed her arms in determination. "Why do you refuse to go to a village? Outsiders are welcomed to use the guest house, even humans."

"If they learn that I am the Fair Defender, they will insist I go the queen and that will delay us for days. It is best that I keep hidden, at least until we have freed our friends. We will keep our distance but you can overnight at Fair Oakwood, just do not tell anyone about the three of us."

Rainflower shook her head at what she saw as foolishness, but she didn't refute the monk's logic. "I will stay with the three of you. Let us find the Oakwood's gathering circle while we still have enough light to gather fallen wood. The fog will return tonight and I would rather be dry and warm than cold and damp."

They never saw Fair Oakwood, for it was over a forested rise, but Rainflower found the gathering circle easily enough. It was a large meadow touched by the long shadows from the trees the lined it. In the center of the meadow was a large ring of mushrooms. In the middle of that circle was an area of clear earth.

"A fairy ring," whispered Adele.

Even Thomas, whose early childhood had mainly consisted of running with a thieving gang followed up by years of isolation in the wilderness with his old master, had heard of these magical places.

"They prefer to call them gathering circles," said Francis. "Be careful to step over the boundary."

"Break the circle and break your luck," replied Adele, repeating something she had heard often.

"No need for superstition. It is out of respect that we do not trample the fragile mushrooms. Listen for yourself; there is no crafting of magic happening here."

But it is innately magical, thought Thomas without saying anything aloud. Tired of standing, he wanted to set his pack down and get to wood gathering, so he moved ahead of the others. There was definitely something magical about this place, even if it had nothing to do with crafted magic. As he stepped into the ring, he felt a change, and suddenly he saw three small trees inside the circle.

Startled, he looked back and saw the others, though Adele seemed confused while Francis smiled. Thom puzzled about the mysterious trees, and then remembered something his master had said about the concealment of fairy rings.

Adele stepped over the circle of mushrooms, smiling as she saw him. "You disappeared when you stepped inside. Only Francis' chuckle kept me from panicking. He enjoyed surprising us."

"Let him have a moment of mirth; this journey cannot be an easy one for him. It was on this mountain that he realized that his master was evil. Decades of service, only to be forced to kill the man to stop the butchering of a fairy village. It was here that his hatred of magic was birthed."

Adele's smile faded as she watched Francis step inside and head toward the center of the circle. "I begin to understand why he detests magic, but even he knows that not all who craft enchantments do so out of an evil heart."

"He knows, but he still thinks the temptation for abuse is too strong. I'm not certain that he's wrong, for it is a temptation to use magic for my own selfish means."

Rather than say anything, Adele hugged him tightly.

He hugged her back, so glad to have her close.

* * *

Their night in the gathering circle was uneventful. They set out the next day in a chilly fog that didn't burn off until an hour later. Two hours after that they finally reached the far side of the mountain and came into view of the archway to enter the second half of the Road. Clouds hung over the entrance, blurring it all from a distance, and Thom wondered if it was always mist-shrouded. Beyond the gate and the mountainside was just sky, a vast blue dotted with hundreds of puffy clouds that slowly drifted northeastward.

"What a beautiful sight," observed Adele as they marched down the final slope leading to the archway.

"But not a good day for traveling the Road," observed Francis. He looked over to the fairy. "It looks to be a day of scrambling and jumping."

"If I can even find a direct route to your friends. It would have been much easier if the day was fully overcast."

"How will you find them in the vastness of that sky?" asked Thom.

"I will not know until we are actually on the Road of Clouds, but I will find a way to them."

"I pray that it will be just a day's journey," said Francis.

Rainflower nodded her agreement, but then suddenly stared past Francis at the skies behind them. "Ten birds fly towards us and they are in formation."

"Rocs?" asked Francis, as they all turned and searched in vain for what the farsighted fairy was seeing.

"Too small for that, but they are definitely birds and not griffins or harpies."

"Giant eagles?" asked Francis. To which the fairy shrugged in uncertainty.

"Will they fly into the archway or over it?" asked Thomas.

"That depends whether they are after us or just following the Road's direction," stated Rainflower.

"Do we have enough time to enter the archway before them?" asked Francis. "Out here we are easy to spot, but inside the enchantment we will be hidden from them."

"We need to move quickly, but we should be able to outpace them," stated the fairy.

All of them began walking faster down the last slope, coming to an unspoken decision to reach the archway before the birds.

"But what if they crowd in behind us?" asked Thom as they hurried along, remembering the terror of the griffin driven to follow them at Sky Tower's archway.

"That will happen if they want to track the Road," agreed Francis, "but I hear something else that may be drawing them."

"What?" asked Thom, even as he became aware of the faint sound of enchantments clashing far away.

"The war for Camelot has moved amongst the clouds. Somewhere out there a battle is happening."

"I cannot hear anything," protested Adele. "Are the sorcerers and wizards at it again? Does it have anything to do with our two friends?"

"At this distance, I cannot tell," replied the monk, "and we will not learn more about it until we get onto the Road."

Adele doubled her pace, almost running. "Then let's get through that archway."

Thom agreed with her, but it was a struggle to keep up. He leaned heavily on his staff as he limped hurriedly after her.

SEVENTEEN

Choices among the Clouds

They made it to the archway before the giant eagles caught up with them. Just before he passed under the heavy clouds hanging over the gateway, Thom looked back and saw that the eagles had passengers that were small and even smaller. He pointed them out to Francis.

"Pixies and dryads, if I'm not mistaken. Rainflower, who do you see riding the eagles?"

Without even looking, she replied, "You have it right, Fair Defender. I have never seen a dryad before, but they fit the description of their kind. I have never heard of either pixie or dryad riding on the Aeti, but they are doing so now."

Francis stopped running and turned to look up. The others did as well. Suddenly, they weren't enemies to fear, but possible allies.

"One of them is dressed much brighter than the others," noted Rainflower.

Thomas thought of Dorthos but then dismissed the idea. The crazy pixie never mentioned mastery of eagles and surely he would have among all his other stories.

"He is making odd hand motions."

"I cannot see them well at this distance," said Francis. "Please explain them to me."

"He repeats three hand motions. He points to himself and then forward with both hands. Next, he holds his hand over his eyes, as if scanning the horizon, and then makes a tumbling motion with both hands. And finally, he pretends to shoot an arrow."

"The pixie trusts that we have a fairy guide who can see them at such a distance. I do not know if he can see us clearly, but we should do the same motions back to them, though changing the arrow shot to a repeat of the tumbling motion." Francis looked at Thom and Adele. "Quickly now, before the clouds obscure us. Join me in signaling them back."

They did so awkwardly and certainly not in rhythm, but they did so twice before the lost sight of the approaching eagles and their passengers. For a moment, they just stood there, looking up at the now vanished birds.

Thomas wondered if they planned to swoop down on them and enter the Road through the archway.

"Are the dryads formidable archers as others say?" asked Rainflower.

Thom wondered if she could still see them, despite the cloud cover.

"They shoot poisoned arrows with great accuracy, but they are not a warlike race. They prefer to hide rather than fight," replied Francis. "But at times, they gift the poison to pixies, so ware them both if ever you confront them."

"My people have no quarrel with either."

"They must be quickly gaining on us," said Adele, turning back to walk out onto the promontory that led to the archway. The others followed as she continued, "Even if they are friendly, I would rather not be bowled over by nearly a dozen huge eagles, should they decide to sweep through the archway. We should get inside and on with our journey."

"Would they want to take the Road?" asked Thom.

"Most certainly," replied Francis. "Road enchantments are constantly moving, although we usually don't feel that motion. It would take a man weeks to walk the width of the realm, but on the Road of Clouds he can do so in a matter of days. Any bird that can drop into the enchantment and fly its length will speed up their travel immensely."

"Can they drop in anywhere along its length?" asked Adele.

"Not so easily near the archway. Because of how the magic works, the area directly above and to the sides of an archway act like a barrier wall, much like the walls of the other Roads."

"So the eagles will have to skirt around the area or dive through the archway," noted Adele, "so I was right that we should hurry and get through before our feathered friends start crowding the entrance."

"That would be best," agreed Rainflower, flying ahead of them and then vanishing as she passed through the gray shimmer. Her two bird escorts followed her in.

Thom was the last one through, trying his best not to limp as he hurried after them. He was ready for it to be slippery on the other side, but he was surprised at the largeness of the landing. There were four benches instead of just two, and there were five pathways of ice heading out into the clouds and another four coming in. Obviously, they were not all paired paths like the distance between the tower and the mountain.

Francis was quick to give them directions as they carefully shuffled over the ice towards two of the half-dozen benches. "Thomas, can you do the Sole Grip enchantment while Adele does the Sole Flight? That worked well the last time. While the two of you prepare to craft, I will go to consult Rainflower. Considering the lightness of the cloud cover beyond the archway, I fear it might not be easy to get to the right Wayrest in a timely manner. Three of the paths are faded and I suspect even the two strong ones will be a challenge. I need to remind her that we are not fairies who can easily flutter across gaps between clouds."

So while Francis talked with her, Thom and Adele crafted their appointed enchantments and made ready to coat everyone's boots. When all was done, the monk came back to get his shoes treated while Rainflower hovered nearby, her bird escorts resting on her shoulders.

So far, no eagles had swept through the archway, but Thom was still tense in anticipation even as he wiped out his and Adele's mixing bowls.

"Are we ready to move on?" Rainflower asked as Thom finally had his staff kindled.

"Are you still certain the fifth path is the best one for us?" asked Francis.

"It is certainly not the best path, but it is the one that will get us to Dripping Branch Wayrest this day. All other paths will take two or more days."

"No great gaps?"

"Not yet, but the cockatrices are already flocking in one area."

Thom gave them both a puzzled look, not understanding of why the presence of the beasts that were half-chicken, half-serpent made a difference.

Francis obliged Thom and Adele with an explanation. "Cockatrices have a love for chipped ice. They will flock wherever the Road has weakened enough to offer them a feast of the frozen slivers. If the little beasts are on the path, then we know that section is close to failing. The Road constantly shifts in this area, as wizards call it to themselves and seek various routes to the far ends of the realm. As it shifts, the ice dissolves in one cloud and new ice forms on a different cloud, changing the path. We will need to be quick, or we will end up plunging to our deaths as the ice shatters."

Thom shook his head at the dire news. "Eagles behind us, cockatrices before us, and crumbling ice beneath our feet, and if we win our way through, we still have harpies to contend with. And I thought walking on clouds was going to be the hard part of our journey."

"Can we get out onto the path?" asked Adele. "I still worry that those eagles will be in here soon."

Rainflower nodded, and started up the path she had chosen. Actually, she flew over the path, leaving it to the humans to test the sturdiness of the ice. As she flew off, she left them with one final fact. "The eagles are no longer behind us. They are now overhead and still going. They bypass this part of the Road. Once they dive into a particular route, I will have a better idea of their intended direction."

Thom was glad to hear that the eagles had moved on, for it meant one less thing to worry about… and yet he wondered why the eagles would even bother dropping into the Road of Clouds. He asked Francis about it.

"They are swift fliers, but even the Aeti can benefit from the speed of the Road's enchantment. Following the right paths will hasten their journey."

Thom wondered what would bring pixies and dryads to the clouds and wondered if they had possibly signaled their intent to his friend. "What were those hand motions they made?"

"I am less than fluent at pixie hand talk, but as I understand it, they are searching for Levitanus as well, and are ready to fight for him."

"That is a good thing," remarked Adele, "but why wouldn't they coordinate their actions with Kane and Vivien?"

Francis shrugged. "We will have to ask them if ever we meet them. Aeti riders are rare among the pixies. Frankly, I didn't know any of them still existed."

He shook his head in uncertainty. "Whatever their mission, we still have ours. Thomas, you need to light our way."

Thom nodded, stepping forward and touching his lit staff to the first block of ice, illuminating it and the next three blocks. They were tightly set, with barely a hair's width between them. To him, it looked like a promising start. But within the hour, he was facing ice blocks that were over four feet apart and now well lined up. Some were higher or lower, or they were angled differently. Although Adele and Francis were more sure-footed, he had to pause with each jump to make sure he would land where he needed. His ankle couldn't handle too many more rough landings. All of this made their progress slower than Francis wanted.

* * *

Two hours later, when they had paused for a moment to rest, Rainflower settled on the ice in their midst as they sat on the ice. They rested quietly for a time, then the fairy spoke up, mentioning again that most magicians used different enchantments that allowed them to travel much faster along the Road.

"You realize which elements are used to make such enchantments?" asked Francis, as he stood and brushed the melt off his traveling robe. "Pegasi blood and wing feathers are two ingredients. Fairy dust is another element used. I think we are fine with the magic we are using."

Thomas and Adele also stood, while Rainflower sprang into the air to hover near the monk.

"Fairy dust?"

Francis nodded, but his focus mainly on where they were going. "Thomas, watch for your next leap. It seems that the road is angling off again."

He followed Thom and Adele in their jump to the next step on the Road, while the fairy kept apace with him.

"Truly?" demanded Rainflower and she wasn't talking about their route.

Francis paused to look her in the eyes. "Yes. Those enchantments that they often use when your kind are guiding them through the Road's twists are enchantments made from dead fairies that have been rendered to powder. Rather evil of them, do you not agree?"

"That is awful," said Adele, who had been listening in. "Do both wizards and sorcerers use dead fairies in their magic?"

"As my old master taught me, 'Fairy dust is the element of choice whenever a magician needs to make something airborne, even himself.' He repeated that lesson to me as part of his justification for wanting to murder a whole fairy village. Magic is brutal in its use of others." Francis shook his head, and looked again at Rainflower. "I am sorry for being so blunt and heartless. I haven't been doing my morning prayers and my soul feels the lack. I will not teach Thomas or Adele any enchantments that use dead beings as elements. There is a limit to how much I will help even my friends."

"Thank you," replied Rainflower. "I was never told that my people were killed to make those enchantments. Now that I know, I will protest to my queen. You are the last magicians that I will ever guide on the Road of Clouds."

Francis nodded. "That is a wise choice. You should also know that my old master told me your kind were rendered and crafted into the original foundations of this very Road. He may have lied to me about that, for he lied about many things, but that was what he claimed."

Thom cursed at the cruelty of it, but then he already knew that pixies volunteered to die for the maintaining of the Road of Leaves so why not use fairies to keep up a floating road? He hadn't thought of it at the time, but he now wondered if they used merfolk the same way to keep the Road of Waters going. He didn't bother to say anything aloud because it wouldn't help matters any. Instead, he sprang to the next section of the Road and concentrated on lighting up more of what lay ahead. But even as he did, he still heard what they were saying behind him.

"I understand better why you hate magic," stated Adele.

"Admittedly, not all magic is so cruel," replied Francis, "but so much of what they call greater magic practiced by the masters of the guild and sorcery alike can be evil; that magic often involves such horrible elements."

Thom paused before making his next jump. "As you once told me, it is a question of *just magic*. Can using magic ever be justified? I think we can use it justly and I think you have shown me how."

"Of course magic can be done justly," sniffed Rainflower, landing on the ice next to Thom and crossing her arms. Although she was so much shorted than him, he felt she was looking down her nose at him somehow. "It is a foolish question. The Fair Defender did just that when he rescued my fellow fairies so many years ago. You ask the wrong question. Instead, ask what is a just and honorable code to impose on magicians so that magic is never abused."

Surprised at her insight, Thom smiled. It was a tired smile, but it was a genuine one. His thoughts went to the League of Barnabas and what Father Justin had told him about their intentions for that group. "You are right, Fairy Rainflower. We need a code of conduct for all magicians and a way to hold all of us accountable."

"Of course I am right. I always am." She sprang into the air and fluttered forward. "Now let us get on with this. I would think you would want to reach Dripping Branch Wayrest well before sunset. No one wants to deal with harpies after dark."

EIGHTEEN

Breaking of Ice

The path continued to degenerate. Once, Thom heard the ice crack under his feet after he landed. For now, the ice held and so he continued. Each ice step became smaller and the distance between them greater. But still he kept going. There was no disagreement on that; all of them were determined to get to Vivien and Kane this day. Thom finally stopped, though, when he encountered something unexpected. The path split in two. The one on the left was wider and higher than the one he stood on; it would be a difficult jump. The one on the right was below him and it seemed the easier jump, but a fog lingered there, making the landing harder to see. "Which way?"

It was too narrow for either Francis or Adele to stand beside him. Instead, Thom knelt and let them look over him to see the two different routes that his staff had illuminated.

"What do you see ahead?" Francis asked of the fairy hovering next to them. "The magic sounds weak on either path."

"We go right. The left one is still developing and leads nowhere. The right one is failing, but is still whole. We should move faster, though, because even the cockatrices know this ice will not last much longer."

Thom nodded and did the awkward drop to the lower ice block. The mists swirled around his feet and again he heard cracking.

Rainflower startled him when suddenly she spoke into his ear; he hadn't realized she had flown so close while he was looking down at the ice. "Keep going. The others will make that drop without difficulty. Light up as many ice steps as you can ahead of us. Maybe it will startle the cockatrices from their ice pecking."

He did as she asked, setting his staff to the ice and concentrating on the way ahead to light it, but he couldn't tell how many steps were now lit. It was just a blue glow in the growing fog.

The next few gaps were small enough to stride over, which was good since it was getting hard to see. They kept close together. Rainflower's two bird companions settled on her shoulders and she remained in the air between Thom and Adele.

After crossing a third small gap, Thomas almost stepped on a dark shape that clucked at him. "What was that?"

"Cockatrice. They swarm the path just ahead," stated Rainflower. "Keep walking. They will scatter out of your way as long as they are not in a feeding frenzy."

"Feeding frenzy over ice?"

"Right before the ice shatters, the birds will go wild. I have seen it before. They will peck at almost anything when they are that excited."

"Hurry up, Thomas," said Francis. "We want to get through this flock as quickly as we can."

Thom shook his head at the thought of dozens of chicken-like animals attacking them, but did his best to limp at a faster pace. He saw another dark shape but it flew away. Then another, but still no clear view of a cockatrice. "Why is the fog so thick here?"

"It is another sign that this section is warming up and dissolving into a rain," replied Rainflower. "Keep your attention on what is ahead. The flock is concentrated on the next section. Can you see them yet?"

"No. How can you? This fog gets thicker with each step. I can barely see the lighted ice beneath my feet. Frankly, I worry that one of us will falter and step right off the edge into oblivion."

"That is a sensible fear. I will do my best to guide all of you, but you cannot just stand there."

Thom looked for her, but saw only a shadow moving through the grayness. He looked over his shoulder, the shoulder that Adele was now holding, and even she was misty and unclear. Behind her, he could only make out Francis' hand on her shoulder and then his shadowy form.

His monk friend seemed to realize he was looking back, for he spoke a few words of encouragement. "Keep going, Thomas. You're doing well."

Thom turned back. Instead of looking outward, he concentrated on the glowing ice below his feet, trying his best to ignore the cracking sounds he heard ahead of him, as well as the clucking.

He gave up trying to see the ice and started using his staff to tap the area in front of him, even though the light of the staff shone back off the walls of clouds and made it even harder to see anything around him.

"You veer to the left," said Rainflower, her voice startling him a bit. "Head toward my voice to straighten out. It is about five more steps to the edge of this block. This way."

He followed her voice until his staff suddenly tapped on nothing. Just air. He was at the edge of this stepping stone of the path.

"You need to make a small jump to the next one. Do not worry; the cockatrices will scatter before you step on them."

That wasn't what worried him. As much as he tried, Thom couldn't see the glow of where he was supposed to jump. For all he knew, he would be leaping off into the nothingness of clouds to plummet to the ground far below.

"Can you see where you're going?" asked Adele in a whisper, "I can't see anything from here."

Instead of answering, Thom concentrated on the glow from his staff. He closed his eyes and focused on that enchantment, trying his hardest to kindle it even brighter, to make the ice glare in its brightness.

"What are you doing?" demanded Francis. "It is so loud."

"Look at the ice," said Adele. "It is like we are standing on a huge lantern or the moon itself; it is so bright."

Thom opened his eyes, putting his hand under his chin to shield the glare from the ice beneath his feet, and finally he saw the next block of ice, a dappled light directly ahead of him. "I'm jumping now. I will light my staff brighter so that the two of you can follow. It isn't that wide of a gap. Just a leg's stretch away."

Adele let go and he jumped, landing to great protests from the cockatrices. He realized the spottiness of the glow was caused by the shadows of the dozens of birds that covered this chunk of ice. The ice made a deep cracking sound as he landed.

"Your light is heating up the ice even faster," complained Rainflower. "We must hurry!"

Adele and Francis made the leap safely, but one of them stepped on a cockatrice and suddenly the clucking turned into a hiss. Then another hiss.

Looking more carefully at the animals sharing their path, Thom made out a creature like an overlarge chicken, but with a snakelike tale and leathery wings that many of them now flapped in irritation.

"They are going into a frenzy," said Francis. "Move quickly but try your best not to jostle them too much or they will stop their ice munching and attack us."

Thom kept going, using his staff to gently shove the birds out of the way. One of them bit hard and he felt it all the way up the wood. He shook the thing off and kept moving. For the most part, the birds were all focused on the ice, chipping at it with their beaks and then slurping up the ice slivers. As they did that, they clucked louder and louder, excited about their feast.

After another five steps, the ice made another loud cracking sound and suddenly the whole block dropped to list to the right. Thom made sure his heels were down and the magic held him from sliding off. It reminded him to keep that enchantment going strong. The birds began to slide, but they dug in their sharp claws and held as they ate even faster.

"Run!" ordered Rainflower from out of the fog. "Toward my voice. You will need some speed to make this next jump." And then she kept repeating 'this way' and 'toward me' to guide them.

Thom broke into a shambling, stuttering run, trying to keep at least one heel was in contact with the ice so that he wouldn't slide away. Where was that fairy? He could hear her but still couldn't see her.

In his rush, he missed removing a cockatrice and stepped on its slithery tail instead. The thing viciously pecked at his bad ankle before he could kick it away. Suddenly, his ankle felt on fire with pain, but he had to keep going.

Tears came to his eyes, but he pressed on, now swinging viciously at any cockatrice that came too close. The ice made another cracking sound and shook.

"Prepare to jump, Thomas," ordered the fairy suddenly. "In one more step you will be at the edge. Can you see the next section? It is about a human arm's length higher than the one you are one, so you need to jump higher."

He didn't slow, even though he could barely make out the glow ahead of him. He rose up on his toes and sprang into the air. He hit the ice hard and flat-footed, so that two enchantments canceled each other and made his footing treacherous. His re-injured ankle flared in pain and went down on his knees in pain, almost dropping his staff as he caught himself. He heard the others land behind him but didn't look.

"We need to keep going," stated Rainflower. Through tear-filled eyes he finally saw her, standing on the ice just ahead of him.

He gave he a nod of understanding but wasn't ready to try standing yet.

"Concentrate on your magic," said Francis with urgency. "Don't let the pain break your enchantments, or we will not make it out of here. We are still in danger."

As if to emphasize the monk's warning, there came a thunderous sound behind him as the ice block they had just left shattered and then shattered again. Suddenly the air was full of agitated cockatrices as they flew away from there now-crumbling feast and sought refuge where the humans stood. As they landed, the little beasts began hissing in agitation. Rainflower quickly lifted off the ice to avoid their vicious strikes, once again becoming just a shadow in the fog.

"They are angry that their meal is gone," said Adele as she helped Thom back onto his feet. "We need to keep going like she says and get away from these little monsters." She kicked one away that came too close.

The next two blocks of ice were thankfully well-aligned. Thom was able to cross the gaps and land just on one foot to keep from further agitating his left ankle. By the second leap, the cockatrices were gone and the fog faded to just a bit of mist.

"You have the path lit all the way to Dripping Branch Wayrest," stated Rainflower as she settled on the ice next to them. "You may want to consider lessening the strength of your enchantment now."

"She makes a good point. In addition, a duller, weaker light will last longer and be less noisy," added Francis.

Chagrined, Thom took a moment to concentrate on his enchantment and to bank the light to a lower brightness. "Can you actually see it all the way to the wayrest?"

"I cannot really see anything that far. What a fairy can do is sense where things at a distance, but the farther away they are the less distinct the impression."

"Think of it like catching something in the corner of your eye," suggested Francis, "or like night vision where you can see the form but not necessarily the details or the colors."

"It is not night vision or corner sight," argued Rainflower. "Why do you always insist on making such comparisons?"

Francis gave the fairy a tired smile. "No, you are correct; it is neither of those things. It is fairy sight and it is unique to your people. That is one of the reasons you serve as guides on the Road, because your kind can perceive the patterns of the Road far better than even the most powerful wizard."

"That is a truer answer," said the fairy. "We should keep moving. There is at least one cloud face to climb and a few more large gaps to jump. This part of the path is more stable but it will be no easier."

NINETEEN

Harpies Ahead

The fog lifted and suddenly there was blue sky all around them, except for their narrow path that now crossed to a towering cloud and climbed up its side. He couldn't see the far side, but wondered why they need to get so much higher in the sky.

Thom looked at it and felt intimidated. "Why does it have to climb so steeply? Why doesn't the Road stay level?"

"The clouds determine the path," replied the tiny female walking in front of him. "Today is a patchwork day, when the clouds float at different altitudes, so sometimes we have to climb or scramble down to get to the next section. The clouds will also drift apart for sometimes hours at a time. Again, we should hurry while our path remains somewhat easy."

Thom shook his head. She considered this easy? Well, there was nothing he could do about it except take the path in front of him, so he took the short jump to the tall cloud and started hiking up the icy stairs, using his staff to keep his weight off his throbbing ankle. Adele and Francis followed. Rainflower chose to fly rather than hike and her two bird companions soared around her, enjoying the sunshine. Thom wished he had wings.

Halfway up, the cloud billowed out and brought a welcome mist around him, because climbing in the midday sun was causing him to sweat and making the icy stairs glisten with melt. He wanted to pause and sit down in the cool of the cloud cover, but he doubted he would be able to get back up if he did. He didn't even look back to check on Adele and Francis because he feared twisting to look down at them might unsettled his fragile balance and send him toppling down the cloud face. Instead, Thomas kept climbing, slowly but steadily.

At the top the cloud mists retreated and he was once again in the bright daylight. Rainflower sat on the path in front of him. In every direction he saw only blue skies. "Why did the Road take us all the way up here? There aren't any other clouds this high."

"There are, once you get beyond to the far edge, you will see where it leads. We are getting close to Dripping Branch Wayrest. Only about two more hours, if the clouds remain aligned."

Thom didn't bother to ask what would happen if the clouds weren't aligned.

"It is so beautiful up here," proclaimed Adele as she caught up with them. "It seems like I can see all the way to the ends of the earth."

"God's creation is truly magnificent," agreed Francis.

Adele's smile suddenly faded. "What kind of a bird is that? Is it one of those great eagles coming back for us?"

Everyone looked in the direction she pointed.

"Too small to be that," noted Francis, "but I cannot tell what it is from this far away. Rainflower, what do you see?"

For a moment Rainflower just stared, then she finally replied. "It is Aello."

"Another fairy is coming to us?" asked Adele.

"Aello is no fairy. Prepare your enchantments, magicians, for the harpy will be on us very soon."

"No!" swore Thom, fumbling his knapsack off his back and pulling out his magician's box. He looked to Francis. "What did you plan to use against them? Tell me now; I need to craft quickly, no matter how tired I feel."

"Craft fireballs," ordered Francis, "but hopefully you will not have to throw any. Remember that harpies are masters of wind, so this one could easily blow that fire back into our faces. Nonetheless, fire can be effective against them. Craft them, but do not use any yet. If it is necessary, I will show you how to get around or under a harpy's windstorm. Right now, I need to guide Adele on how to craft a Tarn's Call and then I will have her talk with this Aello in a way that can't be easily ignored."

Thom realized that Francis was pushing Adele into crafting like a journeywoman. The monk was either desperate or saw great potential in her. Most likely both. He didn't have time to think more about it. Instead, he had to focus on his own responsibility and suddenly realized he had a problem- he was still holding the glowing staff in his left hand. "How can I craft one-handed?"

"Set it down but maintain your mental connection to it," replied Francis. "You have done other enchantments where you kept that link over even greater distances. This is no different."

Thom raised an eyebrow in surprise. That made sense, but he had been too exhausted to consider it. Carefully, he set the staff down between his feet, wanting to make sure there would be no chance for it to roll away and be lost. He needed it for more than just lighting their path; he needed to lean on that wood with every step. Once placed where he wanted it, he cautiously let go, making sure his connection remained. He also checked his Sole Grip enchantment to make sure it was strong. When he felt sure about both, he started preparing for a third enchantment.

He worked carefully, reminding himself about each step. He stirred together powders of Phoenix tongue, crushed Azure Fireflies, and Crested Black Eagle feathers, along with Spotted Pine oil. He then added the mundane elements of oak pollen, black powder, and lamp oil. Finally, he added his spit to attune the enchantment to himself. He coated his dampened hands with white sand, ready to handle the flames, but he didn't form any of the goop into fireballs yet.

When he looked up, he realized that the harpy was now much closer and that Rainflower was back in the air, hovering right above him. Harpies weren't able to hover like fairies, so this one began to circle them, doing so in a rather oblong pattern to keep her flight within the bounds of the Road's enchantment.

He looked over and saw that Adele had just finished her crafting but in the middle of it she had let slip her other enchantment. Thom's boot no longer had a bounce to their toes. She would have to re-craft the Sole Flight once this confrontation was over.

A new wind had begun, flowing in the opposite direction of the air currents that were pushing all the clouds in the sky. It was a wind coming from the harpy. In that wind came the whisper of her voice. "What do we have here? None of you are Founders, yet one of you lit the Road brighter than it has ever been lit. Who are you?"

Even though she was still a fair distance away, the wind pushed her words into Thom's ears, making them distinct and loud even while sounding as if they were a soft whisper. It was a sensation that gave him goose flesh.

The harpy had wings that were eagle-brown and a face that resembled that of a pale, homely woman, but with a flattened nose and pointed ears. Dark hair streamed over bare-skin shoulders and over her feathered back. She had bare human-like breasts and bare arms, but from her waist down she wore feathers and her feet ended in talons. Despite the bare flesh, there was nothing appealing about her appearance.

What caught Thom's gaze as she flew by was her large, angry eyes set in a frowning countenance. This Aello seemed a stranger to laughter and light-heartedness. She looked forever the angry scold and right now her wrathful focus was on them as she circled overhead.

Suddenly, Adele's voice boomed outward, enhanced by the enchantment she had just crafted. "I am Lady Adele and I travel with Rainflower, along with the Fair Defender and the Road Saver. We have come because your sisters have imprisoned my friend and the male who travels with her."

"I have never heard of you, Adele," came the penetrating, insinuating whisper. She said Adele's name as if it were an offensive thing to mention. "Rainflower is known, but she is a mere fairy who cannot make demands of us. As for the males, why would you give them titles as if they were warriors? Virtue and bravery can only reside in the female. All know that truth.

"You ask about our actions, but what my sisters and I are doing on the Road is none of your concern. You should go back to whatever dank castle you crawled out of and leave the skies to those of us who can soar."

"You dare challenge where I go?" boomed Adele back in unexpected anger.

Thom looked at her in surprise, but then he saw Francis whispering to her and realized she was acting as the monk instructed. He hoped Francis knew the correct way to talk with harpies.

"I am a magician and a woman," continued Adele with great volume. "I am no weak-minded male. I demand to know why you are holding my sister captive."

"Your sister? You belong to Vivien's colony? Does your nest abut hers?"

The harpy had come close enough that Thom could now see her face clearly. She looked aside from Adele and locked eyes with Thom for just a moment before looking back at her. "Do you share mates?"

The implication angered him, but he still kept his enchantment in limbo. It wouldn't be wise to start throwing fireballs, at least not yet.

"I claim Vivien as sister, but our sleeping quarters and bed mates are none of your business, Aello. Since when have harpies showed any interest in human habits? I ask nothing about where your colony is located or whose feathers line your nest. No, I only ask that you explain why you have confined my sister."

Thom thought she sounded so convincing, as if she regularly conversed with harpies, even though this was the first time either of them had seen one.

The harpy tightened her circling but said nothing for a time. Her nearness caused Rainflower to climb even higher to hover above her track. Finally, Aello. "You are not who we expected to come for those two. I grant you the right to appeal to my sisters and plea for those two, but I offer no assurance that your wish will be granted. Come to us at the wayrest before sunset and we will talk."

With that, she broke off and flew back in the direction she came, her huge dark wings lifting her even higher and speeding her away.

Thom watched her go and thinking that harpies looked rather fierce. She had no beak for attacking like a bird of prey might, but her talons were wickedly long and powerful and there were spikes on the end of her wings that looked dangerous as well.

Rainflower landed on the ice in front of them. "Trust no harpy. They are known for deceitful words and cruelty. It is always best to avoid them."

"But we have no other path to take," replied Francis. "The Road behind us has shattered to hail and there is no cross path between here and the wayrest, is there?"

The fairy frowned but shook her head. "They are not to be trusted."

"At least she was willing to talk," said Thomas. "For what Bronwen and you implied, I was expecting a raging madness."

"That was just one," noted Rainflower. "When they gather in a horde of harpies, their anger will feed off each other."

"But she implied that they were holding our friends for a reason, which means planning on their part and not merely impetuous anger," said Francis aloud, though he seemed to be more talking to himself than to them. "They have lingered here for days, which also shows their resolve. She said we were not the rescuers they had been expecting. Whose attention are they trying to raise?"

"Do not over-think what they have done. Harpies can hold a grudge for decades, so what is a few days to them? The queen ordered me to guide you, but I do not like guiding anyone toward a possible trap and that is what I suspect lies ahead of us."

"We go with eyes open," replied Francis. "Adele, you can let go of your enchantment. Thom, you should throw those fireballs behind us at the already-ruined Road where they can do no harm."

They released the two enchantments then Francis suggested that Adele craft both Sole Flight and Sole Grip for their next section, to give Thom a rest. Thom hesitantly let go of the magic and watched as Adele handled both enchantments. She did it confidently and he was impressed at how quickly she had learned to handle two enchantments at once. Soon they were hiking along the Road of Clouds again.

They crossed the top of the cloud and saw that there were other tall clouds beyond, though none as tall as this one. They took ice steps halfway down the other side then had a long jump over to another cloud. They climbed more ice steps though this flight tunneled up through the cloud.

As the cloud entombed them, Thom felt the dew form all over him and soon water dripped off his hair and the hem of his insulated robe. The steps were also wet, but thanks to the enchantment Sole Grip, all of them were able to climb without slipping. They also used that odd rolling step, leaning forward just a little to allow Sole Flight to give them a bit of a lift with each step, making the steep climb easier. But halfway through the cloud, the stairs suddenly ended at nothing. Startled, Thom looked around in the mists for the next section.

Adele crowded up behind him. "What's wrong?"

"I don't know where the path continues." It was nowhere at their level. He looked up higher and saw nothing through the mists, but maybe the ice steps didn't light up on their under-side.

He was considering flaring the light again, when they heard Rainflower. "Down here. You must jump down here."

Thom couldn't see her, but following the sound of her voice, he finally saw the glow at least ten feet below them and off toward the side. Rainflower shifted and he saw her as a shadowy that glided between him and the lower path. How would they get down there? He didn't trust his ankle to hold out a drop of that distance and the landing ice block didn't seem especially wide. Even if he landed in the center, he could easily stumble and fall off the side.

"I should jump first," said Adele, "Then I can help you from down there."

Everything in him wanted to protest such an idea; he didn't want her risking more for his sake. But he knew she was right. "Can I do anything to help?"

"Hold my hand. I want to try sitting on the edge and then dropping down. That will lessen the distance."

He helped her get in position, sitting on a corner of the last step, her legs dangling off the side. She smiled up at him once, then looked down and suddenly she was gone. Thom caught his breath as she fell and it seemed to take forever but was really less than the time between two heart beats. The mists trailed after her as she plunged and then she hit the ice below, landing heel first and flexing at the knees to listen the impact.

"I made it," she called back. She was indistinct in the fog but he could tell that she had stepped back to give him room. "Tell me when you're ready to jump."

"Do you want to go next?" asked Thom of Francis.

"No, you go before me. Adele had a good idea of sitting down first to shorten the distance. You should do the same. Here, hold my hand so that you don't slip as you get in place."

Thom made the drop, but landed awkwardly. Adele helped steady him so that he didn't stumble off the side. Francis followed without mishap and the trio kept going, with occasional appearances of Rainflower.

For the next hour, the path was much easier to travel. But then they saw the five harpies waiting ahead of them.

TWENTY

Negotiations

They stood on the edge of another cloud, tiny Rainflower standing with them. There was a small gap to the next cloud and then stairs downward to the landing in front of Dripping Branch Wayrest. From this altitude they could see the harpies waiting for them, perched on the icy benches.

"Five of them," noted the fairy. "That is enough for a horde. They will be dangerous unless one of them is a prima who can intimidate the others. The larger, darker one is Celaeno; she may hold that rank, but I am unsure, since I do not have many dealings with their kind."

"Do we craft enchantments now?" asked Thom, not looking forward to confronting that many. Considering how fast the other one flew, they could easily race toward them as they were descending the ice steps and catching them in a place that would be hard to kneel down, mix, and craft magic.

"Adele cannot yet hold anything else, so she shouldn't. When we get down there, she will be doing most of the talking, since harpies detest males. What do you think, Rainflower? Should Thomas craft magic now in expectation of trouble?"

"There is always trouble when dealing with harpies," she replied. "The correct question is whether coming at them with active magic will cow them or anger them more, and I have never seen a harpy cower toward anything, not even a dragon."

"So, is it worth angering them to have a defense ready... I think it is," said Francis. "Do the rest of you agree?"

"I would feel better if Thomas is ready," said Adele, "as long as it is not too much of a drain on him."

Thom gave her a tired smile. "You are not the only one who can handle two enchantments at once. It will tire me, but not so much that I would lose control of any of them."

"Do what you need to protect us," stated Rainflower. "I am a guide, not one of my queen's warriors. I do not even carry any weapons beyond the small blade that hangs on my belt, and my companion birds are scouts, not birds of prey."

"What should I craft?" he asked of Francis.

The monk grinned. "I know one that will catch their attention. The enchantment is called Founders Fire. Not many know how to craft it, but my old master found out somehow and taught it to me... it was the last

95

enchantment he ever taught me before he became a sorcerer. You will need to let go of the enchantment that lights the staff and the Road, but we will not need that light for this confrontation. Come, I will explain how it is crafted."

Thom followed the monk's very specific directions, an intricate and powerful enchantment that he smeared on the gem of his staff. But as soon as he was done, he struggled to restrain the magic from fully developing. The enchantment seemed eager to get out. Thom, through clenched teeth, asked, "Is this worth it?"

Francis chuckled. He seemed very pleased that Thom had been successful. "This will be worth the effort. You may not recognize the enchantment, but the harpies will and it will bring them to restraint if anything can."

So Thom fought the magic as he rose to his feet and they began their march down that last flight of stairs. Adele and Rainflower went first, then Thom holding tight to a staff whose gem was trying to blaze bright but he kept it under control. Francis came last and, as he walked, he gave Thomas last minute instructions on how to carefully control the fire he would soon be releasing.

Once Thom had a good understanding what he would be doing, Francis passed him to walk directly behind Adele, explaining what to expect from the harpies. He wanted to make sure she kept her demands simple and clear: that they wanted their friends released from the wayrest and allowed to leave.

The ice stairs were in decent shape, allowing them to descend without mishap or delay, and soon they were face-to-face with the harpies.

"Come no closer, humans," ordered the largest harpy, who Rainflower had called Celaeno. She was the darkest of the five, her plumage almost raven black with a hint of a reddish sheen. Thom thought it was a lovely color, although her face looked hideous by human standards. She spoke loudly, without obviously using the wind to carry her words. "Where is the Founder who lit up the Road?"

That question surprised Thom. He almost answered, but remembered that Adele needed to do the talking.

"I will go where I want," replied Adele, purposely taking two more steps before halting. "As for who enchanted the Road to blaze so brightly... that was one of the men in my party. He was the last disciple of one of the Founders."

The harpy ignored Adele's challenge. Instead, she looked curiously at Francis. "The balding one you told Aello was called Fair Defender? He lit the Road so brightly?"

"Not him. The other one."

"But he is just a fledgling," protested the harpy.

"He is a powerful magician," replied Adele. She gave him a slight nod just as Francis had instructed.

Carefully, Thom released some of the power bottled up inside his staff, letting it blaze straight up into the sky. The intensity of the enchantment almost overwhelmed his restraints, but he was able to keep it to just a small amount of power aimed upward as Francis had instructed. A column a glaring light pulsed out from the gem. He had to be careful to let only a little out and aim the powerful light only upward. Francis had warned him that if he let it flare in all directions it might shatter the Road of Clouds as well as burn anyone near. The Road was little more than a shimmer directly overhead, so his enchantment met no resistance as it passed through but it did bring a reaction from the larger enchantment: the Road began to hum and glow all around them, and it began to pulse in synchrony with his enchantment.

"He set the Road on fire!" yelled one harpy.

"We are undone!" cried another.

"It is Founders Fire," stated Celaeno, spreading her wings to dominate the others. It seemed to work, for they calmed down. "How does this young one do such great magic?"

Adele answered just as Francis had told her, for the monk had anticipated such a question. "He was the student of Founder Levitanus. He has also been called the Saver of the Road of Leaves."

"I thought an apprentice saved that Road."

Adele shrugged, a human gesture that probably meant nothing to the bird-woman. "Such was his official rank at that time."

"That was less than a year ago," continued the harpy. "How does anyone, especially a male, go from apprentice to great master in such a short time?"

"He is who he is."

"And he obeys you? He is your mate?"

Adele looked at him and smiled. "He is his own man, but he is also mine."

Thom smiled back at her even though he was still struggling to keep the enchantment contained and channeled. He wished that he could pause and appreciate that look and what she said, but he had to keep the magic controlled and he had never dealt with anything as powerful as this. How long would he be able to keep it contained? What was it that Francis had taught him to craft?

"Why does he do such dangerous magic in the middle of the Road of Clouds?"

"Do we have your attention now?" replied Adele. "Let our friends go free."

"We hold them to force the Founders to hear our petition. We wait for one of them."

Francis leaned close to Adele and whispered urgently, to which she nodded and then turned back to Celaeno. "The Fair Defender has encouraged me to share the truth with you. The Founders are at war, so do not expect them to break off their battling to come here."

"There is no war between them. Merlin and Dalrake have feigned their feud for decades now, but we know it to be a sham. One of them will come since we hold a sorcerer and a wizardess both. They will both be interested in knowing why the two are together because it ruins their story that the two sides are always at odds."

"The damage to the Roads was no sham," replied Adele. "The invasion of Camelot was no fakery. How do you explain those away?"

Celaeno raised a naked arm and pointed at Thomas. "Some were unexpectedly effective even in their ignorance. I think that one spoiled the plans the magicians had plotted."

Thom was shocked at her claim. The harpy had to be wrong. He was not that powerful; everything he accomplished had been more out of happenstance. He did not know Merlin or Dalrake, but it was hard to imagine that those two proud men were in secret alliance.

Adele spoke up before Francis could say anything to her, the harpy's claims have rattled her. "Are you claiming that the attempted kidnapping of the queen, the attack on the king, and the invasion of the city were all planned by both Founders?"

"Maybe Merlin tires of doing Arthur's bidding. I do not know their ultimate scheme behind all this, but we know enough. Merlin and Dalrake play with some deeper game that even their followers do not realize. The Waters and Leaves are both damaged but they are stable and usable, so why did Merlin send almost the whole guild onto those Roads? He left the city conveniently vulnerable to Dalrake's followers."

Francis whispered warning to Adele and this time she showed more restraint. "What is your petition to the Founders? Tell us at least that much."

"End that enchantment and then we will talk."

"Tell us or I might instruct him to turn the Founders Fire at one of your companions. Do you want that death on your hands just because of your intransigence?"

Thom doubted he could direct any of the magic that precisely at one of the harpies. He was barely able to keep it reined in as it shot skyward.

When Celaeno didn't reply, Adele added, "We are here to see our friends released. Do so and we will take your petition to one of the Founders. So tell me, what is it that you want to ask of the Founders."

One of the other harpies spread her wings in agitation. "Tell them, Celaeno. No Founder has come to rescue the couple and I doubt any will. Swear them to taking our petition to the Founders, but let us get this settled. We tire of this business."

"Silence!" hissed their leader, looking over her back. "Is this mission not worth the blood of our sisters? The slaughter must be stopped!"

Suddenly Rainflower spoke up. "Who is harvesting your people?"

Now Thom understood what was happening. Someone had been killing the harpies for their magical elements and that was why they had trapped Kane and Vivien. They were angry and wanted the Founders to order the killings to stop.

"We do not know who is the killer. Considering the reputation of one of those inside the wayrest, we thought we might have trapped him already, but the killings have continued. While waiting here, we have received word of three more vanishing."

So they knew that Kane was the Butcher of Sherwood. Thom was surprised that the bird-women were so well informed.

"Why have you not told my queen about this?" demanded Rainflower.

"Titania would have listened. We have lost fairies as well."

"We are not subjects of your queen," replied Celaeno, glaring at the tiny fairy.

In her frustration, the harpy began to gather winds to her. Thom felt the stir in the air and it worried him, but before he could bring it to Adele's attention, his beloved spoke up.

"I warn you, do not strike at us with the winds. We are not your enemy."

TWENTY-ONE

Founder's Fire

The harpies didn't reply to Adele and the winds continued to swirl around them, gaining speed. The harpies' hair whipped around and their feathers ruffled but none of them were disturbed by it. The nearer clouds were being shredded but, so far, the whirlwind wasn't wide enough to sweep over the humans. However, if it kept growing it would soon hit them and the ice steps behind them.

"When I served at Queen Guinevere's court, her ladies in waiting were rather spiteful," said Adele in a raised voice to be heard over the wind, but she kept it to a conversational tone nonetheless. "They plotted against me time and time again, just because I wasn't what they expected. They feared a woman who wasn't under their domination. Is that the problem here? Do you harpies fear any female you cannot subdue?"

"We will speak to a Founder!"

"There is no Founder here and none of them are coming!" replied Adele, having to yell over the wind's roar. The wind had begun to hit them too now, though not yet with its full force. "They are too consumed in their own squabbles! One of them even faked his own death!"

"What is this? You are claiming Levitanus lives?"

"Cease your winds! I tire of yelling to be heard!" Adele folded her arms, refusing to say any more.

Finally, Celaeno lifted her arm and made a chopping motion above her head. The winds were cut off and suddenly it became perfectly still. Not even the clouds around them moved.

Into the calm Celaeno asked again, "Levitanus lives?"

"As far as we know, he does. He came through here a few days ago as a prisoner of Dalrake and his sorcerers."

"So that is why he did not respond to my greeting," remarked Rainflower. "You did not tell me that one Founder had imprisoned another."

"The Founders truly fight against each other? That is hard to believe, but then it was hard to believe that one of them had died in a fire," stated Celaeno. "How are we to believe one when you have just proven that the other is false?"

"You have heard of the League of Barnabas?" asked Adele, ignoring Francis' effort to stop her.

Celaeno paused, locking eyes with Adele. When she finally spoke, she whispered and a fresh breeze carried her answer just to the humans. "The primas of our people know of it, but not the others. I think your fairy guide is ignorant of the league as well. Is it wise to mention it?"

Adele spoke again, acting as if the harpy had said nothing. "The Founders have broken alliances and now they openly oppose each other. We will share your petition with at least one of them, once we are free of the Road. Just let us rescue our friends and we will get on our way. The two were supposed to be in pursuit of Dalrake when you trapped them."

"Which Founder will listen to you?" demanded Celaeno. "You have just admitted to be opposed to Dalrake."

Adele pointed at Thomas. "He belongs to Merlin's guild and is also Levitanus' last student. I know either Founder will listen to him. Free our friends and we will plead your cause."

Once again Celaeno paused before responding, her look seeming to penetrate through Adele. For a moment, Thom worried he might be forced to fight them with the enchantment he barely controlled now, but then he saw the lead harpy give the slightest nod.

"We have the oath of you, Lady Adele, and your two men. All of the harpies will know about your promise and will hold all three of you accountable to fulfill your vow. Plea our need before at least one of the Founders. Now send one of the men to retrieve your friends. We will no longer keep them captive."

Adele nodded in return. "You have our oath. Francis, go tell our friends that they can leave the wayrest."

The monk obeyed her without hesitation, striding between the ranks of harpies. Instead of asking Adele to end the enchantments on his boots, he removed them at the archway and then passed through barefooted, disappearing into the wayrest. Thom shifted his weight off his aching ankle, working hard to maintain the enchantment he held, while wondering what was happening beyond the archway.

Finally, Francis came back out with Kane and Vivien, pausing only to slip his boots back on. The other two looked suspiciously at the bird-women while the monk just ignored them as he walked to Adele and Thomas.

It wasn't until Kane was past the harpies that he noticed the enchantment Thomas was holding. When he did, he came to a stop and stared open-mouthed at him.

"What is that?" asked Vivien, also noticing the active magic.

Kane turned to Francis, his countenance darkening. "What have you done? You taught him to craft Founders Fire? How?"

Vivien and Adele exchanged a hug, but the journeywoman kept staring at Thomas. "That is a dangerous enchantment he holds. Does he know what he's doing?"

Thom didn't like how they talk *about him* instead of *to him*, but he was too occupied in keeping the enchantment restrained to argue.

"He is ignorant of what he holds," judged Kane, "but Thomas is still in control of it, if barely. That is more than any other wizard or sorcerer has ever done who wasn't one of the Founders. I once saw Dalrake send Founders Fire at a fleet of raiders on the coast. None survived." He stepped closer to Thomas. "Now would be a good time to release it before it explodes in all directions."

Thom nodded but he wasn't sure how to do that without the magic overwhelming his restraints. He looked pleadingly toward Francis.

The monk understood and came beside him. "You will need to slowly widen your column until it is more of a wide cone, letting the power exit the Road without destroying it." Francis paused to look toward Rainflower and the harpies. "Keep away from the air anywhere above this area or you could get caught in the magic."

"We will leave now," replied Celaeno and suddenly all the harpies leaped into the air and flew away, following the Road as it moved past the wayrest.

Rainflower chose to land next to women to keep out of danger.

Thom noticed all this even as he prepared to widen his shield around the magic, to let more of it burn off.

"Go ahead," urged Francis, putting a hand on Thomas' shoulder. "You can do this. I know you can."

Slowly, carefully, he widened the channel for his enchantment and then he let more of it surge out of his staff. For a frightening moment he felt it slipping out of his control, but he fought to keep it tamed and directed.

The magic roared skyward, becoming a beacon so bright it seemed like a part of the sun. The noise of it was deafening to his inner ear, and it seemed to go on forever. But it eventually burned off, ending suddenly as the gem on his staff went dark.

TWENTY-TWO

Exhausted Retreat

Thom would have collapsed if Francis and Kane hadn't been supporting him. He hadn't even realized that the two had come close and started holding him up sometime during the release.

"Sit down on one of the benches," urged Francis, leading him over to the nearest one.

He sank on the ice-covered stone, feeling totally drained. The others came over to stand around him. Rainflower kept at a distance, obviously shaken about what she had just seen.

"He almost killed all of us," whispered Vivien, shaking her head.

"But he didn't," replied Kane, also keeping his voice low. They were all making sure that the fairy couldn't overhear them. "How is it that a journeyman mastered the greatest enchantment ever crafted? How did you know he could handle it?"

"Levitanus trained him for such as this," replied Francis, sounding sad. "He was prepared as a weapon against the other Founders; he was just never told."

"You truly think that?" asked Kane.

"How else would you explain an apprentice who bests a sorceress to save the queen. You knew Narissa; was she so weak to fall to a mere youth?"

"Like everyone else, I thought it a fluke."

"But it wasn't just that time. He defeated Gweir on the Road of Waters and frustrated Dahrake's plans. He survived Horis' torture and helped us fight off griffins."

Thom heard what they were saying and wanted to argue against Francis' reasoning, but all that he could do was shake his head a little. He was just too drained to speak.

"He is so young," protested Vivien, allowing her voice to get too loud, not even noticing Thom's silent protest.

Francis motioned for her to lower her voice. "Do you know how old the Founders were when they started crafting the Roads? They were in their thirties and full wizards. It was only after Arthur succeeded in uniting the realm and the enchantments of Camelot were completed that we saw a more... methodical training of magicians ordered. Before that, many rose through the ranks at a young age, just like Thomas and Adele."

Kane shook his head. "You imply that there is some kind of pact between the Founders and the king to slow the pace of magician training."

"There is, and Levitanus has broken that pact, as has the league by letting Vivien do her instructing as she has. Levitanus has set up the league as not only the enemy of the guild and the sorcerers, but also as the foe of their pact with the king."

Thomas looked up at them and shook his head again and this time found the strength to speak. He tried to keep his voice to a whisper, but still his passion came out. "I am no weapon! Look at me. I'm exhausted and I almost killed all of us. My past victories were more luck or God's mercy than any great skill on my part. Narissa was impaled by something in the winds she herself created. As for Gweir, I vomited on him and that was how I bested him. Vomiting is no warrior's weapon. In Camelot, I was more of a burden than weapon and all of you know that. Many of you had to help carry me because I was so weak."

"I would never be one to puff up Thomas," stated Vivien, this time keeping her voice lower, "but I must admit that his many victories could not have been mere happenstance. Later, we can sort out how he accomplished what he did and whether that was his master's intention. For now, we should get moving. Whatever Thomas did as he bled off that magic into the sky, it is acting like a gong announcing our location. Have none of you been listening to the Road around us? It rings from the magic he just splashed across the heavens. Every magician anywhere near the Road of Clouds will have heard it."

Dully, Thom looked up but saw nothing. He listened and realized that she was right: the very Road seemed to be ringing out. It was not really a change in the Road's magic as much as an addition to it. Rather than an explosive clash, the Founders Fire had caused an extra ringing beat.

"Yes, we should get going," agreed Kane.

"It grows late," noted Francis.

"I will not go back into that wayrest," said Kane. "Better to face the Road at night than to return to that prison."

"Your guide is the same one who left us to the mercies of the harpies," noticed Vivien. "Can we trust her to guide us true?"

"Their queen sent her to Camelot to get help and she came with alacrity," replied Francis. "She has guided us well, despite her quirks and sensitivities." He turned to her and raised his voice. "Rainflower, are you ready to guide us on from here?"

"Where to?" she asked, fluttering closer. "Do we still pursue Founder Dalrake? If so, it will be a hard trail to reclaim. The Road has shifted much over the last few days."

"For now, get us to the nearest crossing," ordered Kane. "From there we can decide the best route forward."

"Night will be on us before we are halfway there," she warned.

"I will light our path well," replied Kane. "You need not worry about that."

The fairy raised an eyebrow. "If you light it to a tenth of the brightness that Thomas can, it will more than enough."

Thom looked up tiredly just as Kane turned to gaze at him again. The master magician gave him a speculative look as he said, "I think there are more stories I will want to hear, but now is not the time. Can you walk, journeyman?"

Thom wasn't sure if he could, but he grabbed his staff and used it to help himself up. He just stood there for a while, swaying just a bit, then he took a few shuffling steps forward. "I… I can walk, but the jumping will be harder."

"We will help as we can," replied Kane. "I want you to eat and drink some because crafting can be as strenuous as smithing, especially with the kind of enchantments you have been making. Adele, can you see that he eats? And you can let go of the enchantments you have crafted; let Vivien handle that."

Thom was too tired to object how Kane was suddenly acting as their leader. Instead, he accepted the plum offered by Adele and began eating methodically, not really tasting its sweetness. When Vivien came around to apply enchantments to the soles of his boots, he merely let others bear his weight so that he could lift his feet. He was too tired to wonder much about what they were doing.

Soon, they were heading away from the wayrest, following the path to wherever it went. He didn't ask how long they planned to travel or when he could rest again. It was enough for him to focus on walking and chewing at the same time. He finished the one and then exchanged her the pit for a second one.

* * *

Thom didn't remember much of their travels. He walked where told, accepting their help to jump and climb. They must have stopped a few times to rest, but he couldn't recall when. It wasn't until nearly midnight that they finally arrived at a cloud crossing, whatever that was. Kane's magic showed that it was a rather large area of now-glowing ice; he had no curiosity about how it held together or its purpose. He was just glad that they were no longer urging him to keep walking; they actually let him sink to a blanket placed on the ice and let him fall into exhausted sleep. He didn't even realize when two others cuddled next to him to share body warmth. He just slept.

TWENTY-THREE

Cloud Crossing

Dawn came too soon and with an icy drizzle. Thom moaned when one of the warm bodies left and then the other did too. He opened up puffy eyes and used the corner of the blanket to wipe the moisture off his exposed cheek.

"You are awake," stated Francis. "How do you feel?"

He took a moment to assess himself, moving to sit up. "I think I'm stronger today. Where are we? I can't remember much of yesterday after I let go of the enchantment."

"We are at a cloud crossing and it is time for some decisions to be made. I'm glad you are awake and can join in on the conversation. Fold up those blankets, one belongs to me and the other to Kane, then join the rest of us; we have a meal to share."

Before getting up, Thom found his knapsack and dug out the balm from Bronwen and slathered it on his ankle. He also took the time to examine his many other injuries, even though the drizzle chilled any skin he exposed. He found the bruises fading and the wounds scabbing. Nothing else seemed pressing, so he put the balm away, got to his feet, and folded all the blankets. His own had been the bottom blanket so he had to shake off an ice crusting before putting it away in his knapsack. Noticing that none of the others were wearing their packs yet, he set it aside and placed the other two blankets on top of it.

"I have a cup of cider for you," said Adele, walking over with two steaming mugs. "Kane used an enchantment to heat it and that makes it so much better."

He took the cup with thanks, wrapping his hands around it and letting the heat waft over his face before taking a careful sip. It was almost too hot, but not quite.

"Kane told Vivien to heat up travel biscuits with cheese and she did so without a murmur. She was surprisingly agreeable with him."

Thom puzzled over Adele's slight smile. Did she suspect a budding friendship or even romance between the two that had been trapped? He shook his head. The fiery red-head wasn't one to become doe-eyed over anyone, especially not a known killer like Kane. Vivien tolerated men; she didn't befriend them.

He followed Adele over to where Vivien held a cloth-wrapped bundle that gave off steam. The journeywoman handed him two hot biscuits with melted cheese in the center of each. Adele took two as well, with Vivien taking the last two. Rainflower declined eating human food, claiming she and her bird companions had already shared some seeds an hour ago.

The five humans stood in a loose circle as they ate and drank, eating quietly and quickly in the ongoing drizzle.

It was Adele who finally broke the silence. "Did we really do it? For once, we have rescued others and no sorcerers or monsters have gotten in our way. The Road itself was hard, but we made it. Vivien and Kane are now free to complete their quest."

"Once again, thank you for freeing us," said Kane making eye contact with each of his three human rescuers and with the fairy, "but I am not certain that Vivien and I can continue our task. As Rainflower said yesterday, the Road has branched and reformed much while we were trapped. My only hope is that Dalrake has gone to his own citadel. At least I know that route."

"That is our best hope," agreed Vivien. "How many more days travel?"

"His keep is farther away from Camelot than most. It will take two days with straight paths, three or four if the Road of Clouds is broken up."

"You will need Rainflower to guide you," stated Francis, "or else you'll waste precious time on detours and broken paths. You cannot call the Road to you all the way there."

"No, you three will need her more," argued Vivien. "How will you navigate the twists of the Road…"

"I will go with either party," stated Rainflower, unexpectedly interrupting, "but before you make a decision you should know that others are coming here."

"Tell us how many and where they are now," ordered Kane.

"One comes from the mountain. Three others come from one of the Road ends. They are farther away but are moving faster because they are flying over obstacles."

"Are there any fairies with them?"

"No. I see no other fairies. There is a roc lurking outside one of the wayrests, most likely waiting for a pegasus to come out so it can eat it. The trio of humans are unaccompanied."

Kane nodded and then looked at Thomas. "Your enchantment has certainly attracted others. I would guess that the Keeper Ellery of Clouds has sent one of his assistant wizards. As for the other three, they could be wizards or sorcerers. I lean more toward the later, considering the magic they are using, but I have been wrong before."

"How are they tracking us without a fairy?" asked Thomas. "I hear no magic and I've seen no purple spheres."

"They are tracking the ripples of power, not us. If you listen carefully, you will notice that the extra noise that the Road is making goes out from that wayrest in waves, like ripples from a rock thrown into a pond. Listen carefully and you will understand."

Thom took a moment to listen more carefully with his inner ear and realized that the noise was passing through the Road's enchantment in waves, like a breeze passing across a meadow. The cloud crossing where they stood was the meeting place of eight paths, four coming in and four going out. It was obvious that the sound came up only one of those ways before passing through and following the four outgoing paths, adding to the usual pulse of their enchantment. Even though he didn't remember, Thom now knew that the incoming path was the one they had used to get here last night.

"We will need to move sideways to get out of this," stated Vivien. "Rainflower, which paths are the ones the others are likely to use to reach this crossing?"

The fairy considered, then pointed at two particular paths.

"That leaves us these two," stated Kane, pointing at the remaining pair, obviously leaving off the one that went back to the wayrest where they had confronted the harpies. "Please describe their condition and how far it is to another wayrest or cloud crossing.

Rainflower went to hover in front of one path, studying it carefully. "This one is strong but meanders from here. We would reach Air Root Wayrest within a day, but it would be another day before we encounter any cloud crossing and that one is only a bypass. It would be very difficult for any of the others to intersect us, but we would end up at the far edge of the Road's paths. Are we heading toward the coast?"

Kane ignored the question, instead asking, "What of the other route?"

The fairy moved to the entrance to that path and studied it for a time. Even in this dreary drizzle and mist, she could way-find to the farthest corner of the maze that was the Road of Clouds. It was a unique skill and Thom could see how an amoral magician could lust for such power.

"This path is still forming, but we would reach Flying Tree Wayrest in less than a day or could push on to the Core Crossing."

"It is that close?" asked Kane, sounding surprised.

Thom had no idea what the "Core Crossing" was, but assumed it was similar to a cloud crossing.

"The route is *odd*. I have never seen one so direct to the Core. It is still forming, so many sections might be soft, but it is clear in its direction. It is almost as if the Keeper placed it just for us."

Kane smiled. "Keeper Ellery is no friend of ours; he is Merlin's man and is also friendly with the sorcerers. Besides, I have never known a keeper to be able to track an individual along a Road. The path was not placed for our sake. Could that path be a possible route for the magician approaching from Cloudholder?"

Rainflower frowned as she considered the possibility. "Yes. There is a way if they turn away from us at the next cloud crossing and follow another newer route. Although it is not obvious, if they follow that route it will also take them to the Core and then they can take the path in front of us. They will get here before the three others."

"Will we get their first if we take that path?"

"I am no foreteller of the future. Most likely we would arrive before the wizard, but we could be delayed in some way that I cannot see from here."

"If a fairy cannot see it, then it is truly far away. From the Core, Vivien and I can find our own way to Dalrake's hold, and it will also simplify the way back to Cloudholder. We take the new path."

"Then gather your things because we need to start now," replied Rainflower.

TWENTY-FOUR

Reaching the Core

Thom felt stronger today than he had in days and he was thankful for that because Rainflower and Kane set a brisk pace. Even with some restored vigor, he was glad he wasn't handling any of their traveling magic. Surprisingly, Kane chose the same enchantments that Francis had, letting Vivien handle Sole Grip and Sole Flight, while the former sorcerer took care of lighting the route ahead of them. The Road was slushy in many areas, but it didn't have any steep climbs or drops. In addition, the drizzly day was thick with clouds so the gaps between sections were small, making those jumps easier too. In all, it seemed a perfect route to travel fast, which they did.

He had enough strength today that he could actually think as he traveled and he had much to ponder. Why did Francis have him craft Founders Fire? Surely there were other enchantments that would have caught the harpies' attention. How was he able to succeed at making such a powerful enchantment? He was an under-trained journeyman, so how could he craft such advanced magic? After an hour of wondering, he was no closer to any answers.

Thom realized that he needed to have a long conversation with Francis, but there wouldn't be any time to do so away from the others. He looked over his shoulder at the monk who was behind Adele in their marching order. If he wanted answers, he had no choice but to ask them openly, so he did. "Why Founders Fire?"

"Because we will be facing far more than mere harpies."

"What do you mean? We are here to free Vivien and Kane and then go back to the city."

Francis shook his head. "Can't you see what's happening around us? I fear that the Founders are finally going to have it out with each other and it will happen here on the Road of Clouds."

"But they've already captured Levitanus," argued Thomas. "I can't imagine Merlin bothering to rescue him."

"By now he has already been freed from Dalrake's hands. We saw the rescue party fly over us only a day ago."

Kane, who was walking in front of Thomas, swore. "What is this? What flying rescue party?"

Francis explained the giant eagles carrying pixies and dryads.

"And you think they will have successfully freed Levitanus?" asked Vivien, who was walking last in line, right behind the monk.

"We will know soon enough. They should fly over us later today if they won."

"What have you gotten us into, monk?" demanded Kane. He had stopped walking and was now turned around to face the rest of them.

"This was not my choice," replied Francis. "Bronwen called on us because she had no one else that could rescue you. We did that, but I don't think we can get off the Road before the Founders clash. Actually, I wouldn't be surprised if Bronwen expected this and sent us to join the league's side."

"She certainly did not send Vivien and I. We left without telling anyone besides the three of you, chasing at the heels of Dalrake and his henchmen. Really, none of that is of concern to me. What you still have not explained is why you taught Thomas to craft Founders Fire."

Francis dropped his usual cheerful countenance, his face growing hard. "I believe his master loves him like a son, but he also used Thomas. He trained him to be a weapon against the other two. I have just brought the weapon to bear in an unexpected way. The enchantment was a challenge to the Founders, even more than a warning to the harpies. I believe all three heard it and it will cause them concern."

Kane shook his head. "You have poked a hornet's nest."

Adele spoke up. "I thought Thomas was your friend and not just a pawn or weapon."

Even with her back turned to him, Thom could tell she was stiff with rage. Surprisingly, he wasn't. He didn't know how he felt toward his friend. Maybe he was just hardened by all the betrayal from Levitanus and the guild… No, it wasn't that. He felt more of a peace about all this, which was strange.

"What were you trying to gain?" asked Kane.

"We should keep moving," suggested Francis. "I will explain as clearly as I can while we walk."

He then said no more until they started marching along the icy way through the clouds. When he spoke, he did so with enough volume so that all could clearly hear. "Do all of you know how old the Founders were when they created the magical protections and travel routes for Camelot? They were maybe ten years older than Thomas is now, and they were at the height of their craft. Yet these days, both sorcerers and wizards insist that only gray-hairs with decades of practice can reach that level. It is a truth that no one wants to talk about, but I have always wondered about it. When I first met Thomas on the Road of Leaves and saw him during the attacks by Sorceress Narissa, I realized that he was not your typical student of magic. It was like he had been trained to become a master but only lacked that last bit of knowledge- the actual formularies for crafting higher enchantments. He was like a great chef just waiting for the recipes. Every enchantment I explained to him, he mastered with almost ease. I've seen students take months to learn even simple magic, but he takes to it like a fish to water."

"That still does not explain why you had him craft Founders Fire," declared

Kane from the front of the line. "Just because he can, does not mean it is wise to do."

"He provided a distraction that I am sure both Merlin and Dalrake noticed. I think it was needed if we wanted to see Levitanus delivered from captivity."

"You assume much, Brother Francis," stated Vivien. "You assume the pixies and dryads were on a mission to rescue him. You assume Thomas' enchantment came at a time when it would be helpful for that mission. And finally, you assume that the Founders were close enough to even notice."

"Kane is not the only one who has been to Dalrake's keep; my master took me there numerous times, always claiming we were sent there as emissaries of the guild. I have a rough idea how far we are from his hold, by way a bird flies. As for the pixies, they told me their mission."

"What is this?" demanded Kane. "None of you said anything about them landing and having a conversation with you."

"They did not, but their leader signaled his plans to me. I know a bit of pixie hand talking."

"So you had Thom ring the bell in hopes that it would help the pixies win their way to Levitanus?"

"That was the hope. We will not know if it worked until we see them again, and I would expect that to happen later today, one way or the other."

"You risked much for what might have been unnecessary," noted Kane.

"Maybe, but Levitanus needs to be freed before the other Founders learn all the secrets of the League of Barnabas. Exposing us is worth that."

"I would agree with Brother Francis," said Thom, surprising himself for speaking out, but he did agree, even if he no longer liked his old master. He needed to be rescued. "This was a risk worth taking."

"I hope you are both right. When do you expect the pixies and dryads to return, and do you expect them to be carrying Levitanus?"

"No reason to get snide," replied Francis. "I doubt even four eagles could lift the Founder, not when they already have passengers on their backs. I anticipate that the pixies and dryads will free him and then let him make his own way back through the Road of Clouds. As for when they will fly back over the Road, I can only make a guess, but I think it is a good one. They should pass over us sometime today. I just hope the clouds clear enough so that we can observe them and exchange hand talk."

"I see no eagles yet," stated Rainflower, who had been listening to their conversation. "However, the magician from Cloudholder has sped up. We need to increase our pace if we want to cross the Core before he gets there."

* * *

They did speed up and, for once, the path cooperated with them. They made good time and came within sight of the Core Crossing of the Road shortly after midday.

The first thing that Thom saw out of the swirling mists was the looming shadow of an immense Cloud Rowan. As they came closer, he realized there more of the trees in a ring around an open field of ice. There were no archways here; this was all within the enchantment of the Road of Clouds.

"It is the Core of the Road," stated Francis. "This circle of Cloud Rowans is like the center pole for the whole Road, keeping all of it in its place even while magicians tug at it in their various travels every day."

As they kept walking, Thom realized there was another path approaching the Core on their right and a third one on their left that was descending a run of ice steps from somewhere overhead.

When he asked Francis about it, the monk replied, "There are dozens of paths connecting here. It is said that every day at least one dies off and another forms, changing directions and altitude. I do not know what lands lie underneath the Core, but it must be the cloudiest, rainiest place in the realm."

"Twenty trees make up that ring, and there are at least as many paths," said Kane. "Be wary, anything or anyone could be in amongst the trees. Keeper Ellery is just as often here as he is at his residence on Cloudholder Mountain, for this is the heart of the Road. Considering that, we must keep our ears alert for any whispers of magic." The former sorcerer signaled to Rainflower and she came back from flying in front of them. "Do you see anyone else at the Core? Any human or being or even beast?"

"It is quiet… almost too quiet. I see nothing except a flock of cockatrices huddling in one of the trees. It is an unusually peaceful midday."

Kane brought them all to a stop. "Not even a stray harpy or a grazing pegasus?"

"No."

The former sorcerer looked back over their group, frowning. Thom saw worry on his countenance, most likely trying to figure out why the Core was so silent. "Where is the one from Cloudholder?"

"A quarter-hour away. That one approaches from our left."

"And the other three?"

Rainflower concentrated, looking off to their right. "They… they are moving much faster and it seems they have a new path as well, but they are still aimed at the wayrest where you were imprisoned and where Thomas set off that enchantment. It appears that they will bypass the Core entirely."

"Something is out of place," stated Kane as he started walking again. "All of us need to be wary."

They reached the ice island without any problems and suddenly were standing between two towering Cloud Rowans that made Thom feel small. He looked up at them, still amazed that such huge trees could be lighter than air. The roots were deeper here than in the wayrests, so they stood on level ice. There was no leaf litter or broken snags either, which Thom pointed out to Francis.

The monk smiled. "These are Cloud Rowans. The breakage will float away until the life dies in it, drifting about as it breaks apart in the weather until they are small enough or old enough to fall to the ground, but there isn't much debris usually because the Keeper's helpers come here regularly to harvest it all for use as elements. The wood can also be worked and carved into things like boxes and cases that can give a buoyancy to heavy objects. These trees make much of what is used to keep the Road of Clouds afloat."

"Enough with the lessons," ordered Kane, walking beyond the trees and into the clearing. "Something is not right here. I sense it but cannot name it yet. Pay attention to everything that is around us, not just the trees."

Thom nodded, ignoring the man's bristly nature. He looked away from the trees and out over the huge ice field that lay within the circle, then he too sensed something different... something nagging at his memory. For some reason he thought of the Shield from Sight enchantment, but he didn't hear its distinct rhythm anywhere. Trying to get a better understanding of what he sensed, he followed the former sorcerer into the empty clearing.

TWENTY-FIVE

Confrontation

The others followed Kane and Thom onto the open ice.

"Do we part ways here?" asked Vivien. "The path back to Cloudholder will not be the same path to Dalrake's castle."

"We will part here," agreed Kane, "and Rainflower should go with them. You and I can make our way from here without a guide."

"Hold your plans," said Francis. "There is something…"

Thom was staring at the large clearing when he caught the faintest whisper of magic. "Something is cloaked out there," he whispered to the others. "It is like a muted Shield from Sight. There is another magician here."

"No," replied Kane, sure of himself. But then he looked more closely and cursed. Quickly dropping his knapsack off of his back and fumbling it open.

Before any of them could craft anything, there was a shimmer and a wizard stepped out of an enchantment, a wizard they all recognized. Suddenly, Merlin was walking toward them.

"What an interesting party. I would not have expected to find all of you together and on the Road of Clouds. The Butcher of Sherwood with the monk who forswore magic, along with two masterless students and one of the queen's ladies-in-waiting." He stopped in front of them and offered a smile that didn't touch his eyes. "What brings all of you up here?"

As the wizard came through the boundaries of his invisibility enchantment, Thom caught a glimpse of something huge still inside, some great beast. He grabbed Francis' arm and whispered warning into his ear, even as Kane stood and put his knapsack back over his shoulder.

When no one answered quickly enough, Merlin motioned toward them. "Surely, one of you has enough intelligence to understand my question. Out with it. Why are you on the Road of Clouds?"

"We are on our way to visit Founder Dalrake," stated Kane. "He is the leader of us sorcerers, after all."

"But you are the only sorcerer here. Those two are mine."

Francis laughed aloud, interrupting the two. "Your guild abandoned both of them and then put a price on his head. Your tether on them is rather frayed, Founder."

Merlin's smile tightened. "What does any of this have to do with you, monk? For one who so boldly renounced magic, you cannot let it go. You have been on every Road when it was disrupted. Why is that, monk?"

When Francis hesitated to respond, Merlin turned away, apparently not really caring for an answer. He looked again at Kane. "Who taught you how to craft Founders Fire? I can only assume it was you, because no one else was in that area of the Road. Did Dalrake show you how?"

It was Kane's turn to smile. "A master revealed the enchantment, but it was not a Founder. I will say no more than that."

"Do not play with me! Who has been sharing the Great Craftings? What other ones do you know?"

Thomas had never heard of Great Craftings before. It sounded like there was magic that they kept secret from even other masters. He wondered who was in this elite cadre. Just the Founders? Maybe the Founders and Keepers? He also wondered why magic seemed to bring out such secretiveness.

"Why should I tell you anything, Merlin?" asked Kane. "I am not a part of your guild."

Merlin stared hard at him, then motioned behind him, letting go of the invisibility enchantment. Suddenly they saw a dragon towering behind him, its golden eyes staring at them.

In a calm voice, Merlin continued. "You will tell me or die."

TWENTY-SIX

Dragon Fire

"Run for the trees!" yelled Kane, turning and doing the same. "He dare not let the dragon attack what is keeping the Road in the air."

Thom's heart raced as he tried to chase after Kane, but his ankle made it more of a slow sprint and the others quickly outpaced him. Instead of tucking his staff under his arm, he had to use it to help support his weight each time his left boot hit the ice. He saw the others dash around the nearest trunk while he was still exposed, but he kept going.

Adele turned and cheered him on even as her eyes widened over something she saw behind him. He dared not look back but tried his best to go even faster. It seemed to take forever and with each stride he anticipated being engulfed in flames or disemboweled by huge claws, yet neither happened.

Adele reached out and he grabbed her hand with the one that wasn't holding the staff. She pulled him forward and threw him to the ground, falling on top of him. Just as she did, something huge passed over them and slammed into the tree, crushing it.

Thomas desperately rolled with Adele so that he would be on top, expecting debris to bury them, but nothing fell. Turning his head, he saw splinters of wood everywhere, but they were all floating away.

"Cloud Rowans," he muttered as he got off of her.

For a moment he forgot about the dragon, but then it roared.

Gulping, Thom stood and looked up to see it flying through the debris to arc high overhead and then dive back toward them.

"We have to keep running," he told Adele as he helped her to her feet.

Just then a shiver went through the Core and it seemed to sag toward them.

"Dig your heels in," ordered Kane from somewhere. "The Road is trying to compensate for the loss of that tree. Once we have our balance, we can confront Merlin."

"No time!" yelled Adele back at him. "The dragon is coming back!"

They all scrambled to get under the cover of the trees. Thom and Adele sheltered under one and Kane, Vivien, and Francis were under a tree on the other side of the shattered one.

The dragon roared through and then climbed into the sky again, not attacking this time.

"This will not stop until you tell me what I want to know!" screamed Merlin at Kane. He still stood where he had been, unaffected by the sudden tilt. "Who taught you such magic? Was it Levitanus?"

"Levitanus is dead," replied Kane, raising his voice to be heard over the distance between them. "From what I have heard, you attended his funeral."

"It had to be one of them," stated Merlin, no longer screaming but still speaking angrily. "Dalrake or Levitanus taught you this. Tell me which one and I will call off the dragon. Be quick with your answer or the beast will burn your companions to death."

"I already told you, neither one, but you will not believe me."

Thom wondered why Merlin was so concerned about one enchantment. It was powerful, but surely it wasn't worth killing others to keep it secret.

"The Great Craftings belong to the Founders. No one else. That you crafted one of the enchantments, means you learned it from one of us. I didn't teach you, so that leaves Dalrake or Levitanus."

"Levitanus is dead."

"No, he lives. Dalrake came through the Road of Clouds only a few days ago with him, but that is something you already knew. What I want to know is which one of them taught you, Butcher. Who has betrayed me?"

"You betrayed yourself," replied Kane, "but you will not believe that either."

Thom wondered why Kane would make such a claim when the knowledge came from Francis who learned it from his old master who… learned it *before* he became a sorcerer. Maybe he did learn it from Merlin somehow.

"Tell me now, or I let the dragon start killing your friends until you do. I have no fondness for any of them, so expect no mercy from me."

Kane laughed a bitter laugh. "No one should ever expect mercy from the great and powerful Merlin. I think you want to kill us all, whether you learn anything from us or not. We are a splinter in your palm, irritating and distracting from your crafting, so you want to yank us out and throw us aside."

"Tell me or watch the others suffer." Merlin paused, likely giving a mental command to the dragon.

Both Thomas and Adele looked up and spotted the monster through the foliage. It was no longer circling and was now diving. This time, wisps of yellow flame escaped from the corners of its maw.

"It's coming for us," yelled Adele, taking his hand and getting ready to run.

"We need to keep behind the tree trunk," replied Thom.

"Can you make an enchantment against it? Maybe something with your staff?"

"I can't craft anything so fast and I don't have anything prepared."

The two circled the tree to get its bulk between them and the rapidly descending beast, but it seemed a flimsy shield, considering how thoroughly the dragon destroyed the other one."

"Should we try running down one of the paths?" asked Adele.

"We can't outrun it. We need to throw ourselves on the ice, cover our travel robes, and hope that they are resistant to fire."

And that it is what they did. He and Adele run a short distance away from the trunk and then dropped to the ice, face down, and huddled under their travel robes, hoods covering their heads and hands pulled under them.

In that position, they didn't see the dragon swoop down breathing fire, but they heard the roar and felt the intense heat.

As soon as it passed, Thom rolled over on the ice to smother any sparks on his robe. Adele did likewise.

The air was full of smoke but once again there was no debris. All the chunks of charred wood, shriveled leaves, and ash were floating upward, while the smoke lingered like smoke normally would. He looked up and was almost mesmerized by the still burning chunks of wood that filled the air above them. The tree was now just a blackened husk.

Then the Core shuttered and sagged even more, tilting them toward the edge. Thankfully, Vivien had kept up the enchantments covering their boots or they would have slid off to their death.

"Where is it?" asked Thom.

"I can't see it through all this smoke," replied Adele. "We need to reach protection before it comes back."

"It will just burn the next tree if we go that way, and I doubt we will survive that inferno a second time."

"Can you make some enchantment to protect us?" she asked.

Thom didn't know how to attack a dragon. They breathed fire, so they had to be nearly invulnerable. How do you attack a furnace? Water? But the dragon flew through rain just a day or so ago. "I don't know what would work," he confessed, tears of frustration coming to his eyes.

"To me!" yelled Kane as he set off running across the ice directly at Merlin.

TWENTY-SEVEN

Sleepy Wizard

Thom was surprised but did his best to run after Kane. Adele was faster, as were Vivien and Francis. By the time Thom caught up with them, Kane had Merlin trapped, standing behind him with a knife to his throat and one of the wizard's arms painfully clasped behind his back.

"Kill me and all of this crumbles around you and all die," said Merlin calmly, not even trying to break free from the larger man. "My Great Craftings are the glue that hold the Roads together. Without me, everything disintegrates or maybe explodes. Do you really want to risk that, Butcher?"

Kane ignored the question. Instead, he said, "Order the dragon to go away; I want it to fly so high that it breaks out of the Road's enchantment. The fairy will make sure that you comply."

"What can you do if I refuse? You seem to think you have the power here, but you are standing in the middle of one of my creations. You need to let me go and then tell me all that I want to know."

Kane calmly replied, "Order it or you will feel the edge of my knife."

"You do not want me as your enemy. There is no where you could run to hide from me. I control all of the realm. Let me go and I will let you live."

"I thought Arthur was the king."

"I am the one who made Arthur; I am the true power of the realm. I control armies, the guild, and even a dragon."

At that moment, the dragon swooped out of the smoke and fog to land on the ice in almost the same place where it had been hiding earlier. Its yellow eyes glowered at them, but it came no closer.

"You kill me and the realm will fall to chaos. It will take decades, if not longer, to reunite even a portion of the lands. Imagine the death and starvation, the injustices and wars that will burn through the countryside without my magical controls. Do you really want that to be on your hands? Let me go, and you and the others will live."

Kane laughed that same harsh laugh again. He pricked the old man's neck, causing Merlin to gasp. "You confuse yourself with God; you are not all powerful. Now send that dragon away!"

Thom saw the anger blazing in the wizard's eyes, but the dragon stirred. Its huge wings stretched out and it leaped into the air, climbing higher and higher in lazy circles above the Core and soon vanished into the clouds.

"Rainflower! Where are you?" yelled Kane.

The fairy came out from behind one of the trees and flew over to them.

"We need you to watch that monster and make sure it leaves the enchantment."

She nodded as she stared up into the clouds. Thom saw nothing, but he didn't have fairy sight. For a while she just watched, then she finally spoke. "It took its time, but it has broken through and is now racing off toward Cloudholder."

"Good," replied Kane. "Not even Merlin can maintain a link with an enchantment interfering, and dragons are too wild to remain docile without a strong hold on them. He will not recapture that one easily."

He took his blade away from Merlin's neck but still hold the Founder's arm behind his back.

"What are you intending to do with him?" asked Francis.

"I will not kill him, even if he keeps reminding me of my reputation as the Butcher, but we cannot just release him. He's too dangerous."

"Take his magician's cache," suggested Vivien.

"Of course, but I think we need more than that. Francis, I know you have renounced magic, but I have heard that you are good at poultices and medicinal liquids. Can you mix something to put the Founder to sleep for a few hours?"

"Without a fire for brewing? Yes, but it will taste terrible."

"Do so. I have no concern about its taste, just that it is effective." Kane turned to Vivien. "Can you and the others gather up some branches and leaves to make a bed for our prisoner. That should make for a light and airy bed. I wouldn't want him to get frostbite while he sleeps off the drink."

Merlin tried twisting free. "You are a fool, Kane…"

"Suddenly you remember my name. That is good. You should know who it was that humbled you, proud wizard."

"I know all of you," replied Merlin, sweeping his gaze over those still near him. "I know that all of you belong to Levitanus' little cadre. It is a shame, because some of you could have risen to become wizards if only you had remained loyal to the guild."

Thomas was well aware that the master magician knew who they were and would never allow them a place among the guild ever again, but they had already declared him a runaway so there was no chance for him anyway.

Merlin was staring at Francis as the monk mixed his sleeping draught, but his words were directed at the man standing behind him. "Kane, how did you become Levitanus' puppet? I know you crafted Founders Fire to distract Dalrake and I, just so that the pixies could free him, but we will soon recapture him, so your plot was for nothing. And now you have revealed yourselves to us. None of you will be able to hide in our midst anymore."

"You have just confirmed that you and Dalrake are more like allies than foes, but I had already realized that. You squabble over who rules, quite willing to waste lives in your battles. Yet when the greater plan is threatened, you two drop your disagreements and show your true commitments."

"We have always been united for the sake of the realm, and that is honorable and even virtuous. We might disagree about who should rule, but we both know that a magician must be the real power behind the throne. We both support Camelot and her magical defenses. We both protect our craft and seek to make it ever greater in service to the greater good. I am proud about what we as Founders have accomplished, even if Levitanus has turned on us."

As Thom held down the branches Vivien broke off, he listened in to the conversation and was astonished at what Merlin had just admitted. What was the invasion of Clas Myrddin or the attacks on the Roads, if not a war between foes?

Kane let go of the wizard's arm. "Take off your knapsack, old man. We will spread your blanket on a bed of Cloud Rowan branches so that you can have a good rest."

Merlin glared but did as told. Kane grabbed the pack and handed it to Adele. "Take out his blankets for the bedding and also his magician's cache."

A bed was made, with one of the wizard's blankest holding down the branches and leaves that wanted to float away and the other set to the side, ready to cover him. His knapsack was placed as a makeshift pillow. The ornate box full of magical elements was set beside the tree trunk.

Francis walked over carrying a cup filled with a dark liquid that smelled somehow bitter and sweet. "Have him drink it all. It will give him a good four hours of sleep without any bad reactions."

Kane nodded then motioned him to the wizard. Francis held out the cup and the glaring wizard took it and drank. Once done, he coughed once and then threw the cup aside, forcing Thom to retrieve it for Francis. "Terrible tasting. Now, why don't you all leave so that I can sleep in peace. The five of you stand around me like you fear I will run off or fight you, but you have already disarmed this magician so leave off your gloating. Again I say, leave me so that I can sleep in peace."

Thom thought he looked much older as he sat down on the makeshift bed, for his intensity was fading as sleepiness came upon him. Thomas wanted to share the harpies' plight with him before sleep overcame him, so he blurted out, "The harpies have been losing people to harvesters. We have pledged to make others aware of this. If the guild is involved, it must stop the killing. You have no right to murder others just for their magical abilities."

"It was not my guild," replied Merlin, stifling a yawn, "but if it were, I would do nothing to stop it. We have the right to harvest all that we need to defend the realm; it is all for the greater good and the magical beings know that."

Thom went rigid at the man's callousness, but didn't strike out.

"Just one more thing, old man," said Kane as he stood over him. "Let me clarify who shared the Founders Fire enchantment. It came from *Wizard Dorlain*."

Thom remembered that was the name of Francis' mentor, the one who had turned evil and tried to kill a whole village of fairies.

Merlin's eyes went wide and he looked rapidly from Francis back to Kane. "Impossible. He died long ago."

"Nonetheless, he is the one who shared your precious enchantment and he was not a sorcerer at the time. From what I remember, he was your favored disciple, although I was only a mere apprentice in those days. Dorlain learned that enchantment from you, so you only have yourself to blame for yesterday's distraction."

"So Dorlain taught it to his student, most likely out of spite for me," stated Merlin, shaking his head in disbelief. "Then the monk held it secret all these years, until he shared it with you. For someone who swore off magic, he certainly worked hard to remember our craft."

Merlin turned his head and pointed a long finger up at the monk. "Shame on you, *Brother* Francis. You have wasted time on worldly things rather than concentrating on the heavenly. God must be disappointed in you."

"In my life I have disappointed and also sinned against many," stated Francis calmly. "Jesus died to forgive those transgressions. It is a salvation He offers to all of us, because we all need it. Would you like to learn more about my Lord?"

Merlin stifled a yawn. "Not today, monk. I seem to be rather tired at the moment."

With that, the wizard lay down and was soon asleep.

Adele set the other blanket over him and then they moved a few steps away.

TWENTY-EIGHT

Turning Back

"What next?" asked Thomas.

"It seems that Vivien and I will be going back toward Camelot with the rest of you," stated Kane. "Levitanus has been freed, so there is no need for us to continue on. It seems Brother Francis' ploy with the enchantment did indeed cause enough of a distraction to allow the pixies to rescue him."

"Where is Levitanus now?" asked Adele. "He may still need help."

"I have no way of knowing. Most likely, he is somewhere in the woods that surround Dalrake's keep. The great eagles are not large enough for humans to ride, but they are strong enough to carry one for a distance. Maybe one of them carried him into the countryside."

"Could he be one of the others that is on the Road of Clouds right now?" asked Thom.

"I have no idea who else lurks on the icy paths and the fairy cannot distinguish individuals until they are close. Is that not true, Rainflower?"

The fairy had been keeping a bit of distance and she looked disturbed, but she answered the question. "Our far sight is not that distinct, especially when viewing through clouds and rain like we do on the Road."

"And what do you perceive now?" pushed Kane.

"The damage caused by the dragon has affected places throughout the paths of the Road. Sections have shifted or suddenly melted. The magician who came from Cloudholder has been forced to retreat and find another route here. The three from the east are no longer heading toward Dripping Branch Wayrest. Upon hearing the magic here at the Core, they changed directions, but now I can no longer see them. They have cloaked, so I do not know if they are continuing this way or how fast they are going. I do not think they fell from the Road because the paths in that area remained stable."

"Did those three come from Dalrake's castle?"

"I did not see where they entered. I was too distracted myself by Thomas' enchantment and then the confronting of the harpies. They called down the Road somewhere in the east, but I cannot say where exactly. Not like the others."

"What others?"

"More have entered the Road and these definitely came from Dalrake's keep. They have entered in a staggered fashion so I do not know if they are together or if some chase others, but it is more than a dozen magicians. Some bunch together, making it hard to distinguish exact numbers at this distance."

"It is getting crowded in here," muttered Kane.

Vivien ran a hand through her red hair and Thom noticed more gray mixed in. "What if that is Levitanus trying to make his escape? Should we do something to help him?"

"We have no way of knowing where he is," replied Kane. "We could easily miss them in this maze of paths and there still is that other group out there somewhere, cloaked from sight like Merlin was. No, I think we can best help by retreating to Cloudholder and getting ready there."

"To do what?" asked Vivien.

Kane shrugged. "I have no great plan. I just know that he will be most vulnerable while outside the Road as he crosses the mountain. We can best help there. Somehow…"

There was a brief silence as they all thought of what might be ahead of them, then Rainflower spoke up.

"Before we go anywhere, I must tell you that this trip has been unprecedented. I am a Road Guide, just like those who lead people through the Road of Leaves or guide boats along the Road of Waters. We are the only ones who aren't humans but we all hold to the same code of faithfully guiding and respecting the privacy of our parties. However, I cannot keep quiet about what happened here. The Core has been damaged. Thomas set off a powerful enchantment that sliced through the Road's enchantment. Kane attacked a Founder! I must report all of this to my queen."

"We would expect no different," replied Vivien, "but first you need to help us to get back to Cloudholder. Once we reach the mountain, you can leave us to make your report."

"Yes, it is as Vivien says," agreed Kane. "You should inform Queen Titania as soon as we return to Cloudholder. But right now, find us the fastest route back there."

Rainflower gave them a solemn nod and then flew off to the far side of the Core to find them the best path through the Road.

As she flew off, Kane took Merlin's cache and shoved the box into his own knapsack. They wouldn't be leaving the wizard with any elements to make certain he couldn't attack them once he woke up. Even Thom realized the wisdom in that, for they would still have at least another day on the Road.

* * *

They spent that night in a wayrest, but they did so uneasily. Kane insisted on guard shifts of two at a time watching from the icy platform to make sure they didn't get trapped inside. But the night was uneventful and they were able to breakfast on berries and nuts harvested in the wayrest, in addition to their travel bread and cheese. As they were getting ready to set off, Rainflower made a disturbing report.

"Someone lingers at the archway out to the mountain."

"Are they blocking the way to Cloudholder?" asked Kane.

"I do not know their intentions. At this distance, I cannot recognize who it is, but it is definitely human. The person keeps passing through the archway, as if watching on both sides."

"What about those who were behind us?"

"It seems Founder Merlin has united with the one who came from Cloudholder. They follow us but we should reach the mountain well before they are close to us. The other three are still shrouded. They might be ahead of him, behind him, with him, or somewhere else entirely. You will have to use your magic to expose them if you want to know more."

"We should be able to hear their magic if they get close," remarked Vivien.

"Unless they can build a shielded enchantment like Merlin did at the Core," said Thomas.

"I have never heard of anyone being able to make such an enchantment that moves," she replied.

Thom raised a skeptic eyebrow and indicated the Road around them. "I know of at least four such enchantments."

"The Roads are different," she stated with a hint of frustration. "The ways were built by dozens of magicians interweaving numerous enchantments. Let me correct my statement for you, journeyman. I have never heard of any one person being able to make a shielded enchantment that moves. Your concerns are…"

"Thomas' concerns are worth considering," interrupted Kane. "Before this week, I would not have thought anyone outside the Founders could make a Great Crafting, but now a journeyman has done so. We should be vigilant as we travel, watching for subtle signs of passing magic, in case someone has found a way to make such an enchantment. No need to scowl at me, Vivien. I know it is a small chance, but you need to admit there is a possibility that we do not know as much about magic as we thought."

Vivien set her hands on her hips and Thom expected her to rant at Kane and himself, but instead she just nodded. Maybe there was something behind Adele's suspicions about the two, for he had never seen the red-haired magician act so… docile. He smiled at the thought, for that was not a word he would have thought described Vivien. No, not docile, but she was rather agreeable, and that was unusual for her.

"There are the others who entered the Road later," continued Rainflower. "All of them came from Dalrake's Keep. They are still staggered and clumped, but all of them are much closer than they were before. It seems that they traveled through the night. It might be some people chasing others, but I see no flashes of magic or other signs of conflict from this distance."

"Whatever happened to the great eagles?" asked Adele.

"That is the last news I bear. I have seen them coming out of Knobby Ground Wayrest. It seems they overnighted there. The Aeti are coming out one at a time, letting smaller beings mount, and then launching into the sky to circle overhead as they await the rest to come out. So far, five are already in the air."

"Would Wizard Levitanus be with that group somehow?" asked Adele.

"I will watch carefully," replied the fairy. "Even at this distance, I should be able to tell if the Aeti are carrying humans in their claws rather than pixies riding on their backs."

"As strong as those great eagles are, I doubt they could carry a human very far," noted Francis, "so please watch for anyone following them on foot."

"If he isn't with the eagles, where would he be?" asked Thom.

"He could be anywhere," remarked Kane, "which is why we are no longer trying to find him. The pixies and dryads rescued him when we could not and now Levitanus could be traipsing across the countryside far from here, or he could be one of the trio who vanished, or he could be among that larger crowd who entered later. Those are only guesses. As I said, he could be anywhere. Do any of you know better?"

Thom thought that his old master would more likely be on his own, either traveling the Road of Clouds alone and hidden or hiking through the countryside somewhere far below, but he had misjudged the man too many times to be sure. He was beginning to wonder if he really knew the man at all, even after having lived with him for over a decade. He could only shake his head, admitting he was ignorant of Levitanus' location.

"So the plan remains that we retreat to Cloudholder and then find a way to prepare ourselves to defend Levitanus there, in the hope that he will pass our way," stated Kane.

The rest agreed since no one had a better plan.

TWENTY-NINE

Enemies Unexpected

They approached the archway with great caution. They were close enough that Rainflower could identify that it was a man holding the exit from the Road. The wizard continued to go through it at times, watching in both directions. With him were two fairies.

"Two?" asked Francis. "When do Road Guides go out in pairs?"

"We do not," she replied. "I suspect the one is a guide and the other is there for our queen."

"Does the human know we are approaching?" asked Kane, "and who we are?"

"If I can see my fellow fairies, then they can see me," replied Rainflower, "but at this distance none of us can recognize details like faces. We do have means to communicate from afar with by exaggerated motions, but that is only done at the queen's orders. It is too limited in what we can *say* and it is also considered uncouth."

"Who do you think it is?" asked Vivien of Kane. "Wizard or sorcerer?"

"It could be either. Guides are assigned to any magician who asks, with no questions about their loyalties. That was the agreement reached by Merlin and Dalrake years ago in order to keep peace on the Road of Clouds. The second fairy means that Queen Titania has her own reasons to watch."

"Would the fairies have seen what we did at the Core?"

"If they were watching at that particular moment, they would have seen most of it. A dragon flaming part of the Road's supports would be hard for even a blind fairy to miss. For that matter, every human on this half of the Road of Clouds would have realized something damaged the Core. Merlin was not subtle in his attack on us."

"All these events should have also caught the Keeper's attention," added Francis. "Maybe the magician watching is the Keeper Ellery or one of his assistants."

Kane nodded. "I thought the same." He turned to Rainflower. "When will we be close enough for us humans to see each other?"

"I would say within the hour, for the path looks strong and fairly straight from here. We will intersect another path once we jump to the next cloud, but otherwise it is clear."

"Do you see anyone on the intersecting path?" asked Kane. "Where does that route come from?"

"I would have told you if I saw others," replied Rainflower. "The route does not come from the Core, but does intersect other paths that lead to where those three vanished, though it would be a rather torturous route from there to here. Do you sense any other magic nearby?"

"No, I do not, but we will watch and listen carefully as we pass the way." Kane turned to the others. "We should move on as fast as we can. I for one, want to get out of these confining ways."

Although Thomas found Kane to be rather abrasive, he was definitely competent and Thom was glad he was leading them off the Road.

"Should we prepare enchantments before getting closer?" asked Vivien.

Kane shook his head. "If we do, he will hear it and just step through the archway; it would be the harpy trap all over again. No magic, if we can help it. We are five to his one; that should be enough to force our way through."

"You assume that there are no others beyond the archway."

"We have no other way out of here, whether an ambush is on the other side or not."

Francis interrupted them. "Merlin or his companion is up to something. One of them is crafting Winged Feet."

They all stopped walking to listen in the direction the monk indicated.

"Your hearing is extraordinary," stated Kane. "I do not know if I would have recognized that enchantment before its completion, but you are correct. One of them crafts Winged Feet."

"That will speed up their approach," noted Vivien.

"But not enough," replied the ex-sorcerer. "We will be done with our confrontation and through the archway well before they arrive. However, it does give us another reason to hurry our pace."

* * *

They crossed the other path without incident and within the hour rounded a thick cloud to finally come in sight of the archway and the icy platform at its base. They stopped for a moment.

Rainflower spoke. "Those are Mistwing and Moonrose with the human. Moonrose is from the queen's court and not a Road Guide."

Thom could see the fairies clearly, but they were new to him. However, he knew the wizard they were accompanying. Thom had spent a night with him at the monastery's guest house, pretending to be his student.

"I recognize the man," stated Kane.

"As do the rest of us," said Francis. "We have all spent time with Wizard Osric. Keeper Bronwen claimed he was far away, which is why the three of us risked walking the Road to rescue the two of you."

"We must ask him about his speedy arrival then," replied Kane.

Thom wondered the same. How had the wizard arrived here so quickly?

Osric had been kneeling over his cache of elements, ready to start an enchantment, but upon recognizing them, he stuffed it back into his knapsack. He stood, slinging the pack over his shoulder.

Once they were closer, the wizard shouted a question at them. "Where is Levitanus?"

"We have no idea," replied Kane, continuing to walk closer. "Merlin admitted that he escaped from Dalrake's keep, but we have not seen him."

"Since when does Merlin confess things to you, Kane? Even if you bring a monk with you, I doubt the Founder would want to whisper his failings to Brother Francis."

Kane actually laughed. "You are right about that. Merlin has no love for the monk. No, we found other ways to encourage him to share with us. Levitanus was freed by pixies and dryads. All we did was craft a small distraction."

Even from this distance, Thom saw Osric's eyebrow rise in bemused curiosity. "You make a Great Crafting and call it a small distraction?"

"Oh, that was not me," replied Kane. "Journeyman Thomas crafted the Founder's Fire."

Suddenly someone new yelled angrily from behind them. "He did it? Levitanus' little whelp?"

Thom turned to find the missing trio. Standing right behind them was Dalrake and two of his sorcerers, and the chief of all sorcerers was angry.

"How dare Levitanus teach him such a thing! Where is that traitor who gives away our secrets to fools?" glared Dalrake.

Dalrake just stood there with fists clenched, but his two companions were rushing to get their element caches out.

"Hurry!" yelled Francis. "We need to get through the archway before they finish crafting."

THIRTY

Dark Passage

Thomas didn't need any more prodding; he started running toward Osric and the archway out. He caught up with Adele as he reached the ice platform and she offered her arm for support. Together, they ran through the gray shimmering gate and came out on the causeway beyond.

Osric was kneeling on the cold stones and furiously crafting magic against those following them. Thom and Adele ran past him, not stopping until they were at the end of the causeway. There they gathered to watch and listen to the wizard's crafting. Thom recognized the sounds; it was a Dark Passage like the one that had almost entrapped them on the Road of Leaves.

"Should we move farther away in case the sorcerers rush through?" asked Vivien.

"I would rather be close enough to help Osric if needed," replied Kane.

The Dark Passage was already forming, with just a hand's width separation from the Road of Clouds' enchantment. It wasn't completely black yet, so Thom was able to see that one of the sorcerers poked his head through the archway and then quickly pulled back before getting caught inside the Dark Passage as well.

"Will this keep Dalrake back?" he asked, knowing that the sorcerer was one of the original crafters of the Roads.

"It will certainly delay the sorcerers," replied Kane. "Look at how Osric is curving his enchantment. The other end hangs over the edge of the causeway. It is a short, enchanted tunnel but they will not be able to just run through it and come after us. Not unless they have sprouted wings somehow."

Osric finished crafting and the Dark Passage darkened so that they could no longer see through it. He stared at it for a moment and then set to meticulously cleaning his tools and putting them away. Shouldering his knapsack, he walked the causeway to where the others waited.

"Now that I have blocked their route, it is time for some explanations. You five will tell me everything as we hike to see Queen Titania."

"Is that a wise destination?" asked Vivien. "Dalrake will get through eventually and he seems determined to pursue us. Delaying at Tuatha Aos Si, the Fairy Queen's court, will bring his wrath on them as well."

"That is not for us to decide, journeywoman. Titania is on the league's leadership council. She has ordered and we must obey. Come."

The humans left the causeway and started up the slope of Cloudholder. The two guide fairies flew with them, while Moonrose stayed to observe the archway. Although there were no paths on the mountain, Osric showed no hesitation in the route he chose, aiming them toward the north, where a stream came out of the woods to water the meadow they were on. They headed that direction as the low clouds began to drizzle on them.

"Now, enough with your questions. It is my turn to get answers. You were sent to rescue Levitanus. Why did you fail?"

Kane and Vivien shared a look and then he spoke, explaining how they were trapped by the harpies.

Osric shook his head in disbelief. "You let them imprison you? You are a master magician; they should be no more than an inconvenience. That was incompetency."

"They were desperate," replied Kane, remaining calm under the accusation. "They were determined to not let us free until a Founder came."

"But here you are, and it only took a journeyman, an apprentice, and a monk who swore off magic. There was no Founder and yet they relented."

Vivien stepped closer as they moved into the trees along the stream's bank. She met the wizard's gaze with her own steely stare. "They relented because Thomas crafted a Great Crafting. Did you happen to hear it?"

"Yes. I was on a path up from the Road of Waters when I heard it."

"The Roads connect?" asked Francis, suddenly interrupting. "Is that how you came here so quickly?"

Osric looked at the monk for a moment before responding, as if weighing whether he should reveal more to one who had abandoned the craft. Whatever he saw in Francis, he chose to answer. "Apparently, the Founders made hidden routes between all the Roads. Only they and the Keepers know of them. This one was shown to me by the Keeper of the Waters because of the dire need to get here."

"I did not think any place along the Road of Waters would be high enough to make such a connection," stated Kane. "Usually, the Road of Clouds needs a mountain or at least a high hill or ridge."

"It was a steep climb on those icy steps," admitted Osric, "and it connected to the Road on a neglected side path that led only toward Cloudholder Mountain, without any intersections where I could redirect toward Dalrake's keep or toward Thomas' impressive display of raw power. When I came out at the archway, Titania had the two fairies waiting for me and I was ordered to wait there to either defend or escort, depending on who came through.

"But back to questions for you five. Did you have anything to do with the damage to the Road?"

Kane answered this one. "Indirectly. Merlin tried to burn us with dragon fire but instead destroyed some of the trees at the Core."

"Both of the other Founders are after you? That is not good."

The two fairies accompanying them were both at a distance, Mistwing was above the trees scanning the skies, while Rainflower was somewhere up ahead.

Nonetheless, Osric lowered his voice for his next question, "Did any of you compromise the league?"

"No," Kane replied, "but they obviously know that Levitanus has rebelled and that some of us are loyal to his cause."

"What of Levitanus?" interrupted Francis. "Have you seen him? We know that he's escaped, but nothing more."

"I hope he has made it away from all of this, but this has gone beyond just him. The leaders have decided that it is time for the League of Barnabas to be revealed."

"Is that wise?" asked Kane. "It is still small compared to the guild or the sorcerers."

"That is for the leaders to decide, not us." Osric's demeanor seemed dark but determined as they strode through the wet, shadowy forest.

Thomas kept quiet as he walked behind the other men. He was glad that his ankle gave him only a dull ache today, making it much easier to keep up. Behind him walked the two women, also in silence.

The forest gave way to a grass and brush-covered slope that led up to a high ridge and Osric choose to climb it, forcing the rest of them to follow. Once they reached the top they paused and looked back. They could see the archway and the shadowy blob that was the Dark Passage.

"Here is where I leave you," stated Osric. "I cannot maintain the enchantment if I go any farther away. You will have to go to Tuatha Aos Si without me. Rainflower will guide you, although I am certain that Brother Francis knows how to find it as well."

"You are rather exposed here," noticed Kane. "I would suggest you drop below the ridge; maybe take cover in that larger clump of brush to our left. Your black cloak will blend with the shadows, as long you keep your hood up to hide your pale face."

Osric nodded. "Good advice. I am far enough away that no magic can surprise me, but it will be helpful if they do not know where I am."

"What will you do if they break through?" asked Vivien.

"I want to hold the enchantment as long as I can to give you time to warn Titania and her people. With their gift of sight, fairies are great at hiding from humans. Only magicians can sneak up on them, so we are making sure they do not. She was one of the earliest and staunchest supporters of the League of Barnabas; we cannot abandon her now with sorcerers heading into her realm."

"You think it an invasion?" asked Kane.

"What do you think? You were one of his men for many years. How will he react when he learns that the fairies have joined the league?"

The Butcher of Sherwood shook his head. "He will not make the mistake I did; he would never slaughter everyone to reap their innate elements. Both he and Merlin are consummate farmers; they do not over-harvest."

"We are mere crops to you?" blurted Rainflower, overhearing.

Kane turned to her. "No, never again to me. But Dalrake and Merlin see magical beings as their own to protect and use. Maybe the better analogy would be comparing you to vassals under a lord. They expect obedience and their share of the magic. Neither Founder will ignore what they see as rebellion from their benevolent rule."

"So you agree with me," stated Osric. "Dalrake will come in force because he will be furious with the fairies. I would expect that the queen and her advisers will be crushed like pests for hurting the crop. That is what we will prevent."

Thom saw that both fairies were upset with being seen as the exclusive property of magicians. He would be too if he were in their place... but then again hadn't the guild treated him as a mere tool to use or neglect as they saw fit? Both the guild and the sorcerers had too much power and it made them tyrants. He sincerely hoped such hubris wouldn't fill the league too.

He looked over at Francis and saw that he was also upset. Thom realized that the league needed his friend to help keep it humble. The monk hated magic, but his love of the land and all of its people would be a conscience to balance the temptation to abuse power. That was why the Father Abbot kept suggesting that Francis should join. The Fair Defender was needed to keep the magic just and fair. They needed him; Thomas needed him.

THIRTY-ONE

Up the Mountain

The fairy Mistwing stayed with Osric, to lend her great sight and to provide a relay from Moonrose, who was still down at the archway. The others hiked on, with Kane taking the lead, and were soon over the ridgeline and could see a deep valley that held a stone residence surrounded by floating trees tethered to the ground.

"What is that?" asked Adele.

"That is the home of the Keeper of the Road," replied Kane. "It also the nursery where they grow new Cloud Rowans to replace those on the Road as needed."

"Why don't we go down there for help?" asked Thom. "Keepers are powerful allies."

"But this one is an ally of Merlin and also friendly with Dalrake. He would likely take us captive rather than aid us. We will bypass Keeper Ellery."

"Might he send out others to pursue us?" wondered Thom, realizing they were rather exposed on the barren slope above the compound.

"Doubtful," replied Kane. "He has four pixies that help with the tree farm, but not students and only one helper magician, and that magician went out to meet Merlin days ago, so who knows where he is?"

"We ignore Keeper Ellery's residence and keep going," said Vivien. "He may not even notice our passing."

So they kept hiking, following the lip of the valley and over another ridge. They dropped back into the forest as they descended into the next nook of the mountainside. Rainflower often flew up above the trees to see what was happening around them, but the vale they were in was quiet. They crossed a fast-flowing stream and started up the next slope and were soon trudging above the tree line again. Thom judged it to be late afternoon, but it was hard to tell with the sun hidden by the thick overcast.

Thom looked back at the ridge where they had left Osric and Mistwing, but he saw nothing of them. "Do we have any idea of what is happening behind us?"

"I will fly higher and see what I can," stated Rainflower.

"Thank you," replied Thomas.

After she soared off, he asked the others, "How much farther to Queen Titania's court?"

"It will be dark by the time we reach Tuatha Aos Si," stated Francis. "If the sorcerers haven't broken through yet, we should be clear of them. I would think they would expect us to be heading across the mountain to the path to Sky Tower, rather than climbing to the mountain's peak."

Thom nodded understanding, but he felt ill-at-ease. Levitanus was free, but somehow it felt like there was still much to finish. What else was left to do? He had no part in revealing the League of Barnabas to the land, for he wasn't a leader in the league... in truth, he wasn't even formally a member of the league yet. So why did he have this feeling of incompleteness? What still needed to be done?

"Will they give up if they can't find us?" asked Adele.

Francis looked to Kane for an answer.

The former sorcerer replied. "If left to their own, the sorcerers would quickly tire of hunting us, but Dalrake is a different matter. He can be as tenacious as a hound pursuing a rabbit, and the others would not dare to anger or disappoint him."

"And he seems rather angry with us," added Vivien. "Especially with Journeyman Thomas."

Thom didn't need that reminder; the sorcerer's angry yell still seemed to echo in his ear.

They all watched as Rainflower descended back toward them. Once near, she reported, "The enchantment trap at the archway has been overcome by some kind of curved bridge between its end and the causeway. At least a half-dozen humans have come through as well as three griffins. I cannot see Moonrose, so she has likely fled into the forest to hide. I also cannot see your wizard friend of Mistwing, but they might still be sheltering in the brush on the other side of the ridge."

"Are they humans warriors or sorcerers?" asked Francis.

"Four of them are already squatting over their mixing bowls, crafting magic, while the other two keep watch and maybe control the beasts that lazily circle over them."

"We should move quickly to get among the trees again before they spot us," stated Kane, encouraging the others by starting to hike up the ridge toward the forest above them. Over his shoulder, he added. "Can you go up again, Rainflower? I expect that the sorcerers are crafting an Eagle's Spying or three, which are like small purple spheres. Watch and see which directions they go."

"Will not her flight catch their attention?" asked Vivien, who was now walking behind the master magician.

"I am hoping that at this distance and altitude, they will not notice her. Besides, fairies are scattered all over this mountain." He turned his attention to the fairy hovering over them. "Look for any obvious signs of magic, especially for small purple spheres that dart about."

Thom nodded as he watched the fairy soar into the sky. Kane expected them to use Eagle's Spying, which made sense. The sorcerers would be vulnerable while they were linked to the flying eyeball-like spheres, but that also explained why two other sorcerers stood watch.

"Hurry up," urged Kane. "We are too exposed on this treeless slope. Even the griffins will easily find us here."

They hiked as fast as they could along the rocky spine and came to the top, where it blended into a sparsely forested slope. Kane pushed on, climbing through the trees, and crested over to an area that was more level, where the trunks were closer together. It was here that Rainflower caught up with them, swooping down through the canopy to settle on a tree branch overhead.

"They are searching in every direction. Two of those purple spheres headed toward the archway that leads to the Road to Sky Tower, but the other one is crisscrossing the land, moving ever closer to us."

"And the griffins?" asked Kane.

"They stay closer to the causeway, making ever larger circles over the meadows and woods in that area. They will find the wizard within the hour, unless he has retreated."

"Is the Dark Passage still intact?"

"It is."

"Then he lingers. He will have to release that enchantment when he flees the area."

"Should I go back to watch more?" she asked.

"Thank you for the offer, but I know how high flying tires your kind," said Kane. "Rest your wings and eat something. If you are too worn you will become an easy morsel for the griffins to catch." He held out a slice of apple to her.

She gave him a hard look but said nothing. Instead, she fluttered to the ground and accepted the slice, which was a huge chunk for someone so tiny. She ate as she walked with them.

* * *

That evening, they stood on another ridge, looking down at a densely forested vale. Beyond it rose the rocky heights that were the summit of Cloudholder Mountain. True to its name, the peak was lost in the clouds, but from what Thomas saw there seemed to be numerous patches of snow on that slope. Even here, in a strong evening breeze, there were wisps of rain that flew past that seemed to dance more than they ought, revealing that some of it was snow.

Thom looked hard through the gathering night, but couldn't make out anything of Queen Titania's court from this distance. Either it was a small place or it was well hidden in the woods. He did notice a few lights among the trees, but they seemed to wink on and off at random moments, faint glows of varying colors.

"From here the Fairy Queen rules?" he asked, not fully convinced.

"There are two fairy villages down there as well as the queen's gathering place," replied Francis. "The lights you see are some of the males performing for their females."

"They glow like fireflies?" asked Adele.

143

Rainflower hmphed in offense and Francis quickly corrected Adele. "I wouldn't compare them to bugs. It isn't done simply for mating. The males will glow during ritual dances, to warn off competitors, and to show pride in their females. It is a subtle way to communicate, with different meanings behind brightness and whether the glow is steady or a rate of blinking."

Thom wondered what part of the males glowed. Was it their wings or their torso? He decided not to ask, to avoid offending Rainflower, and just assumed he would find out soon enough once he saw them in person. He had more important things to worry about, like Dalrake and his intense hatred of Thom. "Might we be leading those angry sorcerers here?"

"It isn't as if the sorcerers are ignorant of where the fairies meet," replied Francis. "It was Dalrake who captured the first Cloud Rowan tree and he was the first magician to walk the heights of Cloudholder. I did not know it at the time, but the reason my old master was up here was to swear fealty to Dalrake. He likely attacked the fairy village in the hopes of bringing them as an offering to his cruel leader."

"Truly?" asked Kane. "All of us sorcerers were told the story of Dolain and how you betrayed him, but not that Dalrake was nearby."

"I did not learn about that part until years later," admitted Francis.

"It was not a betrayal on the Fair Defender's part," interrupted Rainflower. "He upheld past promises made to my kind and by his actions saved hundreds. Do not call him the Betrayer in our presence, for that is just another lie from the Dark."

Kane bowed to her in humbled agreement. "I stand corrected. My apologies for using a slur from my old companions. I know that Brother Francis is an honorable man."

Suddenly, two more fairies flew into view, each carrying small spears.

"Rainflower, you are to fly straight to Tuatha Aos Si," one of them announced. "Springbud will escort the humans that rest of the way. Be quick about it."

Their Road Guide nodded and quickly flew off into the growing darkness.

"As for you humans. You must hurry as well. We have reports of griffins and a roc heading this way, and that is without even considering the oncoming storm."

THIRTY-TWO

The Fairy Queen

Springbud set a grueling pace through the darkening dusk, but it was well into the night before they came within sight of Queen Titania's court.

"It is like a cluster of tree forts," said Thom, trying to make out details in the darkness as he looked up at it. He knew that his reference wasn't a very accurate one, considering the only tree fort he had ever seen was a rickety affair built by children in one the villages he and Levitanus had visited at times. Tuatha Aos Si was a far more masterful build.

In a grove of mature trees were dozens of platforms at various heights, some roofed and some open to the sky. Lanterns hung from the eaves and branches, casting much of it in a warm glow. Beyond the court rose the mountain's summit, a solid wall of stone as a backdrop to the elevated court. Thom could hear a waterfall's roar from somewhere ahead but it was too dark to make out the flow coming off the mountainside. There was a river flowing out from under Tuatha Aos Si, heading off at an angle from their approach. He could make it out by the greater darkness that ribboned through the whitening fields.

As they walked closer, they saw that the platforms were connected by bridges and ramps, but it looked like the fairies just as often simply flew from one to the other. Thom spotted dull-colored males and well as brighter female fairies, but none of them showed any sign of glowing. Instead, all seemed agitated as they strode purposely about the tree platforms or flew here and there.

"They are as stirred up as a wasp's nest," noted Kane, speaking quietly so as not to be overheard by any fairy. "I think there is more going on than just our arrival."

"You think the sorcerers are near?" asked Francis.

"I am not certain, but the court is rarely this busy after dark except during celebrations, and there is nothing festive about their behavior."

"How are we to get up there?" asked Vivien. "We certainly can't fly and I see no stairs."

Springbud overheard that last comment and came closer to explain. "We will lower a basket to lift your packs and staffs, while you climb a rope ladder. Keep heading toward that lower platform while I fly ahead and arrange everything."

By the time they were under the platform she had indicated, there was a lowered basket and a rope ladder that swayed in the increasing wind. It was definitely snowing now, but it wasn't sticking on the ground yet.

The fairy flew down and gave some final instruction. "I would suggest you split your loads for the basket, since it is meant more for hauling produce rather than giant knapsacks and staffs."

"Very well, Vivien and I will go first," volunteered Kane, dropping his knapsack in the woven basket and then more carefully placing his staff. He motioned for her to do likewise, offering a smile to soften his words.

Soon the two of them were up and it was the turn for the last three. Thom looked up at their goal and it seemed so high above. He wasn't certain how his abused body would handle the strenuous climb, but his only other option was to stay down here alone and shiver in the falling snow. So he placed his pack with the ones from Adele and Francis, and then added the staff he now considered his own.

"Go ahead of me," encouraged Adele.

Taking a deep breath, he did so. He climbed cautiously, placing each foot carefully on the wooden rungs. It seemed to take forever, but in truth he was soon up on the platform, thankful to have a firm footing. Vivien handed him his knapsack and staff, while Kane helped Adele and then Francis to stand. Around them were the fairies who had pulled the basket up. Most watched them curiously, while a few drew up the ladder and secured it.

Springbud was standing nearby. She indicated that they were to follow her as she turned to walk up one of the wooden bridges to a higher level.

They followed, having to bend low when passing through any openings because the buildings were more in proportion to tiny fairies and not tall humans.

Finally, they came to a circular platform that was open to the steady-falling snow. Lanterns hung from posts all around the circle. Beyond the platform could be heard the waterfall that plunged off the summit's heights but it was unseen due to much mist in that direction that even the winds couldn't dissipate. A canopy hung over the very center of the platform, suspended by ropes that were tied to the surrounding trees. That canopy fluttered some in the continuing wind. Under it was a backless wooden throne on which sat the Fairy Queen. Thom could understand the reason for the chair having no back, because the queen's wings needed space to furl and unfurl. On either side of her were four more individual benches occupied by a mixture of fairies: male and female, young and old.

Queen Titania had a regal bearing, shimmering in a muted gold color. Though her wings were folded behind her, Thom guessed them to be a similar gold color to her hair and clothes. She was as diminutive as all other fairies, but there seemed a gravitas about her. "Welcome to Fairyland. I apologize for holding court. outside on such a blustery night, but the throne room would be rather cramped with so many tall humans.

"We have already heard Rainflower's report of your adventures on the Road and that will suffice for tonight, but I will ask to hear more details tomorrow."

Her eyes settled on Kane. "Wizard Kane, I will say this since my people need to hear it. Because you have repented from the horrible deeds you did in Sherwood and have striven to make amends these last years, you are welcome among us."

Kane bowed to her; he seemed to be near to tears, which surprised Thom. The ex-sorcerer was always so dispassionate usually.

Queen Titania turn her focus on Francis. "You are always welcome in our midst, Fair Defender. It has been too long since we last saw you."

Francis gave her a sincere smile. "It is good to see you, your majesty. From all that I've heard, you have become a wise and effective ruler since inheriting the throne from your mother. Your people thrive."

"I would never have had that chance if you had not rescued my Fair. I can still recall that day when you stood against that foul and false master of yours." She paused and it seemed she was caught by the memory, and then she continued, "I have heard that you have since left the guild to become a monastic."

He nodded. "I have found serving God more fulfilling than serving mere men."

"That is good, but perhaps someday you will find that you can serve others as a way to serve God. You certainly did that when you rescued the village. Before you leave my court, I will have a proposal for you. It is one that I have already discussed with your Father Abbot." She held his gaze for a moment longer, then looked at them all. "No need to keep everyone out in this cold weather. We will introduce the elders tomorrow, when it will be hopefully drier. Then you can tell us more of your journey along the Road. For tonight, we have warm rooms with dry bedding set aside for all of you. We do not have human-sized guest rooms or beds, but we have cleared two classrooms, one for the males and one for the females. There are others already here that you will be joining, but I trust it will not be too crowded."

The queen stood up and spread her wings, indicating that their audience was over. Two male fairies came forward and asked the newcomers to please follow them to their sleeping quarters.

As they left the queen's presence, Thom and Adele were walking side-by-side and their hands brushed. Smiling in his tiredness, Thom reached over and took her hand affectionately and they walked on holding hands even as they narrowing ramp pushed them closer together. Instead of watching where they were going, they turned heads and stared into each other's eyes as they walked. So distracted were they by each other that neither saw the low arch approaching and both smacked into it. Rubbing his head while also laughing, he kept a hold of her hand as they now ducked and kept going.

The fairies led everyone to a higher platform, ducking under two more low arches as their steps crunched the accumulating slush. At that open deck they separated, Thom kissing Adele's hand before releasing it. The women were guided to a round building to the right and the men toward a rectangular structure ahead of them. The sound of the waterfall was a comforting dull roar in the background.

Thom was tired from the long day. He trudged with Francis and Kane until the stood under the wide eaves of the building. The male fairy opened the small door and invented them to enter, then turned and left, flying off into the snowy night. The three men brushed as much of the snow off their garments as they could and stomped their boots to clear them too, then they bent over and entered the building, through what was to a fairy a grand and tall doorway but to them was a door only half as tall as it should be.

Inside, they found a fire burning, lamps lit, and a group of four pixies.

"Thomas!" yelled one of them in greeting, a pixie in bright clothes so unlike his companions.

"Dorthos? How did you get here?" asked Thom as he embraced the small man.

"I flew. How else does anyone get to the top of a mountain?"

THIRTY-THREE

Founder Vengeance

For the next hour, Dorthos told them about the rescue of Levitanus. It was a rollicking adventure from the way he told it, as they swept in on great eagles to drop inside Dalrake's mighty castle, with dryad arrows taking out most of the guards. He ended it with two eagles lifting the wizard over the walls just as Merlin and his companions came through the front gates.

The tiny chairs and tables meant for fairies had been pushed to one side, leaving a clear floor to the roaring fire, along with a large pile of tiny blankets and pillows for their use. As Dorthos told his tale, the three humans shed their cold traveling robes and made their way to the fire to warm themselves. When the pixie finished with them arriving at the Fairy Court, Kane suddenly applauded as he genuinely smiled.

"I love a rousing tale, Aeti rider. Truly, I do. And yet it seemed so perfectly executed. What have you forgotten to tell us?"

The three other pixie men laughed and one spoke up. "Prince Dorthos polished the truth, but nothing worse than that. It happened much as he said it did, though he left off a few fumbles and eagle pecks. Levitanus is now free of the Sorcerer Dalrake."

"Where is he now?" asked Thom.

"Dalrake? We hear he is on his way here," replied Dorthos, seemingly unoffended by the teasing. "As for Levitanus, we do not know. The eagles lifted him free and set him down in a forest some distance from Dalrake's keep. He fled from there unaccompanied, as he insisted, while we flew back across the Road of Clouds. He asked us to find out what we could of the pillar of light that shot out from the Road just as we were making our escape. Did any of you have a part in that?"

"Consider it our contribution to freeing Levitanus," said Kane lightly. "Where are your eagles and the dryads?"

"The eagles roost as they choose," said Dorthos. "They will return when we call. As for the dryads, they left us to guide Levitanus through the wilds. Dryads have no desire for war; they came along to free Levitanus and then they left to make sure he made it to safety. Before they left, they gifted us with enough dryad poison to coat hundreds of arrows. We pixies came back to the Road of Clouds and Cloudholder Mountain because we are more willing to go into battle."

Suddenly, Dorthos' countenance became serious. "There is something I have left off, but it is not my story to tell. We are not the only outsiders at court tonight. Keeper Bronwen is here too and her tale is a dark one."

"Bronwen is here?" blurted out Kane.

Thom's mind raced even as his heart sank. Keeper Bronwen was in charge of the enchantments that surrounded Camelot. The magic had already been damaged, so how could she have abandoned that duty? Had something catastrophic happened to the whole city?

"What has happened in Camelot?" asked Francis, voicing what was also Thom's concern.

"As I said, that is her tale to tell." Dorthos patted the monk's arm in sympathy. "Maybe we should go over to the women's quarters and have her tell it to you now."

"Yes, we should do that," replied Francis, his countenance revealing that he already expected dire news.

Dorthos nodded and went over to where he had placed his overcoat on one of the small tables. Thom, Francis, and Kane all donned their cold boots and wet travel robes and then let the pixie led them over to the women.

Apparently, they were expected, because a female pixie, the very same one who originally fetched them to the City Keeper's tower, opened the door before they could knock. She beckoned them in. Thom entered with Kane and Francis to find Keeper Bronwen standing next to Vivien and Adele. Vivien's face was tear-stained and Adele was shaking her head in disbelief. Also, there was Sister Myrna and the young girl that was the keeper's apprentice.

"Keeper Bronwen, what has happened?" asked Kane.

"Merlin has gone too far. He ordered the guild council to attack the monastery. There is nothing left but smoldering rubble."

Thom just stared at her, not fully comprehending what she had just reported.

Francis let out a wail of pain.

"But we encountered Merlin at the Core just a few days ago," said Kane. "How could he have made it back to Camelot so quickly?"

"He gave the orders on the same day that Dalrake captured Levitanus and took him back to his castle. Dalrake and Merlin were both at the Keeper's tower that morning, helping to mend the tear in the city's enchantment. Although they dislike each other, they will work together for the sake of furthering magic. Dalrake passed Merlin a note right in front of me." Bronwen shook her head at the gall. "I only learned later that the note told him that Levitanus was still alive and that he was plotting a rebellion with the Father Abbot.

"What I learned was that after the two parted, Merlin read the note and raged. He stormed to the king's castle and gathered the guild council around him. It was then that he ordered them to destroy the monastery and kill whoever was in it, ordering that it be done within a week, as soon as the sorcerers and Mordred were chased out of the city."

Francis regained his voice. "I see Sister Myrna. Did they spare the convent?"

Bronwen shook her head. "All is gone. They slaughtered everyone they found, whether magician or not. They even killed the animals. They also pulled all the buildings down, burning what they could and salting the rest. The Monastery of Saint Barnabas and its accompanying convent are no more. Sister Myrna was with those transporting cargo to the harbor for the evacuation that had already been planned, so she was spared.

"Sister Harmony and the remaining mercenaries fought hard to allow others to escape through Mousehome and then they brought the building down on top of the opening so that the wizards would not find it. She and the men died to save many."

"How did you learn about all of this?" asked Kane.

"I came when I heard the magic battle. Harmony was not that powerful, but she was a clever one. She and the mercenaries kept all those guild magicians at bay because they thought there was a large force of magicians opposing them. But even with their strikes and retreats, one apprentice and a handful of warriors cannot hold out for long. By the time I arrived, it was over.

"I found the three of the guild council overseeing the final destruction, and they were rather boastful in their crimes."

"Who else was killed?" asked Francis.

"I do not have their names, brother. I am sorry. I would not have seen Harmony's corpse if Una had not insisted on showing it to me, along with the mercenaries. She acted like it was a victory for all female guild magicians to kill a nun."

"Evil," muttered Francis.

"Yes, the guild's actions were evil, but Harmony used magic to spare many. Judge the wielder not the tool."

"You have still not explained why you are here," noted Kane. "I would think that Camelot is still very much in need of a Keeper."

"I renounced my position, throwing its duties on those three pompous fools. They gloated over their blasphemous slaughter. They were proud of it, thinking that anything they did was justified in order to stomp out a rebellion against their precious guild.

"They were astonished that I was offended and just stared at me dumbly when I took out the keys to the Keeper's tower and threw them at their feet. Varus even ordered me to take them back, insisting I could not quit my position. With that, I turned and walked away. As I crossed the city to get my personal things from the tower, I started pulling myself out of the city's enchantment. Myrna found me on the streets, while my apprentice Letitia and the pixie staff joined me when I told them what happened while gathering my things. As we left the tower, the three guild leaders came rushing to it because the city's enchantment was already starting to unravel. They will have their hands full trying to keep the magic going."

"Does the council even realize that you are part of the League of

Barnabas?" asked Kane.

Bronwen tilted her head as she considered. "Most likely they are still ignorant, but Merlin will deduce it as soon as they tell him what happened. I do not care if they know or not. I am through with the guild."

Francis was still weeping; Thom went over and put his arms around his friend, crying as well. His grief was not as profound, but he had met many good people at the monastery and it been more like a home than anything else besides Levitanus' cottage in the woods. It was hard to imagine all of it destroyed and so many of the people dead. Sister Harmony had never liked him, but he would still miss the abrasive nun's devotion to truth.

"Why did you come here rather than fleeing down one of the other Roads?" asked Kane.

"I am not certain, but it felt right. It is time for us to stand up for the fair treatment of all magical beings. Where is Osric?"

"He tries to hold the archway against the sorcerers, but they were already winning through. I assume he will be here soon if they do not capture him."

"Maybe it is best that Levitanus is not on the Road. Should we all fall here, the Father Abbot will have at least one master magician to restore the league's ranks."

"You are being rather grim, Keeper," stated Kane.

"Am I? You know Dalrake as well as any of us; he revels in revenge." Her eyes briefly settled on Thom and then returned to Kane. "And now Merlin has noticed us as well. We will make our stand against both of them, but we are not guaranteed a victory. I just pray that the guild and the sorcerers do not unite in coming after us."

THIRTY-FOUR

Taking a Stand

When Thomas ducked his way out of their makeshift men's barrack, he found a cold and gray morning. The snow had continued falling after he had gone to bed and now the land was white under a gray sky. He saw his breath as he looked around. The platforms and walkways had been swept, so some of the fairies must have been working since before dawn to clear the snow and slush. He saw none around except the male who had brought them a slim breakfast of nut bread and dried fruits. The tiny fellow had been astonished that what he thought would be enough for three humans was only enough for one, but he had doggedly provided more food until they were all at least partially satisfied. He had also fed the pixies and was now leaning on an outdoor railing and catching his breath, sweat glistening on his brow. Thom would have thought he would be freezing since he was damp and exposed in this weather, but then he remembered that fairies loved the cold more than others. The man was barefoot and seemed unbothered by it. The fairy's dull colored wings were folded on his back. All the males were of earthen colors while the females were bright shades. It was hard to imagine how such dull-colored men could turn into the bright lights he had seen from a distance.

"Good morning, Thomas."

He looked over his shoulder to see Francis ducking his way outside. "Good morning, Francis. How are you today? I am so sorry for the pain you're feeling."

The monk gave him a weak smile. "The agony will take a long time to calm. Saint Barnabas was my home for decades. Even though Ears and I traveled the realm looking for manuscripts, we were always glad when we were able to return through those gates. That old mule and I survived many dangerous trips; it is sad to think he met his death without me, killed spitefully by magic.

"It is strange that I am thinking of an animal this morning, because there were also so many dear people that I knew that were also killed. My brethren, sisters from the convent, even the mercenaries that the abbot hired. But for some reason, my thoughts go to that stubborn mule this morning." He gave Thom an apologetic smile and that faded to a sigh.

Thom gave his friend a hug, not having any words to comfort him. Francis hugged back for a moment and then pulled away. "I will be fine, Thomas. We have much to decide today. We are bringing Dalrake's wrath on the fairies and that is not something I want to do. I think we should flee before he catches up with us and maybe he will spare these folk."

The fairy that had been serving them, looked over his shoulder and replied, "That is not for you to decide, Fair Defender. The queen is on the league's council and she has discussed this with the others for months now. If she wants to publicly declare that the Fairyland is now aligned with the League of Barnabas, that is her right and we, her people, stand behind her. No longer will we be powders for the boxes."

Francis shook his head. "Deny them what they think is theirs and they will take it by any means. Queen Titania is flying into a dangerous storm filled with terrible magic. Are all of you ready for the consequences?"

The fairy man stood straight, his wings spreading out behind him. His jaw set and his eyes seemed as cold as the snowy ground behind him. "We are ready; we have been ready for decades now. The abuse of magic ends today."

Francis nodded. "Strong words. May your conviction become true. When are we to meet the queen this morning?"

"She will see all of you in one hour," replied the fairy man, launching himself into the air. "I will be back for you then." And with that, he flew away into the dreary morning.

* * *

Thom stood with all the other humans before the queen and her court. Surprisingly, there were other magical beings among the fairies: pixies, a small herd of centaurs, and even harpies. It almost felt like humankind was on trial before the others. The humans who spoke the most were the league's masters: Bronwen, Kane, and a just-arrived Osric. By midday, all tales had been told and the humans were asked to leave the platform while the others had a discussion.

They walked halfway back to their sleeping quarters to linger on one of the smaller platforms. The railings were only knee high, so they were too low to lean on and wooden deck, although it had been thoroughly swept that morning, had a fine dusting of snow on it. So they just stood there, gazing into the surrounding forest as they waited. After a time, Kane spoke up to Osric and Bronwen.

"It is strange to not be the decision makers. I was a sorcerer for too long; I grew fond of being my own master." He smiled at them. "I have been a part of this league for five years now and still it feels foreign to me at times."

"The power needs to be in the hands of those who pay the most," replied Bronwen. "Magical beings give their very lives for the sake of magic; it is only right that they be in charge."

"You have no argument from me on that," whispered Kane. "The league gave me redemption. I thought I was beyond hope for my horrible crimes, but then the league showed God's mercy to me. I have no qualms with this arrangement; I just find it still feels strange at times."

"What I find strange is that you stole Merlin's cache from his very hands," chuckled Osric. "That was a cheeky move, Kane."

"I took it out of desperation, or else he would surely have hunted us down. It has been in my knapsack this whole time. I have not even opened it."

"Well, keep it close," said Bronwen. "We may need to replenish our elements from his cache."

"So you think we go to war?" asked Vivien, interrupting the three.

Bronwen nodded. Osric did as well.

Kane replied, "I think the league's leadership council already made that decision some time ago. Queen Titania would not dare to do this without the agreement of the others. There are only four others of the council on that platform."

"You must be right," said Bronwen, rubbing her face. "I am just too tired to think things through."

"If it is already decided, then why send us away?" asked Thom.

"The harpies were never part of the league before today," responded Kane. "She might be recruiting them. The cruel greed of some wizard or sorcerer might be what it takes to drive those flying brutes into the league."

Osric chuckled. "You still sound a bit miffed about the harpies outsmarting you."

Kane scowled back but said nothing.

"Whatever her reasons, the queen is within her rights as one of our leaders to ask this of us," stated Bronwen. She looked over at Francis, who had wandered away from the rest of them and was staring off into nothing, lost in his thoughts. "We have him to thank for the structure of the league. It was Brother Francis who insisted that magical beings deserved the final say about anything that concerned magic done by us humans. He may never join our ranks, but the league owes much to him."

"He is a good man," acknowledged Thom, "and a good friend. If not for him, I would not have survived any of the Roads that I've traveled."

Francis truly had been the reason he wasn't killed on the Roads of Leaves, Waters, or Clouds. He had taught Thom enchantments, counseled him, and shown him what it meant to practice magic justly.

"The two of you have been through much together," agreed Bronwen.

* * *

An hour later, Dorthos came to retrieve them. "Come along, everyone. We need to make plans. The sorcerers will be here by evening and we need to be ready for them, because we are through with running. On this mountain we will make our stand."

THIRTY-FIVE

Secrets and Pledges

Tuatha Aes Si was arranged in a half-circle against the sheer face of Cloudholder's summit. Within the half-circle plunged the waterfall into a steaming pool that then flowed out from under the Fairy Court to meander across dormant fields and on into the woods. Also within the half-circle was a hot spring whose waters mixed with the frigid flow from the heights, hence creating so much steam. Around the spring, sheltering in its moist warm air, were rows of fruit trees and flowering shrubs. Other trees that filled much of the clearing were aspen, maple, juniper, and pine. Into this forest descended Thomas, Vivien, and Francis, using another rope ladder. The Fairy Queen had asked them to go first because there was someone who wanted to speak with them.

When Thom stepped off the rope ladder, he was surprised at how warm it was down here. The hot spring's heat radiated back from the platforms overhead.

"So you are Thomas of York," remarked a deep yet feminine voice.

Thom spun to find a centaur woman standing in the shadows of the platform. They had told him that mare-woman was down here wanting to talk with them, but she had still startled him. She stood twice his height.

"I am. Are you Thuma?"

She nodded. "These other two, they are Journeywoman Vivien and Brother Francis, who is also called the Defender?"

"We are," replied Vivien as she stepped off the ladder. Right behind her came the monk.

"I requested this conversation before the others came out to survey the battle lines. I understand you three participated in a humbling on the Isle of Mists." It was a statement and not a question.

Thom remembered when they had ridden on centaurs out of desperation. He had sworn to tell no one of this humiliation of the horse-men and he hadn't. He felt certain that was the event she was implying, but he wasn't about to confess something he had promised to never repeat. "We were on the Isle of Mists, yes. We were helped by a herd of centaurs to reach King Arthur before his betrayers could overrun Haven House and slay him."

Francis spoke up, "They honored Levitanus as a *refuge maker* and did what had to be done to avert a catastrophe that would have shattered the realm. It was a brave act on their part, but we cannot share more about their actions."

Thuma actually smiled and then motioned for the stallion-men that were besides her to leave. The two turned and galloped off through the snow-free shadows that were the underside of Tuatha Aes Si, heading toward the snowy field beyond.

"You are their mare-woman," stated Vivien suddenly. "That is the only way you could know anything of what happened that day. Wyndo and the others are of your herd."

"Indeed, I am," she replied. "Come let us walk beneath the platforms and join the others as we survey the field of coming battle. We can talk as we walk."

They had to hurry because of the long stride of the centaur, but she kept it slow enough so they didn't have to run. "My tribe left the Isle of Mists and the Road of Waters after the fighting ended. My men never felt comfortable around others of our kind after what they did. They knew that they had done right, but the feeling of shame still persisted. Too deeply is it ingrained in our hearts that we are not brainless horses, to be ridden by lesser people."

"We have told no one of what occurred that day," assured Francis. "A confidence given is a secret never to be shared."

"Nonetheless, my kind cannot so easily forget such an experience. I had to lead my tribe out of there and eventually we settled on the cold yet green meadows of Cloudholder's slopes. And here we are now, once again sharing a battlefield. That brings me to why I asked to speak with the three of you. I chose down here where the fairies detest to fly and those bothersome harpies would dare not spy on us. I have a boon to ask of the three of you.

"I ask that if you encounter any of my males that you act as if you have not met them before. There are two other centaur tribes that came to the Fairy Queen's call for aid and I would not have any of the others hear about my men having any familiarity with humans."

All three of them readily agreed to what she asked.

As they came out from underneath the platforms, they encountered more centaurs waiting on the leader of their herd. Thuma said farewell to the humans and galloped off with her horse-men to join the leadership group of Queen Titania, Wizard Osric, and Keeper Bronwen. Also with them were Dorthos and the Harpy Commander Celaeno. Thuma joined the group directly, while her horse-men set up a perimeter, ready to protect everyone with their great bows.

As they stood there in the cold shade of the platforms, Francis looked out at the surrounding wilds. He seemed melancholy as he spoke to no one in particular, "I never wanted to be fighting here again."

"It almost seems as if God is pushing you back toward your old craft," stated Vivien. "I know you do not think it is His hand involved, but as long as I have known you, Brother Francis, you have been surrounded by magic. You are like a farmer who has forsworn growing corn whose fields keeps sprouting up on their own, or a trader who refuses to trade wool who gets stranded in the midst of the highland sheep steads. I find it a bit humorous, but not that it is happening here. I understand that Fairyland is a painful place for you."

"I still remember how strongly I felt betrayed," replied Francis, looking over at her. "Crafting magic once seemed like such a wondrous profession, but then I saw the ugly truth behind so much of it."

Vivien nodded agreement but said nothing, and Thom wondered what unfairness she had witnessed during her decades of training. He looked away from both of them, feeling a bit vulnerable himself. He looked out over the gray and white landscape and saw movement among the clouds.

"Are those griffins?" he asked, pointing skyward as two dozen shapes emerged out of the overhead clouds. But then he corrected himself. "No, the silhouette is not of a lion-eagle. They look like beakless birds with hair and a bosom. Those are harpies."

"Needed help," stated Francis.

"How do they move so quickly?" asked Thom. "Their wings are not flapping that quick."

"Harpies have a way with the winds, journeyman," stated Vivien. "You should know that by now."

Eric Loren

THIRTY-SIX

Preparing for Battle

Thom was looking out from the one of the open platforms when a purple sphere came rushing toward them. Coming behind it was a quick-flying fairy. There was no time to hide or try to counter it with another enchantment, so all Thom could do was yell out warning to those around him and then watch it zip back and forth around the Fairy Court. The fairy gave up trying to follow the Eagle's Spying and went directly to her queen to report.

As soon as the enchantment dissipated, Osric went clambering down the rope ladder and then ran to join the centaurs who were already patrolling the forests beyond the fallow fields. Osric would be working to protect horse-men as they harassed the sorcerers from behind.

The rest of the magicians had been split into three groups: Kane, along with Bronwen and her apprentice, were to hold the center; Vivien and apprentice Myrna to the left where the classrooms were; and Thom, Adele, and Francis to the right, in the area where those in residence at the court had their sleeping quarters.

Francis led as they walked bent-over through low arches and along covered walkways. They would have been crawling, but the fairies built with plenty of room for the wings to spread out behind and above them. When they came to the far end of the compound, they had no choice except to sit on the covered walkway, for there was no open area here. At their backs was a series of sleeping rooms, their windows shuttered, doors closed, and occupants elsewhere helping to prepare for the court's defense.

"I feel exposed here," said Thom as he sat on the wooden floor and leaned his staff against a shuttered window behind them, "like a bird fettered to its perch, inside a cage. The roof keeps me pressed down and the floor offers only a thin, wooden shield to my buttocks. I would rather face a sorcerer on the open fields below."

"I'd agree," said Francis, "if they weren't bringing along a horde of griffins."

Thom grumbled but nodded agreement; this would be their best shelter if the bird-lions started swooping out of the sky. He scooted to the edge of the walkway with its low railing and leaned over it to look straight down. "Bare ground below, with no easy way to climb up here. They seemed to have trimmed off all the lower branches of the three trees that hold up this end of the Fairy Court."

"Even the branches above us have been thinned," added Adele as she too leaned over the railing to survey their area. "I see a handful of harpies perched in one of the trees and a trio of fairies in another one."

"Our comrades in arms," said Francis, content to just lean against the building's wall and the let the younger two investigate their area. "But they historically hate each other, so it will not be easy to get them to work together. Fairies see harpies as brutes that are always argumentative and contrary, while harpies view fairies as cowards that would rather flee than confront anything."

"How will they be a help to us?" asked Adele, moving over to sit near the monk.

"The fairies are already spying on the sorcerers," replied Francis. "That is how we know that they come with twelve masters, four journeymen, eight griffins, and one roc. That is also how we learned that they plan to attack in groups of three, with one defending as the other two attack."

"You don't mention Dalrake," noted Thom. "What about him?"

"The fairies report that he has turned away from the archway and instead gone to the Core. None of us know why, but our main concern is the group who has followed us onto Cloudholder."

"Will the fairies be able to help any once we actually start fighting?" asked Thom, also coming over to sit on the other side of Adele. "They look rather frail, no matter how could they are at enduring cold weather."

"Fairies fly fast and see far. However, they can use those innate talents, they will. This is their homeland; they will do whatever they must to prevent its destruction."

"What of the harpies?" asked Adele. "They seem to be here begrudgingly. What can they do besides souring everyone's attitude?"

Francis smiled. "The harpies are committed because the Fairy Queen has promised fairy watchers to warn them of any intruders trying to sneak onto their side of the mountain. For that help, they are willing to join the league and send fighters to help today. The harpies can call the winds to themselves and their voices are loud and intimidating. They are also tough fighters, skilled with spears and bows."

"Will they work with each other and with us?" asked Thomas, wondering if they might end up being more of a hindrance than help. He didn't need a sudden wind gust to send an enchantment awry.

"Both peoples have good reason to work together," replied Francis, "but I expect it to be like hitching a donkey and an ox to the same plow. Do not expect anything neat or quick."

"When do you think the sorcerers will get here?" asked Adele. "And what are we going to do to stop them?"

"The fairies said they will reach us about three hours past midday. As for how to stop them, I would suggest that you and Thomas review what enchantments you know and how that magic might work to discourage Dalrake's friends. While the two of you discuss that, I will try talking with the reluctant allies." With that, Francis crawled around the corner of the building, heading toward an area where there was no roof.

"He is right," said Thom, scooting closer to her. He wanted to hug and kiss her, but he knew this wasn't the time for that. "We should talk about what you can and cannot do. What enchantments have you done?"

Adele smiled and reached over to take his hand, but that was as far as she went. She told him about the dozen enchantments she had done. Some were basics taught all apprentices, like Whisper of Warning, Wizard Light, and Fire Starter, but she had also mastered more difficult enchantments during their fighting around Camelot. Thom only vaguely remembered all that she had done then, so he was glad for the reminder. They discussed how she might be able to us each enchantment to stop attacks on the Fairy Court.

Then Thom offered a serious warning. "You may kill some people. That happens when using magic to fight, so please ready yourself for that possibility. I wish it weren't so. I wish you could just enjoy the wonder of magic without the horrors. I wish you were safely away from here. I wish…"

Adele forestalled his words by putting a finger to his lips. "I am glad that I'm here, because I'm with you and that is where I want to be for the rest of my life, for however long we live. Now, tell me again how to craft and hold multiple Wizard Lights so that it distracts the sorcerers and disrupts their crafting. I want to use the little I do know to make a difference."

Thom smiled and kissed her finger. When she lowered her hand, he answered her question and then continued on with their discussion.

When Francis finally returned, he came with the fairy Rainflower and a harpy named Borea. Somehow, he had convinced the two peoples to cooperate with each other and with the humans. Together, they planned on how best to defend this end of Tuatha Aes Si.

THIRTY-SEVEN

Battle of Tuatha Aes Si

Twelve sorcerers came to attack Tuatha Aes Si. They were organized in groups of three as they marched through the fading afternoon. Before getting too close, two trios broke off, one heading for the west wing of the court and another for the east wing. They had no soldiers with them, but griffins flew overhead, keeping the harpies and fairies at a distance. For some time, they just stood there, looking up at the platforms. But then the first enchantment was crafted. It was a Tarn's Call that was a magical amplification of the crafter's voice. Sorcerer Horis' voice boomed everywhere.

"We are here for the humans. In the name of the Founders, hand them over now. That is their command. Merlin and Dalrake are in agreement that they must be punished for their rebellion."

From the where they kept watch, Thom couldn't see Horis making his threats but he certainly recognized his voice. When he mouthed the name to Francis, the monk nodded. Both of them had suffered torture under that man's direction.

They heard someone craft another Tarn's Call enchantment in reply and then Keeper Bronwen's voice thundered outward. "Founder Levitanus disagrees. We stand with him against those who abuse magical beings in their lust for power. You must leave now. You have strayed from the agreed-to route for those who travel the Road of Clouds and have trespassed into the land of the fairies. By order of Queen Titania, you are to leave immediately."

"You forget your place!" replied Horis, his anger clear. "We provide the havens where magical beings thrive, in return we can take what we need to craft the enchantments that sustain those havens and help to maintain civilized rule over the whole realm. Even we sorcerers recognize the throne in Camelot. On behalf of Dalrake, I declare the Fairy Realm in rebellion. Surrender now or all will be rendered down to their elements!"

Thomas found the words ridiculous. When did the sorcerers show any submission to Camelot? Only a few days ago they tried to overthrow the very king they were invoking now. He said as much to Adele and Francis.

"Their loyalty is to the throne, not to who sits on it," replied Francis. "They want Mordred to replace his father. However, both the guild and the sorcerers are in agreement that Camelot should be the center of it all. They also agree that all magic should be in subservience to the magicians."

Adele shook her head at the hypocrisy. "Convenient that they show loyalty only when it is to their benefit."

Francis crawled to the low railing and looked out over the snowy field. The trio of sorcerers that had come to their side of the Fairy Court had so far done nothing except stand in the snow and study the platforms.

"I give you one minute more to hand over the humans and surrender to us!" came Horis' booming voice from where he confronted the queen and Keeper Bronwen at the center of the court. "Do so, or die!"

Thom heard Bronwen's enchantment fade away, so she obviously planned no answer to the sorcerers. Then Horis' enchantment also faded away.

Francis shook his head at the change. "It is time. They are done with their talking."

He looked around at those who were with them at that far end of the compound, humans and fairies and harpies. "Get ready. With threats so brazen, they will attack soon. Rainflower, please have your people continue to spy out the fields and forests near us to see who is attacking where, and do not forget to look skyward for griffins. Borea, have your harpies ready to drive wind at any fireballs thrown toward us. I will help Thomas and Lady Adele prepare for battle."

Suddenly, they heard magician caches being opened all around the court, including from the trio of sorcerers below them. Francis hurried over to guide Adele as she started pulling the elements she would need to craft Wizard Lights. Thom had no time to watch them because he had his own enchantment to craft.

Thomas stirred together powders of Phoenix tongue, crushed Azure Fireflies, and Crested Black Eagle feathers, along with Spotted Pine oil. He returned the glass vials to his box and pulled three of the mundane elements that were also in there: black powder, lamp oil, and oak pollen. He paused just a moment to listen to what the sorcerers were making. He heard a Shield of Power, Fireball, and third he couldn't readily place. He worried that his own fireballs would not do much against another's, but he could use them to wear down the shield. It was too late to switch anyways; he had to finish this crafting first. He added the mundane ingredients and then mixed all of it, listening carefully to make sure everything was in the correct proportions.

When done mixing, he spat into his crafting and stirred it in to attune the magic to himself and then set the bowl aside. He quickly coated his hand with a powdering of white sand, realizing that his supply would not last that long if this was all that he crafted and there was nothing obvious up here to substitute for sand. He closed his cache, stored it in his knapsack and then scooped the resulting goop from his bowl and started forming two glowing balls.

Surprisingly, Adele was the first to finish and she sent her three wobbling wizard lights racing toward the sorcerers to harass them as they were finishing their enchantments. But then the sorcerer crafting a Shield of Power finished and set a protection over the trio, giving the other two time to finish. One of Adele's lights hit the shield and popped without doing any damage.

"Can you hover one right in front of the shield?" asked Thomas as he made ready to throw his first fireball.

"I will," said Adele, setting one there even as the last one fizzled out.

Taking careful aim, Thom threw one fireball and guided it directly at that little Wizard Light. He hit it so hard that the two enchantments pressed against the shield even as they exploded, creating an effect that was twice as strong as just the fireball by itself.

The magical shield held but started sloughing off sparks and flames.

As Francis helped Adele to clean her bowl and prepare to craft another enchantment, Thom waited to release his final fireball. He held it away from the railing and himself as it dripped flames. His hand was growing uncomfortably warm but, so far, the sand coating was preventing any actually burns. He wanted a clear shot at those hunkered behind the shield and knew that the sorcerer controlling it would have to dissolve it, slide it to the side, or at least lift the bottom edge so the others could release their attacks. So he waited and watched.

Finally, he heard a shift in the enchantment's rhythm and it began to lift higher into the sky, leaving a gap at the bottom. Thom's heart raced as he waited. If he was too late, his fireball would get caught in whatever the harpies planned. Rather than wait for it to lift high enough for a straight shot, Thom would try to ricochet it off slushy ground to get it behind the shield.

Concentrating, he sent the fireball blazing toward the ground just short of the sorcerers. It hit and shattered against the slush, spewing flames in a wide pattern. Some flames bounced off the shield but some flew under the shield and splattered on their legs and magician boxes.

The shield lifted higher, almost rushed in its ascent, and then the other two magicians released their enchantments. One released a glowing green ball of something even as his trouser leg was smoking. Apparently too distracted, his enchantment wobbled as it flew from his hand and almost hit the shield's edge. The sorcerer over-corrected and almost sent it into the ground nearby. Stomping his leg in a vain attempt to stop the smoldering, he tried to get his enchantment under control but still lost it. It splattered on the snowy field halfway to the platforms, instantly dissolving the snow and leaving a green muddy mess that had a sickly glow in the fading daylight.

Thom saw all this in an instant, then realized the other sorcerer had also released his enchantment, which was three fireballs thrown in rapid succession, roaring at the Fairy Court so quickly that the harpies' downwind seemed to have little effect on them.

"Duck!" he yelled to Adele and Francis as the fireballs flew right at them.

Amazingly, Adele kept focused on her crafting, a Teasing of Air even as Francis hurriedly packed her cache and closed it. She added the last element and lifted the bowl to add her spit, then quickly touched the moist powders to her lips and blew toward the rapidly approaching fireballs, adding a twisting motion with her hand as she directed it. A small, spinning air flow grew just beyond the railing and moved toward the fireballs. A harpy's wind caught it and doubled its speed, then one of the fireballs hit it and there was a huge explosion, throwing fire everywhere across the fallow field. The other two fireballs made it through, though they were blown to the side. One passed under the platform. The other splattered all over the covered walkway to the right of Thomas, setting the wood on fire and filling the air with smoke.

Instead of starting his new crafting, Thom was forced to move. He grabbed his staff and his cache and moved past Adele and Francis to the corner of the building that the walkway hugged.

THIRTY-EIGHT

Fire, Water, and Snow

Once again, Thomas found himself facing an attack, but this time he had no great walls to protect him and the ones coming were not soldiers or centaurs. Already the Tuatha Aes Si was burning, and not just near them. A fairy reported there were at least three more fires elsewhere, along something smoldering underneath among the piers and trunks holding the court up.

The sorcerers were behind their protective shield wall, protected by one while the other two crafted their next attack. Thom quickly started crafting too, but Adele needed a moment to recover after that last magical conflict. Francis was calling to the harpies and fairies, asking them to do something beyond the shield, but Thom didn't hear much of it.

He had an enchantment to craft.

Again he went with the Fireball enchantment. He really wanted to craft Hands of Lightning, but he had never made that one and there was no time for Francis to teach him. He crafted as quickly as he could, but the sorcerers were faster and even as he finished, he heard more fireballs roaring towards them.

Adele hadn't even had the time to start and now she and Francis were running past Thom in a half-crouch, trying to move fast without hitting their heads on the low overhead beams. The two hurried around the corner and away from the area, while Thom scrambled to the railing in an awkward, stooped-over stance. With fireballs in each hand, he looked out at the enemy.

Six fireballs were racing toward him.

With a yell of defiance, Thom threw his and then turned, scooped up his magician's box and staff, and throwing himself around the corner.

Fire exploded all around him.

Adele screamed for him to keep moving.

Francis held out a hand to grab him.

He threw his cache and staff ahead of him, and then crawled as fast as he could, even as smoke and flames surrounded him.

Francis caught his wrist and yanked him forward, finally past the flames. "Hurry, we need to move to the next platform."

Thomas agreed, quickly stuffing his box back into his knapsack and taking a tight grip on his staff, once again wondering why he bothered to carry the awkward thing.

The three of them raced as fast as they could hunched over, following the covered walkway around the building to the far side, where they were confronted by a choice. They could climb a ramp to an open platform behind this one or they could race down the backside of the burning building toward the center of Tuatha Aes Si.

Adele started up the ramp and away from the fire, but Thom pulled her back. "That would take us clear of the flames but it will trap us away from the rest of the court. We would have no clear sight on the sorcerers."

She considered and then nodded. "I should have thought of that." And then she raced down the smoky walkway along the building's rear. The two men followed her.

Thom saw no open flames yet, but the building's wall was getting hot and smoke was curling out of every gap in the wooden panels. His fireballs no longer existed. He had maintained his link to them even while being unable to guide their path, but he felt them get pushed by harpy winds and felt when they finally hit something and exploded. It didn't sound like they hit another enchantment, but he wasn't certain as they fled the area. He realized he might never know if they had helped at all.

Adele stopped at the far corner and knelt to look around the corner. She pulled back quickly and reported to the others, "One of the sorcerers is heavily charred and looks dead. The other two are trying to bat away branches and debris that the fairies are dropping on them. The harpies are having an aerial fight with griffins. It is a mess, but we should be able to race to the next platform without getting attacked."

Francis nodded. "Keep leading the way."

Thom followed, wondering how his fireball could have caused so much damage when he hadn't even been guiding it. He hadn't intended on killing anyone, but he knew that might happen. It was saddening nonetheless.

Adele trotted down a ramp to the next platform. This one held three sleeping quarters, with an open courtyard in the center and covered walkways around the outer edge. The center courtyard held some kind of barren tree sculpture or perching structure, but was otherwise bare except for a blanket of snow. Once again, all the doors and windows were shuttered and there were no fairies in sight except the few who were helping to harass the sorcerers. Over her shoulder, she asked, "Do we make our stand on the ramp or under the eaves?"

"We should try something less confining," replied Francis. "We should go up on the roof."

Thom looked at the steep roofline and the clay tiles that were partially covered in snow and shook his head. He remembered when he had tried leaping across rooftops in Camelot and had almost fallen off. "How will we keep our balance and craft while up there?"

"The fairies build their structures with a flat turret at the peak of the roof. They call it a watch perch. See it there?" He pointed to the farthest of the three buildings where they could see more of the roof. "Unlike human turrets, there is no way to get to it from inside. It is just a flat place where fairies can land, offering short walls for protection from the wind and a vista of the surrounding area. It is like a watchman's post, where someone can keep an eye on their surroundings."

"It seems to be rather small," stated Adele. "I don't think all three of us could fit up there and have any room to mix elements."

"There are three buildings on this platform, which means three watch perches. Thom can take one and you another. I will hang onto the edge of yours and offer what help I can."

Thom and Adele saw the wisdom in his suggestion. The watch perches would give them a better viewing of the area without a low ceiling restricting them. So Adele jumped and easily made it up on the nearest roof. Ignoring the snow she now laid in, she offered a hand up to the monk and then to Thomas.

Carefully, the three of them climbed to the summit and onto the watch perch. It was indeed tight with all three of them standing there, pressed against the thigh-high walls that edged it on three sides. Looking down, they could see the remaining two sorcerers fighting off the fairies and harpies that were harassing them.

"We need to help them," proclaimed Thom as he saw three small corpses littering the churned earth, "before more of them are killed."

"You fight from here," said Adele. "It has the best vantage. I will go to the next perch."

Thom wanted to protest that he should be the one jumping over to the other building, but she was right. This was the better view and he was the stronger magician, although he suspected she wanted to take the farther perch to save him from trying another leap with his bad ankle. He nodded agreement and urged her to be careful. Before Francis followed her, Thom quickly asked him what elements he would need to craft Hands of Lightning.

"You think I can just tell you what to throw into a bowl and you'll be able to craft a new enchantment the first time?" Francis actually smiled. "From any other magician, I would think that a conceited and dangerous request but I know you too well. You can definitely master this enchantment, my friend.

"You will need Lightning Bird feather, Thunderbird tongue, Dragon blood, black powder, and lamp oil. Keep a careful ear on the rhythms to make sure they do not speed up or slow down beyond their beginning beat. When you mix, you will need to dip your lit staff into the bowl before adding that final element. The stone will kindle the lightning."

Thom almost asked if this was another master-level enchantment that was supposed to be beyond his skills, but thought better of it. Instead, he just thanked Francis and turned to his task. He leaned his staff into the corner of the turret, then knelt on the wet wood of the perch's floor and pulled out his magician's cache. He found and set aside the vials he would need, then shut the cache to keep the rest of the contents safe. Taking a deep breath he started crafting, doing his best to emulate the rhythms he had heard when sorcerers had crafted this enchantment to attack him. He worked methodically, mixing slower than usual and listening so carefully that the ever-more complex rhythm stayed sound, not speeding up or slowing down. Finally, it came time for him to kindle his staff and dip it into the mixing bowl. After all the practice on the Road, he was able to light it confidently, but when he set the glowing gem to touch the mixture, there were three sudden throbs and then silence. Eyes going wide, Thomas pulled out his staff and set it clattering into the corner as he fumbled for the final element.

Why had it gone silent? Was it getting ready to explode?

He paused as he was about to pour in the final mundane element of lamp oil. The mixture was still ominously silent but was now starting to glow. Should he add it now? Would this help or would it worsen? What had he done wrong?

Levitanus had lectured him too many times over the years to never leave an enchantment half-done, so he swallowed his fear and began mixing in the lamp oil.

Suddenly, he heard three more loud throbs and then the rhythm came back, steady and at the same pace as it was before. He kept stirring even as he took a ragged breath. The mixture began to steam and glow even brighter, with flashes of light in it, telling him it was ready. He spat in it to attune the magic to himself, set aside his staff, and then plunged all ten fingers into the hot mixture. It wasn't hot enough to burn, but it certainly was uncomfortably warm and sent his fingers to tingling. He pulled out his hands and held up his hands with the fingers spread apart as lightning sparked from finger to finger.

THIRTY-NINE

Hands of Lightning

Awkwardly, Thom got to his feet, being careful not touch the low walls, the floor, or his staff. The last thing he needed was to set his roost on fire. Once up, he looked to see what the sorcerers were up to.

They had heard his crafting and had reacted by one of them putting up another shield wall while the other was crafting his own Hands of Lightning.

Thom didn't want to waste all his energy on a useless attack, so he tried to point only his left pinky finger at the shield. The energy from both his pinky and his thumb shot out, one striking the shield and the other shooting over it to hit the tree directly behind them. The strike didn't seem to weaken the shield much and now he had only eight more strikes left.

He had thought the challenge would be crafting Hands of Lightning, but trying to use the magic was just as difficult.

He decided to try a concentrated attack and flicked the remaining three fingers on his left hand at the shield. This time there was noticeable damage as the sorcerer's shield began to burn and cascade flames on the snow in front of it. Unfortunately, the fire was only in a small area and it didn't seem to go all the way through the shield but more like sloughed off its top layers.

Thom had only a handful of lightning left. Five blasts to get to them before they attacked him in return. The one crafting his own Hands of Lightning was already to the point where his mixing bowl was glowing.

What could he do to stop them? How could he shatter that shield?

Just then, he heard Adele release what she had been crafting and he was surprised at what she had made. It was a new enchantment he had never encountered before. He knew it was a water-type of enchantment, but it took a moment to realize what it was doing. The enchantment was a blue mist that moved into the clouds and caused them to let go all the moisture they held. The enchantment reminded Thom of a Cloud of Mist but instead of gathering the moisture into a fog, it was pulling the water out and forcing it to fall. She had crafted something that was far greater than a mere apprentice-level enchantment.

It was like a tiny blizzard heading for the sorcerers. Adele's enchantment climbed through the low clouds, high enough to pass over the shield and then stopping on the other side. Suddenly, the sorcerers were caught in a sleet and snow storm that fell only on that small area. Thom lost sight of them in the downpour.

He waited before throwing his last strikes, even though the magic was eager to escape, sparking between his fingers and giving him painful shocks. He didn't want to interfere with Adele's magic and he needed to see his targets.

Finally, the storm let up to reveal two men struggling to get out from under a pile of slushy snow. At that moment, Thom struck. Following Adele's example, he shot two finger bolts above the shield, at a large branch of the tree the stood under. There was a spark-filled explosion and the branch broke off and plunged at them. Thom was aiming for the sorcerer crafting Hands of Lightning, but the branch glanced off another and deflected, striking the shield-maker instead.

The sorcerer collapsed into the snow, his shield shredding.

At that moment, the other sorcerer threw a handful of lightning at Thomas.

Desperate, Thom threw himself to the floor of the turret, accidentally kicking his mixing bowl and sending it skittering down the roof to fall in the central courtyard. Lightning slammed into the low wall, sending chunks of stone everywhere, including at him.

He ignored the stone shrapnel as he landed painfully on his side in an attempt to keep his hand free. It worked; his remaining lightning still danced between those three fingers. Somehow, he had kept his three lightning strikes from going off, so he still had a way to strike back.

He just lay there for a moment, stunned and expecting another attack. But none came. When the worst of the pain subsided, he used his other hand to carefully leverage himself to a sitting position. Still no attack, but then he heard it and he realized the sorcerer was now after Adele and Francis.

As fast as he could, he pulled himself up by grabbing what was left of the wall so that he knelt on the rubble and could see the sorcerer below. Thom sent his last lightning bolts searing at him while he was distracted.

Somehow, the sorcerer realized he was being attacked. He suddenly turned, threw his last lightning strikes at Thom, and then dove to the side. Realizing his own danger, Thom let go of controlling his attack and dropped to the wet floor. His own attack would miss because the sorcerer had jumped out of the way, but the sorcerer seemed to still have his magic under control and he could hear it screaming in his direction. He covered his head in anticipation of a terrible explosion, but instead, he felt a great wind ripping across his perch. Curious, he turned his head and saw, through watering eyes, two harpies overhead causing the windstorm somehow.

The lightning exploded, but on roof tiles well away from where Thom sheltered. As the wind died down, he waved thanks to the harpies and then looked over the wall to see what was left below. Somehow, his lightning strikes had not missed the sorcerer after all. He guessed more harpy help there too. It looked like the man was down with a singed robe and shattered magician's cache, but he seemed to be moving a little.

Thom looked to the other building where Adele and Francis had been and found only a gaping hole where the watch perch had been, smoke and flames angrily dancing in the opening. But before he could despair, he heard her crafting from nearby. Looking frantically, he finally spotted both of them in the central courtyard below. Adele was kneeling over her mixing bowl while Francis stood watch. He recognized the enchantment as the same one she had used to soak the sorcerers.

Relieved that both were hale, Thom picked up his staff and started a slow and careful descent from his fractured perch. He made it down without falling. As he approached the others, Adele completed her enchantment and it triggered a storm over the burning building, dumping a blizzard's worth of snow and frozen rain on the fire and extinguishing the flames. So much water poured off the roof into the courtyard that Thom had to step back to avoid the splash of the temporary waterfall. As the smoke dissipated, she moved the storm over the perch where Thom had been crafting and put out the smoldering fire there as well. Finally, she let go of her enchantment with a sigh of relief and the storm faded away.

As the weather returned to its dreary self, two fairies and a harpy came winging down to see them. Before they landed, Thom quickly asked if either Adele or Francis were injured, but they assured him they weren't.

"Lady Adele, you must stop the rest of the fires as well," stated Rainflower as she landed on a perch-like structure in the center of the courtyard. Thom was sure they would be insulted if he called it a perch, but that was what it reminded him of.

"She does not have the stamina or skill to extinguish all of the fires," answered Francis for her. He motioned around them at the smoke wafting through from other fires among the platforms of the Fairy Court. "We will do what we can, but the sorcerers are our first concern. If we do not stop them, then all Tuatha Aes Si will be destroyed."

The harpy also settled on the roosting sculpture, folding her wings behind her. "Speaking of sorcerers, two of those below still live. Should we pummel them to death?"

Thom imagined the harpies dropping rocks and branches on the helpless men and thought it sounded like a cruel and drawn-out death, even for sorcerers.

"No, I do not think so," replied Francis. "They could be of greater use to us as captives. Thomas, can you go down there and take away their caches and staffs and then bind them?"

Thom nodded, for it sounded the sensible thing to do. "I will, if Rainflower can tell me where the nearest rope ladder is. It is too far down to jump."

"Do it quickly," urged Francis, "because we need to help fight off the rest of the sorcerers. This battle is not won yet."

As if to emphasize that fact, all of them heard and saw a great explosion in the sky over the center of the Fairy Court.

FORTY

Taking of the Queen

Thom went to tie up the wounded sorcerers while Adele and Francis would do what they could with the fires that still burned at this end of the court. He found one of them unconscious but breathing steadily. The other one was awake but moaning over his burnt legs. The third sorcerer was most certainly dead, buried under debris dropped by the fairies and harpies. He bound the two who were still alive, both their hands and feet, then he pulled them out of the muck caused by Adele's storm enchantment and left them covered with blankets from their knapsacks. It was only a temporary solution but that was all that he could provide. If the remaining battle went well, he would come back before they froze out here.

He found only two element caches intact and shoved them into one of the knapsacks he had taken from the men. The three magician staffs were too bulky to carry back up the rope ladder, so he buried them in the snow four trees over from where he had placed the two survivors. Leaving the rest of their supplies out of their reach, he hoisted the second pack onto his back and hurried back toward the rope ladder he had descended.

While crossing the turned-up and muddy ground, he looked toward the center of the Fairy Court and saw too much of it was lit up by fire. He also saw two of the giant eagles flying in his direction. On one of them rode a pixie dressed in bright colors. When Thom realized that they were heading straight for him, he stopped and waited, knowing it would be easier for them to land away from the platforms.

As they landed, Thom recognized Dorthos by his bright clothes, which was so different from the earthen tones preferred by all the others. Only he dismounted; the other pixie stayed away.

"Thomas! I see that you and the others have done well here. That is good, but the rest of the Fairy Court is in shambles and aflame. We need you and Adele and Francis. Osric is dead, as are half of the centaurs. Bronwen is wounded and her apprentice killed. Kane is wounded. Vivien is the only one uninjured and she had to give up the western wing of the court to help the others. The apprentice magician-nun is also dead."

The report stunned him. He had expected that the others were still fighting, not that they were close to being routed. "What can we do?"

"I hope much, but you know magic better than I. Whatever you do, it must be quick, before the others arrive."

"What others?"

"Fairy watchers report that Merlin and many of his wizards have come to the mountain and even now are approaching Tuatha Aes Si. Bronwen states that they do not come to our aid."

They had left Merlin doused with a sleep potion and stripped of his magician's cache; he would not come here as an ally. He must have crossed Cloudholder after the sorcerers came through the archway. Thom had no idea how he was able to call the wizards to his side so quickly, but they must have been ready at the archway to Sky Tower section of the Road.

"I must get to Adele and Francis and let them know what's happening. Thank you for informing me, Dorthos. What will your people do?"

"We will fight as long as we must. Some call me Deranged, but I still have hope of victory."

Thom nodded in approval of the small man's determination. "God willing, we will win and the League of Barnabas will be established so that neither wizard nor sorcerer will openly oppose it again."

"That would almost be a miracle," admitted Dorthos, "but I have seen greater surprises in my life. Let us drive them off, my friend Thomas!"

Thom ran for the rope ladder, ignoring the ache of his ankle, while Dorthos remounted his eagle and went aloft. Thom found the others on the bridge to the first place they had made a stand. Adele had extinguished the worst of the flames but the platform was probably still beyond repair. Thom saw that both their faces were smeared with ash, showing that they likely went too close to the flames at some time, but he said nothing about it.

"It is done," stated Adele in a tired voice. "The fire will smolder in the center, but it won't spread any further. Did you get the sorcerers secured?"

"Two still live. They are tied up and covered in blankets against the cold. I also recovered two caches. But we have worse things to face." And then Thomas told them what Dorthos had reported. It was sobering news to share.

Adele raised a soot-covered hand to her mouth in shock. "Not Myrna! Poor Vivien; she will have taken the loss of a student hard. And now she is all that is left to defend the others? We need to help her."

"We will need to hurry if we want to make a difference," said Francis. "The sorcerers will press any advantage they have before the wizards arrive."

The three of them hurried back to the three-building platform and this time took one of the outer walkways around to the far side. They climbed a ramp to the next platform and once again ducked their way around the outer walkway to the far side. They stopped there to stare.

They finally had a good vantage point on the center of Tuatha Aes Si and saw fire everywhere.

"There's Queen Titania," said Francis, pointing to where the fairy royalty struggled to fly away from a tether around her leg. Even as they looked, they saw a griffin dive at her forcing her low enough for two sorcerers to grab her and bring her back to the ground.

Other fairies tried desperately to get to their queen, as did the remaining harpies, but the griffins fought them away and then some magician threw an enchantment at them that made every being and beast in the area fall out of the sky, temporarily paralyzed. Even as Thom watched, the sorcerers rushed on the fairies and harpies, quickly binding them, and muzzling the harpies' mouths to prevent them from fighting back with any windstorms. They ignored the griffins.

"Where's Vivien?" asked Adele.

Thom looked around and couldn't see her through the smoke and flames, yet he did hear someone crafting an enchantment on the far side of the central platform. The person worked quickly and with confidence that for some reason reminded him of the journeywoman. "She might be over there, crafting a Twist of Air."

"I think you're right," agreed Francis, "but how are we going to get over there to help her? There are at least six sorcerers between us and her."

"Can we also rescue the queen?" asked Adele. Tired as she likely was, she radiated determination and Tho was so proud of her. She was so strong.

"We can try," he said, looking back to where the fairies and harpies had been knocked from the air. They were now all bound and were being led toward two wooden cages that were held four sorcery journeymen. At first, Thom didn't understand why they needed to keep holding the cages, but when one shifted to close the cage door behind their captives, that cage began to float away. Thom then understood that they were built out of Cloud Rowan wood, making them lighter than a feather.

"How will we get to her?" asked Francis. He too was watching the cages. The journeymen walked them to the edge of the platform and then jumped off the edge and both cages floated down to the ground below with the student sorcerers clinging to the carrying arms. "Titania will be even harder to reach than Vivien."

"I don't know how yet, but let's start by getting to Vivien, Kane, and Bronwen. The Lord willing, we can work with them to turn this rout into a rescue."

Francis shook his head but also smiled. "Your faith encourages mine, Thomas. Yes, the Lord willing, this will turn around."

"Can we distract them enough to cross behind them?" asked Adele.

"I think I can do that, if Vivien keeps her enchantment going long enough," said Thomas, quickly pulling out his magician's box, bowl, and pestle. He remembered a fight he and Vivien were in at Haven House while on the Road of Waters, where he sent a Twist of Air into a hail of Fireballs. The explosion had been huge. Something like that should send the sorcerers running and give them a moment to get through.

As soon as he started crafting, Francis protested, "Fireballs into a Twist of Air? That kind of collision could hurt her."

"I know," he said even while he continued. "When I did it, she had to slap me to get me to my senses. I trust Kane or Bronwen will be there to help her recover from any backlash."

"You are making more fire?" asked Adele. "Isn't there enough burning? How are we supposed to get through a wall of flames?"

"Get crafting, my beloved. You are good at magical rainstorms, so make one to soak a way through the firestorm I will be causing."

Thom crafted quickly yet confidently. When done, he coated his hands with sand he found in one of the sorcerer's caches he had taken, and then formed two huge fireballs. He made ready to heft the first one at the whirlwind that Vivien had sent into the sorcerers, taking careful aim. He threw the first one, paused a moment, then threw the second one. He guided them with his mind and hearing, through the smoke and flames, directly at that Twist of Air.

When fire met wind, both enchantments exploded, flattening everything that was on that platform.

Thom was pushed back by the explosion even at this distance, but he was able to keep standing. He looked over at Adele, worried because she was actively crafting, but she had been kneeling and Francis had stood in front of her as a shield. She was fine and finishing off her crafting.

Thom looked at the platform and saw nothing but flames. The sorcerers that had been there were rushing to get away, having no time to craft any enchantments to protect themselves.

FORTY-ONE

Faith among Wreckage

Thom ducked under a low arch and then strode down the ramp toward the blazing platform. Behind him came Francis and Adele, and with her came the storm. She directed the storm to pass him and suddenly it was pouring down on the fires in a tight area directly in front of them. Thom saw that it started as snow, but the intense heat quickly turned it to rain. Yet Adele kept it going and soon the area had no active flames.

Thom walked out onto the still warm wood, avoiding the spots where it seemed to have burned all the way through, but there were not many of those. Adele kept the storm going, clearing a way across the platform, and soon the three of them were on the other side, looking up at a platform where the other magicians were sheltering.

"You three are still alive," proclaimed Kane as he sat with his back to one the small fairy buildings. He was cradling a bloody arm and his face showed griffin claw marks. His attempt at sounding hail was ruined by a coughing fit that sucked the cockiness from his face. "I..." He cleared his throat and started again. "I take it the fireballs came from you. It caused quite the nasty backlash on Vivien."

Thom ignored his mild rebuke as he walked closer. He noticed Vivien laid out next to him and an injured Bronwen laying next to her, propped up on an elbow as she applied a damp rag to the unconscious journeywoman's face. Thom turned back to Kane as he came to stand before him. "They have Queen Titania."

Kane nodded, now having to look up at Thomas. "They also have Leader Celaeno from the harpies. Dalrake sent his lackeys here to stop the league and to capture a fresh batch of element-sources." The ex-sorcerer motioned around them with his good hand. "It looks like they accomplished both for him."

"Not yet, they haven't," argued Thom, feeling a new anger rising inside of him. "We can rescue their captives."

"Who is this *we*?" asked Kane. "No one is left to join you except Adele, and she is a mere apprentice."

"I am here too," stated Francis softly but firmly.

"You are a great teacher, Brother Francis, but she is still an apprentice no matter how much you guide her."

"I am also the Fair Defender," stated the monk. "Thomas, give me those extra caches. I will join you on this hunt of sorcerers."

"You are returning to the craft?" asked Bronwen, speaking for the first time.

Francis took the captured knapsack from Thom and started rummaging through it. He pulled out the magicians' caches and opened each one, quickly reviewing their contents, then stuffing them into his own knapsack. He also took a mixing bowl and a pestle. He dropped the captured pack that now only held whatever stuff Thom had failed to throw out earlier.

As Francis swung his own pack onto his back, he finally replied to Bronwen. "At least for today, I will craft. I'm needed to right these wrongs."

"Go with God, Fair Defender," the Keeper replied. "I know you will craft justly."

"You will need a staff," said Kane, holding out his to Francis.

The monk shook his head. "The guild is coming. You will need that yourself."

Kane smiled. "I hope the fairies succeed in slowing them down, because if they arrive soon, I will not have the strength to do much against them. Take my staff; I will find another somewhere around here."

Francis took it with thanks while Thom told Kane about the two sorcerers he left tied up and where he had hidden their staffs.

Adele came over and knelt over Vivien. "Will she recover soon?"

Thom came and knelt beside her. "I wish I could have spared her the shock, but I couldn't think of any other way to clear out those sorcerers."

Before anyone could say anything else, Vivien moaned. She opened her eyes and looked up at the two of them. "I should have known. Just like you did at Haven House."

Thom smiled. "This time you were the one who crafted the Twist of Air."

Vivien struggled to sit up, flinching at some pain somewhere. She waved off Adele's attempt to help. "I will be fine; I just had the air knocked out of me by this foolish wizard."

Thom raised an eyebrow at his sudden *promotion* by her. She scowled at him, then suddenly winked and gave him the briefest of smiles.

"Well, if you are going to be fine, then we should get going," stated Adele. "Night is approaching and the sorcerers have already fled."

She gave Vivien a careful hug and then stood up.

Thom would have stood up too, but Bronwen grabbed his arm. "You must be careful, Thomas. Dalrake's men are not running away. They go to where his power is greatest. They go to where Dalrake is waiting for you. He was the Founder who crafted the heart of the Road of Clouds and no one knows this Road better than he does. He lures you to where he has the greatest advantage. It is certainly a trap."

Thom nodded as he gently removed her hand from his arm. "I understand, but I have no choice. I will not let him torture and kill those fairies and harpies. I must do all that I can to get them away from him."

"I know you must go, but still, I worry that we will lose you too." Bronwen fiddled with something stuffed behind her dress' belt, drawing out three small pouches. She held them out to him. "You have learned so many of the secrets of the masters that you might as well learn one more. These lead-lined pouches are used to pre-craft enchantments so that we can use them almost instantaneously. You stop just before completion and then store them in a pouch that almost completely shields the elements from detection by others. Each pouch has a small opening through which you can maintain your connection with the almost-finished magic but you will need to practice maintaining that faint link or you will feel the burn of elements going unstable. Not all enchantments can survive the tension of being almost-complete, but we have learned of a handful that can. When you are free of here and have entered the Road of Clouds, take a moment to prepare some of these enchantments to have at hand. The ones that I know will survive being almost-complete are Twist of Air, Hand of Lightning, Fireball, Osric's Blade, Shield of Power, and Wormbore. There are likely more, but those six will endure a pause before you add that last element or final tuning with your spittle. Do you know any of them?"

Thom took the offered pouches and put them behind his own belt, making sure they were snug. He knew three of the six. He had no time to learn the others, so that would have to be enough. "I know half of them," he admitted to her.

"Good. Then go with God's favor and confront Dalrake. Bring him back to face justice if you can, but he must be stopped somehow, no matter what it does to the Roads."

"Is there anything we can do for you before we leave?" he asked, knowing that his leaving would put her and the others in an even worse position.

"No. We will hold out against the guild. I am just thankful that we are not facing both wizards and sorcerers at the same time. For once, we need to put magical beings above humans. Titania and Celaeno are the future leaders of the League of Barnabas, far more so than us. Stop Dalrake and free his captives." She gave him an encouraging smile.

Thom bowed his head in respect to the former Keeper and then stood and followed Adele and Francis away from the ruins of Tuatha Aes Si.

FORTY-TWO

Leaving Cloudholder

They found a rope ladder that wasn't burned and climbed down to the ground. As they were moving away, Rainflower joined them from somewhere. "You go after the queen."

Thom nodded to the fairy hovering in front of them. "And all the others, including the harpies. We also go to stop Dalrake from doing this again."

"Then I will be your Road Guide. It is only fitting that my last service as a guide is to confront the Founder who has brought so much grief on my people."

"What about the defense of the Fairy Court? You will not stay to help?" asked Francis.

"We have no court without our queen. The others who remain will defend our lands as well as they can, but I doubt they will make their stand among the ashes of Tuatha Aes Si. There are stronger places in the realm where they can withstand the wizards."

"I am thankful you are with us," said Adele. "Your eyesight will help us find the quickest way to catch them and might reveal any traps they plan Will you be able to see them even in the dark?"

"We can see in night or storm," replied Rainflower, "but we cannot see through an obscuring enchantment, which is why we could not see through Wizard Osric's enchantment that he set at the archway to slow the sorcerers. Once we reach the edge of the mountain, I will be able to see across the Road of Clouds, but it will be a blurred view because I will be looking through the enchantment. I will see much better once I am on the Road of Clouds myself and not trying to view it from outside."

"Well, please use your great sight now and tell us which way the sorcerers went," said Francis.

"They are approaching the ridgeline directly east of here," said Rainflower, pointing in the direction, "but they are delayed by a clamor of harpies that are harassing them. There are also two of the great eagles circling them and the pixies are raining arrows down on the sorcerers. It looks like the sorcerers are sheltering behind the cages and two of them have pulled out their magician boxes."

Thom suddenly heard the elements exposed, faint at this distance but obvious because he knew that they were doing so. Francis and Adele nodded that they heard it as well.

"Let's get going," he said, setting off at a jaunt that he hoped his ankle could endure. Adele and Francis came right behind him, with Rainflower flying overhead.

* * *

Thom knelt in the snow to check for life, but the harpy was dead. He shook his head as he looked around the battle site. One dead sorcerer and three dead harpies littered the slope. From what Rainflower told them, one of the giant eagles had been injured but was able to glide far enough away to escape a fatal blow. Now only one eagle and two harpies were left, still harassing the sorcerers as they retreated back toward the entrance to the Road of Clouds.

Sunlight had drained from the day and it was starting to snow again. He could barely see the nearest trees on the slope and they were just black shadows in the night, but Rainflower told them that the sorcerers weren't stopping so they didn't either. Thom and the other humans could hear a Shield of Power up ahead, so the sorcerers were defending themselves from any aerial assault.

Keeper Bronwen's ointment for his ankle was more efficacious than Thom realized, because he was able to hike through the night with only a little bit of throbbing and no new weakness. For that he was thankful, as he was for the thick travel robe for the Road of Clouds because it ended up being a very cold night. They didn't stop because they could hear from the magic that the sorcerers kept going.

When dawn lightened the gray sky, they were on the ridge where Osric had made his original stand. Thom thought of that and then remembered that the kind-hearted wizard was now dead. Thom felt sadness that he never had the chance to get to know him. All of this fighting was so wasteful of valuable lives, and it was all because some powerful people insisted that everyone else should submit to them.

As they stood there and tried to see the archway through the morning gloom, they suddenly heard an end to the Shield of Power.

"What is happening down there?" asked Francis of Rainflower.

"They have fled through the archway but two sorcerers linger on the landing, with the magician's boxes at their feet."

"They prepare to attack anyone who might dare follow them onto the Road," noted Thom.

"They have also left five griffins on this side of the archway to guard the entrance."

"Five of them?" asked Thom, remembering how hard it was to battle just one of them.

"My eyesight is not failing, human. Can you not see them prowling the causeway?"

"We will take your word for it, Rainflower," said Francis smoothly, "but how will we get past them? Does anyone have an idea?"

"You might ask the pixie."

Francis gave her a quizzical look.

"The pixie guides his Aeti mount toward us and the harpies follow him.

186

You should be able to see them shortly as they come out of the mists, especially considering the gaudiness of his attire."

Thom smiled. It was good to hear that Dorthos had survived, because it couldn't be anyone else on that eagle.

Soon, there were with two harpies and the pixie standing with them. Dorthos did the introductions, naming the harpies Alcyone and Thisbe.

"There are two sorcerers and two sorceresses," reported Dorthos. "With them are four journeymen who are guiding the two cages. They left five griffins at the archway, chained to keep them from wandering away but with enough slack that there is no way to sneak past them. Another three griffins continue with them onto the Road of Clouds."

"Is it certain that they are heading for the Core?" asked Francis.

"I did not overhear anything concerning their intended destination." Francis turned to the two harpies. "Did either of you?"

The two exchanged a look and then one said, "I heard one say that Dalrake would not be happy with the losses and another replied that at least they were returning with important captives."

"Is there any way for us to bypass the gateway?" asked Thomas, not looking forward to dealing with that many griffins, even if they were chained.

"All of us, except you humans, can fly over and drop into it," stated Rainflower. "Is there a way to get the three of you airborne?"

"The Aeti could carry you, but only one at a time and with a significant break between each. We had a special harness when we rescued Levitanus that allowed two to share his weight, but I do not have that harness here, nor do I have another bird to help carry you."

"Even if we use magic to lift us into the air above the Road, it would be too great a drop for us to survive," stated Francis, "but there might be another way."

He turned around and looked down the valley on the other side of the ridge. "We can use a Cloud Rowan and float in."

Dorthos laughed. "Take one of Dalrake's precious trees and then use it to get to him? I approve of that."

"You would steal a tree?" asked Thom, surprised that Francis would suggest it.

"We will ask Keeper Ellery to borrow it."

"And what if he denies you?" asked Rainflower, sounding cynical.

"We will need to be very persuasive."

"If he will not agree, we can whip winds into his tree farm," suggested one of the harpies. "Those tethers cannot withstand a harpy gale."

"Let us hope he is sensible enough that we needn't resort to that," replied Francis, starting off in their new direction.

For a time, Dorthos walked with them. Thom looked over at the small man he had first met at a tower on the Isle of Mists. He was impressed by the pixie's courage and fortitude, but he also wondered why Dorthos was still here. He had completed his mission of rescuing Levitanus. "May I ask why you are helping?

Is it for revenge on the sorcerers who killed so many of your people?"

Dorthos looked up at him and shook his head. "Vengeance belongs to God, not me. For too long I let anger eat me up my sanity, until they now call me Dorthos the Deranged. No, I am here because the League of Barnabas is worth fighting for. They have captured important leaders of the league and I would see them freed."

"The queen," stated Thom, nodding.

"And Celaeno. Once the harpies have fully embraced the league, I would not be surprised if she ends up on the leadership council. Is that not why you are here too? To see the imprisoned freed?"

"Yes. But I also want to stop Dalrake from killing more."

"How will you stop him? Would you kill to stop a killer?" He paused, and Thom could tell from his hard look that the pixie didn't approve of anyone being a one-man judge and executioner. "I would suggest it would be better to bring him to justice."

"Who would hold one of the Founders to justice?" asked Thom. "The league's leadership council? The king?"

"King Arthur seems a fair man."

Thom had his doubts that Merlin would ever allow his fellow Founder to be tried. The wizard needed Dalrake to maintain his precious Road enchantments and the magical shield over the city. But the pixie was right that they shouldn't be pursuing Dalrake or any of the sorcerers to get revenge. They needed to capture as many of them as they could and then turn them over to the king or the league's leadership council to decide their fate.

"One other thought before I return to the Aeti. I see that you are still fond of Lady Adele, are you not?"

Thom smiled. "Of course I am."

"That is good. Do you know what is my greatest accomplishment in life?"

Thom gave him puzzled look at the rapid shift in topics. "Would that be becoming a prince or an Aeti rider?"

"No, Thomas. My greatest accomplishment was marrying my beloved. There is nothing better than finding the love of your life and then pledging yourself to her."

Thom nodded, even as he remembered it was the loss of that wife that had driven Dorthos insane.

The pixie seemed to know what he was thinking, because he said, "Even with the pain of my love's death, it was worth it. Do not miss your opportunity."

With that, the pixie fell back and called down his great eagle. He mounted and went aloft. Thom continued walking, his eyes on Adele who was ahead of him. He did love her. Very much.

* * *

Thom walked among the trees with awe. He strained his neck as he looked up at them. From below, each tree's roots spread to cover twice the area of the crown. The greenish roots reminded him of a huge bush of grass turned upside down, but had an outer layer that was whitish and thinner. Most of the trees floated well above the ground, but a few had been pulled lower for tending, and walking past those lowered ones he saw that the frilly root-blades were fleshy instead of knobby, and the outer white layer seemed more like a papery-layer reminding him of onion peels if one could slice onion peels into long thin strips. There were ladders leaning on the lowered Cloud Rowans, obviously used by the non-flying helpers- most likely pixies because they were known for their skill with plants.

Francis noticed his interest and remarked, "God's creation is full of wonders. The roots are that way to gather moisture out of the air, much like a normal tree gathers water from the ground. Beyond that, I do not understand how Cloud Rowans thrive; there hasn't been much written about them."

"Where are all the workers?" asked Rainflower. "Usually they are laboring on these lowered trees, pruning and feeding them. They put the trimmings in those stone huts so that they don't float away, but I see no one over there either."

"The residence chimney emits smoke," stated one of the harpies. "We will find someone there."

When Francis informed the pixie that answered the door that they would be borrowing one of the trees, he became agitated and insisted that they could not without the Keeper's permission. Unfortunately, Keeper Ellery was absent, as were his two assistant magicians. Ellery was off doing repair work, which he did often according to the pixie. The two assistants had gone to Camelot in response to a summons from Merlin.

"But the Keeper is not here and time is pressing," argued Francis. "Surely, there is someone else here who helps oversee the tree farm."

"Well, there is Lilandra, but she will never approve anything that might damage her dear trees."

"May we talk to Lilandra?"

The pixie assistant complained about not wanting to bother the other pixie and Thomas got the impression that he was intimidated by the female. Eventually, he went to find her, shutting the door on them and leaving them out on the porch.

While they waited, the harpies flew off to consider how best they could blow a Cloud Rowan over the Road. Dorthos brought the Aeti to a landing near the residence, but he remained on the huge bird.

Finally, the door reopened and an elderly but muscular pixie woman confronted them. Thom realized that her face tattoos were the same red color as Dorthos', which meant she was of the Clan Brythoni. "Who are you people and what is this babble about taking one of my trees?"

"On behalf of Queen Titania and the League of Barnabas, we ask to borrow one of your trees to allow us quick entry to the Road," stated Francis.

"This valley is not part of the queen's realm," she replied bluntly, "and I am furious with their kind after all my fairy workers fled two days ago. I am already short four pixies who are busy rooting the new trees at the Core. I need the rest of my people here, not gallivanting about on some whim of their queen. How am I to get my trees properly topped without fairy workers? Answer me that." She glared at Rainflower, who was hovering nearby.

"As for this league you speak of, I have never heard of it. You trespass here. Begone!"

"I would ask you to reconsider," shouted Dorthos from his mount. He was not angry; he just raised his voice to be heard over the distance.

She looked over, apparently not having notice the Aeti or its riders before then. Her mouth fell agape. "Prince Dorthos? You have mounted the Aeti. We are at war?"

"The Aeti riders mounted not for war, but to rescue Founder Levitanus from his imprisonment by Dalrake. This borrowing of one of your trees is needed to get these magicians onto the Road so that they can rescue others that the sorcerers have unjustly captured. Please allow us to use a Cloud Rowan to reach the Road because the archway has been blocked by fierce griffins."

She paused for a long moment, then nodded. "Let me help you find the best one to ride. If you pick one that is too young, it might splinter during flight."

* * *

An hour later Thomas was sitting on a tree limb as the Cloud Rowan soared over the Keeper's residence. Adele and Francis sat on other limbs around the tree, each of them carrying a handsaw. Lilandra had given a quick lesson on how to prune branches to help lower the tree without causing any lasting damage. There were three tethers wound around the trunk so that they could unroll them and use them to anchor the tree when they were done. His staff and Francis' staff were bound to the trunk below them, the wound tethers serving to keep them secure.

The harpies had provided the wind to get the tree moving in the right direction, while Rainflower spied out the best place to drop onto one of the Road's paths. She had to make sure it was a path going in the right direction and aimed toward the Core.

Thom had hoped they might be able to catch the sorcerers while they were still on the Road, but he soon realized that there was no way a floating tree could ever be as fast as a magical path that sped its walkers across the sky. The view from up here was spectacular as the clouds broke up enough to let the morning sun light the sky. He looked back over his shoulder at Cloudholder Mountain. It was still cloud-enshrouded, the sunlight lost to grayness. Even though they were moving into more sunlight, it still felt like they were heading into a darker place.

FORTY-THREE

Return to the Road

Riding a floating tree was quite an experience for Thomas. The only sound was the rustling of the leaves as the harpies kept up their wind to direct its flight. They rose above the pathways of the Road of Clouds, although the enchantment made it hard to see the Road from outside of the magic. Once they reached their desired altitude, they carefully sawed off a set of branches, letting off enough foliage to stop their ascent. It still seemed so odd to Thom that the cuttings didn't drop to the ground far below, but instead floated off into the heavens.

Rainflower perched on one of the air roots and studied the Road of Clouds to find the best place for them to set down. She would decide where they needed to go and give those directions to Adele, who would then yell them out to the harpies. Both the fairy and the harpies seemed to prefer having the human intermediary.

"Will we be able to get ahead of the sorcerers?" asked Thom of Francis. He would rather rescue the fairies and harpies before having to face Dalrake.

"No, we will be behind them. You forget that the Road of Clouds is always in motion. The enchantment speeds their steps so that they are well ahead of us now, and the longer we take to get onto the Road ourselves the farther ahead they will get."

* * *

Thom stood on the icy platform as he checked the tautness of a tether. All the times he had sat on the benches outside of wayrests, he had never noticed the tethering rings at the bottom of each bench. They had brought the Cloud Rowan down into the Road of Clouds right next to a wayrest and were now securing it. Thom had been the only one to get off to do the securing and he'd been replaced by Dorthos' Aeti, which was now perched on top of the tree to add weight. In addition, the harpies were blowing wind down on the tree to keep it from floating off. The great eagle didn't seem to mind the wind blowing on it and the tree, but Dorthos didn't seemed too pleased. Francis wanted it done this way rather than cutting off more branches to force the tree down, but he didn't explain his reasons for wanting to maintain its buoyancy.

Once Thom had the lines secure, he waved off the harpies and watched as the tree strained against the lines, but the restraints held. Satisfied, he yelled for the others to come down. They had to use the tether lines to shimmy down, since there were no ladders here, but soon Adele, Francis, and Dorthos joined him. Rainflower and the harpies also glided down to the landing. The great eagle was content to roost on top of the tree, which was for the best.

"So now we go on by foot," stated Thom.

"No, now we go into the wayrest and sleep for a bit," replied Francis. "We have been up for almost two days straight. We need rest or we will make too many mistakes and could fail at our tasks."

"But the sorcerers will get far ahead of us."

"Rainflower reported that they too have gone into a wayrest."

"Then this would be our chance to catch up with them."

Francis shook his head. "They are on a different pathway. If we ran now, maybe we could get to Dalrake before they do, but that would just put them at our back. We need at least a few hours rest."

Adele came up and took his hand. "He's right. We need to rest, my beloved Thom. We need to be alert when we face Dalrake again. This time I do not want him escaping like he did on the Road of Waters and in Camelot. He needs to be stopped or else the killings and corruption will only get worse."

Thom looked into her blue eyes and nodded. He trusted that both of them knew best, even if he wanted to keep going. "Let's get inside then and out of this cold. Who will take first watch?"

"I will take watch," said Rainflower.

"And I will join her," said one of the harpies, "because two are better than one."

That settled, everyone else entered the Wayrest. Dorthos laughed as he entered, "Wen I saw the tree farm of young Cloud Rowans I was impressed, but when you see these trees up close and in full growth in awe inspiring. I am intrigued by them… such an intricate root system and look how the foliage gathers the air's moisture and then brings it down to form these pools."

And with that, the pixie wandered off as well.

The harpy Thisbe wasn't impressed by any of it. She simply flew to the nearest stout branch and roosted there, soon burying her face into a wing.

That left the three humans to themselves. They found some grass bunks freshly grazed and then realized that there was a pegasus in here as well, still grazing in a back corner of the Wayrest. They left the winged horse alone as they settled down for a quick meal and then some much-needed sleep.

Adele ate and was soon asleep. Thom ate and settled on his grass bunk but couldn't fall asleep immediately. Instead, he propped up his head with his elbow and took a moment just to gaze at her.

"She loves you as much as you do her."

Thom turned to see Francis watching him with a smile.

"She is now a lady, while I'm still just a journeyman magician."

"Do you think she will let a newly-won title come between the two of you? You should know her better than that."

Thom looked back at her sleeping form. "It would be selfish of me to ask her to give up being one of Queen Guinevere's attendant ladies for me. I don't even have the right to call myself a journeyman; the guild will banish me soon, if it hasn't already."

"You have a new home among the League of Barnabas, as does Adele. Now get some sleep; you need it, especially since you and Dorthos are taking the second shift at watch."

"As do you," stated Thom as he laid down.

"I will, but first I want to spend some time in prayer. Good night, Thomas."

"Good night, Francis."

* * *

Thom yawned as he wrapped his hands around a mug of hot cider. It was near the end of Thom and Dorthos' turn at watch and the day was already lightening around them into a cloudy dawn. Francis was up early to prepare food for all of them and had come out with two mugs just a few minutes ago. Now that Francis had embraced magic again, he was using it for practical things like warming food with magic.

His turn on watch had been uneventful. He and Dorthos had kept moving because it was too cold to just sit, and they had talked some. Mainly, the pixie talked while he listened. Dorthos shared about his younger years and when he first met the female pixie he eventually married. As Thom listened, he thought of Adele and how wonderful it would be to marry her.

"So when will you marry her?" asked Dorthos suddenly. "If you wait too long you may lose your chance at true love."

"What do you mean?"

"These are troubling times, Thomas. You will face dangers not just today, but for many days or even years to come. Do not wait until all is calm before you promise yourself to her, because days of peace may be many years away. She deserves your pledge soon, if not today. She deserves to know that you are committed to her."

"But Adele already knows my devotion to her," he protested.

Dorthos gave him a sad smile. "I am talking about more than hand-holding and passionate kisses and whispered affections. Does she not deserve your vow to marry her?"

"A betrothal?" He had not thought of making such a formal pledge. Neither of them had family or a home parish where such betrothals are usually done.

"I believe that is what you humans call it. Among us pixies, we announce our intentions before our tribes' elders and even add the pledge to our facial tattoos." He indicated an intricate circle tattooed on his left cheek. "On the day of our pledge, half the circle is done, with the other half completed when the pledge is fulfilled."

Thom's eyes went to the red ink on his cheek. Over time he had grown so used to Dorthos' Brythoni clan tattoos that he hardly noticed them, but now he looked again, realizing that they were a story announced on the body for all to read.

"We humans often pledge with rings," replied Thom, wondering where he would get the money to make such a purchase, since his money was mostly hidden in Clas Myrddin and it was doubtful he could ever get back inside the guild house. Even if he had the money, where would he find a ring maker?

"Do not get caught up in objects and symbols," said Dorthos, almost as if he knew Thom's thoughts. "More important were my words than my tattoo. Pledge yourself to her, Thomas."

Thom realized the mad pixie was talking sense. "I will."

"Now?"

"Why not? Let me go talk with her and see what she thinks."

FORTY-FOUR

Love Expressed

Thom passed through the gray shimmer of the gateway to enter the wayrest that was part of the Road yet not part of it. He looked around and saw Adele sitting next to where Francis was cooking a morning porridge. His heart was racing as he walked over. He was so focused on her that he actually tripped on one of the thousands of gnarled roots, staggering forward but fortunately not falling. He quickly recovered, embarrassed.

She looked up and gave him a sweet smile. "Good morning. Is all well outside?"

"Uh… yes, it is… it's a good morning and also it's fine outside." He felt his face redden as he stumbled to answer. "Cloudy… but fine."

"Good. Sneaking up on the Core and rescuing the others is going to be hard enough without having to push through another storm."

"Thomas! Good morning to you. Are you ready for some breakfast?" Francis held out a bowl of steaming porridge.

Thom took the bowl, muttering his thanks, and sat next to Adele. He realized now that she had a half-empty bowl in her lap. He was too nervous to eat, but he still lifted a spoonful toward his lips and blew on it, not knowing was else to do.

"That smells wonderful," announced Dorthos. He had followed Thom inside. "May I have a pixie-sized serving, Brother Francis?"

The monk gave a smaller helping and Dorthos started eating it while standing next to Francis' magical fire that made no smoke and caused no harm to the roots that were the floor in here.

Frustrated with now having an audience, Thom looked at the pixie with a pleadingly.

Dorthos grinned and winked. "Brother Francis, have you seen to flowering on the far side of the tree? While most rowans are not as flamboyant in their blooms, I really appreciate how the Cloud Rowans show off their colors. I noticed this cluster last night before going to sleep. Come, let me show you."

As the monk and pixie went to inspect the tree blooms, Thom took a deep breath and prepared to ask Adele about becoming betrothed. He set the untouched bowl of mush aside and turned toward her, but then he saw Rainflower fluttering towards them.

He tried to wave the fairy off, but then Adele looked up and he turned his hand motion into a brushing of his hair.

"Is something bothering you?" asked Adele, giving him a concerned look.

"No. I'm fine. Everything's fine... I... I... um..."

"What are you babbling about?" asked Rainflower as she hovered over the two of them. "Is there something happening outside?"

"No, nothing is happening outside. Dorthos says that the Aeti is calm, which means there is no danger or strangers nearby and I hear no magic besides the Road itself."

"Then why are you stuttering? I could smell your nervousness from across the wayrest. Most talk about our fairy gift of great eyesight, but our sense of smell is also far greater than you mere humans and I can smell your fear and worry."

Thom gritted his teeth to keep from yelling, thinking furiously how he could get the fairy away. "Maybe I am a little worried about what is out there. Could you go and take a look for me? Maybe you can spot trouble that I could not hear."

"I will gladly do so if it will sooth your fears." The fairy fluttered off to the shimmering gate and passed through.

"You don't smell any different to me," said Adele. "Maybe a bit ripe, but we all are in need of baths after so many days of hiking across sky and mountain."

Great! He stank. This was not turning out to be very romantic, but he pressed forward nonetheless. He had to, because there was no guarantee that both of them would live through this coming day. "Adele, there is something I've been wanting to talk to you about."

"Yes?" She looked at him intently and he almost lost his courage.

He swallowed, trying to clear his throat, then just blurted it out. "Would you become my betrothed?"

Adele laughed, and at first he thought it a laugh of mockery, but she instead threw herself around his neck. "Of course I will, my beloved Thomas. When we are through with all of this we will do a formal betrothal pledge."

He hugged her back fiercely, but then pulled back enough to see her face. "No. I want to do this now. We have no promise of our troubles ever ending or a time of peace arriving. We should pledge now to marry. I understand waiting for a better time for our actual wedding vows, but our betrothal shouldn't wait any longer. What do you say?"

"Here? Now? Who could witness our betrothal?"

"Francis can oversee it and we will have a pixie, a fairy, and two harpies as additional witnesses."

* * *

It was a hurried ceremony, but the others were agreeable to the slight delay for something so joyous. Francis guided them through what such a pledge entailed, telling them what couples often swore. It wasn't a usual ceremony because they weren't in a church before a priest. Instead, they were speaking before a monk while standing on trees hanging in the air.

Francis explained the importance and solemnity of such a pledge, but also shared how it was a joyous moment too. He shared what should be in their pledges, including a formal title for each of them. Thomas chose to identify with his craft rather than with his birthplace since he hadn't been back there in so many years, so he would go by Journeyman Thomas rather than Thomas of York. Beyond that, the pledges were to be short but specific, heartfelt and also respectful before their Lord. Adele would be addressed as a lady, since she now had such a title by decree of the king.

Thom and Adele had no fancy garments but each wore a flowery wreath hastily woven by Rainflower. The harpies sang a beautiful song, which was completely unexpected.

Francis began the ceremony. "I have grown to love the two of you, and my heart overflows with joy at seeing you taking this pledge. I am no priest, just a simple brother of the Benedictine Order, but I am honored to serve as your guide through this ceremony of promising to marry one another."

He motioned for them to face each other and to take each other's hands. "Marriage is a commitment before God to a life spent together and it should be entered into with careful consideration. That the two of you are willing to start with a betrothal to get married shows your commitment to one another. We will keep this a simple ceremony, so I will just ask the two of you to make your pledge to marry before God and the rest of us. We will leave the extra flourishes and polished words for the day of your wedding, may that be a better day when there is peace and time to truly celebrate." Then he nodded for the two of them to begin.

Thom spoke first, repeating some of what Francis had suggested but saying it all from his heart. "Today I, Journeyman Thomas, swear before God and these witnesses that I will one day take you, Lady Adele, as my wife. I love you and will remain faithful and loyal to you until that day of our marriage and for the rest of our lives together. I pledge this to you, my beloved Adele."

Then she spoke. "Today I, Lady Adele, pledge before God and these witnesses that I will one day take you, Journeyman Thomas, as my beloved husband. I bind myself to you, in faithfulness and trust that God has brought us together and that His Spirit will guide us in our life together. I pledge this to you, my dear Thomas."

Francis smiled at both of them. "With your shared pledge of troth, we recognize that Journeyman Thomas and Lady Adele are now betrothed to marry. May God bless their coming marriage with joy, peace, and love."

And with that, their brief ceremony was done and it was time to face the dangers of the day.

FORTY-FIVE

Center of the Road

As they gathered outside the wayrest, Thom had a question for Dorthos. "What will happen today? Do you think we can get the prisoners away from the sorcerers?"

Dorthos shrugged. "My companions and I were able to get Founder Levitanus out of Dalrake's keep, so anything is possible."

Thom looked out from the icy platform at the clouds flowing past. "When you rescued me from the courtyard at Clas Myrddin, did you ever imagine the two of us would end up standing among the clouds?"

"We have traveled far and seen many sights," agreed Dorthos.

Thom agreed, taking a moment to look at Adele who was talking with the harpies. Becoming betrothed to her was also something unexpected, and it was so wonderful.

Francis walked over and put a hand on his shoulder to break his happy stare. "We need to prepare."

He agreed, and they called over Adele, because she was the only other magician among them.

Thomas and Francis filled the pouches that Bronwen provided, but Adele waved off the offer to have one because she doubted she had the discipline to keep an enchantment at the cusp of completion. Francis filled his with an almost-complete enchantment of Hands of Lightning, while Thom filled the remaining two with Fireballs and Hands of Lightning. Thom put them inside his travel robe, putting them in pockets in the lining that seemed made to holding such pouches.

Once done, they all set off.

* * *

The approach to the Road's Core Crossing was surprisingly unobstructed and apparently unobserved. Rainflower confirmed that there were no fairies with the sorcerers besides those in the floating cages and none of the sorcerers sent out an Eagle's Spying, so none of them seemed concerned about being followed.

Francis took charge of their traveling enchantments, covering their boots with far more Sole Flight and adding extra power to that enchantment with the use of his staff. Although he warned Thom and Adele that their steps would be turning into huge leaps that would be harder to stop, they still almost overstepped the icy way. It was a far more awkward lope across the clouds that called for constant attention, but they moved at three times as fast as before. Their flying companions had to strain to keep up.

The question was, how close could they get without being noticed? The Core was not separated from the Road's pathways, so magic could be heard. How long would it take before Dalrake and his followers noticed other magic being used? Thom asked that of Francis during one of the pauses they took to recenter their leaps.

"We will keep this up for another hour," the monk answered. "It is a risk, but we need to get there before they start killing and rendering their captives. Once closer, we will wipe our boots partially to lessen the sound and then I will add a shield to cloak us and our magic. Keeping so many enchantments going will keep me busy, so when we get to the Core, I want you and the harpies to sneak up on the cages and release them, hopefully without the sorcerers noticing."

"Will you be concealing us?"

"For as long as I can, but I think Adele and I need to be away from you. It will be best for us to be able to attack from multiple directions once we're discovered."

Thom agreed with him, though he wished their plans were more detailed.

* * *

They were able to get much closer than Francis expected, due to the excessive amount of magic being used at the Core. There was so much of it that they even heard it around Francis' shield because the sound echoed through the Road's walls and floor. Whatever they were doing, it caused the Road to shiver a few times and even caused a sudden drop that sent all three of them airborne for a moment. In that moment, Thom overheard familiar sounds from up ahead, even while he fought to keep his balance.

"What is happening?" asked Adele as she regained her footing on the ice.

Francis repositioned his magical shield to keep them hidden. "It is something to do with the trees again."

"Have more been destroyed?" asked Thom.

"I don't think so," Francis replied, then motioned for Rainflower to come closer from where she flew above them. "Can you see what they are doing with the trees up ahead?"

"The Keeper has planted replacements for the ones destroyed by the dragon," she replied. "It looks like he and his pixie helpers are finishing up the lacing of the air roots into the ice of the platform. Such work takes time or else the trees will not thrive. Whenever a tree is replaced, it causes ripples through the Road."

"That explains why he wasn't at his residence," noted Francis. "We should have pressed that pixie woman for the information before we left, but at the time I was just glad to have gotten permission to borrow a Cloud Rowan.

"Rainflower, where will this pathway bring us onto the Core? Will it be near the new trees or close to the captives?"

"This pathway comes out on the west side of the Core. The damaged trees were on the south side. Everyone is at that end, including the captives. The pixies are around the new trees. Keeper Ellery stands back from them, next to the large weighted bundles of deadwood, where he oversees their work. The sorcerers and their journeymen gather beyond them but still near the replants, with the cages in their midst. In the clearing there are three griffins huddling together for warmth and a giant roc that is three times the size of an aeti."

"Where is Founder Dalrake?"

"I am uncertain at this exact moment, but he was with the others recently. I have seen glimpses of him, but the roc is between us and the sorcerers' camp, so my view of them is limited. I can see the Keeper's group better, for the deadwood bundle isn't too tall and the griffins are easier to see past. The two parties are definitely staying separate."

"Will Keeper Ellery side with Dalrake?" asked Thom, knowing that keepers were strong magicians.

Francis replied. "I'm not certain. He isn't part of the league, that much I do know. He has been a keeper longer than any of the other five, having been in charge of Leaves and then Waters, before coming to Clouds when it was finished. He has allowed all to travel the Clouds, whether wizard or sorcerer."

"Someone allowed them to build those cages out of Cloud Rowan wood," noted Adele. "He either approved it or chose to ignore what the sorcerers were doing. Either way, he is not trustworthy."

Francis nodded agreement with her assessment, but said, "We still need to go to the Core, whether Keeper Ellery will help or harm us. We could wait, but the longer we linger on a pathway, the likelier it is that they will find us and we have no room to avoid their attacks here, no trees to hide behind, and no way to spread out. Instead, we will use his activities as a distraction for us. Come, we need to get onto the Core while he and his workers are still doing their replanting."

"I heard open caches ahead during that moment when your shield slipped," said Thomas to Francis. "I think three, but it was such a brief moment that your shield was disrupted and it's hard to pinpoint where they are located when all the sound is funneled along the Road's path."

"Rainflower, do you see any open magician caches?" asked Francis.

The fairy flew higher, but she couldn't fly very far to either side due to the limits of the Road's enchantment. The harpies stood on the ice nearby and watched her without comment, while Dorthos on the aeti circled far overhead in a tight, oblong that kept the bird within the Road's enchantment. The fairy went up almost as high as the great eagle, then came back down to report. She only saw one cache for certain, and that one was at the feet of Keeper Ellery.

"That was to be expected," noted Francis, "because Cloud Rowans do not normally spread their roots into ice like they do here at the Core. Ellery had to set certain enchantments to encourage such growth. I am more worried about any other caches that are open. I think that they are expecting some kind of rescue attempt and that they are using the caged captives as bait to lure more of us in. If they had other intentions, they would have carried them on to Dalrake's keep or would have begun the slaughter and rendering already."

"But still we go on," said Thomas.

"Of course," replied the monk. "I will hold the shield until we enter the Core, then we will need to use the trees for cover. Adele and I will move toward the new trees and that pile of deadwood, using it all to shield us from attack for as long as we can. In the meantime, you sneak in the other direction with Rainflower and get to those cages."

Thom didn't like the thought of separating from Adele, but saw the reason. She and Francis would try to keep the sorcerers' attention so that he could get to the cages. "What about the harpies and Dorthos?"

Francis looked back at the harpies standing on the ice behind them. "I ask that the two of you do whatever you can to distract the roc and the griffins to keep them off of us. But be cautious around the sorcerers, for they have enchantments that can knock you out of the air."

"We will fight with breath and claw and voice," replied Thisbe.

"We will fight to victory," added Alcyone.

Then Francis made exaggerated hand gestures to a still-flying Dorthos, apparently telling him the same thing in pixie hand speech. Once satisfied that the pixie understood, he motioned them all to move on.

FORTY-SIX

Unseen Lightning

They entered the Core without anyone raising a cry against them, and then they separated.

Thomas carefully yet quickly dodged from tree to tree around the north side of the huge ice landing. He kept his element cache stored, and instead pulled his knife as he ran. He also had his sword as a weapon; he meant to keep to a mundane defense for as long as he could. By quick count, there were nine trees between their entry path and the cages, so the sorcerers' camp was almost halfway around the Core. He kept count. Eight more trees. Seven more.

Rainflower flittered along one tree ahead of him. She had the advantage despite her brighter colors, because she was able to fly among and behind the tree canopies, keeping as much foliage as possible between her and the sorcerers' camp, while Thom had to hurry across the exposed gaps between the tree trunks. Six more.

As he hurried, Thom watched with his eyes and with his inner ears. There were definitely two more open caches out there somewhere, their elements making quite a bit of noise. One was near the cages, but the other one was harder for Thom to place. He heard it, but it was more like an echo of it coming from different directions. He had no time to figure out what that meant, though, because he saw that the roc was stirring and one of the griffins had launched into the air.

"God, please protect Adele and the others," he whispered as he ran to get behind another tree trunk. Five left. Four gaps crossed and so far no one seemed to have noticed him.

He heard fireballs being crafted in the sorcerers' camp, but so far Ellery hadn't joined in. Instead, it sounded like he had grabbed his cache and moved closer to the deadwood for shelter while still leaving the cache open and ready.

The harpies were obviously stirring trouble because, even at this distance, he could feel a stiff breeze and hear their cries.

Thom was breathing heavier now as he pressed against the cold bark of a Cloud Rowan. He was thankful that his ankle was holding up. He heard the sorcerer who made the fireballs throw them, and it wasn't toward him. Francis responded almost instantly, obviously having pulled his almost-complete enchantment out of the holding pouch from Keeper Bronwen, activating it and throwing it.

Suddenly the shadows sharpened around Thomas and he realized there was a bonfire to the south of him. Either Francis or the sorcerer had hit the deadwood pile and ignited it.

More caches opened everywhere, as sorcerers and some of their journeymen started crafting. Thom also heard two others crafting apart from them and guessed it to be Francis and Adele.

The roc screamed at the sudden light and heat and it lumbered backwards, toward Thom, but he had no time to watch what it would do. Instead, he used the distractions to run past the next tree and on to the one beyond that. Four. Three.

He still heard one other cache and that person was also crafting, but he still couldn't locate where they were. They were crafting Hands of Lightning. It seemed closer, but not. It was like he was hearing the echo of magic.

Rainflower was still a tree ahead of him. She caught his attention and pointed forward and showed three fingers on her dainty hand, so apparently one of the four journeymen was either away from the cages or was down.

At that moment, the roc roared and leaped into the air as one of the harpies blew hard against it. Rainflower was buffeted by the sudden wind and leaves filled the air as they were ripped from the trees.

Whoever was crafting Hands of Lightning finished, but Thom saw no one with lightning arcing between their fingers. He heard it, but it was muted...

Suddenly he noticed that the blown leaves were disappearing in front of him. It was like they were going behind a screen... a shield...

Thom's eyes widened as he threw himself to the side even as he yelled out warning to Rainflower.

In front of him a Shield of Sight and Sound dissipated and there stood three sorcerers, one of whom threw lightning at Thom.

He hit the ground hard and then fast crawled toward the nearest tree even as he felt the lightning gouge into the snow-covered ice only an arm's length away. He kept moving, scrambling to his hands and knees and then throwing himself behind the trunk.

He heard Rainflower scream and he peeked around the tree to see her ablaze in the sky and then plummeting to the ground. He swallowed the urge to gag at her unfair death.

Lightning hit the trunk even as he quickly ducked behind it, and he realized that the one magician in the middle who hadn't been crafting was Dalrake. The Founder had anticipated his attempt to rescue the captives and had set a trap for him.

Thom still had his knife in hand, but what was that against lightning? His other hand was already full with the smooth wood of the staff, so he fumbled with his travel robe to get inside and sheath his blade. As he did his hand brushed one of the prepared pouches of magic and the elements responded. He had forgotten that he had some almost-ready magic. He dared not try to craft anything now because they would have time to rush him as he worked, but those two enchantments nagging in the back of his head were almost ready. Was it time to use what he had prepared? Which enchantment?

He carefully got back to his feet, hugging the tree in front of him and keeping it between him and the nearest sorcerers. What now? How was he going to get to the captives by using one of the enchantments he had ready?

From behind him the roc had taken off, but he heard the griffins and harpies battling and the harpy winds were whipping Thom's hair and clothes. There was so much burning that it was casting his shadow on the tree trunk he was hugging. He was tempted to turn around to see what was happening, but he needed to keep focused on the enemy that was closest.

He could hear the nearby sorcerer that still held a hand-full of lightning and he was coming closer. One of the other sorcerers had started crafting a new enchantment of Fireballs. He wondered if that was Dalrake crafting or if the Founder was still holding back.

Thom realized that if he didn't move soon, they would surround him and kill him. He reached inside his travel robe again and pulled out one of the pouches. It was time for him to fight back.

FORTY-SEVEN

Floating Fire

Thomas squatted over the pouch, setting his staff on the ground so that he could have both hands free. He rubbed both hands with snow that he scooped from the ground. It wasn't as good of a protection as a sand coating, but it was all that was available without taking the time to dig out his cache, and there was no time for that.

The sorcerer with lightning was almost on him and the other one crafting fireballs was nearly done. He needed to act now.

With both snow-covered hands, he opened the small bag and reached inside to embrace the almost-complete crafting of Fireballs. He spat into the elements to attune it to himself and then moved it quickly away from his face as the heat and brightness shown through the opening.

He realized he had sequenced this wrong, but it was too late; he should have pulled the paste out first before completing the enchantment. The bag's outer cloth caught fire even as he pulled his hands free. It fell to the ground, a charred mess.

In each hand he held a large fireball and his hands were blistering from the heat.

Screaming in agony and defiance, Thom ran from behind the tree and threw the fireballs in quick succession, one at the sorcerer with lightning and one toward where he heard the other enchantment. He threw and then dove to the ground, sticking his stinging hands into the snow to alleviate the burning.

Looking over, he saw his first fireball hit the extended hand of the lightning bearer. The two enchantments clashed and then exploded in the face of the sorcerer, throwing him back as he screamed. The other fireball was heading toward the sorcerer who had just thrown a fireball back at him, but between them stood Dalrake. The Founder reacted to the fireballs flying from both directions by releasing an enchantment he had prepared beforehand, and suddenly a Shield of Power surrounded him. The dome of magic sheltered the great sorcerer, sloughing off and deflecting both fireballs upward, sending a shower of sparks and flames into the tree branches overhead.

Thom realized he was still in danger and scrambled to his feet. Desperate, he ran back for his staff, grabbing it with a reddened and painful hand. As he looked around, he realized the clearing was full of floating wood that was ablaze. The deadwood pile had caught on fire and burned through its bindings, so now the wood filled the air, some floating up into the sky while others lingered just above the snow. All of it was drifting toward the north end of the Core because of the winds the harpies had started. Floating fire and it was heading right at him!

There was smoke and fire everywhere. Behind and above him, he could feel the heat from the trees starting to burn overhead. He looked toward where the prisoners were being held, but he saw nothing in that direction except more smoke and flames. He could hear that Dalrake still held the Shield of Power. Of the two other sorcerers, the one was doing nothing magical while the other was crafting again and it sounded like Hands of Lightning.

Thom knew that this was his chance to get to the cages, so he started running. He made it only halfway to the next tree.

As he ran, he heard a powerful enchantment released. It was a Deluge far greater than the ones Adele had used at the Fairy Court, and Thom was fairly certain that it had been crafted by Keeper Ellery. That made sense, since the Keeper would want to protect the precious Cloud Rowans that were the heart of the Road.

Even as he ran, Thom could hear the great downpour of water hitting what was left of the deadwood piles and a burning tree. He also heard the magic moving rapidly toward him as it chased all the burning wood floating over the Core. Maybe the sudden storm would hide his approach to the cages, but it sounded more like a waterfall than a rain fall and he feared it might just flatten him rather than just mask his steps.

He kept running. The cages were just three more trees away, but they could easily have been a half-a-kingdom away for all that he could get there.

To his left, Dalrake lifted his shield to create a gap to shoulder height. He probably kept it in place over his head to protect him from any falling flames. The Founder suddenly brought out another enchantment, one almost finished. Thom heard the magic and felt new fear as he realized it was something he had never faced, something to do with wind and ice.

He ran as fast as he could, wanting to get a tree between him and Dalrake, but the distance was too great. An ice storm roared at him even as a deluge of water was bearing down on that end of the Core. Realizing it was too late to find refuge, he desperately threw himself to the ground and rolled up in a ball, with his back toward the oncoming ice storm.

Shards of ice sliced into him like hundreds of knives, cutting into his knapsack and through his thick travel robe. They kept coming, slicing through his clothes and into his back and hands that covered his head.

He yelled in agony, unable to do anything to stop the onslaught.

But where he could do nothing to stop the magic, the Deluge from Ellery washed over him and the two enchantments clashed, caused a terrible lightning storm all around him. The flying ice was replaced by the thunder of water that knocked him flat.

When the downpour finally passed, Thom struggled to his hand and knees. There was blood dripping off his hands and shoulders where the ice had pierced him. Judging by the pain, he probably another half-dozen such wounds across his back. He could also hear the unmistakable sounds of elements coming from his shredded knapsack, which meant an ice shard had penetrated his magician's box and broken some of the vials.

He lifted his bruised face and looked to where Dalrake was. The Founder was still standing and dry as can be, his Shield of Power having kept him safe. As Thom watched, the sorcerer had the dome lift again so that there was an air gap around him. Instead of another attack, he yelled out some kind of whistled call that was answered from far overhead.

Thom gulped as he looked skyward to see the roc returning, diving directly toward him.

"No!" he yelled. He couldn't die now. He was so close to getting them freed. Dalrake wasn't stopped yet.

Thom took his staff in both hands and jammed it into the snow-covered ice in front of him and lit it brighter than he ever had.

The light exploded out from the green gem, lighting like a tiny sun. The whole staff lit up and then the ice that made up the base of the Core started shining too. All of it shone so bright that Thom closed his eyes against the glare.

The roc screamed at the hurtful glare but it was in the middle of a dive and couldn't stop. A roc is just too huge to suddenly change course. It dropped on top of Thom and its talon came over him, his planted staff driving into the bird's foot and exploding inside.

The roc's scream turned into an angry screech and it yanked its talon away as the rest of the bird hit the ground hard.

Thom was thrown back by the shattered staff, pieces of wood piercing his arm as he tried to cover against it. He bounced off the feathery breast of the giant bird and landed with a thud and then everything blacked out.

FORTY-EIGHT

Captured

"Polin, is he still alive?"

"He breathes. I had to staunch the blood flow from his arm wounds. I couldn't get out all the staff wood, but the worst is pulled and he will not die too soon."

Thom heard the words but it took a moment to realize that they were talking about him.

"Then get him up and take him with us. That is Levitanus' whelp. If anyone knows where my fellow Founder hides, it will be him."

Someone poked him in his side. He knew he should be reacting, trying to get away, but he had no strength left.

"Stand up," ordered Sorcerer Polin, poking him again.

Thom groaned and opened his eyes. The sorcerer who tried throwing fireballs at him was standing there. He tried to bat the man's foot away but failed.

The man kicked him this time, causing Thom to grunt.

"Get up now!"

He followed the kick with a swing from his staff.

Standing nearby and watching without emotion was Dalrake.

So close. So vulnerable.

Thom remembered the almost-finished enchantment in a pouch and was surprised that his mind had somehow maintained a link to it. The magic was still there and ready to use. If he could just get it out…

Another kick and stick whack. "Move."

Thom struggled to his hands and knees. He was about the reach for the pouch when he remembered what he needed to complete the enchantment. He need not just his spit, but also his staff… his staff!

He looked around and saw pieces of it everywhere, except for the end that was jammed into the roc's foot. The bird sat nearby, glaring at him.

"Your staff is in splinters," stated Dalrake, seemingly aware of what he was looking for, "and your shattered magician's cache is leaking its contents into your knapsack. You are done, whelp."

That explained the jumble of element sounds that filled Thom's inner ear.

Polin forced Thom to stand and then brought his hands behind his back and tied them together. Thom submitted to the manhandling because he had no choice. His thoughts were too jumbled to think of any way to escape or fight back.

Dalrake seemed to be waiting for Thom to respond to him, but Thom said nothing and that seemed to anger him.

"And where is your precious Levitanus? He is no leader, but a coward. First, he faked his own death and now he has fled and abandoned all the work to you. I am here with my followers, but where is he? Run off to his backwoods cottage, most likely. How can you serve a man like that?"

At that moment, Thom realized a truth that had been troubling him since the Road of Waters. He was no longer Levitanus' disciple, even should they ever be reunited as teacher and student. There was much he could still learn from his old master, but he was now being called to serve something larger than a mere human. Nor was he called to devote himself to something as selfish as the guild or the nebulous pact of sorcerers. His calling was to serve humanity through the League of Barnabas. "I do not serve Levitanus, but we both serve another."

Dalrake laughed. "Who is that? Merlin? He's far weaker than I, which is why he recruited Levitanus as the third Founder. For decades, the two of them have schemed to suppress my powers, but no longer. When Levitanus faked his death and ceased his enchantments in support of the Roads, he helped me. Now, Merlin can no longer use him against me. Your master is a nothing."

Thomas met the sorcerer's gaze. "I don't serve any mere human…"

"Ha! What then? Do you claim to be led by God like that crazy monk?"

"No, although I believe God favors our cause. I am a part of the League of Barnabas and we serve at the behest of our leadership council. There are no humans on that council. The ones ruling are the magical beings you have abused for decades. Does that frighten you, sorcerer?"

"What pig slop are you trying to shovel? Are you claiming that you take orders from pixies and fairies and merfolk? No human should debase himself in such a way. We are meant to rule with magic." Dalrake shook his head at Thom's claims and then turned his attention to the sorcerer restraining the youth. "Take him over to the camp. I will not listen to more of the insanity he babbles. Tell Horis to start questioning him, and this time I expect answers. I want more about this league and who belongs to it. I want to know where these vermin hide, especially since Merlin burned down that monastery. Tell him to get this boy to talk. I will have no repeat of the fiasco that was his interrogation at Clas Myrddin."

Dalrake strode off through the slush caused by the Keeper's rainfall, passing around the injured roc that was using its beak to try pulling the head of Thom's staff out its foot. Sorcerer Polin shoved Thomas to follow, aiming toward where the rest of the sorcerers were gathered.

With the magical storm done, Thom could clearly see the cages and the three journeymen guarding them. They didn't pass close enough for him to see any of the prisoners, but he did get a good look at the three who kept watch. Two were middle-aged with thinning hair. The third was closer to Thomas in age, but still a good ten years older.

Thom wondered what had happened to the fourth journeyman, then saw the body in the mud with an arrow in its neck. Who could have shot that? Then he remembered Dorthos. He resisted the temptation to look around for the mounted pixie, but that was the only one who could have accomplished such a feat. Hopefully, the mad prince and his giant eagle stayed out of sight of that enraged roc. Even if he killed no others, this meant one less to fight off when Thom rescued the fairies and harpies, and he was still determined to do that.

The three journeymen sorcerers stared at him as he was forced to walk past them, but he couldn't tell what they thought of him. Most likely, they thought him too young to be a threat. At the moment, that assessment was correct, though it had nothing to do with his age.

Two trees beyond the cages they came upon the other sorcerers. They were two men and two women, all of them gray-haired veterans of magic. He recognized one of them from the dungeon of Clas Myrddin. It was Horis and he seemed to recognize Thom too.

"Is that Levitanus' journeyman-child?" he asked as Polin pushed him in that direction.

"It is indeed," replied Polin, "and Dalrake wants him singing all that he knows, especially if he knows where Levitanus is hiding. This is the one that somehow learned how to make Founder's Fire."

"Him? It is hard to believe the boy could craft something that powerful."

"We heard that the Master Slayer taught him the enchantment."

"Francis? He is here too, along with some journeywoman I do not recognize. He is back to crafting magic. The two of them have angered Keeper Ellery with all the fires they have started."

Polin laughed. "From what we saw while waiting on this one to trigger our trap, I would say you and the others also had a part in angering Ellery. Fireballs came from both directions."

Horis stepped closer to Polin. "The last person who laughed at me lost three fingers. I will let it pass this time, but for next time would you prefer that I break fingers on your left hand or right?"

Polin frowned. "I have handed him over, do to him whatever you must; he is no longer my responsibility. But I will say this: you are a sick man, Horis. You may be Dalrake's best interrogator but you enjoy the suffering of others too much."

"All of life we face suffering. I merely concentrate it." Horis then turned his back on Polin in dismissal, concentrating on Thomas instead. He looked him over then pulled him closer, taking the sword from Thom's side and inspecting its sharpness. "I will find good use for this blade, for peeling your skin and chopping off wings. I think you will appreciate that I will wield the weapon you planned to use to liberate them as the very thing that maims and kills them. And once we capture the other two magicians, I will use it on them too." He took the sword belt too and buckled it on himself.

Thom felt a surge of rage and tried to break free of his bonds, but his hands were tied tight behind his back. So he used his body instead, charging at Horis and intending to ram him to the ground while he was distracted buckling on the sword belt.

The sorcerer was unsurprised. He merely stepped aside and whacked Thom with the flat of his own blade, sending him sprawling. Unable to catch his fall, he did his best to roll on his shoulder but it was a painful and awkward landing.

FORTY-NINE

Dragon Returned

It took a moment for Thom to roll over and sit up. He wasn't sure what to do next to get to his feet.

"You are so easy to bait, boy," mocked Horis, but his focus wasn't really on him. He was looking to where Dalrake was gathering the other sorcerers for some quick orders, then the four headed off toward the still-smoldering deadwood and the trees beyond.

"They go to capture your two friends," stated Horis, noticing Thom watching as well. The four passed another magician that was heading toward the camp. "And now Keeper Ellery comes to complain to the Founder. As if securing tree debris is more important than stopping traitorous magicians."

Thom thought it odd that a *sorcerer* would label anyone else traitor, but he said nothing.

"Well, I need to get to my work," Horis said calmly, walking behind Thom and yanking him to his feet. He whispered into his ear, "Were shall we begin? You resisted much during your last sessions, but I think you will be more motivated to share this time." His warm breath tickled the hairs in ear. "Once you realize that talking will spare *her* pain."

Thom tensed at the implied threat to Adele.

"Ah, that is it. You are one of those chivalrous ones. Who would have thought that of a thief's son? Sometimes my thorough knowledge about every magician in the land is actually more of a hindrance. When I arranged your torture at Clas Myrddin I assumed your affection for the monk would be enough to break you. Your hunger for a father figure should have weakened you. I had been wrong to assume the lack of women in your life made you callous toward them.

"Is it that you want to protect all women or is the one with Francis somehow more important to you? Maybe a mother figure or someone you see as an older sister or beloved aunt. Who is she? Is it Vivien who troubles us?"

Thom realizes that Horis can't imagine anyone young being powerful enough to fight against full sorcerers, so he is unaware that Adele was no gray-hair. Thom silently prays that Adele and Francis don't get captured.

Horis stops whispering and instead pushed Thom to move toward the nearest Cloud Rowan. Forced to walk or fall, Thom complies, but as they get near, Horis grabs his back and shoves him hard against the tree, slamming his face into the rough bark. He bashes Thom's face into the tree twice more, splitting his lip and causing his nose to bleed profusely.

The sorcerer pulled Thom back for another bash but paused. Thom was facing outward and saw only clouds and one pathway off to the right. But behind him he heard the roc give a challenging shriek at something.

"What is that?" muttered Horis to himself. He let go of Thom in his distraction.

Thom turned and was about to ram into the sorcerer when he too was distracted by a thunderous roar from something in the clouds overhead.

The injured roc screeched again as it stared skyward, desperately flapping its wings as it tried to get airborne. Then, out of the clouds, came the plummeting shape of a dragon. The monster dove directly for the huge bird and crashed on it before the lumbering roc could get away. With another mighty roar, the dragon blew fire over the bird's head and then sank teeth deep into its neck.

Blood and feathers flew everywhere as the dragon fought to complete its death blow. The giant bird flapped its wings feverishly a few more times and then went limp, as the dragon feasted.

Thom recovered first and rammed his head into Horis' face. The surprise hit sent the sorcerer sprawling. Thom ignored his ringing ears and pressed in, stomping on the man's right hand and then kicking him in the side and on his right leg a few times, hard. It was nothing Thom enjoyed but he had to make sure that the torturer was unable to fight back.

Once certain that Horis was unconscious, Thom dropped to his knees beside him and worked to get the man's knife out of its belt sheath. It wasn't easy to do with his hands tied behind his back, but Thom was able to get it freed and turned the blade around so that he could start cutting at his bindings.

As he worked on the ties, he watched as Ellery cowered behind the very tree he had been hit against. Meanwhile, Dalrake just stood there and cursed Merlin for sending the dragon to attack.

The dragon looked at the yelling Founder, but then turned away. Instead, he focused on the four magicians that had been crossing the central clearing on their way to attack Francis and Adele. The four were running away, catching the beast's eyes and driving its killer instinct.

Thom sawed faster at the ties. He needed to get free. Horis moaning behind him further emphasized the need to get his hands unbound.

He lost sight of the fleeing sorcerers as the hulking dragon chased after them, then the beast roared out a stream of fire. Even though the fire's roar was deafening, Thom still heard some screams over it.

"He's killing my sorcerers!" yelled Dalrake, even as he knelt over his cache and began furiously crafting.

The Keeper didn't bother with magic. He also ignored Thomas, choosing instead to run past him and then down the nearest pathway away from the Core.

The dragon turned and flamed again, and another victim screamed in death throes.

Finally, Thom's bindings frayed and he was free. Jumping to his feet, he looked back at Horis and saw him stirring as he moaned. If that man came to his senses, there would be no escaping. Not liking it, Thom picked up the man's staff and then hit him on the head with it, trying to keep it soft enough not to kill him but hard enough to keep him down for a little longer. He also kicked twice more in the right leg.

Horis moaned louder and rolled over, but did nothing else. Thom wanted to retrieve his sword from the man's side, but he was now laying on it. He would have to be satisfied with taking Horis' knife and staff.

What to do now? Thom looked around. The cages weren't that close, but Dalrake was. Thom still had that almost-complete enchantment of Hands of Lightning and now he had a staff to complete the crafting. Raining lightning down on the sorcerer definitely sounded appealing, especially with the Founder looking the other way. But before Thom could do anything, Dalrake finished what he was crafting and was suddenly surrounded by a Shield of Power.

Thom growled to himself at the opportunity missed. Sending lightning at him now would just slough off that shield.

Once his shield was in place, Dalrake began crafting a second enchantment, without the first one showing any flickering or weakness. This was not a Sight and Sound Shield, so Thom heard what he was making. It was lightning too.

Thom realized that he was exposed just standing here, so close to Dalrake and a moaning Horis. If Dalrake turned his head, he would see Thom immediately.

Knowing that he would lose any kind of lightning fight, Thom moved to hide behind the wide bough of the Cloud Rowan, which took him a bit farther away from the captive and bit closer to his friends, but both groups were still too far away for him to reach. Dalrake didn't seem to notice his breaking free, but it would not be hard for the Founder to locate him with Thom's cache leeching elements and creating so much racket on his back.

The dragon hunted another magician, but this time the prey threw magic back at the beast. The Fireball enchantment didn't seem to do more than anger the monster. It roared and half-ran, half-slithered after its intended victim.

Thom moved around the tree trunk to watch the dragon's progress and realized it was Francis that it was chasing. "Lord, protect him," he whispered.

And then Adele stepped out from behind another tree and strode out to confront the dragon. She looked so confident and bold, an enchantment ready to throw. Even without a magician's staff, she looked like a master of their craft in her stance against the charging monster.

Thom wanted to yell at her to get away.

She stood there, defiantly. Waiting Why was she waiting?

The dragon roared, its inferno-like maw opening to flame Thom's beloved.

"No!" he yelled, unable to resist. He would have charged at the huge beast, but it was too far away.

At the last minute, Adele threw her enchantment. Rings of power surged from her and the enchantment was first golden yellow but then turned blue as the deepest lake as it expanded and rushed at the monster. A flood of water slammed into the dragon's face, extinguishing its flames.

Thom was shocked at the power in her crafting, and impressed.

The dragon shook its head, confused for a moment at losing its fire, but then it charged at Adele in a fit of rage. It might not have fire, but it was still a huge monster with great talons and sharp teeth.

FIFTY

Leaking Magic

Thom ripped open his travel robe and scrambled for the magic pouch. He knelt and set the open pouch on the ice, then finished the enchantment with the staff he had taken from Horis and with his own spit. He plunged both hands in and came out with lightning blazing across his fingertips.

Knowing it was only seconds before the dragon overran Adele, He sent all ten fingers' worth of lightning at the beast in one combined blast.

Thom's attack stopped its charge and definitely hurt the monster, but one strike hit its maw and actually reignited its internal flames.

The dragon changed direction and now charged toward Thom.

He ran behind the far side of the tree, coming in sight of Dalrake in his protective shield.

The sorcerer glared at him. The Founder spoke and his voice was a bit muffled by the shield but was still clear. "I will take care of you after this interruption from Merlin. You can try running but I will find you, for I am a master of the Roads."

Thom didn't reply, but instead looked for shelter from the coming inferno.

"There you are!" yelled Horis, who was now on his feet, one hand against the same tree trunk for support.

Startled, Thom pulled away from the tree and was suddenly in the open right behind the sheltering Dalrake.

"Come here!" ordered Horis, lumbering after him.

Thom chose to run for the tree on the other side of Dalrake, even as he feared he was drawing the dragon's eyes. He ran as fast as he could, even as Horis jogged after him, obviously pained where Thom had kicked his leg.

He didn't look at the fast-approaching dragon, but he could hear it. He expected to be incinerated at any moment, but then he made it to the tree's wide girth, dropping to the ground behind it and covering his head.

Behind him, he heard the dragon roar of fire at Dalrake, Horis, and the surrounding trees. He felt the heat wash over him but then it was gone. He lifted his head and then crawled around to look past the tree. Horis was a burnt husk, while Dalrake stood glowering at the dragon from within his Shield of Power enchantment. The dragon loomed over Dalrake, frustrated at not being able to burn him.

Overhead, the tree was burning, so Thom decided to retreat to the next tree in the circle, keeping the burning tree between him and the dragon. Once safely behind that tree, he debated whether he should fight here or go challenge the three journeymen guarding the captives. Either direction, he wouldn't be able to sneak up on any magicians, not with his element-saturated knapsack loudly announcing his presence to everyone in the area. He really needed to do something about that before he tried anything else.

Fearing that the dragon might soon tire of playing with the Founder and come look for him, Thom swung his ripped knapsack off his back and opened it, finally confronting his damaged magician's box. He pulled out the wooden box and found the lid cracked where the ice shard had stabbed through. Carefully opening the lid, he found far more damage inside. Ten glass vials were shattered, the powders mixed with glass shards and each other and ruined by moisture. Another four vials were cracked but intact.

Carefully, Thom removed the remaining vials and then turned his box over to shake out as much of the debris as he could. He set it down and replaced the surviving vials, then he just started at the mess for a moment. What should he do now?

A frustrated dragon's roar reminded him that he didn't have much time.

He decided to reuse the lead-lined pouches that Bronwen had given him, but since he didn't have an easy way to clean them thoroughly, he decided it would be best to refill them with the same two enchantments. Even though neither of those would be effective against a beast that breathes fire of its own, it was all that he had. He crafted the replacement enchantments even as he considered what to do about the dragon.

He almost-finished the last enchantment- Fireballs- and poured the contents into the remaining pouch, then he took the last two ingredients, the mundane items of black powder and lamp oil, and premixed them in a vial and stuffed that into his belt next to the one pouch.

As he finished those final preparations, he finally thought of a possible answer for attacking the dragon. He would try a Twist of Air as a way to redirect the dragon's fire back at it. But when he looked inside the damaged magician's box, he realized one of the needed elements wasn't there. No Twist of Air.

What to do now? How do you kill or chase off a dragon? But why was the dragon his problem?

Suddenly, Thom smiled. The dragon wasn't his problem as long as it wasn't attacking his loved ones. The dragon was Dalrake's problem at the moment.

What he really wanted to do was to rush across the Core and find out if all was well with Adele, but that would be foolish. Such a dash would just attract the dragon and its killing inferno breath. For now, he needed to concentrate on his duties on this side of the Core.

Thom decided it was time to free those prisoners while the Founder was distracted by Merlin's pet.

He grabbed his knapsack and turned it upside down, emptying its contents and trying to get out as much of the spilled elements as he could. He shook out his clothes and stuffed them back in. He then carefully closed the magician's cache and stored in the backpack too. It still announced his presence, but at least it wasn't as loud as before.

One last thing he had kept out was the balm from Bronwen. He opened the jar and slathered it on his ankle, feeling first a chill and then warmth in his throbbing joint. The pain already lessened as he closed the container and added it to his pack. That should be enough to make it through whatever was still ahead. He couldn't do much about all the other cuts and bruises, but none of them seemed more than superficial, which was a good thing.

He shouldered the knapsack, but realized it still made too much noise. The journeymen would hear him coming. Grunting, he took it back off and set it against the tree and stepped away from it. He was still making noise, and it wasn't from the pouches.

What else about him could be covered with element powders?

He took off his travel robe and turned it around, finding the back of it was covered with snow-smeared powders that wouldn't be easy to brush off.

Realizing he had no other choice if he didn't want to be easily found, Thom decided to give up his warm outer robe. He laid the robe next to his knapsack and headed off. At least the long and heavy robe had protected his shirt, trousers, and boots from being element-stained as well. He was now free of the revealing sound of magic and he was ready to sneak up on those journeymen. The cold was starting to nip at him but he wouldn't be without the robe for too long. One way or the other, this was all going to end very soon.

Thom scrambled to the next tree, working to keep out of sight of both the dragon behind him and the guards up ahead. In one hand he carried Horis' staff and in the other he held Horis' knife.

Soon, he was close enough to overhear the three journeymen still guarding the captives.

"The one with the spilled cache is no longer moving," one of them observed. "The person using a Shield of Power is also standing still. Why do you think they are not moving?"

"The dragon, of course," hissed one of his companions. "They are probably hiding from it. You saw the size of that monster. I would hide too if I dared break from this duty."

"Go ahead and run, but no cowards become sorcerers."

"I am not running, and I will become a master far sooner than either of you."

The other two strongly denied that, declaring they were more worthy for promotion. It turned into a three-way whispered argument over who was the better magician.

FIFTY-ONE

Facing Other Journeymen

Thom used their arguing to sneak closer, ducking low so that one of the cages obscured his approach. Once he was almost on top of them, he set the knife and staff on the ground and grabbed one of his pouches. He added the pre-made mixture of black powder and lamp oil and then lifted the pouch to his face to spit into the enchantment and attune it to himself. Quickly, he plunged both hands into the pouch and came out with two huge fireballs.

"Resist and you die!" he yelled as he stood up and surprised the three. "Drop your staffs and lift empty hands above your head."

"You are only one and we are three. I would say the odds are in our favor," said a balding journeyman, who then dove behind the other cage even as he fumbled his knapsack off his back.

The other two were startled by his sudden move and hesitated just a moment, which was to their rue. Thom hit both of them with fireballs.

Screaming, they both fell to the ground and started rolling in the snow in an attempt to extinguish the flames.

Thom didn't hesitate. He grabbed his staff and ran around the two cages to where the first journeyman was crafting fervently. Rather than use lightning on him, Thom saved that last enchantment and just kicked the man's mixing bowl away from him, scattering the half-completed enchantment.

"Fool!" exclaimed the sorcerer-in-training, even as he fell to the ground, clutching his cache to himself and turning his back to the quickly unstabilizing magic.

Thom turned his back to the magic too, but he ran to the front of the nearest cage and started working on their latches to free those inside.

The disturbed enchantment exploded, sending bowl shards and splatter everywhere. It rocked the cages and one of them started floating away.

Thom stopped trying to open the other cage and grabbed for the one getting away. He desperately worked the latches on that one even as it lifted him from the ground. He wrapped one arm over the top of the cage, and tried to grasp its edge even while also holding his staff. With his other hand he worked the wooden latches, even as he was aware that his grip was slipping. He saw out of the corner of his eye the three journeymen getting to their feet and advancing toward him, holding their staffs like weapons.

Finally, he got the latches undone and threw open the cage door, letting go of his hold on the thing and dropping back to the snow-covered ice. The captives were all winged beings. They could fly out on their own.

A he dropped to the ground his ankle complained, but he was too focused to pay it much attention. He still had another cage to open and the journeymen were almost on him.

Desperate, he ran to the cage, but he was on the wrong end. The door he had already started unlatching was turned more toward the sorcerers and it would be sure death for him to bend over that and expose his back to them. Thinking quickly, he grabbed the side of the cage and lifted while pushed, getting this one airborne too. Once it was floating, he was able to turn it so that he could get to the door. He got his hand on one of the latches but then the cage was yanked away from him.

Looking up, he saw two the journeymen at the other end, spinning the door away from him. He had to let it go because the third one was almost on top of him, ready to jab him with a glowing staff.

Thom raised his own staff and prepared to defend himself, but then the journeyman sorcerer disappeared behind an explosion of colorful wings. He screamed and then fell to the ground, bleeding from a hundred small stab wounds, as the dozen fairies pulled away.

The sudden attack startled the other two and Thom was able to wrestle the cage away and turn it around. He started working feverishly at the latches while the fairies started harassing the remaining two journeymen, who were now swinging the staffs wildly in the air, trying to keep the fairies away.

The second cage opened and out rushed harpies, flying past him and straight at the two men who were still fighting off fairies. As Thom watched, the fairies parted and four harpies dove at the men, making swift work of them. Two bloody bodies dropped to the snow.

"Thomas, you did well."

He turned and saw the Fairy Queen and Harpy Commander both exiting the cage. It was the queen who had spoken and he gave her a small bow of acknowledgment.

"Humans can sometimes be helpful," admitted Celaeno. The harpy gave a fierce stare but then a slight nod of approval.

"Well, now that we are free, we should get to our next task," said Titania. "The flames from Thomas' fireballs are not completely extinguished, so we should make our torches and light them so we can do what we have decided."

"Agreed," said the Commander Celaeno, barking orders to her people, who then flew to the nearest trees and broke off branches to use as torches. The quickly lit them from the remaining embers of Thom's magic and set about starting fires among the trees.

Titania called her fairies to do the same, and soon the they were working on the next tree over to also set it on fire.

"What are you doing?" asked Thom.

"Celaeno and I have decided that the Road of Clouds shall end now. No more will we allow our kind to give themselves for its upkeep. This is over. No more killing for these murderous enchantments. We will burn up the Core and let the rest of the pathways unravel, and then we will go to the Keeper's place and cut free all the Cloud Rowans. Ellery is banished from Cloudholder and may not return on penalty of death."

"Dalrake is still out there on the Core," warned Thom, pointing toward where he had last seen him. The Shield of Power was still active, so likely he was still hiding under it to avoid the dragon. "He will fight your plans."

"Then we will kill him," replied Celaeno. "He is a human; he has no wings or place in the skies. He too is banished from our lands."

"We know the danger he poses," added Titania, "and we ask your help in resisting him. You are a great magician, but it is not our place to order you to do this; we are not the full council of the league. We merely ask."

"I will help and, if possible, will capture Dalrake so that he can face the leadership council's justice."

The tiny queen nodded agreement. "We will go around the circle away from him so that we can ignite as many trees as possible before he realizes what is happening."

The one surviving journeyman was climbing to his feet, but stood very still when two harpies flew close.

"Drop your knapsack," ordered Celaeno, flying over too. "And your staff. You will then run down the nearest pathway and you will not stop until you get to the shelter of a wayrest. If you try coming back, you will be killed. If you linger on the pathways somewhere, you will also die. Hide in a wayrest and you will likely live. Drop your bag now."

The frightened man complied, lowering his pack to the ice and placing his staff next to it.

"Now go! Run!"

As soon as he was gone, the harpy leader beckoned Thomas over. "I noticed your knapsack is gone and earlier the sorcerers mentioned that it was shredded and spilling elements. Take this one's cache and switch staffs if you want. We need you able to craft."

Thom nodded and knelt over the leather knapsack. He threw aside all the clothes and belongings, keeping only the mixing bowl, pestle, and the lead-lined box. He set the box down and opened it briefly to see what he had to work with. Only half the vials were full and they were placed haphazardly, but it would work. He quickly closed it to cut off the sound and stuffed it back into the knapsack. He then adjusted the packs straps and swung it over his shoulders. "Let's go."

FIFTY-TWO

Burning Trees

Thomas hurried along the outer circle of the Core, past two already-burning trees and on to where two more were being lit by the fairies. Titania and Celaeno landed next to him.

He still had something painful to share with the queen, so he finally did so. "Queen Titania, I need to tell you that Rainflower was killed by one of the sorcerers. She gave her life trying to rescue you."

The queen's wings stopped moving for a moment. "I wondered if any of my kind guided you here. She was one of our best Road Guides and she will be missed greatly."

They fell into silence for a time, then the queen spoke up again. "Thomas, you need to refrain from any magic so that your position remains unknown, but keep an ear open for any other magic being crafted. Is the Founder still occupied with the dragon?"

Thom nodded his understanding. "His enchantment is still going; I can only assume that he is still under it and the dragon looming nearby. I hear no other magic."

"Dalrake will notice the fires soon enough," said Celaeno, "then he will tire of the dragon and chase it off, so that he can come investigate what we are doing."

"Why did Merlin send the dragon?" asked Thom.

"I doubt he expected to trap Dalrake like he has," said Titania, "but I believe he wants to weaken the sorcerers. He fears Dalrake, knowing that he is the strongest of the Founders. He wants him alive because he has an important part in all the great enchantments around Camelot and its Roads, but he doesn't want the sorcerer becoming dominant. The dragon was not sent to help us. Merlin uses it to make sure that Dalrake is weakened and cannot overthrow him as the king's counselor and the preeminent magician of the realm."

"Merlin is a pompous fool," huffed Celaeno. "He too needs to be banished from the slopes of Cloudholder."

"Agreed," replied Titania.

The three of them kept moving as another tree started burning.

Suddenly, two of the fairies broke off from starting fires and flew toward them. "Ware the edge!" one of them yelled.

Thom, who had been concentrating on hearing Dalrake's enchantment, turned and lifted his staff in defense just as another beast rose up out of the clouds to fly directly at them. It took a moment for him to realize what approached, then he shouted. "Hold your arrows. It is an Aeti!"

The giant eagle came climbed out of the mists and landed on the edge of the Core, letting its sole rider leap off.

"Dorthos!" yelled Thom, running at him in joy.

"Thomas!"

Thom bent over and gave him a strong hug. "It is good to see you alive."

"I thank God that you live too, and you succeeded in releasing the captives. Good for you!"

"What about Adele and Francis? Do you know if they are well?"

"I just left them on the other side of the Core. Although battered like you, they live." He turned to Celaeno. "Unfortunately, Thisbe and Alcyone were both killed, one by the dragon the other by a sorcerer. My condolences to the Harp."

The commander of the harpies nodded back to him. "We will mourn our brave sisters once the battles are done."

Dorthos turned back to Thomas. "I came here because Francis and Adele heard Fireballs thrown and then all this fire started. I am confused. Why do the fairies and harpies set even more fires? Hasn't the dragon set enough ablaze?"

The queen answered him. "We have decided that it is time for the Core to fall, Prince Dorthos."

"Would that not be a decision for the whole council?"

"Without our innate magic, the constantly shifting pathways would fade within a month and Celaeno and I have decided we will no longer let our kind be sacrificed for such things. We will refrain from shattering the half of the Road of Clouds between the mountain and the tower, but only for now. We expect the others to agree with us that it is time for the Road enchantments to end. There was a time when such costly sacrifices were needed to unite the realm under Arthur and to bring about peace between humans and magical beings, but that time is over. The king needs to keep his realm together like all other human kings, with trade and prosperity, strong forts and fair laws. Let the humans start sacrificing for this man. We magical being have lost too many loved ones. It is their turn now."

"I agree with you," said Dorthos softly, "but it is still a decision for the full council. We are not despots like the Founders. We must resist sinking to their immorality. As Francis has discovered, there can be just ways for use magic, and in the same way we must rule justly too."

Titania smiled. "Lectured to act more sane by Dorthos the Deranged. God has a sense of humor, even in the midst of all the pain."

Dorthos gave her a small nod as he smiled back. "He does indeed. Now, how can I help with destroying the Core?"

"Go back to the Fair Defender and Lady Adele. Tell them our plans and have them meet us across from where Dalrake faces the dragon. The humans will need to work together to stop the Founder."

"Do you plan to kill him?" asked Dorthos.

"He deserves it, but a death sentence would have to be the ruling of the council," she replied. "We will try to capture him, or at least drive him away so that we can destroy this part of the Road of Clouds."

"I will do as you ask." With that, Dorthos took a running leap onto the eagle's back and soon they were gone, dropping below the Core to fly to the other side without being seen.

"Let us see how many trees we can set on fire before either the dragon or the sorcerer interrupts us," stated Celaeno.

They only made it to one more tree before Dalrake reacted. He motioned for the queen. "What can you see over there? I hear more, as if the Shield of Power has lifted higher, and I hear another enchantment being wielded."

Titania rose higher into the sky and then shouted down. "It is as you said. The dome around seems to be higher, judging how the dragon fire is coursing over it. And now it looks like Dalrake is throwing icicles at the beast's legs and belly."

They all heard an angry roar from the dragon as it was cut by the ice shards.

Thom heard the Shield of Power suddenly end, but the ice enchantment kept going.

"The dome is gone and now Dalrake is throwing icicles at the dragon's maw."

Again the dragon roared, but this time it seemed more pained than angry, and even Thom could see it lifting into the sky.

"The dragon flees," reported the queen.

At that same moment, Thom heard the ice enchantment end and a new one start immediately, meaning it was something he had prepared ahead of time. It was Hands of Lightning.

"Everyone take cover," warned Thom. "He wields lightning now and can probably reach this far."

Lightning shot outward, but not at them. Instead, the sorcerer aimed at Thom's shattered cache that was so obviously making sounds from behind a tree not that far from Dalrake.

The enchantment met the exposed elements and there was a blast and then an even bigger one as Thom's whole cache exploded. The harpies and fairies looked to him for an explanation.

"He destroyed my knapsack and robe," explained Thom. "Most likely he thought it was me."

For a moment, everyone held their breath. There were no sounds, except the crackle of the already burning wood. There were no magical sounds except from the Road of Clouds itself. It seemed that Founder Dalrake was also listening.

Suddenly, Dalrake started crafting again and Thom recognized it as the Downpour enchantment that Adele had used so effectively at the Fairy Court. The sorcerer was going to extinguish all the fires.

Thom swung off his pack and would have pulled out the cache in it, but

Titania ordered him to stop. "Not yet, Thomas. It will take all of us to defeat Dorthos."

"But he will put out all the fires we've started."

"We will light them again once we have dealt with him. For now, resist exposing our position. Instead, let us move away from the burning trees and go find Brother Francis and Lady Adele. We will need to work together to bring the chief sorcerer to justice. This is not something that you can do by yourself. You are part of the league now, so let us do this together as the league."

Thom put his knapsack back over his shoulder and nodded. "I... I appreciate that." He meant that. It felt good to have others on which to depend.

FIFTY-THREE

Trapping a Founder

When they met Adele, Francis, and Dorthos, Thom was overjoyed. He rushed forward and swept Adele off her feet, spinning her around as he hugged her tightly. Only then did he admit to himself that he had been worried that she might have been killed. Tears of relief ran down his dirty face.

She kissed him and then gently touched his bloody nose and matted hair. "What happened to you?"

He brushed a loose strand of hair out of her soot-stained face. "Much happened, just like it did to you."

They kissed again then separated. Behind them, Dalrake's enchantment was sweeping ever closer as it extinguished one fire after another.

"He is certainly powerful," noted Francis. "This Downpour has kept going for nearly a quarter of an hour now and has doused almost all of the fires at the north end."

"I hope it exhausts him," said Dorthos. "That will make his capture much easier."

"I doubt that it will," replied Celaeno. The harpy leader turned to her fairy counterpart. "Are there any other foes on the Road?"

"I wondered the same. While Dalrake is distracted with his enchantment I will send four of my fairies up to see what is out there."

The fairies climbed into the sky, disappearing into the clouds, but with their great vision they were able to see through such obstacles and took the time to spy out the pathways all around them. When they finally came back down, one of them made the report for all of them.

"There are no others on the Core besides us and the sorcerer. Merlin has entered the Road, but he and five other wizards linger at the archway to the mountain. They have with them a tethered fairy that we think he is forcing to view the area. The dragon is flying back toward us, but it is staying within the Road so it will take a bit for the beast to return."

"We will have to deal with guild magicians once we are done here," stated the queen. "What of Ellery or the journeyman sorcerer?"

"We saw neither, so they have either fallen off the Road or they are in one of the wayrests."

"Or they hide behind a Shield of Sight and Sound," noted Francis. "That was how Dalrake nearly caught us at the archway."

"From what I understand, not many are strong enough to craft such an enchantment. I cannot imagine that Keeper Ellery would be brave enough to make one and come back here. He has never struck me as fearless, just sly as he has played Merlin and Dalrake off each other for years, making both of them think that he was their man."

"Then we should take him now," stated the Harpy Commander, "before that dragon complicates things again."

"Agreed," said Dorthos.

Queen Titania motioned for everyone to get closer. "Time for us to make our plans for trapping a Founder."

* * *

The humans ran across the open center of the Core under the cover of Dalrake's storm, letting the rush of water obscure their approach. The harpies flew into the storm too, their sturdy feathers able to handle the beating of water. The fairies chose to fly over it, as did Dorthos and his Aeti.

By the time the Downpour moved past, they were halfway across the clearing to Dalrake. The sorcerer was so concentrated on his enchantment that, at first, he didn't notice them.

Thom ran at the front because he was the only one with an enchantment pre-made. He kept going until Dalrake finally saw them and let go of his Downpour enchantment.

Stopping where he was, Thom pulled out his last pouch and set his staff to the mixture inside it, sparking it to life and then spitting into it to attune it to himself. He dropped his staff and jammed both hands inside, coming out with blue lightning sizzling across his fingers.

He pointed his right hand at Dalrake and released all five bolts at him, but the sorcerer saw it coming and ran to the side, putting a burnt tree between him and the lightning.

Thom did his best to bend the power around the trunk, but he missed with every one. Worse, he heard Dalrake activating his own Hands of Lightning.

"Scatter!" shouted Thom. "He is about to attack!"

Behind him, he heard Francis and Adele both crafting. They were not heeding his warning.

Thom pointed his one remaining hand's worth of lightning at the sorcerer but didn't release it yet. He steadied his left arm with his right hand and waited for Dalrake to step clear of the tree.

Dalrake moved out into the open and raise a hand with lightning arcing from finger to finger.

Thom released the lightning from his pinky. Paused, then released the power from his ring finger. Paused again.

Dalrake sent a whole handful of lightning bolts streaking toward him.

Thom maintained his position to make sure he hit his target. He released a bolt from his middle finger, then paused again. Willing all three at his target.

Adele yelled for him to drop to the ground.

One of his bolts actually hit one of Dalrake's, exploding in mid-air and taking out all of his and most of Thom's, but one was still going.

He released the lightning from his last two fingers and then dropped his arm but kept his eyes locked on the target.

Dalrake dodged to the side and released his remaining handful of lightning bolts. All of them were aimed at Thomas.

Adele threw Wizard Lights in an attempt to interrupt the attack, but missed. She yelled for him to drop, but he was determined to guide his magic to the target.

Some more bolts brushed against each other and veered off in an explosion. Two of Thom's remained, while four of Dalrake's were coming directly at him.

Dalrake dodged again and then threw himself to the ground, while Thom refused to move even though he was risking death.

Francis finished his enchantment, a Shield of Power that he set directly in front of Thomas, so close that it almost touched the tip of his nose.

Thom lost connection with his lightning and swore, not even noticing that Dalrake's attack splattered right in front of his chest.

Francis' shield held, so Thom lived.

Thom's lightning barely missed, so Dalrake was alive but injured.

The harpies swarmed him, ripping the knapsack from his back and taking away his staff.

Francis dropped the Shield of Power and all three of them hurried over to see their captive.

With them came Titania, Dorthos, and Celaeno.

"What do you want with me? Let me go!" demanded Dalrake.

"We will not," stated Titania, hovering at a safe distance even as Francis tied the sorcerer's hands behind his back. "You are to go on trial for the many crimes you have committed."

"In who's court? Arthur would never dare to try me."

"You will go before the League of Barnabas for the murder of so many of our people."

"It was not murder, foolish fairy. It was rendering down for the good of all society, a sacrificing of a few to save the realm. That is not murder; that is righteous action."

"The leadership council of the league will rule on that."

"You are not taking me in front of any court of jesters. Who would even try to run a council with magical beings? How would a dryad communicate? Will you add a pond to your court for the merman? How about a shovel for all the centaur droppings? What a farce!"

Thomas came over and helped Francis lift the sorcerer back to his feet, then Thomas picked up Dalrake's knapsack, while Francis grabbed his discarded staff.

Dalrake struggled against his bonds the whole time, ordering them to undo the ties and to give him back his belongings. He called them thieves and cowards.

"Can you three send fireballs at the trees to restart the fires?" asked Celaeno. "We should get it burning and then get moving out of here. I would suggest we head back to the wayrest we visited last night."

"You are going to set fire to the Core? Are you insane? That will destroy the Road of Clouds, the greatest achievement of mankind."

"We should gag him," suggested Dorthos. "His complaining is already hurting my ears."

"If you are going to kill me, you should do it now," challenged Dalrake. "Go ahead, and see how long any of you live afterward, because if you kill me all the great enchantments of Camelot will unravel."

"He really needs that gag," repeated the pixie.

Thom did his best to ignore him as he opened up the Founder's knapsack and dumping out the belongings. He kept the magician's cache and then added the one he seized from the journeyman, along with Dalrake's mixing bowl and pestle. Everything else he left behind as he put the pack back over his shoulder. He hadn't looked inside, but he was fairly sure that he now had a full supply of elements again.

FIFTY-FOUR

Chasing and Being Chased

It took an hour for the three magicians to craft and throw enough fireballs to restart the fires because they had to walk around the Core to get near the trees they wanted to burn. When enough were finally on fire, they returned to where the fairies and harpies were waiting with the bound Dorthos.

"We should hurry," said Queen Titania. "The dragon is moving faster than we expected. We want to be away from here before it arrives."

At that moment, Dorthos suddenly pulled free and ran off among the burning trees. The harpies started following then pulled back as the flying embers became too much. It was up to the three humans to recapture him now.

Thomas was already tired from walking all over the Core and now he was having to run under a burning tree. The only good thing was that the burning branches that broke off tended to float upward rather than come crashing down, but the air was still full of smoke and embers and those glowing remains that were almost ready to disintegrate. "Can you see him?" he yelled to Francis and Adele.

"He weaved around the trunk up ahead," replied Adele, "but now he's gone again."

"I'll go toward the far side. You and Francis circle the near side. He couldn't have gotten very far."

Thom came around but saw nothing of the man. Adele and Francis showed up, but no Dalrake. Looking in all directions through the smoky air, he finally spotted him on the ground beside the charred remains of one of his sorcerers. He must have tripped over the corpse.

"There he is," he said pointing him out and starting to walk toward him.

"What is he doing?" asked Adele.

Thom more carefully and saw that he was doing something behind his back. Thom's eyes widened as he realized what the Founder was attempting. "He has a knife from that body and is sawing through his ties."

Right then, the bonds snapped and Dalrake rolled over, reaching inside his travel robes for a pouch that he spat into.

"Watch out!" Thom yelled. "He has another enchantment."

They scattered, as Dalrake rose to his feet with a fireball in each hand. He threw the fireballs but missed with both. He then turned and kept running.

"How many more almost-finished enchantments do you think he has left?" asked Thom as they started chasing him again.

"I was certain he was already out," replied Francis. "I would have thought no one could sustain more than two enchantments at the cusp of completion, but he had at least three in addition to the active magic he was using."

"At least he can't craft anything new," said Adele, "because Thomas has his knapsack."

They continued their hunt, but they now kept closer together. Dalrake was an old man but he had already shown that he was still agile and strong, and they did not want him overpowering them to get at their knapsacks. As long as he had no new elements, he was limited in what he could do and there was a chance that they could recapture him without any more injuries.

Thom dodged a smoldering branch that floated past. He couldn't see Dalrake anywhere. It was like he had disappeared into the smoke. Frustrated, he motioned the others to follow him out into the central clearing. Once clear of the worst of the smoke, he motioned to the nearest fairy and asked her to spy out where Dalrake had gone. She concentrated and then pointed. "He is at the edge of the Core."

"He might be trying to flee down a pathway," noted Adele.

"The harpies have already considered that," the fairy responded, "and there are two at each of the nearer entrances. He will not escape that way."

"Where is the dragon?" asked Francis.

"It will be here soon," stated the fairy. "It never left the Road, but merely flew up one of the pathways to shelter at the platform outside one of the wayrests. Do you think it still being guided by Founder Merlin?"

"Yes," replied Francis. "The bond to the wizard will not be broken until one or the other leaves the Road's enchantment. Are not Merlin and other wizards lingering just inside the archway?"

"They are still there," admitted the fairy.

"Is Merlin trying to help us or the sorcerers?" asked Adele of the monk.

"He helps only himself. I do not know his mind, but I would guess that he wants the league shattered and Dalrake weakened. How he hopes to accomplish both by sending that dragon, I cannot guess. The beast is a brutal weapon that cannot be easy to guide."

"But I thought Merlin and Dalrake work together," argued Thom.

Francis smiled grimly as he looked around the clearing. "Sometimes their interests overlap, that is all. My old master told me decades ago that Dalrake disdains the wizard, while Merlin envies and fears the sorcerer. Dolain was wrong in so many things, but in that assessment I think he was correct."

"What are we going to do now?" asked Adele. "I don't think we can catch Dalrake before the dragon arrives."

"You're right. We need to prepare, but where?"

Thom looked around too. There was the partially-eaten corpse of the roc and a small bundle of deadwood that hadn't caught on fire, but nothing substantial in the center of the Core. Around the edges, fifteen of the twenty trees were either burning or smoldering. "Should we shelter under the trees that aren't burning yet?"

"Do we have time to run over there?" asked Francis of the fairy, pointing to the newly-planted trees on the south side.

"No," she replied.

"Then we make our stand right here. Adele, craft a Downpour enchantment, like last time. I will craft an Icicle Storm because it seemed to work when Dalrake used it. As for you Thom, I'm not sure what you should make…"

Thom did. "I will craft Founder's Fire, but I will not use it unless your two enchantments don't succeed."

"That is a desperate move, but you're right. Merlin has sent the dragon to eliminate all of us. We need to stop it or we will die."

"Are you certain of that?" asked Adele. "It seemed to go after the sorcerers more than it did us."

"The only sorcerer left here is Dalrake and the dragon only played with him. Merlin isn't sending the dragon back to kill Dalrake because he needs the sorcerer to maintain the Camelot enchantments. The dragon returns to now hunt all of us. Let us get to crafting while we can."

They knelt in the churned snow with their back to each other, opened their caches, and gathered what they needed to create the enchantments that they hoped would stop the monster racing toward them.

FIFTY-FIVE

Kill or be Killed

The first thing Thom saw of the dragon was its yellow-glowing eyes and then suddenly it was there, sweeping the smoke and embers aside as it roared into the air over the Core. It came out directly in front of Adele and she did not flinch at its huge size. His brave beloved stood there, her hair whipped by the downdraft and her skirts tugged back. She released her enchantment and it went out from her like ripples in a pond, first yellow and then turning to a dark gray as it pulled rain from the clouds all around them.

By the time it hit the dragon, the Downpour was like a huge waterfall, thundering on the beast and pushing it toward the ground. The dragon shut its mouth to save its internal fire and glided over them as it dropped lower. The Downpour enchantment follow it, soaking the three humans in passing.

The dragon hit the ice hard as the water forced it down, but it fought against the cascade and turned to glower at them.

Adele's enchantment finally wore out and the Downpour lessened to just a hard rain.

Angry, the dragon threw its head back and roared its defiance and they saw that its fires were not extinguished this time.

Through the rain, Thom saw Dalrake run out from among the burning trees. He lost sight of him as he went behind the dragon.

Harpies appeared, swooping in on the dragon and shooting their deadly arrows at it. Most were just an annoyance to the beast, but one punctured its left eye, which made the dragon scream in rage and spew fire all over the sky.

Two harpies crashed to the ground, engulfed in flame.

A flight of fairies flew past, led by Titania. They shot arrows as they circled the dragon's head. The monster roared and spewed more flames, frying the last four in the line.

Francis released his enchantment and suddenly a storm of icicles shot at the dragon, slicing into its chest, wings, legs, and head. The beast stood against the onslaught, glowering at Francis as it endured, and Thom realized that this wouldn't stop it either.

Having no choice, Thom worked to complete his enchantment before the ice attack ended. He needed to use Founder's Fire against the dragon or it would kill all of them.

As Thom mixed the last elements together, out of the corner of his eye he saw Dorthos fly in with his great eagle.

As he lifted the mixing bowl to spit into it, he saw the Aeti dive close and Dorthos shoot with his dryad-poisoned arrows.

Thom finished attuning it and set the bowl on the ground. With his hands, he directed the whirlwind of power skyward.

As he looked at the dragon, he saw the Aeti complete its pass and at the last minute the dragon's tail rose and smashed into the side of the eagle. The bird faltered and Dorthos was thrown off of it. Thom watched in horror as the pixie fell from the sky and thudded on the ice.

"No! Not Dorthos too!"

Thom released the enchantment, aiming it directly at the monster that had just crushed his friend. A blinding light shot outward from him and hit the dragon, burning it and cleaving it into two. And the Founder's Fire didn't stop there, but shot on like a beacon of death. For just a moment, he saw Dalrake highlighted in its glare and then he was no more. The power also hit one of the perimeter trees and obliterated it, then roared on through the sky.

For a moment longer, the power roared out from Thom and then it just ended.

He staggered from the intensity of it. Then he staggered again as the Core suddenly shook and then sagged toward the now-missing tree.

"You did it!" shouted Adele, coming over and hugging him.

But he was in no mood to celebrate. He hugged her back, but then let go and started walking to where Dorthos had fallen. Adele and Francis came with him.

They skirted the bloody and burnt mess that was the leftovers of Merlin's beast and searched for the small man among all the churn and gore. They might have missed him, but his Aeti had survived and it came to land next to its fallen rider.

When they made it there, they found Prince Dorthos the Deranged was still alive, but just barely.

Crying uncontrollably, Thom knelt beside him.

Dorthos opened his eyes. "No tears, Thomas. No tears. I… have lived… a good life." He coughed up blood and groaned in pain, but then continued. "I have fought the good fight of life. No tears for me. Now its time for me to go to God and also to finally see my beloved Hestani again. Ah, that will be a glorious reunion."

"Can we do nothing to help you?"

"You have done so much already, young Thomas. Dragonslayer." He turned his head and looked at Francis. "Can you pray for me Brother Francis? It is time for me to leave this mortal shell of mine."

"I will be honored to pray for you, Friend Dorthos, Prince of Clan Brythoni, Rider of the Aeti, and cherished spouse of Hestani." And then Francis prayed, asking God to take Dorthos into his embrace and reunite him with his loved ones that have gone before him.

By the time the prayer ended, Dorthos was dead.

FIFTY-SIX

Fall of the Road

The Core shook again and sagged more.

Queen Titania and Commander Celaeno flew over and both paid their respects toward Dorthos, but the queen also told them that they needed to hurry.

"The Core will fail soon and with it will go much of the pathways. You need to leave; you cannot fly away like we can."

"We will fly too," responded Francis. "We used a Cloud Rowan to get onto the Road of Leaves. If you can find the wayrest where it is tied, we can use it to get back."

The queen nodded and soared up into the sky to find where they would be going.

"Did any of you see where Founder Dalrake went?" asked Celaeno.

"He is dead," stated Thomas. "He was standing behind the dragon when the Founder's Fire killed it. The fire kept going and caught him too."

"I saw the same thing," confirmed Francis, while Adele nodded agreement.

"Well then we have even an even bigger reason to flee the Road of Clouds," stated the harpy. "Without his magic all of this will unravel very quickly. We need to get going."

"What about Dorthos' body?" asked Thom. "We cannot just leave it here to fall from the sky when this place disintegrates."

"We should let his mount carry his body," said Adele, looking up at the giant eagle that had remained calmly at his side.

Francis nodded agreement. "If it will let us tie the body on its back. Let us try."

"Allow me to sing to it and calm it down," said Celaeno, who then began a lovely yet sad song. A dirge without words.

As the harpy sang, Francis and Thomas lifted the broken body of their dead friend and brought it to the eagle. The bird actually knelt lower, allowing them to reach the riding straps on its back. They set Dorthos there and secured him. Francis even added the rope belt from his monastic robe to make sure the body would not fall off.

Once done, they stepped back and motioned to the Aeti that it could now leave. The giant eagle spread its wings and leaped into the sky and was soon gone from view into the clouds, carrying the body of Dorthos back to his people.

* * *

Titania found them the quickest route to the wayrest and they set off at a run, passing through the burning trees and then up the right pathway. Behind them, the Core groaned and sagged even from all the damage done to it. They were too exhausted to keep running, but Francis gave their boots more Sole Flight than Sole Grip and they used it to take huge leaps to chew up the distance. More than once a harpy had to help redirect their jumps to keep them on the path. But they made it to the wayrest and the waiting tree. Everyone was too tired to go any farther, so they went inside the wayrest and slept that evening and the whole night, not waking until morning.

When they came out, the connecting pathway of the Road was gone. The wayrest and its attached platform were just floating in the gray sky. Thankfully, the attached tree was still there too.

From what the fairies could see, Merlin and his wizards were gone, having retreated to the last remaining section of the Road of Clouds and were now halfway back to Sky Tower and Camelot. There were no other magicians to be seen, though the Keeper and that journeyman might be in one of the many other wayrests that were floating about the sky, for almost all of the Road of Clouds on this side of Cloudholder had melted away. So they no longer had to fear any magical attacks.

With the help of the fairies and harpies, they got the loose tree back to the Keeper's Vale and brought it down at the tree farm. The pixie workers were still there and helped to secure it. While that was going on, two fairies arrived and met with the queen to update her on everything that had occurred during her imprisonment.

Once the humans were safely on the ground, Titania urged them to stay there and rest. "I have informed the pixie workers that Ellery is no longer the Keeper and that he is banished from the mountain. Celaeno and I have different plans for this place, but for now the three of you should rest here. We will have Kane, Vivien, and Bronwen come here to join you."

"They are still alive?" asked Adele. They had all been worried about leaving the three behind with the guild wizards approaching.

"They are fine. Merlin never assailed Tuatha Aes Si. Instead, he and his guild magicians fought the griffins and then the sorcerers who held the archway. Once they had it secure, they stayed just inside the Road, so that Merlin could direct his pet dragon in its attacks."

Thom was glad to hear the news. The only thing that would have been better would have been the capture of Merlin to face justice, but that wouldn't likely happen any time soon. King Arthur needed that evil magician, probably more so now that the Camelot enchantments were failing.

* * *

It was a month later and the six humans were still in the Keeper's Vale. In that time, the remaining half of the Road of Clouds disintegrated and now Cloudholder Mountain was no longer linked to Camelot, so there was no longer a fear of a guild attack on the land. Every few days a fairy or a harpy would check on them to see how they were doing, but today the queen and the commander were coming to see them.

Thom stood with the others in front of the Keeper's house, enjoying one of those rare moments when the sun broke through over the land. He had his arm around Adele's waist and felt at peace.

Queen Titania came with six attendants, as did Commander Celaeno. They all landed nearby and then the two leaders approached the humans.

"It is good to see all of you hale," said the queen. "We have come to bring you news of the league. Levitanus made it safely to the new monastery that Abbot Justin has begun building in the wilderness. It has also been decided that this Keeper House will be turned into a second school for the league. The council has also decided to add two positions here: one person will oversee the school and the other... well, the other is one we want to offer to you, Brother Francis."

Celaeno continued the conversation. "You have been called Fair Defender for what you so bravely did in the past, but now we want you to be known as the Defender of Fair and Harp. We want you to use your magical skills to help keep Cloudholder safe, not only for fairies and harpies, but for all magical beings that will be seeking refuge on these slopes. Will you take this job?"

Suddenly, Titania was holding out a magician's staff to him, along with an old magician's box. "When you renounced your craft, you abandoned these two items at the Fairy Court and I have kept them safe all these years. I offer them back to you as a symbol of your return to magic, with the promise that you will only be asked to practice your craft justly, in service to others. The Father Abbot will allow you to continue as a brother, but with these added duties. Will you accept our offer, Francis?"

Thom's eyes filled with joyful tears for his friend, especially after he nodded acceptance.

Eric Loren

WAYS OF CAMELOT
4-Book Arthurian Fantasy Series

1- Road of Leaves
First Book of the 4-Book Ways of Camelot Series.. Available in paperback and e-book.

2- Road of Waters
Available in paperback and e-book

3- Camelot of the Roads
Available **September 15, 2023** in paperback and e-book.

4- Road of Clouds
Available **October 15, 2023** in paperback and e-book.

Eric Loren

About the Author
Eric Loren

Eric is an American author of fantasy, science fiction, and dystopian novels.

His writings include the Ways of Camelot series, the upcoming Tag Warren series, and the Cirian War saga.

The son of immigrants, he can speak his parents' tongue, though with a decidedly American accent. He studied our collective past and our present (holding a degree in both History and Religious Studies), and still enjoys learning about the world's diverse cultures and beliefs.

Eric currently lives in California, enjoying the sunshine and natural wonders of that unique state. He is married to his beloved Amy and has two wonderful sons.

Learn more about Eric at his website:
http://ericloren.com

www.ingramcontent.com/pod-product-compliance
Lightning Source LLC
Chambersburg PA
CBHW070743180626
46818CB00007B/2968